Join the FREE Preferred Reader Program

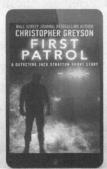

JACK & JILL AND THE BLUE LIGHT KILLER

This time, there's murder on Jack's doorstep...

Jack takes out the trash and comes face to face with a lifeless body in the dumpster. With no attempt to hide his crime, the killer left his gruesome handiwork on full display, wanting it to be discovered. Is this chilling message directed specifically to Jack?

When the body count rises, and more suspects emerge, Jack is ordered to join forces with recently transferred Detective Jill Reyes. As they plunge headfirst into the investigation, each new piece of uncovered evidence suggests one of their own may be the killer, leaving Jack to wonder who he can trust. Will Jack be able to outsmart this cunning murderer and catch the killer? Or will he become another victim in their sick game of life and death?

ALSO BY CHRISTOPHER GREYSON

The Girl Who Lived

One Little Lie

The Woman Beneath the Stairs

The Dark

Pure of Heart

The Adventures of Finn and Annie

The Detective Jack Stratton Mystery-Thriller Series:

And Then She Was Gone

Girl Jacked

Jack Knifed

Jacks are Wild

Jack and the Giant Killer

Data Jack

Jack of Hearts

Jack Frost

Jack of Diamonds

Captain Jack

Jack of Spades

Jack & Jill and the Blue Light Killer

Kiku - Rogue Assasin Trilogy

I'd like to dedicate this book to Kathy Tolich. She's the dear wife of a friend of mine and a wonderful beta reader. I'm very grateful for how much she lets me monopolize her husband's time. So to Kathy — thank you.

JACK & JILL
AND THE BLUE LIGHT KILLER

WALL STREET JOURNAL BESTSELLING AUTHOR
CHRISTOPHER GREYSON

GREYSON MEDIA

Chapter One

Tyrell Miller sat in the last booth of the diner, pressing his hand against his right leg to stop it from shaking. Beads of sweat quickly dotted his brow as he wiped his forehead with a napkin. He took another sip of water, but his mouth was dry again before his glass was back on the table.

The little bell above the door chimed, and a mountain of a man strode through. Carlos Delgado's bushy eyebrows bunched together, forming a continual line of thick black and gray hair. His forehead wrinkled into deep troughs while his lips pressed together tightly in a thin line.

The waitress stayed behind the counter as the angry-looking man lumbered toward Tyrell, the diner's lone occupant.

Tyrell didn't know if Carlos was mad because Tyrell had asked him to meet him. Carlos always seemed angry whenever Tyrell was around, but this was different. He looked ready to kill.

Slipping out of the booth, Tyrell held out his trembling hand.

Carlos shook it with the strength of a man who worked manual labor his whole life. He sat without saying a word.

"Thank you for meeting me, Mr. Delgado," Tyrell said.

Carlos slid into the booth and swallowed. Not trusting his shaking hands, he didn't dare try to take a sip of water to dampen his mouth. "Would you like something to eat or drink?" Tyrell asked.

Carlos shook his head and continued to stare, silently studying Tyrell.

Tyrell exhaled. He placed his hands on the table and then on his lap. That felt like too much of a submissive position, so he crossed his arms, but that seemed too defiant, so he settled on placing his hands back on the table. "Your daughter and I have been together for five years next Monday, sir." The deepening scowl on Carlos's face made his stomach sour. "So that's our big anniversary. I've been thinking and praying, and I wanted to get your opinion... I mean, permission or blessing to ask Rosa."

Carlos's thick, calloused hand stroked the rough stubble on his chin. His eyes narrowed. Like a bear debating about eating an unsuspecting hiker, a deep rumble built in his chest and reverberated in his throat.

Tyrell sat up straighter and lifted his chin. "I want to ask Rosa for her hand."

"Doesn't she need both of them?"

"I understand if you're hesitant considering my past, but... what?"

A broad grin spread across Carlos's face. He reached across the table and grabbed Tyrell's arm. With both of Carlos's beefy hands wrapped around Tyrell's, Carlos shook his arm so hard that Tyrell's teeth clattered. "Of course, it depends on what Rosa says, but if she agrees, I will treat you as my own son."

Tyrell's jubilation rose but just as quickly came crashing down. "If she agrees? You think she may say no?"

Carlos chuckled. "The first rule of marriage is you never know what your wife will do! If you're asking my opinion, of course, she will say yes. She has always been your biggest advocate."

"I can't tell you how much that means to me, Mr. Delgado. And I want to assure you and your wife that I will be a good husband. I've changed. As far as what I used to be like — "

"Stop." Carlos pointed a thick finger at his face. "You are a new creation. You've given your heart to the Lord, and He forgave your sins. Who am I to bring them up again?"

Tyrell exhaled and settled back into the seat.

"Of course," Carlos continued, "if you fall back into those ways, I will break your legs and then your arms and then — "

"I won't. I won't." Tyrell sat back up.

"I'm kidding!" Carlos laughed. The table shook as he set his massive elbow down. He held out his hand, his index finger and thumb close together. "Maybe I am a little serious. Keep that in mind. Now tell me your plans!"

Tyrell took a deep swig of water and tried to relax. Over the next hour, he had the nicest conversation with Carlos that he'd ever had. They talked about Tyrell's plans to take advantage of a management program at work and Rosa's continuing her nursing degree. Two men in gray coveralls entered the diner and ordered the special while Tyrell spoke with Carlos. One was Hispanic, the other Black. Tyrell showed Carlos the small diamond ring, and the man bragged to everyone like Tyrell was about to present his daughter with the crown jewels. The waitress, the men, and even the cook called out their congratulations.

Tyrell and Carlos said goodbye in the parking lot, with Carlos promising not to tell anyone, especially his wife. As

Carlos drove away, he rolled down his window and said, "Keep that in mind. If you ever want the world to know something, tell Mrs. Delgado. I love her more than words, but she can't keep a secret to save her life!" He beeped twice and drove off into the night.

Tyrell jogged to his car, feeling like an anvil had fallen off his shoulders. He was so happy he felt like he could run home. His Honda was older and had almost 70,000 miles, but he paid it off. Plus, the car had never broken down on him, not once.

Pulling out of the parking lot, he pulled out his cell phone to call Rosa, but he dropped it like he had picked up a snake. Rosa was smart. She already suspected he had planned something big for this anniversary. If he called her now, she may check his location. And when she did, she'd see that Carlos was nearby. She'd put two and two together and spoil the surprise.

Tyrell laughed and rolled down the window. All this over-thinking was driving him crazy. So what if Rosa figured out he was planning to ask her to marry him? It would calm his nerves a bit if she knew.

The night was so beautiful he'd rather walk than drive, but his apartment complex was in the boondocks. Leaving restaurant row and the lights of Darrington behind him, he turned onto Livingston Road to travel by the pond. The day he met Rosa there was the happiest day of his life. He couldn't believe a woman as pretty as she was would love fishing even more than he did. He had just taken up the hobby, and it showed. After casting out his line 3 times, he got it stuck in a tree. Rosa took pity on him and came over and gave him some advice. He was hooked on her ever since.

He thought about trying some elaborate proposal, like tying the ring on the end of the fishing line, but he was so nervous already that he settled on getting down on bended knee and begging. He knew just the spot, the little sandy beach next to the large rock where they met.

Blue lights flashed in his rearview mirror, and a siren clicked on and off.

"What did I do?" Tyrell checked his speedometer. The speed limit was forty-five, and he was under fifty. "Darn it."

He pulled onto the side of the road, hoping the cruiser would pass him, but the police officer turned in behind him.

Getting pulled over in the middle of nowhere set him on edge. After all, he had done nothing wrong. He glanced again at his phone. He thought again about calling Rosa or texting her, but that would make her worry.

The sharp rap of metal on glass made him jump. The policeman outside his window banged on the driver's window with a large metal ring.

Blinded by the officer's flashlight, Tyrell shielded his eyes with his right hand as he powered his window down with his left. "Good evening, officer. I —"

"License and registration."

"Certainly. The registration is in my glove compartment. I'm getting it now." Tyrell leaned over and got his paperwork. "Can I ask why you pulled me over?" He handed the cop his license, too.

"We'll discuss that in a minute." The police officer shined his flashlight on Tyrell's license and then back in his face. "Step out of the car, please."

"What? Why?"

"Your name is Tyrell Miller. You live at 1500 Livingston Road, apartment 43?"

"Yes, sir."

"You have an active warrant for your arrest."

"That's not possible." Tyrell's hands shook. No matter how

hard he tried, somehow, some way, his tainted past always seemed to pollute his present. "There must be some mistake."

"Step out of the car. You can straighten it out later."

Tyrell wiped his hand down his face. "Is there any chance you can let me drive my car home? It's five minutes away."

"I won't ask you again to get out of the car."

Tyrell's hands balled into fists. This was absolutely ludicrous. Now, he'd have to get bailed out and pay for a tow and impound. He gasped. "Look, I'm about to get engaged. The diamond is on the passenger seat. I can't leave it."

The police officer shined the light on the box and then back in Tyrell's face. "I'll secure it. Last warning." He opened the door.

"Okay. Okay." Tyrell got out of the car.

The large cop grabbed his shoulder and spun him around. "Hands on the roof."

Tyrell complied, and the officer patted him down. "I've been clean for over five years. I haven't even gotten a library fine. This has to be a computer glitch."

"You have a rap sheet of forty-three previous charges." The cop jerked Tyrell's arms behind his back. The click of the handcuffs had an all too familiar ring.

"Most of those were petty thefts, but I did five years. The DA threw the book at me and charged me with everything you can think of. I paid my debt."

"You moved up to carjacking."

"I only drove the first car. I had no idea what they were going to do."

"You stole the first car." The cop jerked up on Tyrell's arms and marched him toward the cruiser.

"I've changed. I'm working two jobs, attending church, and even getting married. You'll secure that ring, right?"

They reached the police cruiser, but the cop prodded him past it.

Tyrell stiffened. Why wasn't he placing Tyrell in the car?

The cop shoved him from behind.

Tyrell stumbled and pitched forward. The tar rushed toward his face. With his hands cuffed behind him, there was nothing he could do to break his fall. He shut his eyes as he braced for impact.

The policeman caught him by the collar of his shirt.

Tyrell's face stopped inches away from the pavement. "Thanks." Tyrell gasped, collapsing onto his knees.

The cop jerked him back. Something cold and metal pressed against the side of Tyrell's head.

"NO! PLEASE!"

Chapter Two

"It smells like something died in here," Jack muttered as he cinched the trash bag closed with the speed of a rodeo cowboy. The odor stung his nostrils, and he hurried for the apartment door. Recently married, it still took some getting used to having a wife to inspire him to pay attention to the little things, like making sure the kitchen didn't smell like a garbage dump or, in this case, the morgue.

"I'm taking out the trash," Jack called out.

"Does Lady need to go?" Alice yelled from the bedroom.

"No. I took her out five minutes ago," Jack shouted just before the front door swung closed. He headed toward the stairs at the back of the building, holding the bag to the side and hoping whatever rotted didn't leak out.

He descended the two floors and shoved open the rear door. The cold air of an early spring evening was a welcome change from the frigid winter, but a far cry from his recent honeymoon in the Bahamas. He jogged across the rear parking lot, holding the trash bag as far away from himself as possible.

The gravel crunched beneath Jack's shoes as he crossed to the large green dumpster. Using the plastic of the trash bag to cover the palm of his hand so his skin didn't touch the metal, he raised the lid and froze.

He stood there staring at the dumpster, blinking rapidly.

"No way."

Taking a deep breath, he gazed at the body lying on top of the trash inside the dumpster. The corpse lay face down with the legs twisted at an odd angle. The hot, familiar glow of adrenaline clicked on and pumped through his veins. There was a murder at his doorstep, and he had a family to protect. You can take the soldier out of the war, but the war in the soldier remains. Mentally and physically, he switched to DEFCON 1. He forced himself to breathe normally and remain calm with the words he'd repeated so many times before — "Stay frosty."

Jack slowly closed the lid. He took out his phone and called dispatch. "This is Detective Stratton. I need to report a Code 54."

"Affirmative. What is your location?"

Jack recognized Beverly's voice. The dispatcher was a friend and had been to his home several times. "Behind my apartment in the rear parking lot. The body is in the dumpster. I'll secure the scene."

"Roger that. Sending available units."

Jack hung up the phone, and his eyes widened. Alice had just returned from finding her grandfather, an ex-Ukrainian general with a price on his head, now living in the U.S. under an alias. On top of that, Alice went with Kiku, a member of the Yakuza, to find him. Wherever Kiku went, she left a trail of bodies behind.

Jack raced back to the building and thundered up the stairs.

Taking them three at a time, he shoved open his apartment door. It crashed into the wall with a bang.

Andrew, Alice's grandfather, an older man with a barrel chest and thick gray hair, stood at the kitchen island dicing carrots. When the door burst open, he raised the large chef's knife, ready to fling it straight at Jack.

Jack held out his left hand while yanking the door closed with his right. "There's a body in the dumpster outside." He panted, trying to catch his breath. "Did you put it there?"

Andrew thought momentarily, shook his head, and returned to dicing carrots. "No. I hope you are hungry. I'm making my special veal."

Jack stood there blinking. He just told Andrew there was a body in the dumpster, and it didn't faze him in the slightest.

Once again, Andrew stopped chopping. "Do you need a hand moving this body? I'm happy to help."

"What body?" Alice asked as she stepped out of the bedroom.

Jack rushed over, grabbed her by the wrist, and dragged her into the bedroom, kicking the door closed behind them. "There's a body in the dumpster!"

"Who?!" Alice's green eyes grew as large as emeralds.

"I don't know, but do you need me to narrow it down?! Did your grandfather put it there?"

"No! I was with him the whole time since we've gotten back." Alice's eyes widened again. "What about Kiku?!"

"You don't know if Kiku dumped a body in the dumpster?"

"You never know with her! People are always trying to stab or shoot her, and then she kills them. Maybe she did it after she dropped me off?"

Jack yanked open the bureau and grabbed a burner phone Kiku had given him. "She was my next guess."

"She should have been your first guess, not my grandfather."

"Did Kiku drive on the way back? Did you check the trunk?"

"We loaded the car up with my grandfather's things. There's no way a body could have fit in there."

The phone rang, and Kiku answered. "My apologies for keeping your new bride away from you for so long, Jack. And congratulations on solving your first case."

"Another one just fell into my lap."

"That is wonderful."

"No, it isn't." Jack paced. "There's a body in my dumpster, and you're the prime suspect for putting it there."

"And why would you consider me a suspect? How was the person killed?"

"I don't know yet. I took out my trash and found the body, called the police, and then realized he may have been someone coming after you. Was it self-defense?"

"I am flattered that you are watching out for me, but no, I did not kill anyone in Darrington on this visit."

"So, this body in my dumpster has nothing to do with you?"

"This time, no."

"What do you mean 'this time'?"

"Do you *really* want to know that information, Detective?"

Alice tugged his arm and whispered, "She only kills bad guys now."

Jack covered the phone. "Kiku kills people that Kiku thinks need to be killed."

"You are correct, Detective," Kiku said. "But I assure you, I have no knowledge regarding the body currently in your dumpster."

Sirens sounded on the street below.

"Got it. Thank you for being honest, Kiku." Jack said.

"Give my love to Alice. It sounds like you need to go. Good-bye." The line went dead.

Alice moved to his side. "If Kiku didn't kill him, who did?"

Jack tossed the phone into the trash. He had several more and never used the same one twice to call Kiku. He opened the bedroom door and said, "That's what I need to find out."

Chapter Three

Jack burst out of the apartment building door as a police cruiser, its lights blazing, raced into the parking lot and skidded to a stop. A familiar police officer got out: Calvin Green. The veteran cop stood a little under six feet. In his late forties, his tight shirt strained over his bulging muscles.

Calvin grabbed his hat and exited the car. He swaggered across the parking lot, his hand resting on his gun belt. His eyes narrowed when he recognized Jack.

"What are you doing here, Stratton? We're in the city limits."

"I found the body," Jack said, trying to catch his breath.

"You did?" Calvin stopped. "What were you doing out here?"

"Taking out the garbage." Jack pointed at his trash bag lying on the ground and then up at his apartment. "I live there."

"I thought you sheriff types preferred the suburbs. Did you disturb the crime scene in any way?"

"No. I'm a germaphobe, so I covered my hand with the

trash bag when I lifted the dumpster lid. Because of that, my prints won't be on it. Other than the lid, I didn't touch anything." Jack crossed his arms. "I called the Sheriff's dispatch. What are you doing here?"

The radio in Calvin's cruiser squawked, and more sirens sounded in the distance.

"You're in the city limits. Last time I checked, this is city police jurisdiction."

"I don't want to start a turf war— "

"Nothing's started." Calvin lifted his chin. "Yet."

Jack squared his shoulders but avoided the staring contest, which Calvin seemed determined to start. Jack's father always said to avoid a fight if there was nothing to win. Calvin didn't have the clout to change jurisdiction, so there was no point in arguing with him.

A second city police cruiser pulled into the parking lot and stopped behind Calvin's. Sergeant Emmett Wilson got out and strode over. Emmett's fifty years made his frame thicker but not fat. His black hair was peppered with gray, and streaks of silver highlighted the sides. He strolled across the parking lot, resembling a friendly Wyatt Earp in how he walked slightly bow-legged.

They weren't related, but if Jack weren't aware of that fact, he'd think Emmett was Calvin's older brother. The men had been partners for years. Jack wondered if the same process of married couples looking like each other over time extended to cops.

"Hey, Calvin. Jack." Emmett gave a friendly wave. "Congratulations on both the wedding and the promotion. I heard you were a super cop, but how'd you get here so fast?" Emmett hammed it up as he glanced around the parking lot. He even held his hand against his head and pretended to search the sky.

"He found the body," Calvin said, never taking his eyes off Jack. "Stick around, Stratton. I'm sure our detectives will want to interview you."

Jack shook his head. "Seeing how this body is outside my home, and the Sheriff's department technically has jurisdiction over the county, this is my case."

Calvin's brown eyes hardened. "I thought you wanted to avoid a turf war, not start one. What is your problem, Stratton?"

"I don't have one. But if you're still miffed about losing the Cowboy Shoot, let it go."

"This has nothing to do with that." Calvin's finger jabbed the air in front of Jack's chest. "This is city jurisdiction."

Emmett ambled over to stand between the two men. "How about we let the boys and girls above our pay grades decide?"

"There's nothing to decide," Calvin snapped. "I'm calling the Chief." He marched over to his cruiser.

Emmett eyed Jack.

Jack shrugged.

"You're not going to call Sheriff Morrison?" Emmett asked.

"Why spoil his dinner?" Jack crookedly grinned. "Besides, there's no reason to ask, anyway. The Sheriff's department has jurisdiction."

Emmett scratched the back of his neck. "I'd be the last guy to tell you your job, but traditionally, City calls you guys in. You don't come uninvited."

"True. But I'm going by an older tradition."

"What's that?" Emmett said.

"Finders keepers. I found the body. It's my case."

Emmett laughed, but it quickly faded. "Try to cut Calvin some slack. You heard, right?"

Jack pressed his lips together and shook his head.

"His daughter Emma was murdered out in California six

months back. Nice kid. She was visiting an aunt, and some three-strike loser out on bond carjacked them."

The news hit Jack like a punch in the gut. He was all too aware of the pain that loss carved through a person's heart. Jack glanced over to Calvin, who stood with his back to them, talking into his phone. A wave of guilt washed over him. Aunt Haddie was right. You never knew what someone else was going through. "Thanks for the heads-up," Jack said. Have you got any tape?"

Emmett fished a roll of yellow police tape out of his pocket and held it up. "I thought you fellas would need some. How wide of a perimeter do you want?"

Jack surveyed the parking area. The lot was tar, and the area surrounding the dumpster was gravel, so the chance of getting footprint impressions was nil. Still, with the advances in forensics, the wayward hair or discarded pieces of gum solved cases. "We'll set a two-level. I'll tape off around the dumpster, and then we'll cordon off the entire parking lot. Do you have cones in your cruiser?"

"A few."

"While you grab those, I'll start."

Jack created a twenty-yard square around the dumpster. He frowned as he stared at the trash container. They'd have to sift through every piece of garbage. Jack closed his eyes and pinched his nose between his thumb and index finger. Had Alice, her grandfather, or Kiku thrown anything out that he didn't want the police to find? With his stomach twisting into a knot, Jack finished his tape barricade.

Emmett returned carrying the cones. While he placed them at the entrance and taped off the parking lot, Calvin stood beside his cruiser, talking on his phone.

Jack cocked an eyebrow. Everyone in Darrington knew Emmett. He was practically the face of the Darrington P.D. He recorded public service announcements and gave talks throughout the city to bolster their community policing programs. Why would a Sergeant do the grunt work while Calvin called the station?

Jack remembered Calvin's daughter. Emmett was probably keeping an eye out for his friend.

Calvin strode forward with a broad smile and stopped two feet away from Jack. He crossed his beefy arms. "Our detective is enroute."

Jack tried to flash a friendly smile. "Who's covering? Price? Medina?"

"New hire. Transfer in from Monterey. Detective Reyes."

An unmarked Ford Interceptor pulled into the parking lot with its emergency flashers on.

"Speak of the Devil," Calvin said. "I'll let you introduce yourself, Stratton. I can't wait to see this." He laughed as he walked over to Emmett.

The driver's door of the Interceptor opened, and a woman exited. Five foot six, fit, she wore her long black hair pulled back in a ponytail. Dressed in a blue-collared shirt, khaki pants, and a brown blazer, she wore her gold badge on her hip and her service weapon in a shoulder holster. She adjusted her glasses as she strolled toward Jack.

"Officer Stratton?" She smiled and extended a hand. "Detective Jillianna Reyes. Everyone calls me Jill. I've heard a lot about you. You found the body?"

"I did." Jack shook her hand. "It's Detective Stratton, now. I'll be taking jurisdiction on this case."

"You're with the Sheriff's department. This is within the city limits."

"Calvin mentioned you were recently hired, so I don't know if you know exactly how jurisdiction functions out here.

The sheriff has law enforcement authority over the whole county — including the city. I'm calling this case."

Jill scrunched her nose, and her head tipped to the side. "Not yet, you aren't. Chief Hill wants me to take it. He's clearing it with Morrison as we speak."

The last thing Jack wanted was to sour the Sheriff's Department's relationship with the police any more than it already was. Still, he wasn't about to roll over. "That's too bad. I didn't want to spoil Bob's dinner. His wife Meg makes a pot roast on Sunday that melts in your mouth. Tell you what, until this gets settled, let's make a truce. We'll start this as a joint investigation. A democracy where we both call the shots."

Jill crossed her arms. Her lips pressed together in a grimace, indicating her feelings about his proposition. She glanced at her watch. "I suppose I can handle that for the next five minutes." She flashed a slight smirk as she walked toward the dumpster.

Jack cleared his throat.

Jill stopped.

Even with her back to him, Jack could tell she was miffed from her rigid posture and the lengthening of her neck.

Jill glanced over her shoulder. "I'm going to get a look at the body. Would you like to say something about that, Detective Stratton?"

"Jack is fine. We should hold off examining the body until the techs run the dumpster for fingerprints. Mine won't be on it."

"You opened it. You must have touched the lid."

"I'm a bit of a germaphobe, so I covered my hand with the trash bag when I did. When I saw the body, I let the lid down gently. It's been dry as the desert, and with all the pollen, the killer may have left prints. I didn't want the lid crashing down to knock them off. Hopefully, the techs get something."

Jill didn't turn around. Maybe she was debating what he said or trying to come up with an argument.

"If you have a better suggestion, I'll listen," Jack said.

Jill shook her head and motioned Jack out of the immediate area. "Why don't I ask you a few questions while we wait for crime scene?"

Jack followed her over to Mrs. Stevens' car.

"Is this dumpster for your building only?"

"Yes. It's three floors and three apartments on each floor."

"The parking lot isn't gated. Do you have a problem with people dumping trash?"

Jack shook his head. "Not that I know of. I've never heard Mrs. Stevens complain. She owns the place."

"Walk me through what happened tonight."

Jack took a deep breath. "My wife just got home and —"

"Where had she been?"

"Visiting an old family friend." Jack swallowed. Since Alice's grandfather had a price on his head, he had to use an alias, but Jack didn't know what it was.

"Who? Where?"

"I haven't gotten all the details from my wife yet. She had just gotten home when I went to take the trash out. Anyway, I get to the dumpster —"

"Back up a minute. You have no idea who your wife went to visit?"

Jack shrugged. "We have a very trusting relationship."

"Trust is one thing. Blindness is another. How long was she gone?"

"A couple of weeks."

Jill pulled on her gold stud earring. "And you don't know where or with whom your wife went for two weeks?"

Jack tried to figure out a way to derail her current line of questioning. "Alice and I are newlyweds. I'm still discovering how this whole marriage thing works. Who gets what side of the sink in the bathroom, what side of the bed she wants to sleep on, that kind of stuff."

"Her going away without you having a clue where she went is in a completely different league than agreeing on whether the toilet paper roll should hang over or under."

Jack laughed. "That was funny."

"I didn't mean it as a joke." Jill crossed her arms.

Running footsteps made Jack turn.

Alice skidded to a stop beside him. "Sorry to barge in! I'm Alice Stratton, Jack's wife."

"Nice to meet you. Maybe you can explain where you were for the last two weeks and why your husband didn't know."

Alice smiled up at Jack, but one look into her eyes filled him with terror. She was about to make up a story on the fly, and that was a skill she was surprisingly bad at. "I know it's hard to believe because of his macho exterior, but Jack is the sweetest, most thoughtful man in the world. That's why I married him. And you know how some brides get cold feet before the altar? Well, I had a meltdown *after*. Being so unselfish, Jack thought I should get away and clear my head. So, I did."

Jill's gaze ping-ponged between Alice and Jack. "And where was this?"

"Florida. But what does that have to do with the body in the dumpster?" Alice asked.

"Did you take out the trash with Jack?"

"No."

"Then how do you know that there's a body in the dumpster?" Jill stared at Jack. "Officer Green informed me he saw you running out of the apartment building when he arrived. Did you fail to secure the crime scene, Detective Stratton?"

Jack cringed internally. "Like I said, I'm new to the whole

marriage thing, and right after I called it in, I wanted to make sure Alice was okay. So, I ran upstairs, but I came right back down."

"But you did leave?"

"Yes."

"We were watching out the window, and nobody came to the dumpster while he was upstairs," Alice added.

"We?" Jill asked.

Alice turned to Jack. Her green eyes were as big as plates and had *help me* written all over them.

The back door of the apartment building crashed open, and Andrew appeared carrying a trash bag. "Jack? Alice? What's going on?"

Jack's eyes rolled up, and he stared at the evening sky.

"I take it you're the friend Alice went to see?" Jill asked.

"I am Aino Oja. It's difficult for Americans to pronounce, so you can call me Andrew."

"You want to spell that for me?" Jill took out her phone. "Better yet, do you have any identification?"

"Of course." Andrew set down the trash bag and took out a worn wallet. He handed Jill a Florida driver's license. "I am a naturalized citizen originally from Estonia. Alice's mother was my cousin's second aunt."

"And you were in the apartment when Jack said he found a body?"

Andrew glanced at Jack, who gave a slight nod. "Yes."

Jill waited for him to elaborate, but Andrew said nothing more. She turned to Jack. "Still, you should have stayed at the crime scene. I'll have to note in my report that you left."

"Oh, no," Andrew shook his head and clicked his tongue. "You have it all wrong. Jack had a good reason to come upstairs. I was cutting carrots and... uh," he glanced at Alice.

"I screamed!" Alice blurted out. "I thought he cut himself, and I shrieked."

Jack felt like he'd just guessed the correct answer in math class. "And since the apartment window was open, and I heard the scream, I had to ensure civilians were safe. That supersedes securing the scene, according to department policy."

All three of them smiled and nodded.

Jill's eyebrows traveled in different directions. "Seriously?"

"We better go see when the techs are getting here," Jack said. "Thanks so much, Alice and Andrew. I'll talk to you in a little bit. You've been so helpful. Why don't you go back to the apartment now?"

"I still have more questions for them," Jill said.

"I'm sure you do, but we should get right on processing this." Jack's phone pinged in his pocket, announcing a text message. He pulled it out and scowled. He read Morrison's text twice to make sure he hadn't read it wrong. SPOKE WITH CHIEF HALL. I WANT THIS TO BE A JOINT INVESTIGATION WITH THE CITY. I'M SURE YOU'LL WANT TO DISCUSS IT IN THE MORNING.

Jill held up her phone and scowled. "Looks like we will be working together on this after all."

Jack stuffed the phone into his pocket. "I'll talk to the Sheriff about it in the morning. But until then, truce?"

Jill made a face like she swallowed a bug.

"You can go call your chief and argue with him about his decision now, or you can help me figure out who dumped a body on my doorstep. Your choice, but I'm not backing off."

Jill thought about it momentarily and held out her hand, which Jack shook.

"No offense," Jill said. "But I didn't think it was a good idea for you to take this case because I'm worried you'll take it personally."

"I take every case personally." Jack pointed back at the dumpster. "But you haven't seen the body yet. The corpse is lying on top of the trash bags. Whoever put him in there made no effort to cover him up. They wanted the body to be found. So yeah, I worry that this may be personal."

"Do you have a lot of enemies?"

Jack vainly tried to stop the sarcastic grin spreading across his lips. "It's a lengthy list. And I've got a bad habit of adding to it. I hope you had dinner. It's going to be a long night."

Chapter Four

Jack stood staring at the dumpster, eager to find out the identity of the deceased man inside. Before they could do that, the techs needed to photograph the scene. More flashing emergency lights added to the glow as the crime scene van pulled up and parked in the street. He and Jill met in the middle of the parking lot. The door slid open, and Dr. Lai climbed out. The petite woman gave a friendly wave.

Jack was used to calling her Mei, but considering her recent promotion and the fact they were in the field, he opted for formality. "Detective Jill Reyes, this is our Medical Examiner, Dr. Lai."

Dr. Lai blushed. "Please call me Mei." She tucked an errant strand of her shoulder-length dark hair behind her ear and adjusted her rectangular blue-and-pink glasses.

"It's a pleasure to meet you," Jill said.

"Are you Jack's replacement partner?" Mei asked.

Jill shook her head. "This is a joint investigation. Both the Sheriff's department and the city police are taking part."

"I heard about Ed's leg, Jack. Is he all right?" Mei tied her hair into a ponytail.

"Ed's doing great. He's taking some time off while it heals," Jack said. "He'll be back soon."

Mei pulled some gloves out of her pocket and frowned. "If it's a joint investigation, I guess that means every report will need to be doubled. That's going to mean a mountain of paperwork. Still, I'd rather be safe behind my desk than riding shotgun with Jack." Mei laughed. "Jack tends to get shot at quite often."

Jill chuckled until she realized Mei wasn't joking. Some of the color drained out of her cheeks.

"What do we have?" Mei asked.

Jack closed one eye like he was staring through a sniper scope as he recalled the details. "Black male. He looks to be in his mid-20s. 5 foot 8 or 9 inches tall. Average build. 150 pounds. Short, black hair. He's dressed in a white-collared business shirt. Blue jeans, black sneakers. He has a probable gunshot wound to the back of his head."

Jill did a double take. "I thought you only caught a glance at the corpse?"

Mei grinned. "Jack is extremely observant. You'll enjoy working with him. As long as you don't get shot or blown up." She laughed again.

From how Jill's brow furrowed, he hoped Jill would request off the case on her own.

"There's a layer of dust on the dumpster. The techs might be able to lift some prints." Jack explained.

Mei crossed her arms and thought for a moment. "We'll work from outside in. I'll start the paperwork while the techs process the ground around the dumpster. I'll call you when we open the lid?"

"Sounds like a plan," Jack said, then turned to Jill. "We

should sweep the perimeter to see if we can find the original crime scene."

Jill nodded. "I don't think I've ever heard of someone getting murdered inside a dumpster."

"There's always that first case, but seeing how there wasn't blood on the trash bags, I doubt it. You sweep clockwise, I go counter, and we meet at six?"

Jill winked and gave him a thumbs-up.

Fanning out, Jack took his time looking for evidence of violence as he circled the parking lot. Even with the victim being shot in the head, finding the initial crime scene would still be difficult. Most people thought police work functioned as it did on TV, and there'd be a pool of blood with the murder weapon sitting beside it like a pirate's treasure marked with a bright red X. But actual reality didn't work that way. Jack stared at the landscaped area surrounding the building. With so many areas of dark mulch and low-growth shrubs, you could dump a gallon of blood, and the vegetation would soak it up so the spot would blend in.

When Jill caught up, he'd reached nine on the imaginary clock he had divided the parking lot into. She'd searched the unfamiliar area twice as fast as he did. She was either hyper-observant or rushed. Since the crime scene techs were searching that area, too, he decided not to go over it himself and further aggravate the working arrangements.

"Do you want to split up to canvass the neighbors?" Jack asked.

"Why don't we have uniforms do that?" Jill said.

"You know the saying; you never get a second chance to make a good first impression? I think that goes for potential witnesses, too. I like to watch their reactions when they first hear the news. And their memory is fresher."

Jill crossed her arms. "Seeing how we have time to kill, how about I take your apartment complex?"

Jack clicked his fingernails and tried to appear nonplussed. Because of the situation with Alice's grandfather, it already looked like Jack was hiding something — which he was. He smiled and nodded. "Go for it. But, before we start," Jack said. "I need to run upstairs and get my badge, gun, and body camera."

"The Sheriff makes detectives wear body cameras?"

"No. I think he should, but it helps me with notes."

Jill's lips pursed together. "I guess you like being thorough."

"That, and it helps if I bring in a suspect who has been injured. I like having the camera as an eyewitness to prove I didn't do it. Be right back." Jack sprinted for the house.

Taking the stairs three at a time, he burst into the apartment. Alice and Andrew sat at the kitchen table, eating dinner, with Lady lying on the couch. Alice and Lady got up, and everyone began talking immediately, including Lady, who growled and barked.

"I only have a second, so you need to listen," Jack said. "I made a mistake —"

"In calling the police?" Andrew nodded as he cut up his steak. "I agree."

"I am the police," Jack said, somewhat miffed.

"He didn't mean anything by that," Alice said.

"I most certainly did." Andrew took a large bite but continued to talk and chew simultaneously. "In my country, you handle things like the man in the dumpster yourself. You do not involve the government."

"In America, we call the police," Jack said.

"But you said yourself — you are the police. So, you still should have handled it yourself." Andrew shot back.

"The mistake I was referring to was I didn't ask you what

your alias was." Jack grabbed his gun, badge, camera, and a leash, which he handed to Alice. "Alice, can you come with me and bring Lady?"

"Of course." Alice fastened the leash to Lady's collar. "If you're going to do what I think you're going to do, you're brilliant!"

"He just admitted he made a big mistake." Andrew took a sip of milk. "Don't lie to puff up his ego. It's not good in a marriage."

Jack's mouth fell open. He was about to set Alice's grandfather straight when she grabbed him by the hand and dragged him out into the hallway.

"He takes a little while to get used to," Alice said as Lady tugged her along.

"Lady, stop." Jack's head spun with everything going on and all he needed to do. "Before we go outside, are we going with the story that your grandfather is Aino Oja from Estonia, an old family friend?"

"He's got all the paperwork, so why not?"

"Oh, I don't know. Maybe because it goes against the oath I swore as a detective?"

"You made another one when you married me." Alice flashed him that smile that melted his heart and his will. "So, they kind of cancel each other out, right?"

Jack leaned down and kissed her. "Sometimes I think it would be nice to live in this other world of yours."

Lady barked and yanked Alice forward and toward the stairs.

"Here's the deal," Jack said as they went outside. "Morrison paired me with that other detective to work the case together. I know zero about her, so say nothing and follow my lead, okay?"

Alice saluted, but he knew that with his impulsive wife, that was no guarantee of compliance.

Jack whistled loudly as he came out of the door, then cupped his hand to his mouth and called out, "Listen up, everybody! Gather round."

Mei and the crime scene techs formed a wide circle around Jack, Alice, and Lady.

"What is that?" Jill pointed at Lady from a distance.

"This is Lady, my King Shepherd," Jack explained. "And she's the best tracking dog I know. I should have thought of her first."

Jill shook her head. "She'll have to wait for the techs to process the prints like the rest of us. We can't open the dumpster until then, so she can't get a scent."

"Lady has a traumatic past," Jack said. "But it makes her the best cadaver dog there is. She only needs to get close. Ask around later."

Mei raised her hand. "I'll vouch for her."

All the techs raised their hands, too. One said, "She helped find the person who murdered those women last year."

"And the Giant Killer." Another added.

Jill shrugged. "That's good enough for me. I'll watch from over here, though."

"If you all could stay back for a moment, I'd appreciate it." Jack walked toward the dumpster with Alice and Lady following.

As they got closer, Lady froze. Jack and Alice crouched down next to her. The poor dog whimpered, and her ears laid back on her head.

"Sorry I have to ask this of you, girl," Jack said, swearing the dog understood him. "But I need your help."

Alice patted Lady's back. "You can do it."

Jack led Lady over to the dumpster. Lady's nose wrinkled. She pawed the ground and barked.

"Yip, yip," Alice said.

"Yip, yip?" Jack raised an eyebrow. "I knew we should have used German to train Lady."

"I don't know German." Alice shrugged. "And this way, no bad guys can confuse Lady because only you and I know her commands."

"Only you know them. What does yip, yip mean?"

"Start tracking."

Lady sniffed the air and placed her muzzle close to the ground. She slowly moved out a few feet and stopped.

Still keeping her distance, Jill craned her neck to look at the spot and frowned. "She didn't go very far."

"She didn't have to." Jack squatted down next to Lady and peered at the ground. Dark spots speckled the grayish-white gravel. Jack pointed to a tech. "Greg, you need to flag this spot."

Greg hustled over and handed Jack a marker, then quickly retreated.

Jack didn't blame Greg for being nervous around Lady. She was an intimidating dog, and her reputation for taking down bad guys in the police department had already grown legendary.

"Yip-yip," Jack said.

Lady sniffed the air. She trotted toward the parking lot entrance and back again. Jack repeated the command twice, but she responded the same way each time.

"Good girl," Alice stroked her back.

"Give her some steak," Jack said, then cringed.

Lady bolted for the apartment, dragging Alice after her.

"Sorry!" Jack said. *Steak, outside,* and *walk* were three words that made Lady freak out.

Jill strolled over. "You think you found something?"

"Lady did." Jack pointed at the spot where he set the flag. "Blood. And look at the gravel pushed up there. The piles are about five feet apart."

Jill nodded. "It looks like someone backed a car up, took the body out, and dumped it."

"They'd be in and out in less than two minutes. No muss, no fuss. Hopefully, someone saw something."

Two techs came forward. One carried a camera and the other several evidence markers.

"Thanks, guys." Jack stepped back so they could get to work, then turned to Jill. "What's your contact information so I can give you a heads-up when Mei calls me?"

After Jill's information was entered into his phone, Jack headed for the building next door. The house stood on the corner of the street, a well-kept duplex in a neat row of similar facades. A wrought-iron fence that had been polished to a shiny black separated the little patch of yard from the sidewalk, while the cool blue hues of the wooden exterior looked like they had just been painted. The windows were framed with delicate white lace curtains.

Jack climbed the steps and stopped. The door to the house was a deep mahogany color, with a brass knocker. He rang the doorbell. There was a long silence, and then footsteps sounded from inside. The door opened, and Mrs. Singh, an older woman, answered. The brightly colored sari she wore almost engulfed her slight frame. Her eyes grew large. "Oh, Jack. Whatever is going on?" She said, her voice thick with her Pakistani accent.

"We've had a tragic situation occur in the parking lot out back," Jack said. "We believe it is an isolated incident, and you're not in danger. I'm here officially from the Sheriff's Department, and I was hoping to ask you some questions."

She nodded and stepped aside. "Please come in."

Jack followed her into the house, which had a warm and inviting atmosphere. The walls were lined with bookshelves, and the air carried the faint scent of incense. The living room was tidy, with a couch, a loveseat, and two recliners.

"Arahm and his sisters are visiting their brother in Phoenix. With my back acting up, I decided not to go. I'm so glad you stopped by. I was getting a little nervous about all the commotion outside."

"Speaking of commotion," Jack sat on the loveseat while Mrs. Singh settled into a recliner. "Did you notice anything before the police arrived? And if you need to recline your chair for your back, please go ahead."

"Oh, thank you." She picked up a remote. A motor whirled, raising her legs and easing her body into a reclining position. "Before the police came? I don't think so." She pressed her lips together and thought for a moment. "Mostly, I lay here watching TV. I only left the room to go into the kitchen for some tea. I didn't hear or see anything odd."

"Do you have cameras in the house?"

"We have a doorbell camera, but that's it."

"That could still come in handy," Jack said. "Would you mind getting me the footage for the last few days?"

"Not at all." She picked up her phone. "Where should I send it?"

Jack gave her his Sheriff's Department email. His hopes rose — how he loved cameras. But when Mrs. Singh showed him her phone, reality set in. They'd angled the camera down, and it didn't record any of the street. Most people set up their cameras to catch porch pirates, not murderers driving by on the way to dump a body.

Jack wrapped up the interview with Mrs. Singh and four other neighbors before Mei called him back to the parking lot. It was almost eleven, and the lights in his apartment were still on. Even though Alice had a big day tomorrow, he knew she'd wait up until he returned.

Once the techs were finished processing the ground, they gathered around the dumpster. Jack stood on Mei's right while Jill waited on the left. With crime scene techs each taking a side of the lid, they slowly raised the cover and set it back.

Jack stared down at the corpse, and his anger rose. Aunt Haddie had raised him to believe that every person was created by God and, therefore, special. Yet here was a man with his whole life ahead of him, brutally murdered and tossed out in the trash. He didn't know the man or his name, but he and Jack were now connected. Jack had sworn an oath to uphold the law. Finding this man's killer and bringing him to justice wasn't a job for Jack. It was his mission.

Chapter Five

Jack snuck into his bedroom and quietly closed the door. Alice lay in the bed, facing the opposite wall. He didn't know if she was asleep, but she had a big day tomorrow, so as quietly as possible, he undressed and slipped under the covers.

Alice rolled over and pulled herself against his side. "Hey, Babe." Her green eyes were bright but sleepy. "How'd it go?"

Jack held his petite wife close and let her warmth seep into his body through the oversized t-shirt she wore. "Narrowing it down. No big leads."

"Did your new partner suspect anything about my grandfather?"

"Best case scenario, she thinks we're all very odd. Worse case, she starts digging. We'll have to get on the same page about your grandfather's cover story tomorrow. Speaking of tomorrow, are you excited?"

Alice bit her bottom lip and nodded quickly. "Are you still nervous about my doing it?" She asked.

"Bounty hunting is dangerous."

"You did it."

"Only because I got kicked off the police force. I still don't understand why you don't go into law enforcement."

"I'm still catching bad guys."

"But you'd have backup." Jack placed his right hand behind his head. "You'd be a great cop."

Alice blew a raspberry. "I follow the rules less than you do. How long would I make it on a police force?"

Jack opened his mouth, closed it, and chuckled.

"See?" She pressed closer. "Do you think I won't make it as a bounty hunter?"

Jack stared up at the ceiling. "This will probably come out wrong, so don't get upset. But Aunt Haddie always taught me to tell the truth in love. And seeing how I love you, I need you to know my concerns. I know you can find the bad guys. Bringing them in is what worries me."

"So, you think I can catch them, but not keep them?" Her eyes narrowed.

"Yes. But it has nothing to do with you being a woman. Take a firefighter for an example. If I were trapped in a burning building, I wouldn't care if that firefighter was purple. I only care if they can get me out of the building. If they aren't physically able to do that, I die, and they might too."

"You think I'm not strong enough?"

"I'm not saying that either. There's always someone out there stronger than you. I could never put cuffs on Chandler. He was way too strong. But I knew that, so I wouldn't even attempt it. I worry you'll have a chip on your shoulder and try to use force to take down people you can't, and you'll get hurt."

"That's why I have the taser, pepper spray, a baton, and mace. And Bobbie G is helping me."

"Still, most of the people you are going after will be stronger than you."

"You're teaching me Martial Arts." Alice let go of him and rolled onto her stomach.

"Also called the art of self-defense. You're going to be on *offense.*"

"You're freaking me out a little bit."

"You need to be freaked out a little bit." He draped an arm over her shoulders. "A little fear is a good thing. Remember, you've got nothing to prove."

"I know I don't."

Jack frowned. "Then why don't you take Lady? She makes big guys wet their pants."

Alice smiled but shook her head. "She can't fit in my Bug comfortably. I'd have to borrow your car."

"It's our car."

"I think Lady scares Bobbie G."

"He'll get over it." Jack shrugged.

"That's not the way to treat a partner. Bobbie is nice enough to split the bounty fifty-fifty."

Jack pulled her close and kissed her. He stared into her eyes. "I love you so much, I worry."

"Right back at you." She kissed him tenderly. Her hands traveled up his back, sending flashes of lightning across his skin everywhere she touched.

Jack reached down and grabbed her hip.

Alice gasped, but not in a good way.

"What's wrong?" Jack let go.

"My grandfather is here!"

Jack stared at the bedroom door and listened. Besides their breathing, the house was quiet. "He's probably asleep."

"What if he isn't? He could hear us."

Jack leaned in to kiss her neck. "I'll be quiet. Totally stealthy."

"I'm serious, Jack. You're loud. The bed's loud."

"You're loud, too."

Alice frowned. "See! He'll hear."

"Not if we're quiet."

"I don't know if I can be."

"It will be fun to try." Jack impishly smiled.

Alice scooted over to her side of the bed, pulling the blankets around her like a shield. "I'm not comfortable doing it with him here."

Jack rubbed his hand down his face. "But he's living with us now. Are we never having sex again until he moves out?"

"Just give me a couple of days."

"A couple of days?"

"You can go a couple of days."

"I'm a guy."

Alice rolled her eyes. "You made it months before we were married."

Jack nodded sagely while trying to give her his best seductive look. "But that was before the buffet was opened 24x7."

Alice laughed. "The buffet is closed — temporarily. Please?"

Jack lay on his back, folded his hands behind his head, and shut his eyes. He hadn't foreseen this coming when he agreed to Alice's grandfather living there. Now, he had to find another place for Andrew to live.

Who was he kidding? Alice and Andrew had spent a lifetime apart. Jack couldn't ask him to leave. He'd have to figure out a way around Alice's uncomfortableness. Maybe he could soundproof the bedroom? Or... Jack's eyes snapped open. He had just thought of the perfect present for Andrew — noise-canceling headphones.

Genius.

Chapter Six

Alice strolled through the doors of Patton's Supply. It didn't feel the same since the old owner, Benny Duggan, sold it and moved to Florida to retire. Benny was a diehard Patton fan. He even dressed like him and went everywhere in military clothing. Benny was unconventional, to say the least, but Alice liked the eccentric man.

She took out her phone and ran down her checklist — pepper spray refills, Taser cartridges, and another pair of handcuffs.

The store was divided into four sections: guns and ammo, hunting and fishing, police and tactical, and knives. She found the fact they dedicated an entire section to knives a little disturbing, but she soon found herself drawn along the rows upon rows of items whose packaging cried out for her attention.

Grateful Jack had selected her gear when she started bounty hunting with him, she only had to pick up refills. She wouldn't know where to begin if he hadn't helped her. There were dozens of choices for brands of pepper spray and even options for how to carry and deploy it. She decided on two cans of pepper spray: a gel and an aerosol. The gel was best used if it was windy or there was a chance of blowback. She selected the type she could carry on her belt clip and picked up a third one on a keyring for when she went jogging or for undercover work.

Stopping at the handcuff section, she frowned. They only had three sizes of non-flex handcuffs: standard, oversized one, and oversized two. She wanted a smaller size, so she waited to check online later.

After getting the rest of the items on her list, she wandered into the police and tactical section of the store. Shelves and racks contained everything from uniforms and badges to bullet-proof vests and emergency lights. They had it all.

Alice stopped at the lighting section and grabbed their most powerful flashlight. Not only would this thing light up the night, but she could temporarily blind someone if needed. A car-mounted spotlight caught her eye. They even had one in blue that would match her Bug.

With her basket filled, she headed to the checkout counter.

A large man behind the register leaned on the counter, his palms flat against the glass. He was in his fifties, six feet tall, with a shaved head and stout. His neck was thicker than Alice's waist, and his broad chest looked like he had lifted weights. His name tag was written in black permanent marker: BUD. "Good morning. Picking up some presents for your boyfriend?"

"They're for me." Alice set the basket on the counter and took out her wallet.

Bud's jaw went slack, and he ran a hand over his bald head. "I sure stuck my foot in my mouth. Sorry about that."

"No worries." Alice's smile disappeared when she realized she had forgotten Taser refills. "I forgot to grab something. I'll be right back."

"Take as long as you need. Hey, Brad! We've got a customer that needs some assistance."

A man who resembled a softer, much younger Bud appeared at the end of the counter and set down a cardboard box. His name tag read, BRAD. "I can help you if you like."

"Thank you." Alice smiled as he followed her back to the Taser aisle. "I need some Taser refills."

"Be sure to show her the new concealed carry pocketbooks we got in," Bud called out. "Or what about those new ladies' keychain weapons? One has sparkly hearts, but an extendable three-inch stainless steel blade is inside." Bud called after them.

"Unless you need something like that, ignore my Dad. He's the king of the upsell." Brad said.

"I'm on a budget." Alice drove the thought of the pay cut Jack took when he rejoined the sheriff's department out of her mind. "I better stick with the Taser refills."

"Did you know the LE Taser and civilian versions use the same cartridges? LE Tasers have a five-second power cycle when the trigger is pulled, even if it's held down. The cartridges merely fire off the darts and confetti for future ID. But the LE model can shoot further. They're good out to thirty feet, while yours is limited to fifteen."

"I didn't know that." Alice grabbed three of the correct replacement cartridges from the rack. "LE? Law Enforcement?"

"Yes. Be careful when using the pepper spray and the Taser. The spray is flammable."

"The Taser makes the spark, and whoosh — instant barbeque! My husband warned me."

"I'm Brad, by the way." Brad held out his hand, and she shook it.

"Alice Stratton. Thank you for your help."

"Your husband wouldn't be Detective Jack Stratton, would he?"

"One and the same," Alice said proudly.

Brad's mouth fell open. "No way! I met him. He came to speak at the Citizen's Academy."

"That's the police ride-along program, right?"

"They do that and tour the jails and courthouse, too. It's unbelievable. I'm going to the police academy next year."

Alice stopped when they reached the counter.

"He should have been going this year," Bud said as he took the cartridges from Alice. "But the fellas running things over there wouldn't know a good cop if he fell in their lap."

"It was good advice, Dad." Brad took Alice's empty basket off the counter. "I tried to apply at the police academy, and they wanted me to make sure I could pass the physical first."

"It's ridiculous," Bud said, ringing up Alice's items. "Crime is through the roof, and they won't let him join. Besides, a little meat on the bones helps when cuffing a drunk. Believe you, me. And I know what I'm talking about. Nineteen years on the force." Bud pointed at a cardboard display on the counter. "With you being a young lady and all, have you considered a date rape detection kit? Say you're out at the bar and wonder if someone tried something with your drink."

"She's married, Dad."

"Still, you can't be too safe. And the kits are on sale."

"I'm good." Alice nodded. "But you might know the answer to this. I wanted to get a second pair of handcuffs. I've got the standard size, but if I put them on me, I can slip out of them."

"Not if you put them on right," Bud said. "A lot of people, cops included, don't make them tight enough. And seeing how you're petite, you gotta make them real tight, or someone can slip out of them." Bud held up the spotlight Alice had picked out. "You're not some kind of whacker, are you?"

Brad rolled his eyes. "She's Detective Stratton's wife. He's the one I told you about. He caught the Giant Killer!"

"Oh, yeah. He's the guy you were fanboying all over."

"What's a whacker?" Alice asked, unsure whether to be upset or not.

Brad gently placed a hand on her shoulder. "My dad's kidding. He didn't mean any offense."

"A whacker is a wannabe cop," Bud said. "We get them in all the time, but never a female." He winked and chuckled.

"You should look them up online," Brad said. "There are lots of videos of guys pretending to be police officers. Some even pull people over and write them tickets."

"I'm not pretending to be a cop," Alice said. "But is it illegal for a regular person to use that spotlight?"

"That depends on how you're using it," Bud said. "You can't use it while your car is moving or on a highway. Other than that, it's a great buy. Do you want some replacement bulbs?"

Brad cleared his throat. "If you put that on your car, there's a chance you'll get pulled over."

"She's a detective's wife. She'll be fine." Bud pointed to the display on his left. "What about one of these Thunder Pens? A mini stun gun in your pocket. It's on sale." Bud grinned hopefully.

Alice glanced at the pink taser the size of a marker and caved in.

"Wonderful!" Bud's smile widened. "You'll love it."

"What do you do for work?" Brad asked.

"I'm a fugitive recovery agent."

Brad raised a skeptical eyebrow. "Are you serious?"

Alice took a deep breath.

"From that look on her face, I'd say she's serious," Bud said. "And do you know what I say? Good for you. Back in my day, they'd never let a woman work for a bounty hunter, even in the office. Are you a secretary?"

"Dad!" Brad's voice rose high.

Bud's mouth fell open. "There I go putting my foot in my mouth again. I'm sorry. I didn't mean any disrespect. It's just you must weigh a hundred pounds wet. Are you really working out in the field? It must be as a spotter or decoy, right?"

"Don't you listen to me?" Brad said. "She worked with Jack before he went back to the Sheriff's Department."

Bud opened and closed his mouth. His eyebrows knit together as he stared at Alice. "I apologize if my words came out wrong. Like I said, I was on the force for nineteen years, so I know how rough it can be on the streets. But good for you for trying at least."

Alice nodded, but Bud's words were like throwing gasoline on the self-doubt growing inside her. She pressed her lips together and tried to keep her hand from shaking as she tapped her credit card against the machine. "Thank you, both. It was nice meeting you." Alice grabbed the bag and spun on her heels.

"Thank you!" Bud called after her. "Come again."

She hurried for the exit. Maybe she was a fool for trying to make it as a bounty hunter, but she brought valuable skills to the job. She helped Jack catch plenty of skips, and she and Bobbie G would make a great team. Besides, she needed to help make up for the lost revenue.

Shoving open the door, she gulped in the fresh air. It did nothing to quench the fears burning inside her. It only fanned the flames. Perhaps Bud was right — maybe she was making a huge mistake.

Chapter Seven

Jack sipped his coffee at his desk in the Sheriff's station. The black liquid was as bitter as he remembered it but still made him smile. Settling back in his chair, he stared at his computer screen. It didn't take him long to organize the results of the initial canvass. Both Jill and he came up empty. He kept glancing toward the door, expecting the detective to come rushing in any minute, but she was probably at the police station giving her update to the Chief.

Jack flipped to the next page of his notebook. It was a bulleted list of reasons why he should handle the investigation alone. It wasn't that he didn't like Jill or think she was incompetent; he simply worked better alone.

Footsteps sounded in the corridor leading to the rear parking area. Sheriff Robert Morrison smiled as he strolled into the office. Bob, a tall African American man in his late fifties, wore the tan uniform of the Sheriff's department without the hat. His curly black hair was short and graying at the temples. "Good morning, Jack. Got a minute to bring me up to speed?"

"Yes, sir." Jack stood and snapped to attention.

Bob sighed.

Jack shrugged. "Sorry, sir. The Army and Sheriff Collins made it a tough habit to break."

"I don't know why Art insisted on everyone acting like he was the bridge commander, but don't do that with me. It freaks me out when you do."

"Sorry, sir."

"Bob is fine." Bob unlocked his office door and held it open for Jack, who followed him inside.

Inside the office, a large wooden desk and a high-back, wheeled chair were positioned in front of the far wall. Behind the desk were shelves with pictures of Bob, his wife Meg, and their two sons and a daughter. Another framed picture of Meg sat on the desk. There were other photos, too—Bob with friends, family, and law enforcement personnel. The desk was uncluttered.

"So, Jack." Bob crossed behind the desk. "What do you have for me?"

Jack sat in one of the two rigid chairs before the desk. "On the initial canvass, Detective Reyes and I came up empty. No one heard or saw anything unusual. We're pulling video footage from homes and contacting businesses in the area. We got a hit on fingerprints for the Vic. Tyrell Miller. Twenty-eight. His prints lit up the system. Tyrell has a long list of priors but finished parole and has stayed off the radar since he got out."

"Do you think this is related to what he went to prison for?"

Jack tapped his pen against the page. "I've checked that angle out. Tyrell stole a car and acted as the getaway driver in a carjacking. He went to jail, but the two other guys were minors, and they walked. One moved to Florida and is in prison there now, and the other OD'd a year ago."

Bob rubbed his chin with the edge of his thumb as he

slowly shook his head. "How am I not surprised that if someone was going to find a body in his dumpster, it would be you?"

"It's funny you should phrase it like that."

Bob sat up and placed his hands flat against the top of the desk, bracing himself for what Jack was about to say.

"If you drive down my street, there are five or six dumpsters in either direction that would make a better dumping spot for a body. They're more out of the way with less lighting and fewer eyes on them. Why didn't the killer use one of them?"

"You know, killers sometimes aren't thinking too clearly right after the fact. But back it up. Are you sure they drove, and he wasn't killed in the parking lot?"

"That, I'm positive. I brought out Lady to track. She only pinged around the dumpster. We found tire marks. The techs couldn't get tire prints with the gravel, but they got wheelbase width. That will only rule out smaller cars, or something big like a truck or Hummer. There was a blood spot on the ground that came back human. Mei will run DNA, but odds are it's Tyrell's."

"Anything else?"

"There was no attempt to cover up the body." Jack continued. "They dumped the body in, closed the lid, and left. If I didn't find it, the next person to take out their trash couldn't miss it. They wanted the body to be found."

"Maybe they panicked?"

"It's possible, but there was a flattened cardboard box and other bags right there. They only needed to pull the cardboard over the body, and you wouldn't see it. Typically, someone tossing a body wants it to stay hidden so it goes to the dump."

"Why would they leave it in plain sight?"

Jack leaned back in the chair and crossed his arms. "That's the million-dollar question. The killer may want to send a message."

"To you?"

"It's my apartment complex. Everyone living there cleared our background checks and aren't the types to make those kinds of enemies."

"Did your landlady have you run background checks?"

"Alice ran them on everyone. She's protective."

Bob chuckled, but his laughter quickly faded. "You're right about that. I wouldn't want to get on her bad side. Did you know this Tyrell Miller?"

"I checked his past arrests to see if I made any of them. On an old shoplifting call, I was a backup officer. I think he was already cuffed and in the cruiser when I arrived, but it was a long time ago."

"Still, that's something we need to consider. And that's another reason I'm removing you from this case."

Jack stood up. "What? There's no way you're taking me off this case."

"First off, sit back down. Second," Bob pointed at the monogrammed title on his shirt. "I'm the Sheriff, so I decide who gets what case."

Jack sat as he struggled to right his derailed train of thought. He'd gone in intending to get solo custody of the case. Now, he needed to shift gears to stay on it. "With Ed still out of commission, there's no other day shift detectives to assign to this case."

"Which is why I'm turning it over to the city police."

"Respectfully, I disagree."

"I assumed you would."

"But not for the reason you're thinking." Jack's eyes darted around the room as he tried to devise an excuse that would work on Bob. He stared at the picture of Bob's wife and pointed, "Meg!" He said a little too loudly.

"What about her?"

"Put yourself in my shoes, Sheriff. Imagine you were me. It's night, and you go to take out the trash, but you find a body."

"That could only happen to you, Stratton."

"Humor me. Pretend it happened to you, and you're the one who found a body in the dumpster only feet away from your home. You'd have to tell Meg. And what would her reaction be?"

Bob rolled his eyes. "Are you kidding me? She would go ballistic. She'd want to move."

"Exactly. But you don't want to move. So, what would your wife want you to do?"

"Catch the killer," Bob said.

"Because that's what you do. Right? You catch bad guys, so she expects you'll find this one and make her safe. Now imagine you went to work and came home. You open the front door. Meg rushes up, gives you a big kiss, and asks, did you catch him? But you have to say no. I'm not even looking because my boss says I can't. What do you mean can't? Why not? That's what you do! You catch bad guys, and you won't even try?" Jack sighed and held his hands up like a beggar pleading for scraps.

"You're laying it on a little thick," Bob tugged on his ear, a sign that he was debating what to do.

"I'm not. I know Meg. She'd march down to the Mayor's house and give her what for."

"Meg would give it to her in spades." Bob's eyes went wide. "Do not send Alice down here. Seriously, Jack. I just said that I wouldn't want to get on her bad side, and I don't."

"Me? I would never do that, but I can't guarantee what Alice will do. Who knows? She could go to the mayor or some news outlet. But are you going to put me through that? How would you enjoy living with Meg under those circumstances?"

Bob set his elbow on the desk and rubbed his forehead with his thumb and forefinger. "Why am I always stuck between that proverbial rock and a hard place with you, Stratton?"

Jack grinned. "Look on the bright side. I've got a lot of motivation to catch this guy fast!"

Chapter Eight

A bell chimed over the door as Alice walked into Titus Bail Bonds, a tiny office sandwiched between a rundown nail salon and an old pizza parlor in the middle of a rough neighborhood downtown.

Even though the office had just opened for the day, two people sat in the small waiting area. One was an older man who watched Alice with red-rimmed eyes. The other was a young pregnant woman who appeared so mad she was ready to explode. Alice immediately processed the possibilities. A father bailing out a kid, and it wasn't the first time. From how sad he looks, it's probably not the last time he'll do it. The young girl is probably helping a man she hopes will be there when the baby is born. But he was sure to get it from her when he got out.

"What is up, my married girlfriend?" Shawna's rich voice filled the room. She was a short, heavyset woman ten years older than Alice. She wore a wig that was more orange than red, and her matching dress strained at the seams, about to burst open.

"Morning, Shawna."

Shawna pressed the buzzer to let her into the back office. Before Alice could even get through the door, Shawna scampered over on her five-inch heels and hugged her. "I can see from the smile on your lips that married life is treating you just fine." Shawna wiggled her eyebrows. "Do tell. Do tell."

Alice grinned. She had known Shawna all her life. Michelle, Alice's foster sister, and Shawna had been good friends.

"Aren't you the one who said never kiss and tell?" Alice blushed and tried to change the subject.

Shawna drew her head back quickly and stuck out her tongue. "Me? Oh, no, no, no. I love to hear the details. Spill!"

Alice felt like her cheeks were on fire. "Is Titus in?"

"Oh, I get you. You're doing that "keep work and private life separate" thing. That's fine. You want to dish someplace more private. We'll have a girl's night, and you can tell me all about your love life!" She laughed as she hurried over to her desk and picked up a manila folder. "Remember to keep the bail piece and the bond with you. They're both certified. I'm sorry that your login wasn't ready, but it looks like IT fixed the problem. They emailed me this morning that your account just started working. I call those computer miracles. But I wish you could have had a chance to fill out all the paperwork online. It's going to take you an hour to do it now."

"Actually, IT emailed me last night. I logged in and filled everything out." Alice glanced at the floor as guilt gnawed at her moral compass. She'd been a hacker her whole life, and when Shawna told her that IT was having a problem with her new account, Alice wanted to get started so badly that she couldn't help but hack the computer system to fix the problem.

Shawna grabbed Alice's hand. "Wonderful! Now, don't you be nervous. Titus can be a bit of a bear, but you got this." She glanced at her watch. "You're early."

"I like being prompt." Alice read the label on the folder—Oren Dorcey. Why is that name familiar?" She flipped it open. Inside was a mugshot of a man Alice knew. "Scoops!"

Shawna laughed. "I thought that bonehead had turned his life around. Did you know he's dating Imani Wilson?"

"Isn't her father Emmett? The police sergeant?"

Shawna whistled low. "So, you better catch him before Imani's father does. That man thinks the sun rises and sets over his little girl. If Emmett catches him first, they'll be scooping dirt on Scoops 'cause he'll be six feet under."

Alice stared at Scoops' mugshot. One look at his pudgy face, and she relaxed, grateful her fist skip wasn't a seven-foot weightlifting beast. "What did he do?"

"It's all a big mess. Scoops spent six months inside and thought he was good. But the DMV did some computer upgrade and found a boatload of unpaid tickets."

"He had to get bailed out for unpaid tickets?"

"Scoops' rap sheet is a mile long, and we're talking a mile-high pile of fines, so the judge locked him up. But Imani bailed him out and was straightening the whole thing out."

"Why did he skip?"

"Because he's a moron." Shawna's expression softened, and she shook her head. "Maybe he fell off the wagon? He was a drunk but had a year of sobriety. I don't know why he'd throw that all away, but if you don't find him fast, it's gonna be bad. Even if Imani straightens out the tickets, they'll throw the book at Scoops for jumping bail."

Alice exhaled. "I was hoping to start on a case with a little less pressure."

"Not on this one. The clock's ticking! And poor Imani is the one who put up the bond."

"What's her address?" Alice pulled out her phone to take notes.

"Put that away." Shawna pointed at the folder. "I got your back. It's all in the file."

"You're the best."

"Why, thank you. Yes, I am." Shawna patted her fake orange curls. "I don't know if I'd start with Imani if I were you, but Jack had his methods, so you've had an outstanding teacher."

"I just hope I paid attention in class."

Shawna's desk phone clicked to life. "Shawna?" Titus called over the speaker. "Alice Stratton is due here soon. Tell her I'm out of the office."

Alice's heart sank, and her mouth dropped open.

Shawna's eyes grew large. "She's standing at my desk right now and heard you."

The microphone clicked off. Behind Titus's closed office door, something slammed.

Alice stared at Shawna, hoping for some answer as to why Titus wanted her to lie, but her friend only shrugged.

The microphone clicked back on. "Send her in."

Alice debated about leaving, but Shawna gently touched her shoulder and gave her a little push.

"Don't let him give you any garbage. Stand tough." Shawna said.

Alice nodded, but Shawna said this, knowing she didn't have to go inside Titus's office. Alice was the one who had to face Titus alone.

Shawna opened the door and stepped aside as Alice walked in.

Titus J. Martin sat behind an immense oak desk. He was in his mid-forties with a medium build. Dressed in a pressed white shirt, steel-gray tie, matching pants and black leather shoes, he looked as if he'd be more comfortable in a corner office on Wall Street than here. His fingers flew over the keyboard before he triumphantly reached over and clicked the mouse. "I just had to finish an email." He stood up and thrust out a hand.

Alice shook it but didn't sit down. "If now isn't a convenient time to talk, we can reschedule."

Titus shook his head. "No. I might as well get this over with. Please sit down."

Alice sat in one of the chairs before his desk and cradled the folder in her lap.

Titus set his elbows on the desk and steepled his hands. "I've been giving a lot of thought to you working here, and I don't think it's a good fit."

Alice's chest caved, and her gaze moved to the floor.

"Don't feel bad about it," Titus said.

Alice took a deep breath and looked up, careful to meet his eyes. "I'm not feeling bad, Titus. Right now, I'm upset and confused. I turned down a different job because you said I could have this one."

"At the time, I meant it. It was your wedding reception, and Jackie was there. What was I going to do? Rain on your big day? But we need to be realistic. This is a tough job."

"I know it is because I've already done it." Her voice rose despite her trying to keep her composure. "I've caught several bounties for you already."

"Those were Jack's bounties."

"I helped catch them," Alice said.

"Don't make this ugly. I like you. I do. That's part of the reason I can't let you try to do this job. I can't risk it."

"All I'm asking for is a chance. If I don't catch Scoops, you don't owe me anything. There's no risk on your end."

"I'm not talking about money. What would I say to Aunt Haddie if you got hurt?"

Alice crossed her arms. "If I were you, I'd think about what you'll say to Aunt Haddie if you go back on your word."

"That is not fair!" Titus jabbed a finger toward her. "You can't go getting Aunt Haddie involved in this."

"You brought her up," Alice said. "I can do this job."

Titus leaned back and eyed Alice. "No, you can't. And it's not because you're a woman, so don't go giving me any female empowerment speech."

"Then why?"

Titus picked up a pen from his desk and clicked the end. "To be a bounty hunter takes something you don't have. Ruthlessness. That's not a bad thing, Alice. You're nice. The world needs more people like you."

Alice pulled out her phone and opened her remote terminal app. As she typed, Titus continued to talk.

"I've heard there's no one better than you on computers. There must be a million jobs for someone with your skill set. You could work from home. Do you have any idea what I'd give to do that?"

"That sounds like a wonderful idea," Alice said as she frantically typed. "Will you be selling the bail bonds business?"

Titus scowled.

Alice was too angry to be intimidated. She pressed a couple more keys and held her breath.

Titus's computer monitor beeped, and the screen flashed. Titus sat up in his chair, his feet stomping on the floor. He grabbed his mouse and shook it. "What is this?"

"What is what?" Alice asked innocently.

"Look at my screen. It's a picture of a hand giving me the finger." He turned the monitor so she could see it.

"Oh, that's bad." Alice slowly shook her head. "It looks like you've been hacked."

Titus wiggled the mouse and mashed the keyboard. "Who would do that?"

"Probably someone ruthless." Alice smiled.

Titus's eyes widened. He pointed at her phone. "Did you just do this? This isn't funny, Alice. Undo it."

"Me?" Alice stood up. "I'm not ruthless enough to do something like that. Have fun getting a new computer system. I'm sure starting over won't be easy. Maybe you can do some of the work from home?"

"Stop right there!" Titus slammed his hand down on the desk.

The door to Titus's office clicked and slowly swung open. Shawna stood outside with her arms crossed, nervously looking between Alice and Titus.

Titus glared at Shawna. "Were you listening at the door?"

Shawna demurely touched her chest. "Why, I'd never. I came in because I can't access my computer. Everything is locked up."

Titus stared at Alice until the veins in his temple throbbed. "Fine. I'll try you on one bounty. But you have to do it alone. No help from Bobbie-G or Jack."

"That's not fair!" Shawna said.

"Life's not fair!" Titus shot back. "Well? Is it a deal?"

Alice's stomach tightened, but she forced herself to flash one of Jack's roguish grins. "All I was asking for was a fair shot. It's a deal."

"You have one week. Now fix my computer!" Titus looked ready to grab the monitor and throw it across the room.

Alice pressed several buttons on her phone to unlock the computer system.

Titus's computer beeped, the screen returned to normal, and he flopped onto his chair.

Alice winked as she walked past Shawna.

Shawna shut the door and whispered, "That was awesome!"

"Not really. It certainly wasn't how I thought my first day would start."

"I am so sorry."

"Don't be. I'm glad he decided to give me a shot."

"But he only gave you a week!" Shawna shook her head. "Not even Jack could catch Scoops that fast."

Alice swallowed but lifted her chin. "Then I better get started. Because there's no way I'm giving up."

Chapter Nine

Jack parked his Charger in front of the Kent Building, shutting off the engine but not getting out. He loathed going to the morgue. The pall of death hung over the building. He stared at the modern, two-story complex that housed all the police forensic offices and the morgue, but even with the sun shining, there seemed to be a haze casting a shadow over the area. He wasn't superstitious, but he'd guarantee the place was haunted. Besides, he couldn't avoid descending into the pit if he wanted to solve this case. Forensics are indispensable to law enforcement. Bodies held secrets that, if found, helped the police catch killers that otherwise would walk free.

Pulling out his phone, he texted Jill. She was bound to get upset he was going to speak with the M.E. without her, but he couldn't afford to slow down so she could keep up. He hit send and got out of the car.

Tires squealed as a dark green, four-door sedan that screamed "I'm really a police car", barreled into the parking lot. Detective Jill Reyes scowled as she skidded into a space. She must have been mad because the first time she tried to close the car door, it caught on the seat belt with a loud crunch. She yanked the door back open, flipped the seat belt out of the way, and slammed it shut. "Detective Stratton, what a surprise finding you here."

"Whatever do you mean, Detective Reyes?" Jack tried unsuccessfully not to smile.

"We agreed last night to speak with the medical examiner together, did we not?"

"Yes, we did. Do you have your phone on silent?"

Jill yanked out her phone. "Don't say you tried to text me because..." She glared at the screen. "This text just came in."

"I just got here. Of course, I was going to give you the professional courtesy of waiting until you arrived."

"Sure, you were." Jill thrust her chin out.

Jack exhaled. He could picture his mother standing beside him with her arms crossed and a disappointed expression. *Treat others how you'd like to be treated.*

"You're right. I wanted to talk to Mei before you arrived because I don't know how you operate. That was wrong, and I'm sorry. Truce? I'll buy lunch." Jack offered.

Jill eyed him suspiciously for a moment before she exhaled and relaxed her shoulders. "You don't have to do that. Let's make sure we're on the same page from now on."

"Sounds good. Have you gotten the morgue tour yet?"

"I have. It surprised me how advanced your lab is. They had money to burn out in California before all the budget cuts. Our labs are all state-of-the-art, but yours is right up there with them. I take it you and the M.E. are friends?"

"Mei and I go back a ways. She just got promoted, but don't let that fool you. She's exacting. Dots all the I's, and she's unflappable on the stand."

"That's pretty high praise."

"Mei deserves it. She's a little shy, which can seem aloof to some, but she's a wonderful person."

The front doors of the building swooshed open. Jack and Jill headed to the elevators and the basement. Jack felt like he was being lowered into a crypt as they descended. His nostrils flared, and his mouth went dry. The stench of death permeated the building and always clung to Jack even after he left. He already wanted to take a shower. The bell dinged, the doors opened, and a chill swept into the elevator. The air was dense and cold, seeming to press in from all sides.

Exiting the elevator, Jack knocked on an office door with an engraved metal plaque: Dr. Mei Lai, Medical Examiner.

A moment later, the door opened, and Mei greeted them, smiling. "Good morning. Please come in." Mei's white hospital coat nearly touched the shiny linoleum floor. The petite woman gave a friendly wave and held the door open.

"Thank you for seeing us so early, Dr. Lai," Jill said.

"Please, call me Mei. Everyone else is so formal."

They followed her into her office as Mei moved behind a large oak desk and held her hand toward the comfortable-looking leather chairs in front. Jill sat on the left while Jack took the seat on the right. The M.E. sat back in her chair, and her smile disappeared. "You're here regarding the Tyrell Miller case?"

"That's right," Jill said. "Have you performed the autopsy yet?"

"I have. I like to present my findings in three ways, with varying levels of graphic detail depending on how squeamish you are. If you're sensitive, I can give you an outline or provide you with the written report; I'm almost done putting it together with photographs. If you want the most thorough walk-through of the autopsy report and have a strong stomach, I can explain what I discovered while we review the body together."

Jill swallowed. "I'm up for a walk-through."

Mei nodded. "Certainly. I know Jack can handle it. We keep the morgue as clean as possible, so you must scrub and put on gloves, booties, paper gowns, and respirators. Follow me."

Ten minutes later, Jill stood with her back ramrod straight and her eyes glued on the double doors leading into the examination room. It appeared that she wanted to run in the opposite direction but would push ahead to get the job done.

Jack respected that. He shoved open the door. An earthy smell hung in the air, tinged with the scents of unknown chemicals and citrus, undoubtedly to help mask the unpleasant odors. Jack and Jill crossed the room to Mei, who stood beside a body laid out on a stretcher covered with a sheet.

Mei pulled the sheet off Tyrell's face, and Jill lost all color in hers.

Jill's breath came in halting little puffs. "I'm good. I can do this," she said, more to herself than anyone else.

"The deceased is male, black, twenty-eight-years-old. I estimate the time of death between six and eleven p.m. last night."

"So, someone killed him shortly before Jack found him?" Jill asked.

"Body temperature would indicate that. The official cause of death is a single bullet wound to the rear of the skull that penetrated the brain. The caliber of the bullets is a nine-millimeter."

"Bullets?" Jack repeated.

"Three more shots were fired postmortem into his abdomen. All shots were fired at close range." Mei took a penlight from her lab pocket. She angled Tyrell's head, moving his hair aside so they could see the entrance wound. "You'll notice the stippling on the skin here." She changed the direction of the light to illuminate his stomach. "And here."

"How do you know the headshot was first?" Jill asked.

Jack answered before thinking. "There's blood splatter on top of the stippling of the head wound." He met Mei's gaze. "Sorry. I'm sure you were going to point that out."

Mei nodded approvingly. "No. That was a very keen observation. And you're correct. Because of that fact, it's clear the victim suffered the head wound first."

Jill's eyebrows knit together. "If they shot him in the head, why shoot him in the gut afterward?"

Mei shrugged. "That, I can't help you with. But I recovered the three bullets from the torso, mostly intact. The other broke into several pieces when it penetrated the skull. I've sent everything to ballistics with a rush."

"Thanks." Jack winked.

Mei glanced at Jill. "Jack has one speed, fast. So, I assume everything with him is a priority." Mei moved to the middle of the table. "The victim also has two areas of bruising. You'll notice the discoloration on his knees and around his wrists."

"Tyrell is five-foot-nine," Jack said. "The bruising on his knees could explain the downward trajectory of the shot to the head."

"But not why the killer fired three more rounds," Jill said. "If you shoot someone in the head, why shoot them again?" She didn't wait for Jack to answer. "Unless it was a rage killing."

"Any idea what caused the bruising on the wrists?" Jack asked.

Mei shook her head. "They're faint but noticeable on both arms. I've photographed them, and we'll try to enhance the pictures."

"We may be looking for two perps," Jill said. "One grabbed Tyrell by the wrists and pulled him forward onto his knees. Then the other shot him in the head."

Mei thought about the theory for a moment and nodded.

Jack kept his mouth shut. Jill's idea was plausible, but it was far too early to settle on anything. "Anything else?"

"We're processing Tyrell's clothes now, looking for foreign fibers. I'm afraid that's all I have so far."

Jill asked, "Were any drugs in his system?"

"Please allow me to explain a bit about our protocol. We ran two drug tests: blood and urine. Both tox screen tests were negative."

"Any evidence of alcohol?" Jack asked.

"None. Alcohol leaves the body rather quickly, but if he had been drinking, it would have shown up. His liver shows past abuse." She pointed over to a cart with several containers holding organs.

Jill started coughing.

Jack shook Mei's hand. "Thank you, Doctor. We'll let you know if we have additional questions."

Mei nodded, and Jill made a beeline for the exit.

"I'll finish the written report and get that to you as soon as possible," Mei said. As Jack turned to follow Jill, Mei called after him, "I'll email you when the results are back."

Jack waved as he passed through the door. He wanted to get his hands on the ballistics results, but without a suspect or gun to match them to, they were worthless. Mei did everything in her wheelhouse to uncover the secrets Tyrell's body held. Now, it was his turn to hunt down the murderer that executed him.

Chapter Ten

Jack drove to the Sheriff's station to run a complete background check on Tyrell Miller while Jill returned to her office to update the Chief. He needed to find Tyrell's next of kin to make the notification. It was the part of the job he hated most, but he wouldn't pawn it off on someone else, especially in a murder investigation. He had to be there to witness the reaction of the person he told that their loved one was never coming back. Even though it felt like he was stabbing himself, Jack had to see how they behaved because most people were murdered by someone they knew.

Worse still, every time he made a death notification, he couldn't help remembering all the people he lost. He hoped his pain could somehow help him deliver the news, but it never felt like it did. Every situation was different. A mother finding out their son was never coming home, a wife realizing she would have to tell her children their father was killed, and teenagers grasping to understand that they are now orphans — the horrible combinations seemed to have no end.

Parking on the side of the Sheriff's Department, Jack

walked to the front entrance. A man exiting held the door open for Jack. Jack mumbled a quick 'thank you' and crossed the foyer. A middle-aged couple was filling out a form at the desk along the wall. A young woman stood before the window, speaking with the duty officer.

"Hey, Jack?" A familiar voice called out.

Jack grinned. His friend Donald Pugh was working at the front desk. Donald was Jack's age and height, but Jack had twenty pounds of muscle on him. Donald was the type who never could seem to gain weight, even if he wanted to. He pushed his hat farther up his sandy brown hair and waved Jack over. "Can you come here a second?"

"Sure, Buddy." Jack stopped next to the young woman standing in front of the window.

"This is Rosa Delgado." Donald nodded to the slender woman in jeans and a yellow top. "She wants to file a missing person's report. I tried to explain that we can't start—"

"I don't mean to complain officer, but I know something is wrong." Rosa's dark ponytail bounced as she held her phone before Jack's face. "See?" The phone's screen displayed a map with a red dot on the road beside a lake. "This is where he was, and it just stopped. My father and I went out there, but he was not there. Something bad has happened to Tyrell. I know it."

At the mention of Tyrell's name, Jack's expression switched to the neutral mask of a police officer, but inside, his stomach clenched as if he'd been struck in the gut with a sledgehammer. "Why don't we discuss this in a conference room?" Jack said, holding his hand out to the door on the left.

"Thank you," Rosa exhaled. "Thank you for listening."

"Of course. Give me one second." Jack tried to smile. Internally, his heart felt the crushing weight of what he knew the outcome of the conversation he was about to have would be. He turned to Donald while Rosa walked to the conference room door and whispered, "Do me a favor, Donald. This may turn into a loss of life notification, and I'd appreciate it if you could covertly call for a female officer to come into the room with us."

Donald's eyes rounded. "Oh, man, are you serious? I feel like such a jerk. I didn't know."

"You did nothing wrong. Just make sure you do it on the down low and not over the speaker."

Donald nodded.

Jack crossed to Rosa and held open the door. The conference room was small. A rectangular table with six chairs, three on each side, sat in the middle. A whiteboard hung on the wall to the left, and windows looked out to the parking lot, but their shades were drawn. Jack flicked on the light and motioned to the closest chairs.

"Tyrell was supposed to call me last night," Rosa said as she sat on the edge of her seat. "He met with my father and then..." She gulped air, and her lip trembled. "Nothing."

"Rosa," Jack leaned forward, so she had to look him in the eyes. "I need you to take deep breaths. I'm going over to the cabinet in the corner to get you a water bottle. I'll be right back, all right? Look at me and nod."

Rosa swallowed and nodded. "I'm sorry. I've been up all night and flipping out a little."

"I understand." Jack hurried over, grabbed a bottle of water, and gave it to her. "Why don't you take a drink? I'm going to write some notes." He slid a pad of paper and pen on the table closer to him. "Let's start by getting some information about Tyrell. What's his last name?" He held his breath.

"Miller. Tyrell Miller. He's my boyfriend. He's twenty-eight years old. I have a few pictures I printed out." She handed Jack two separate photos.

Jack stared at the face of the man he'd seen earlier that morning at the morgue. Tyrell was standing in front of the fountain in the city park. His friendly smile looked genuine. "Does Tyrell have any family in the area?"

"No. He never had a relationship with his father, and his mother passed away a few years ago. They lived in Chicago. Tyrell came out here with a friend when he was seventeen."

"No brothers or sisters?"

"No. Why?"

Jack took a deep breath.

Someone knocked at the door.

"Excuse me for one second, Rosa." Jack stood and opened the door.

Officer Kendra Darcey, twenty-six years old, a former army officer and all-cop, stood at attention somberly.

Jack gave her a slight nod.

Kendra's lips pressed into a tight, thin line, but her eyes glistened. She was a warrior who'd seen combat but was still human. He could see it written all across her face. This was the last place she wanted to be and the last thing she wanted to be doing, but she'd do it — because if she didn't, someone else would have to.

"Rosa, this is Officer Kendra Darcey, and I've asked her to join us."

Rosa shook Kendra's hand.

Kendra moved a chair to sit next to Rosa on the right.

Jack sat back down and stared into Rosa's eyes. He watched dread slowly fill them like storm clouds rolling off the ocean. She knew what was coming, but Jack needed more answers first. "Do you know why Tyrell was out at the lake?"

Rosa shook her head and then shrugged. She closed her eyes, sniffed, and nodded. "I think I do. He was going to propose. Our fifth anniversary is today. That's why he met my father at the Waffle Shack. He wanted to ask his permission. The lake is where we met."

Kendra opened her hand, and Rosa took it.

"Did Tyrell drive out there? What kind of car does he have?"

"An old Honda Civic. Red. I don't know the year."

"Was he with anyone?"

"My father said he left alone." Rosa's eyes widened. "He showed my father the ring. He had it with him! Something terrible happened. Right?"

"I'm so sorry, Ms. Delgado, but last night we found the body—"

Rosa covered her face with her hands. "I don't want you to tell me. I don't want to know." She burst into tears.

Kendra draped her arm around Rosa's shoulders.

Rosa collapsed into her. She screamed and cried as if someone had ripped her heart out. It was a pain so deep that Jack knew a part of her was dying. He knew because it happened to him. No matter how much time, therapy, and prayers, the grief that tore Rosa apart now would forever leave its scars.

Jack forced himself to keep his eyes open and his expression somber. All he wanted to do was run out of the room, catch the person responsible, and make them pay, but Rosa didn't need that now. She needed him to be there. The minutes turned into an hour, but Jack and Kendra let her cry. When Rosa looked up, her eyes were vacant and distant.

Kendra squeezed Rosa's hand and softly said, "I'll give you a ride home. Is there someone there for you to be with?"

"My mother is home. Daddy is at work."

"I'll need to speak with your father," Jack said. "My partner and I will stop by later today. Kendra will take care of you."

Rosa nodded, but Jack doubted she fully understood what he was saying.

Kendra helped Rosa out of the room and toward the exit.

As Jack watched them go, his anger rose. A man was dead. His girlfriend was traumatized, and for what? Was this a robbery gone wrong? Had someone seen the diamond ring at the Waffle Shack and followed Tyrell to the lake to steal it?

Jack took out his phone and texted Jill. "Meet me at the Sheriff's Station. We've got a killer to catch."

Chapter Eleven

"You can do this. You can do this." Alice sat in her little blue Volkswagen Beetle, gripping the steering wheel to stop her shaking hands, trying to psych herself up. "You've done this before. It's simple." She exhaled, and her body sagged back against the seat. "It's simple when Jack is here."

A wave of doubt slammed over her. Jack had spent his whole life working on becoming a police officer. It was easy for him because he reprogrammed his DNA. She hadn't even finished High School. To support Aunt Haddie, she dropped out. She had her GED but no college, and certainly no police training.

She hung her head and closed her eyes.

A tremendous gust of wind made the Bug sway from side to side, but it reminded her of when Chandler got into Aunt Haddie's station wagon a long time ago. Alice was supposed to go to field hockey tryouts but hid in the car instead.

Chandler, a giant of a man even in high school, clamored into the backseat behind her, making the whole automobile bounce. He sat there, a huge grin on his handsome face. "Can I interrupt your little pity party?"

"I don't want to talk about it."

"Aunt Haddie said you don't want to go to the tryouts. If it's because you don't want to spend hours running up and down a field chasing a ball, I completely get that. That's fine, and we can get a pizza slice instead. But if it's because you're afraid you won't make the team, move over because I'm driving you."

Alice scowled.

"That look might scare other people, but not me. Speaking of fear, what are you afraid of?"

"I'm not afraid. But there's no way I can make the team. I've only had two lessons. All the other girls played last year. I can't compete against that."

"Maybe you can't. Maybe you can. You won't know if you don't try."

Alice rolled her eyes. "Thanks for the try-try-again speech, but you didn't hear me. I don't have the training."

Chandler chuckled. "That's not true."

"You're not listening." Alice raised her voice. "I only had two lessons in gym class!"

Chandler wiggled his finger in his ear. "Take it down a few decibels, please. You may not have formal training, but I believe God prepares us for what we want to do."

Alice groaned. "Please give me the try again speech instead of a sermon. I get enough of those from Aunt Haddie."

"Maybe you should listen more." Chandler grabbed the seat back and leaned over it to look at Alice. "Look, it's kind of like the Karate Kid."

"God is like Mr. Miyagi?"

"No, but Mr. Miyagi used some of God's techniques to train Daniel-san. I believe God does the same for Alice-san. For example, how many games of tag did you play growing up?" Chandler answered before she could, "Probably a bazillion. And how often did people tag you? They didn't! Shawna said it was like trying to catch a greased pig."

Alice scowled.

"That's a compliment," Chandler continued. "And you played street hockey. You've got a million-mile-an-hour slapshot."

Alice grinned. Jack had taught her how to shoot. But her smile faded. "I don't even know if they let you shoot like that. I don't know all the rules."

"Rules, you can learn. But you've got the speed, the moves, and ten times the determination to at least try it."

Alice opened her eyes and blinked back tears. She missed her foster brother so much it hurt, but the funny thing was, the older she got and the more she thought about him, the softer the pain became. Looking up at the ceiling, she whispered, "Please tell Chandler thank you," and exited the car.

The Greens lived in a two-story house on the edge of town. The house was older but freshly painted a pale yellow. It had white trim around the eaves and windows. On the porch was a swing with a faded plaid canopy and a rocker made of wood with a deep red cushion and a floral pillow. To the side of the yard sat a birdbath. The property had two maple trees, one to the left of the porch and the other to the right. The house had a well-manicured lawn, but it was a dull green due to the weather.

The porch steps creaked as Alice climbed them. She rang the bell and waited.

Footsteps rushed down the hallway inside. Imani, a young woman in her early twenties, yanked open the door. The blaze in her large brown eyes cooled as she recognized Alice. Imani leaned against the doorframe, resting her shoulder against the wood. Her hair was piled high on her head, bound with colorful beads and ribbons that blended into her dark curls. A red bandana partially hid the scar on her forehead. "Hey." She exhaled. "If Aunt Haddie sent you over to make me feel better, nothing can right now. But thanks."

"Titus sent me."

Imani gasped. "Is Oren all right? What's wrong? Why would Titus send you? Did they catch him? Is he hurt? Nothing went wrong with the police, did it?" The questions flew from her mouth like bullets fired from a machine gun.

Alice placed a gentle hand on her arm. "They haven't found him yet. That's why I'm here."

"Wait." Imani pulled at her oversized gray sweatshirt. "I thought Jack stopped chasing bounties. He's a detective with the Sheriff's Department now, right?"

"He is. But I'm still working for Titus."

Imani crossed her arms. "No offense, but I hoped that Bobbie G was going after him. I begged Bobbie to smack Oren around once he caught him."

Alice gave a tight-lipped smile. "Titus assigned the bounty to me. Do you have time to talk?"

"Sure." Imani opened the door and held her hand out to the living room on the right. "Not that I want to spend another second of my life discussing that no-good player. What an idiot I was for believing him."

Alice shut the door and followed Imani as she continued to vent.

Imani spoke in a mocking tone, pretending to be Scoops. "'*I've changed, baby. I'm a new man. No more playin' the game for me.*' Ha! What a load of garbage." Imani pointed to the couch. "You can sit there, but I can't sit. I'm so mad I'll start busting stuff. Do you want a drink or something?"

"No, thank you. It sounds like you don't want to talk about

it, but can you explain why Oren was arrested in the first place?"

"Unpaid tickets!" Imani shouted at the ceiling. "Who goes to jail for freaking unpaid tickets? The whole thing is a bunch of stupid anyway. My father looked into it anonymously, got it?"

"I'm married to a cop." Alice grinned. "I get it and won't say a word. What did Emmett find out?"

"The DMV was upgrading their computer system, and they did an audit. It turns out Oren had close to a hundred unpaid tickets. The thing is, he may have paid them as part of his restitution. It's all screwed up because of the computer system, and Oren's public defender moved, and no one can find the files. My dad was straightening everything out. Worst case, Oren would owe some money, but it wouldn't even be that much."

"Then why did he run?"

"When you find him, you ask, but I'm not gonna. I'm gonna slap him upside his head so hard he won't be able to form a sentence for a week."

"You haven't heard from him?"

"Heard from him? Are you kidding me? I'm the last person he'll call. I put up his bond. If you don't catch him, I'll be out of that money, but it doesn't matter now."

"Why do you say that?"

Imani's lip trembled, and she hid her face in her hands. Her shoulders shook, and she sobbed.

Alice rose and led Imani over to the sofa. "It's going to be all right."

"It won't." Imani cried. "Even if Oren walked through the front door right now, it will never be right. Not with my father. My daddy trusted Oren. It went against his gut as a cop, thinking Oren could change, but Daddy gave him a chance. He said it was the Christian thing to do but look how Oren repaid him. All the cops he works with told him not to do it, but Daddy did it for me, and this is how Oren repays him. This is what he thinks of me?"

Alice squeezed her hand. "Maybe something happened? Oren had a drinking problem before. Maybe he fell off the wagon?"

Imani shook her head. "He would have reached out to his sponsor or me. Oren knows I could understand that. He did something bad. Broke the law bad. That's why he's hiding."

Alice took out her phone. "Can you give me his sponsor's contact information?"

Imani nodded as she took her phone out of her pocket and shared the name and number. "You can try him, but I already did. He hasn't heard from Oren, either. I bet he's headed to Florida and his cousin's house."

After writing that address, Alice asked, "Can you think of anywhere else he would go?"

"He wouldn't go to his sister's. Mary hasn't heard anything from him at all. And she'd tell me. We're like best friends now. Besides, he knows she'd smack him around worse than I would."

"I don't want to worry you, but why are you so sure he did something bad and not something bad happened to him?"

Imani's lips pressed together, and she stared at her phone.

Alice waited. Remaining silent was a trick Jack taught her to get people to talk, but it was so hard to keep her mouth closed.

"Tibet," Imani whispered.

"Tibet Olson?" Alice pressed.

Imani nodded. "She saw Oren running behind the closed K-Mart."

Alice sat up straight. "When? What time?"

"Friday night. I don't know what time."

"Why would that make you think Oren did something wrong?"

"Because a cop was chasing him."

Chapter Twelve

Jack stood at the door, watching Kendra drive out of the Sheriff's Station parking lot with Rosa sitting in the passenger seat. Every person deals with death differently, but he'd felt what Rosa was going through. Was she gazing up at the sun and wondering how it kept shining now that Tyrell was gone? Or was she puzzled that the earth continued to spin, and her heart still beat even though Tyrell's had stopped?

"Stratton!" Jill yelled as she stormed into the foyer. "I can't believe you."

Jack slowly turned around. He didn't know why she was so upset, but he wasn't in the mood to deal with it. "If you're going to say my name like that, please attach the title detective in front of it."

Jill's face turned crimson. "I'll call you a detective when you behave like one. You broke your word!"

"I suggest you take the level of your voice down a couple of notches."

"Do you think you're going to make me shut up? I don't care if the whole sheriff's department hears me!"

Donald stepped back from the window, picked up some papers, and pretended to read.

"Neither do I. But there are civilians in here as well, and they don't need to hear you. So how about we continue this one-sided conversation in the conference room?"

Jill marched over to the door, ripped it open, and waited.

Jack strolled through. He tipped his head slightly, smiled, and said 'thank you', too.

The wall shook as Jill slammed the door behind them. "First, you try to ditch me and go to the Medical Examiner's office by yourself. And now I find out that you notified next of kin without me?"

"Hold on a second."

"No, you hold on. I don't know if the Sheriff told you, but he and my chief thought excluding you from this case would be a good idea. The Chief asked for my opinion. And what did I do? Despite everyone telling me you're a cowboy who doesn't play nice with others, I tell him I'm willing to try. Do you know why? Because everyone also said that even though you're an undisciplined, unmanageable miscreant who always bucks the system, you were a good guy."

"Miscreant? That has a nice ring to it, but I am a good guy."

"Good guys don't lie to their partners."

"Back up and give me a minute to explain. One minute. You can time me."

To Jack's surprise, Jill lifted her arm and clicked a button on her watch.

He started talking fast. "First off, you're right about the M.E. I didn't text you until I hit the parking lot because I wanted to talk to Mei alone. That was wrong. I apologized then and thought we'd put that behind us."

"We did, but you lied to me and went and spoke to Rosa Delgado without me."

"That couldn't be helped. Ask Donald at the front desk what happened. We agreed when we left the M.E. that I was going to come back here to check—"

Someone knocked hard on the door, and Donald stuck his head in. "Sorry to interrupt, but Jack needs to get to Sheriff Morrison's office ASAP. It's an emergency."

"What about?" Jack asked.

Donald shrugged. "Bob was so upset on the phone I could barely understand him. But he said Stratton like five times."

"Can you go and see—"

The speaker in the ceiling clicked on, and Sheriff Morrison's voice boomed across the room. "Detective Stratton, report to my office immediately!"

Jack turned to Jill. "I'll be back as soon as possible, but I promise you there was nothing I could do to avoid speaking with Rosa. Ask Donald, he'll tell you. I'll be back in a minute."

Jill bit her lip.

As Jack hurried down the hallway, he tried to figure out what her expression meant. He'd seen that look before — biting the bottom lip, rounded eyebrows, and a slightly wrinkled nose. He hoped she was wondering if he was telling the truth, but she appeared guilty of something.

Shoving those thoughts aside, Jack strode through the main office with everyone silently staring at him. They all heard the announcement summoning him and watched him like a man going to the gallows. But he'd done nothing wrong. He had nothing to worry about, right?

He was no longer sure of that fact when he walked through the door.

Bob sat at his desk, staring at a pen he clenched in both of his shaking hands. "Shut the door." He said without looking up.

Jack did, and the click of metal boomed in the quiet office. "What's going on?"

"What's going on?" Bob repeated, the pen cracking in his hands. "I just got off a conference call with the Mayor, her staff, their Human Resources department, and the Chief of Police."

Jack pulled the chair back and sat down. "Seriously, Bob, I don't know what all this is about."

Bob slowly raised his head and stared at Jack with his mouth ajar, his brows knit together, and one eyelid blinking like a light on the fritz. "This is one of those moments when I need you to refer to me as Sheriff Morrison." He set the pen down and folded his hands on his desk. "You, Jack, were the subject of the call."

"Me?" Jack asked, stalling for time as he tried to think of anything he could have done that would have risen to this level of bad. He scratched his neck. The only thing he could come up with was Alice's grandfather, but if they knew who he really was, the Feds would be involved, not just the mayor. "You're going to have to give me more information to go on, Sheriff Morrison."

Bob's knuckles turned white as he gripped his hands together. "When I agreed to let you stay on this case, you assured me you would give the city full cooperation. We're not even a day into it, and I'm already dealing with threats of lawsuits."

"What?" Jack laughed but swallowed it down as soon as he realized Bob was serious. "This can't be about the disagreement Jill and I had. It just happened."

"No, it didn't. Do you know Detective Reyes is the first female detective the city police have ever had?"

"No, but..."

"As such, the Mayor is very proud of her—so proud she checks up on Jill's progress with the Chief. When she heard how you were treating Detective Reyes, the Mayor organized that emergency conference call. You stonewalled Jill at the

M.E.'s office, and then you went to interview the victim's girlfriend on your own."

Like a powder keg going off, the raw emotions of recently telling Rosa that her boyfriend had been murdered ignited his frustration, blasting it into anger. "Hold on a second. This whole thing is so overblown that I don't know where to begin. Today is the first full day we have worked together, so we're both figuring out the dance. Yes, I went to see Mei alone, but I texted Detective Reyes when I got to the parking lot and apologized for not texting her sooner. We both agreed to try better."

Bob raised his voice. "Yet you made the death notification without her?"

"I had no choice. Ten minutes ago, I had to tell a young woman that the man she loved was murdered. That's what I just dealt with, and now I've got you and Reyes screaming at me, and neither of you will let me explain."

Bob's eyes widened, and he sat up in his chair. "You're right, Jack. I apologize."

Jack accepted his apology, but the Sheriff's words did little to cool his anger. "You know what? Talk to Donald. He'll explain. He was working at the front desk when Rosa Delgado came in. She wanted to file a missing person report and wouldn't take no for an answer. You know, that's what happened with Alice and Aunt Haddie when they tried to file a report on Michelle. They got the runaround when they went to the police station. I swore I would never do that to anyone. So, I talked to Rosa, and she told me her boyfriend's name was Tyrell Miller. She knew something bad had happened to him based on the look on my face. She knew he was gone. What was I supposed to do, leave her hanging until Reyes came in?" Jack's hands slapped the arms of his chair, and he stood. "If the situations were reversed and Reyes did what I did, I would have understood."

"You would have. Why did she call the Chief?"

"Because she never let me explain before she assumed the worst and started screaming at me." Jack wanted to add, like you did, but left that part off. "Permission to leave your office, sir."

Bob opened his mouth and closed it. Maybe it was because of his friendship with Jack, or he noticed Jack was ready to explode. Either way, he said. "Of course."

Jack forced himself not to slam the door. He marched through the office and headed for the parking lot, pushing his frustration out of the way. Now wasn't the time to get emotional. He wasn't about to lose control and get kicked off the case. He needed to catch the man who killed Tyrell.

Chapter Thirteen

Jack trudged up the stairs to his apartment. The stink from the morgue clung to his clothes, and the conversations with Reyes and Bob left a foul taste in his mouth. All he wanted to do was shower, brush his teeth, and return to work.

He opened his apartment door, pulled it closed behind him, and set his keys in the dish on the table next to the door.

Andrew strolled out of Jack's bedroom, dripping wet with nothing but a towel around his waist. The bear of a man was covered in a carpet of wet, gray hair. "Hello, Jackie!" Andrew smiled as he left a trail of water across the floor. "I am making a classic lamb borscht for dinner. You will love it. Tender chunks of lamb, loads of beets, onions, carrots, cabbage, and fresh dill."

"It sounds fantastic, Andrew, but I'm only here for a few minutes. I have to go back to work."

"No, you don't. You're promoted. Have one of your men do it."

"It's part of a homicide investigation. I can't do that."

"Oh," Andrew nodded, sending water flying in all directions. "In that case, I will make you a bowl, and you can take it with you."

"I'll have to take a rain check. I'm going to jump in the shower myself and head right out. Speaking of which, don't you dry off in the shower? My landlady will kill me if I mess up the floors."

"I'm sorry. I'll clean it. It's these towels. What are they made from? Plastic? I will have to pick up some Mersin towels. Mersin is a small town in the Aegean region of Turkey. With a couple of their towels, you could stop up your Mississippi. Completely dry and baby soft."

"Sounds great." Jack headed for the bedroom. "Do you know where Alice and Lady are?"

"Lady took Alice for a walk!" Andrew laughed. "Never have I seen a dog like that. Alice should ride her! Lady is bigger than wolf."

"If she comes in, let her know that I'm in the shower."

"I will. I will."

Jack headed through his bedroom and into the bathroom. He grabbed a towel, mopped from the tub to his bedroom doorway, and quietly closed it. The day had set his temper on a hair trigger, and the last thing he wanted to do was get into a fight with Alice's grandfather. He put his gun on the bureau, undressed, and headed for the shower.

The hot water washed over him, and he felt fantastic for about ninety seconds. The steam trailed off, and the water ran cold. Muttering and swearing under his breath, Jack switched to a Navy shower. Shutting the water off, he soaped up from head to toe. But before he could turn the water back on, the bedroom door slammed open and shut, followed by the bathroom door.

"Who is texting you from 617-1090?" Alice asked, her tone clipped.

"I don't know! Hold on." Jack reached for the faucet and cringed as the icy blast hit him. "Your grandfather took all the hot water."

"Don't go blaming my grandfather. I did a load of laundry, too. Who is this person?"

"I don't know. Why are you reading my text messages?"

"I'm not. But are you worried I am?"

Jack stuck his face under the freezing water and opened his eyes. "Alice, I've had a really hard day so far, and it's not over yet. Can you please tell me what you're so mad about because you're not making sense? If you're not reading my text messages, how can you be so upset about a text someone sent me?"

Alice pulled the curtain back a little and wiggled her phone. "Whoever sent this text to me must have thought my number was yours. Listen to this. *Jack. I don't even know where to begin. I had you all wrong, and I'm so sorry. All I wanted was for us to be together. Now I understand you wanted me to be with you, but you couldn't tell me that because she was there. I'll do anything to make it up to you. See you tonight.*"

Jack shut the water off, wiped his hand down his dripping face, and chuckled. "That sounds really bad taken out of context."

Alice crossed her arms. "It sounds horrible in any context. Who is this?"

"My new partner. I can explain."

"How about you start with her wanting the two of you to be together?"

Jack jumped out of the tub and wrapped his arms around Alice.

"You're all wet! No! Stop! I'm upset!"

He ignored her protests, picked her up, and set her down on the counter with a kiss. "Everyone else has doubted me today. I need my wife to believe in me. Okay?" He kissed her again and didn't stop until her tense muscles relaxed.

Alice flashed a lopsided grin. "I do. Explain."

It took Jack fifteen minutes to tell her everything that had happened between the morgue and Morrison's office. Once he was done, Alice pulled him close and laid her head against his chest. "I'm sorry you went through that, buddy. And I'm sorry I jumped to conclusions."

"You, I understand. I'd be miffed if some guy texted me like that, thinking I was you. What must have happened is when Jill took down your number the other night, she must have texted Stratton and not checked if it was you or me."

"As a detective, isn't she supposed to do that?"

"She's human. It happens. I'm sorry, but I can't stay for dinner. I'm heading right out."

"Where?"

"The last place we know Tyrell was alive — the lake. We have a BOLO out for his car, but nothing has turned up. The forecast for tomorrow is rain. I can't risk losing evidence if the first crime scene is out at the lake."

"You're a good man, Jack Stratton."

Standing there in only a towel, Jack pulled Alice close. "If you knew what I was thinking right now, you might not say that." He kissed her neck.

"You are so bad. Stop!"

Jack's hands shifted down to her hips. "You want to try for a little ninja make-out session when I come home?"

Alice wiggled her eyebrows. "Wake me up."

"I will. I'm taking Lady with me."

"How come?"

"She's the best tracker in Darrington."

Chapter Fourteen

Jack pulled into the scenic overlook beside the lake and shut the car off. The Charger rocked on its chassis as Lady paced in the backseat, eager to be released. He opened his window and breathed in the cool, fresh spring air. The sun was setting over the trees on the other side of the lake. The golden light sparkled on the water as if the lake were dancing to a melody only nature could hear.

He stared across the shimmering span and up the hill to the place where he'd found Michelle's body. The pain was still deep, but it wasn't the raw, searing agony that made him want to drown it in whiskey anymore. That wouldn't do anyone any good. More importantly, Michelle would hate him for doing that. She would be the last one to want Jack to go through life in mourning. He pictured his little foster sister bounding out of her room at the break of dawn. Her brown eyes were wide, and her hair streamed out behind her as she rushed outside to see what adventure and opportunity the new day held.

Jack smiled at the memory, exited the car, and opened the back door.

Lady bounded out. She set her massive paws on the ground and stretched.

"No running today, girl," Jack said as he attached the leash to her harness. "Today, you track." He pulled an evidence bag out of his pocket. Mei had released one of Tyrell's socks to Jack. Holding the bag under Lady's nose, he let her take a few long sniffs.

Headlights shone at the entrance to the overlook, and Jill's car pulled in. She parked beside the Charger and got out but stayed next to the door. "You didn't say you were bringing the wolf."

Jack raised an eyebrow. "You saw she's an excellent tracker. Why would you have a problem with her being here? Are you afraid of dogs?"

Jill shook her head. "That's like asking me if I'm phobic about kittens when I'm standing in the lion's den. That's no dog. It's Dogzilla."

A long, low rumble of a growl escaped Lady's throat.

Jill held up her hands. "I meant that as a compliment."

"She's not mad at you. She's tracking. Yip-yip, Lady."

Lady started trotting along the road's edge.

Jack let out more leash so Jill wouldn't feel so intimidated. "Bring her a steak if you want to get on Lady's good side. You'll make a friend for life."

"I think she could eat the whole cow." Jill hurried to catch up to Jack. "We don't have much light left."

"Lady doesn't need it. But the forecast is for rain tomorrow, so we don't have a choice."

"Then let's hope Lady is as good a tracker as you say she is." Jill took a flashlight out of the inside pocket of her coat and quickly zipped it up.

"Is Darrington cold compared to Monterey?" Jack asked.

"I'm always cold. Maybe I should have transferred to Arizona?"

"Why'd you pick Darrington? Do you have family out here?"

"Nope. But I needed a change. It was the Emma Green case that got to me. I was the lead investigator on her murder. Both Calvin and Emmett Wilson came out to California."

"Emmett did, too? That's a good friend."

"Emmett was Emma's Godfather. Calvin named her after him. It was all so senseless. A guy sticks a gun in the driver's face at the red light and orders Emma and her aunt out of the car. Both women complied and handed over their pocketbooks. The guy shot Emma and drove away."

"Did you catch him?"

"The guy's brother lived in Dallas, and he went there to lay low. SWAT raided the apartment, and the guy tried to shoot his way out. He died on the scene. The part that kills me is that he never should have been walking the streets. He'd just been arrested for armed robbery and possession with intent and was already awaiting trial for domestic battery. The DA let him walk with no bail, and the next day, he murdered Emma. I took some time off and decided to tell Calvin in person. Once I got here, we talked about policing. The more he and Emmett spoke about Darrington and how things worked here, the more I realized I needed a change. Law enforcement in California has devolved into a catch-and-release program. The cops joke that we should install a revolving door on the jail, but it's true."

"And you liked Darrington enough to move?"

Jill shook her head and gave him a lopsided grin. "I was at the point of anywhere but California. I could have easily thrown a dart at the wall. But while I was here, I saw the opening for a detective position, interviewed, and as they say, the rest is history."

Lady stopped.

Jack held up his hand in a fist.

"Is that a signal for the dog or me?" Jill asked.

"Sorry. Army habit. She found something. Come here, girl."

Lady trotted back to them, and Jill moved out into the road.

"She's harmless," Jack said.

"I don't believe that for a second." Jill shined her light in front of where Lady had stopped.

The light shimmered off a sizeable dark splotch. The stained area covered a three-foot section of the tar and spilled onto the dirt on the side of the road.

Jack rubbed Lady's neck. "Good girl. You are the best. I owe you a steak."

Lady barked and wagged her tail, but then she sniffed the air and backed away again.

Jack undid her leash and took out his key fob. The Charger's lights flashed, and the back door opened. "Go lay down, girl."

Lady turned and bolted back to the car.

"That's so cool," Jill said. "Her doggy door is automatic?"

"Comes in handy," Jack said. "That dog has saved my life a few times. I'm telling you, they don't get better than Lady. But she had a tough past and hates blood." He returned to the spot she had triggered on and pointed at the stain. "And looking at the color, texture, and Lady's reaction, that's definitely blood."

"Could it be roadkill?" Jill asked.

"Could be, but I doubt it. No carcass and no tire prints in the blood." He shined his flashlight up and down the tar. "And if someone hit an animal large enough to hold that much blood, you should see broken headlights or some car damage. We need to get the crime scene techs out here."

"Agreed." Jill pulled out her phone.

Jack flicked on his flashlight and circled the dried pool, walking in the road as he scanned the ground. The dried circle of blood was over four feet in diameter. Even if they hadn't found Tyrell's body, one look at the amount of blood lost and it was clear the person had died.

Jack angled his flashlight along the side of the road, illuminating fresh tire tracks. "I've got tire prints." He called out. Careful to stay on the tar, he moved closer. The rich soil and soft ground around the lake made it easy to see a car had recently parked there. Depending on the quality of the prints, they could use tire castings like fingerprints for identification. But just as fingerprints were limited, you had to find the car to match it to the castings. Still, they were gathering forensic data, and that was invaluable.

"They're on their way." Jill stood next to him. "Looks like someone parked here."

Jack walked along the side of the road a little further. "Two cars parked here."

Jill stood gazing up and down the street. "So, Tyrell comes out here to look for the perfect place to propose. He pulls over, and then the killer stops behind him. Why?"

"Rosa said that Tyrell had a diamond engagement ring with him."

"But a robber wouldn't know that," Jill said. "And from what I know about Darrington, people don't randomly pull over and mug someone."

"Tyrell showed the ring to Rosa's father at the Waffle Shack. If someone saw it, they could have followed him."

"Looks like we need to speak to Carlos Delgado."

Jack moved to the edge of the tar and frowned.

"We should wait to check the ground until the techs arrive with lights," Jill said.

"I agree. I'm not touching anything." Jack squatted down and drifted the light over the line of shoe prints left in the soil.

"I think we're looking for two perps now," Jill said. "Both cars are missing. That would take two drivers."

Jack pointed at the shoe prints. "I'm not certain. The shoe prints overlap and cross over each other. All the prints are on the driver's side of the cars. If it were three people, one would have needed to get out on the passenger side."

Jill examined the ground from a distance and nodded. "It's still possible. Or maybe it was a few guys, and the ones in the backseat got out?" She reached for the bare ring finger of her left hand, her lips pressing into a tight line.

Jack had noticed the fading tan line on her finger, but why the ring was missing was the last thing he'd ask. He'd let her bring it up first if she wanted to discuss something personal.

Jill pointed down the road. "What's in that direction?"

"More lake. It's five and a half miles to the nearest house."

"Assuming the killer came alone, he would have driven away in his own car. If that's the case, where did Tyrell's car go?"

Jack turned to stare at the lake. "Looks like we need to contact the dive team, too. The lake brings up another question — seeing how Tyrell was killed here, why not just dump the body in the lake? Why bring it back to Darrington?"

Chapter Fifteen

Matt Yates sat in his recliner, holding a beer, and watching his 90-inch curved screen, brand new TV. He had his doubts about the crappy wall in his trailer supporting his latest loot, but it was nothing some two-by-fours and screws couldn't compensate for. He'd thought about pawning it, but the cops were still paying too close attention to him, and he wasn't up for driving to another county to sell his latest haul.

He changed the channel until he found an old Stallone movie. He couldn't remember the name, but Sly was shooting someone, and that's what mattered.

Matt slurped his beer and powered back his chair. Maybe he should watch a spy movie to get some ideas. All the home security cameras were becoming a nuisance. He'd learned from his mistakes and worn a mask this time, but the police said they had a witness who spotted someone who fit his description. That meant his body. He grabbed the Alabama pillow his sister had given him for his birthday off the floor and stuffed it under his stained t-shirt. Would something that simple work? Would the cops end up looking for a fat guy?

Matt chuckled and downed the beer. He should get one of those fat suits. Then the cops would be searching all the gyms and giving a hard time to all the porkers on treadmills. He'd call himself the fat bandit and become famous! He laughed and cracked open another beer.

Over the explosions blaring from the TV, he heard a noise outside and froze. Matt bolted out of his chair, raced into the hallway, and dropped to his knees. He slid the heater grate to the side and yanked out the hidden pistol. Crouching down, he moved to the side of the front window and peered out.

Relieved it wasn't some rival crooks looking to steal the stuff he stole fair and square, he exhaled when he saw the police car. There were guys out there who'd kill for the merchandise he got his hands on. But the cops had to follow the rules. There's no way they could get a warrant so fast. They were probably back to hassle him again.

He walked to the hallway, pulled the heater grate to the side, and hid the pistol. Then he returned to the living room to ensure he had left no paraphernalia or anything else in the open that would give the police probable cause to search the place. Satisfied it was clear, he waited for the pounding on the door.

The movie on the TV cut to a commercial. That commercial ended, and another one started. Puzzled, Matt peeked out the window again. The marked cruiser sat parked in the driveway with its lights off. He couldn't tell if anyone was inside.

"What are they doing?" he muttered. He gasped and dashed to the back door. Leaving the kitchen light off, he checked, and the door was locked. "Ha!" Peering through the barred door and out into the darkness of the backyard, a sense of empowerment washed over him. He'd installed bars on all the doors and windows. There was no way the cops or anyone else could kick it open. They could even use a battering ram but weren't getting inside.

Relieved that a SWAT team wasn't surrounding the house, Matt stomped to the front door. Sweat matted his t-shirt to his back. He stared outside until his eyes watered, but he didn't see anyone.

The commercial break ended, and the movie played.

Matt grabbed his beer from the cup holder and swigged half down. The cops must be screwing with him. The guy was calling for backup. Soon, the police would have him surrounded. He yanked the front door open and glared past the barred gate on the door at the parked cruiser. "This is private property! Get out of here."

No one answered.

Matt finished his beer, crumpled the can in his hand, and pitched it through the bars toward the driveway. "I know you can hear me. Leave now. You ain't got a warrant, so get off my land."

Outside, crickets chirped.

Matt grabbed the handle of the barred door and pushed it, but it didn't open. He turned the handle again. The metal latch clicked, but the door wouldn't budge.

"What the...?"

Someone had wrapped a chain around the railing, connected it to the bars on the door, and padlocked it. Why would the police lock Matt inside his house?

"This ain't legal."

Inside the police cruiser, a small flame appeared. There was someone inside. Were they smoking?

"Hey! You can't do this. This ain't legal. Take this chain off!"

The driver's door to the cruiser opened. The cop got out of

the car, holding a large glass bottle. Fire danced up the cloth rag fuse stuffed into the mouth.

"Hey! Stop right there!" Matt let go of the door handle. He couldn't see the police officer's face because of the flames, but this was all sorts of wrong. "Wait, a second. Hold on!"

The cop ran forward, drew back his arm, and threw the bottle. The fire streaked across the night sky and straight at Matt.

Matt dove out of the way. He tripped over the recliner and sprawled on the living room floor.

The Molotov cocktail shattered against the door's bars, and flaming liquid ignited everything it touched, including Matt's legs.

Screaming in pain and fear, Matt ripped his jacket off the couch and extinguished his burning jeans. Most of the accelerant had landed in the hallway. He could not get to his pistol because of the fire.

The TV sparkled, cracked, and shut off. A second later, all the lights went out, but the living room glowed in the flames.

Matt tried to reach the kitchen, but the fire prevented him from going that way. He rushed to the window, but it was barred shut. He kicked the wall. The drywall cracked, but the siding held it from breaking.

Someone pounded on the wall next to the front door.

Matt turned. A cloud of black, acrid smoke hit him in the face. His eyes and lungs burned. He gasped and fell forward onto his knees. Coughing and choking, he crawled toward the front door.

The cop stood on the steps. He was removing the chain holding the gate shut.

Matt ripped the blanket off the couch and tossed it over the flames before the door, smothering them. Crawling, with tears streaming down his face, he reached the bars as the cop yanked the chain free.

"I surrender. I surrender." Matt, still on his knees, raised his hands and looked up.

The police officer aimed the barrel of a gun straight at Matt's face.

Matt stared down the black tunnel and saw a spark —

Chapter Sixteen

Alice pulled up to the side entrance of Tibet Olson's apartment complex. The building was four stories tall and sat on top of a huge hill next to the power lines entering Darrington. Alice drove between the two stone pillars that marked the route to the parking lot. She felt a wave of anxiety crash over her as she stepped out of the car and onto the driveway. Her hand was as steady as a rock when she was with Jack. Now, it shook like Jello during an earthquake. Why was she so nervous? She grew up with Tibet. All Alice was going to do was ask her some questions. There was nothing to freak out over.

Alice took a deep breath and grabbed her bag from the back seat. She trudged up the hill, her boots crunching the gravel beneath her feet. As she reached the entrance of the building, she pressed the button for Tibet's apartment. A few moments later, Tibet buzzed her in.

The hallway was empty and silent. Alice stepped inside, her heart beating faster. She walked to the elevator and headed to the third floor. Stepping out into the corridor, she passed door after door until she reached 322.

Alice stepped to the side and knocked. It was a habit Jack instilled in her. Police stood to the side so they didn't get shot through the door.

A chain rattled, and the handle turned. "Alice!" Tibet grinned. The petite woman was four years Alice's senior, but she had always been so kind to Alice growing up. Tibet seemed to have a perpetual smile on her face. "What brings you by? I wish you had called. I have to leave for work in half an hour."

"I won't hold you up, but I'm here because of my job."

"I heard you were working with Bobbie G as a bounty hunter." Tibet grabbed Alice by the hand and pulled her into the apartment. "You're like my hero. Aren't you freaked out? You worked with Jack before, but Shawna said you're flying solo now. You're crushing it, girl!" Tibet held her fist up.

Alice blushed as she returned the fist bump. "I don't know about that. I'm striking out right now, which is why I'm here. I spoke with Imani, and she suggested I talk with you."

Tibet set a hand on her hip. "I don't think there's a stupider man on this planet than Scoops. Imani is so far out of that boy's league that she's playing a different sport! And what does he do? He goes right back to his old ways. He fooled me too, though."

"What do you mean?"

"Friday night, I ran into him at Sonic. I shouldn't be eating there, but I had to work overtime and was behind on shopping and yadda-yadda. But their mozzarella sticks are so good I had to get some, you know? Anyway, Scoops was pulling in when I was pulling out."

"Was he alone?"

"Yeah. So, I ask him how he's doing, and he goes on and on about Imani. She's the best thing that ever happened to him. He's sober and turned his life around. He goes on about his new job and how in love he is, and I believe every word! How stupid am I?" She placed her hand on her chest, rocked her hip to the side, and rolled her eyes.

"When was this?"

"Friday night. Around 8:30."

"What happened after that?" Alice asked.

"After the day at work that I went through, all I wanted to do was go home and eat dinner with a glass of wine or two. Don't judge, but Mozzarella sticks were the closest I could come to Italian. It was so nice that I went out on the balcony." She jerked her thumb toward the sliding doors behind her. "That's when I saw him."

"Do you mind me looking?"

"Not at all." Tibet walked through her living room to the apartment's balcony, where she opened the slider.

Alice and Tibet stepped out into the crisp morning air. Two chairs sat next to a small table in the corner. The city of Darrington stretched out before her. Down the hill on the left was the Sonic. Directly across from the balcony and below was the old K-Mart.

"I heard something, and I stood up," Tibet explained. "I saw Scoops running like the Devil was chasing him."

Alice peered down the hill at the parking lot far below. "Are you certain it was Scoops?"

"A hundred percent. When I saw him at Sonic, he wore a bright red and white Chicago Bulls jacket. And do you remember what he looks like when he runs? He sticks his butt back, and his arms dangle behind him like a giant chicken."

Alice laughed. "Yeah, I never understood why he ran that way. He thought it made him faster, but he always came in dead last."

"When I saw the cop chasing him, I understood why Scoops was running."

"Was it the city police or the Sheriff?"

Tibet's nose wrinkled. "I assume City, but from here and at night, it's hard to tell their uniforms apart."

"Was he white or black?"

Tibet shrugged. "He was wearing a hat, and to tell you the truth, I didn't get a good look. I was so mad at Scoops that I went inside and called Imani."

"So, you didn't see if the cop caught him or where Scoops went?"

"It took me a minute to find my phone, and when I returned, they were both gone."

Alice reached into her pocket and removed a business card. "If you think of anything else or hear from anyone where Scoops is, will you please let me know?"

"Of course I will." Tibet frowned. "I wish this could somehow have a happy ending for Imani, but it can't. Her father will never trust Scoops again. What an idiot. Why would he throw all that away?"

"When I find him, that's the first thing I will ask."

Chapter Seventeen

Jill waited behind Jack as they stood on the front steps of Carlos Delgado's house. Footsteps shuffled down the hallway, and the door slowly opened. An older, tall, muscular man stood there. His complexion was gray, and the dark circles beneath his eyes betrayed a lack of sleep. His shoulders were rounded, and his arms hung limply at his sides.

"You must be the Detectives," Carlos said, stepping back into the hallway. "My wife told me you would stop by. She's not here." He shuffled toward an opening on his right and led them into a tidy living room. "They're at the church making arrangements."

The living room was simple, with modern furniture. A large plasma screen TV hung on the wall opposite the front door. A small bookcase on either side of it housed DVDs, video games, and books. There was a brown leather couch, a coffee table, and a recliner with a throw blanket in front of the TV. The floors were light hardwood. The walls were covered with family pictures, including ones with Tyrell, and three crosses hung on the wall.

Carlos sat in the recliner while Jack and Jill took the couch.

"I'm very sorry for your loss," Jack said. "We're here to ask some questions to discover who did this to Tyrell. I'm Detective Jack Stratton with the Sheriff's Department." He inclined his head toward Jill.

"I'm Detective Jill Reyes with the City Police. This is a joint investigation." She took out a tablet.

Carlos nodded but kept staring at his hands. "I'll do whatever I can to help."

"You were the last person we know of who saw Tyrell. Can you please tell us why and when you met with him?"

"Tyrell asked to talk to me at the Waffle Shack the night he..." Carlos drew a shaky breath, "the night he went missing."

Jill sat ramrod straight. Her voice was normal in tone and volume, but it was loud and brash compared to Carlos's. "Why didn't you meet here?"

"Tyrell didn't want Rosa to know what he was meeting me for. Rosa is my daughter. Tyrell was asking for her hand. Not that he had to, but I was—" The muscles in Carlos's thick forearms flexed as he squeezed his fingers together. "He didn't want Rosa to know."

"You met at the Waffle Shack on Willow? What time was that?" Jack asked.

"About seven. Seven thirty."

"Was it crowded?"

"No. We may have been the only ones there. I wasn't paying attention. When I came in, I was trying to look mean. Menacing."

Jill's fingers tapped loudly on the tablet's screen. "So, you weren't happy that Tyrell was marrying your daughter?"

Carlos looked up, his face pinched. "No. I couldn't be happier."

"Then why were you trying to scare him?" Jill pressed.

"I was pretending. I knew why he asked me to come." Carlos looked at Jack. "I was ribbing him, you know. Make him sweat. A joke to tell at the wedding."

Jack nodded. He understood why Jill was leaning into Carlos but disagreed that it was the right time to do so.

"Pretending?" Jill asked. "Tyrell had a very checkered past. Understandably, you'd be hesitant about him marrying your daughter."

Carlos sat up straight and placed his large hands on his knees. "No, I wasn't. Tyrell had changed. He got a job that he worked hard at. He went to church."

"Just because he started attending church doesn't make him a saint." Jill continued, "Any more than standing in a garage makes you a car."

Carlos's expression hardened.

Jack shifted forward on the couch. "I understand where you are coming from, Mr. Delgado." Jack pointed at the three crosses on the wall. "I think I'm going to be like the thief crucified on the right. When I get to Heaven, and someone asks me why I'm there, the only thing I can say is that the man in the middle told me I could come."

Carlos exhaled. "That's what I'm trying to explain. Tyrell changed. God can do that for a person. It's a miracle, and I saw it. Tyrell was different." He pounded his chest. "I'm still so much like the old me. So much hate and anger are still inside. But the Lord turned Tyrell into someone special."

"So, you were fine with Rosa marrying a felon?" Jill asked.

Carlos stood. His hands balled into fists.

Jill jumped to her feet, and so did Jack. He moved slightly in front of Jill. "Mr. Delgado, I'm sorry we must ask these questions. Please understand that statistically, people are murdered far more often by someone they know. We simply need this information to rule you out as a suspect."

"Fine. Ask, and catch the real killer. But know this: I had nothing to do with Tyrell's death."

"Where did you go after Tyrell left?" Jack said.

"I came home. Ask my wife and Rosa. Rosa can prove it, too." He yanked his phone out of his pocket. "There's this program thing on here that tells Rosa where I am. Check it." His hands shook as he removed his watch. "This thing does, too. I'll even take one of those truth tests."

"That won't be necessary, but I would like to check your phone to see the exact time Tyrell was at the restaurant and when he left. This is very helpful." Jack said.

Carlos's dark eyes met Jack's. "You understand me. You've hurt like me, haven't you?"

Jack's jaw flexed, and it felt like a spear pierced his heart when he recalled everyone he'd lost to violence. "My father was stabbed to death before I was born. My brother died next to me in the war, and my sister was murdered. I have some understanding of your pain, but everyone is different. You grieve for Tyrell like a father for a son, and your heart is breaking for your daughter's pain. I can't promise I will catch the person responsible, but I will do everything I can to bring Tyrell's killer to justice. I give you my word."

Carlos covered his face with his hands and slumped, weeping into the chair. He grabbed a tissue, blew his nose, and stared at Jack. "What else do you need to know?"

"Did Tyrell show you the ring?"

He nodded. "He was so proud you would have thought it was the Queen's jewels."

"Was it expensive? Do you know how much he spent?" Jill asked.

"Tyrell worked hard but didn't make much. I don't know about those things, but it would have meant the world to Rosa."

"Did anyone else see it?" Jack asked.

Carlos wiped his nose and balled the tissue in his hand. "The waitress. But there were two guys at the counter. She told them Tyrell was going to propose. One made a joke. He hummed the death march, but we all laughed, and he did too."

"What did these guys look like?"

"A little younger than me. They had gray coveralls. Maybe they were mechanics? One was black, and one was kinda white."

"Kinda white?" Jill repeated.

Carlos kept his eyes focused on Jack. "I think he was South American. He looked like that big wrestler turned actor. But he wasn't muscular. Just average."

"Do you mean the Rock?" Jack asked.

"That's it. But he had hair — brown hair."

"Were these two guys still in the restaurant when you and Tyrell left?" Jack asked.

"Yeah. We walked by them."

"Who drove away first, you or Tyrell?" Jack asked.

Carlos's pupils hardened into black spheres. "I did. Do you think those guys have something to do with this?"

Jack's heartbeat sped up. He recognized the look on Carlos's face — the hunger for revenge. "Mr. Delgado." Jack waited until Carlos's eyes locked with his. "Those two men could simply be hard-working guys who stopped to get something to eat. Detective Reyes and I are going to check everything out. But you must take care of your daughter and wife and leave the police work to us. Do you understand?"

The muscles running along Carlos's jaw flexed. He didn't answer immediately, which was a good sign he was thinking it over. He held up his hand and pointed at Jack. "You give me your word. Will you do your best to find the man responsible?"

"I will."

Carlos nodded. "Then I will leave it to you."

After checking Carlos' phone and watch to determine the exact time he left the Waffle Shack and confirming that both pieces of technology had come directly back to the Delgados' house, Jack and Jill headed for the car. Jack took the driver's seat while Jill circled to the passenger seat.

Once inside, Jill's head tilted toward her left shoulder. She looked at him sideways and said, "While you have my deepest sympathies for your losses, we missed an opportunity in there."

"For what? To kick a grieving guy when he's down? The guy freely offered his phone and his watch and agreed to a polygraph."

"I've known guilty people to do the same."

"Me too." Jack shot back. "While I haven't completely ruled him out because I don't trust anybody, so far, he checks out. And seeing how he was talking and answering every question, why would you risk getting him upset and having him shut down?"

"He only gave us the watch and phone after I pressed him. How do you know he wanted Tyrell in his family? No offense, but are you considering that Tyrell was black and Carlos is Hispanic? I know Hispanic fathers."

"I think we're going to need to have a conversation about race. Let's start by saying that I spent most of my childhood being raised in a predominantly black foster home that was an international melting pot. So, I think people are one race — human. I don't care if Mr. Delgado was purple and Tyrell was green. Mr. Delgado is the type of man that if he didn't like Tyrell, he wouldn't let anyone put pictures of Tyrell all over his living room."

"That's a good point. I wasn't saying he's a racist. Maybe he is, or it could be the fact that no father in his right mind wants his daughter dating a convicted felon."

Jack grabbed the steering wheel with both hands to keep

them from waving all over the place. "While we have a job to do, we have to keep in mind that he just suffered a traumatic loss. I agree that we have to ask the hard questions, but you used a sledgehammer to do it. Next time, take a more delicate tact."

Jill yanked her seatbelt into place. "Thank you for that suggestion." She stretched the word out so far she spit on the windshield. "But my interview techniques work."

Jack wanted to ask at what price but kept his mouth closed. He started the engine and pulled out onto the road.

Jill grabbed a napkin from the glove compartment and wiped her spit off the glass. "Where are we headed, Detective?"

"To the Waffle Shack." Jack stared straight ahead. "We need to check out the employees and find out who those two guys are."

"I'm thinking that they followed Tyrell. Remember the bruising on Tyrell's wrists? When I saw it, I thought someone could have held onto Tyrell's arms and yanked him onto his knees while someone else shot him. We're looking for two guys." Jill crossed her arms.

Jack kept his eyes on the road. He was too frustrated from going back and forth with Jill to correct her again. They may be looking for two guys. They could also be looking for a single killer or a gang. You needed to focus as a detective but never put blinders on. And Jill was already zooming in on her theory.

Jack pictured Mr. Delgado and the pain etched on his face. Once again, he heard Rosa's cry of anguish. Jack needed to find the killer as much for them as Tyrell. They needed closure. The pain would never heal, but if he could soften it somewhat, he'd stop at nothing to give them that little bit of peace.

Chapter Eighteen

Alice drove past Sonic and to the deserted K-Mart. The sign was gone, but the outline of the letters remained on the front of the building. Moss and grass grew through the cracks in the parking lot. Pulling around, she stopped in front of the truck entrance. Someone had moved some of the parking curbs to block off the back of the building to vehicle traffic.

The lights on her Bug flashed as she locked the doors. The hum of traffic in the distance echoed off the cement retaining wall. Even armed with pepper spray and a Taser, the hairs on the back of her neck rose as she walked between the graffiti-covered walls. She passed the closed loading docks until she reached the rear parking area.

A tall chain-linked fence separated the old shopping center from a slope, which descended to a large drainage basin and an auto dealership below. Alice slowly approached the fence. It was so tall it stood almost twice her size. Maybe ten feet. She took out her phone and snapped some photographs. There was barbed wire on top, but it was missing in several sections. Still, she wondered how Scoops got over it with a police officer chasing him.

Trash littered the ground along the fence. Bags, bottles, and old shopping carts lay scattered in both directions. The grass leading down to the drainage area was tall and wild.

She noticed the fence jutted out to her left, forming a boxed-in area with a separate gate. More pallets stood leaning against the fence inside, but a red piece of fabric stuck on the barbed wire caught her attention. She walked to the gate, which was ajar, and stepped inside the pen. She moved to the corner and peered up at the foot-long piece of bright red and white fabric.

After snapping photographs of the cloth hanging off the fence, Alice climbed onto a stack of pallets and stretched to grab her prize. She dropped back onto the ground and stared at the cloth like a puzzle piece. She didn't need to see the original picture to know what it was. Scoops must have climbed the fence here. The red and white fabric with the tip of a bull's horn still visible made that clear.

Sticking the cloth into her pocket, she stared at the other side of the fence. Driving to the car dealership at the bottom of the hill to check it out would be much easier, but what would Jack do? He'd climb over and follow the way Scoops had run.

A metallic clink sounded behind her.

Alice spun around.

A man stood in the middle of the gate opening, blocking the way out. His grayish-yellow hair was long and pulled back in a ponytail. He wore dirty, camouflaged pants and army boots, but his brand-new Chicago Bulls jacket caught Alice's attention. "Where are you going, girly?" He shoved his hands deeper into his coat's pockets.

Alice swallowed. If he charged her, she'd never be able to climb the fence in time to get away.

The creepy-looking man's eyes brightened as his eyes traveled up and down her body.

Alice lifted her chin. "Where'd you get that jacket?"

"Do you like it?" He smiled, revealing brown and yellow teeth. "I'll sell it to you. But it's expensive. How much money do you have?"

"I don't want to buy it, but I'll give you five bucks to tell me where you got it." Alice reached into her front left pocket and pulled out a five.

Jack had given her the advice of separating your bribe money. You never wanted anyone to see you pull out a wad of cash or your wallet.

He frowned at the bill and shook his head. "It'll cost more than that."

"Ten's my limit." She folded the bills and walked over to the side of the fence bordering the K-Mart parking lot. She stuffed the bills through the chain-link and flicked them out. They fluttered to the ground.

Alice's impromptu plan made her smile inside. When he went to retrieve the money, the man would walk away from the gate, and that would be her chance to run.

The creep didn't move. His eyes narrowed, and a lecherous smile spread across his face. He pulled his hand out of his pocket.

Alice's throat tightened.

The man held an object in his hand. With the flick of his wrist, a seven-inch-long blade snapped open. "That's not enough cash. What are you willing to give me to sweeten the deal?"

Alice took a deep breath and ripped out her pepper spray and Taser. "How about you give me the fire sale price because if you don't tell me where you got that jacket and get out of my way, that's what I'm giving you!" She held the pepper spray higher. "Flammable liquid." She rocked the Taser left and right. "Spark. And considering how much booze you have in you, when the firefighters arrive and find your crispy little pile of ash, they're going to think it was a case of spontaneous human combustion."

"You're crazy!"

Alice grinned. "I like to think of myself as very determined. This is the last time I'm asking. Where did you get the jacket?"

The man dropped the knife on the ground and raised two shaking hands. "The guy left it on the fence. He never returned, so I took it."

"Start backing up and tell me what you saw."

"This guy was running like his butt was on fire. A couple of seconds later, a cop comes tearing after him. The guy went over the fence like one of those gymnasts, but his jacket got snagged on the barbwire. I thought he was done for, but he slipped out of the coat and kept running."

"What about the cop?"

"He didn't catch him. He stopped at the fence but didn't climb over."

"What did he look like?"

"I didn't see him."

Alice raised the pepper spray.

"I swear I didn't. Cops don't like me none, so I hid when I heard him."

"If you didn't see him, how do you know it was a cop?"

The man rolled his eyes. "It's like hearing the bad ice cream truck. They jingle and jangle and wear those hard-heeled shoes. Cops sound like cops. You don't have to see 'em to know it's them."

"And the cop never said anything?"

"Not a word. He just left."

"So, you heard the cop leave, and the guy he was chasing never returned?"

He nodded. "I stayed up half the night expecting him to come looking for the jacket, but he didn't."

Alice tilted her head toward the fence, where she had dropped the money. "Go. Get it."

The man eyed her suspiciously. "How do I know you're not going to turn me into a s'more?"

"Because you answered my questions. Next time, answer them when I ask, and I'll give you more. But tell your friends, if you cross me, it won't end well."

The man nodded and hurried over to get the money.

Alice forced herself to walk calmly over to the alley. She kept a lookout for the creep in case he followed her, but once he snatched the money off the ground, he scurried back to the shadows of the loading dock. She didn't know if he had forgotten the knife or was waiting to get it, but either way, he wasn't coming after her.

Once she reached the alley, she sprinted back to her car. Fear, doubt, and the recall of her past, sexual abuse crashed over her. She fought back the tears, but they streamed down her face. She yanked the driver's side door closed and locked the car. Her breath caught in her throat, and her hands shook as she reached for the ignition button. She tilted her head back and screamed at the ceiling. She would not allow herself to fall apart. If she did, the monster who abused her as a child would win.

Gasping for breath, she laid her head back against the seat. She doubted the police would be able to do anything about the creep, even though he had pulled a knife on her. A faint smile flicked across her face. The scumbag wouldn't try anything like that on anyone else soon.

All she wanted to do now was go home and shower, but she

couldn't give up. Scoops was driving when Tibet saw him in Sonic. Where did his car go? It had to be close by. She shifted the transmission into drive. She would continue the hunt but needed to be more situationally aware. This wasn't a game she was playing. She was hunting the most dangerous prey on the planet — man.

Chapter Nineteen

The radio in Jack's car crackled to life. Donald's voice buzzed with excitement. "Detective Stratton, come in."

"Jack's fine, Donald. No need for titles."

"It sounds good saying it. Listen, you're gonna want to head over to the lake. The dive team got a sonar hit on a car where you told them to look. They're getting ready to go in the water."

"Thanks, Buddy!" Jack held his hand out, and Jill returned the fist bump.

She settled back in her seat and said, "Time for the berries and cherries!"

Jack hit the lights and sirens and headed for the lake. It was only a short drive, but the anticipation made it feel like a longer trip. They flew down the back roads and arrived at the lake in minutes.

"Something's off," Jack said as they neared the spot. "There's only a van parked at the boat ramp. The boat's in the water, but there should be more cars and other divers here."

"How small is your dive team?"

"There's four of them and some volunteers, too." Jack pulled off the road and parked next to the van.

Lieutenant Grant Strickland of the Sheriff's Department circled the van as they exited the car. The short Texan had a big smile and a booming voice. "How's it goin', Stratton? Look at you. I took a little sabbatical, so I haven't gotten a chance to say congratulations on the gold shield. I heard you got hitched, too?"

"Guilty as charged." Jack shook the man's hand.

Grant was a holdover from Sheriff Collins's era. He'd moved with Collins to Darrington but stayed when the Sheriff retired.

"Country, this is Detective Jill Reyes from the City Police. We're investigating the Miller case."

"Nice meetin' you, ma'am." Country wiped his hand on his pants and held it out.

"Country?" Jill repeated the nickname.

"I'm a music fan." He hooked his fingers in his belt and rocked over on his right hip. "And since there's only one kind of proper music, country, some fellas on the force started callin' me that, and it stuck. What do you prefer? Detective, ma'am, Jill, or do you have a nick?"

"Jill is fine."

"Are you sure? Jack and Jill? I heard you're from the West Coast. How's Hollywood sound to you?"

"That has a nice ring to it," Jack said.

"All righty then, Hollywood it is." Country nodded.

Jill made a face. "Jill is fine. We got a call that you found the car?"

"I was only on the water for about twenty minutes when I picked it up on sonar. I got it marked with a buoy. The car didn't go far, and it's only sittin' in about twenty foot. Check it out." Country took out his phone and moved to stand between

Jack and Jill. "This here is a recordin' of the feed. Y'all move closer so you can see."

A video began playing on the screen. It was grainy and in orange and black.

Country pointed to the bottom. "This here is the lakebed. The square thing I'm passin' is a sunk boat, I figure. And this rectangle is the car." He paused the video. Even if Jack wasn't too familiar with sonar feeds, the outline of the car was crisp and distinct.

"Are you going to scuba dive to the site to make a visual confirmation before we initiate a recovery effort?" Jill asked.

Country chuckled. "You speak fancy, but I think I got what you're saying. And the answer is yup."

Jack asked, "Where's everyone else?"

"Two of the guys are helpin' Fairfield P.D. search the river for a pitched gun used in a stickup. My other two divers are also part of the forensics team. There was a fatal fire last night, so they've got to investigate that. Procedure says I can't dive alone. I can put the boat in the water and use sonar, but I can't go under unless another diver is with me, so we gotta wait. Sorry."

"I'm certified to dive, but Collins wouldn't let me join the team," Jack said.

"Well, old Art went and retired. Bob says the team is mine, so guess what?" Country grabbed both of Jack's shoulders. "You made the team. Congrats."

"That can't be all that's needed for him to dive," Jill said.

Jack stared at her with wide eyes. He made a cutting motion over his throat.

"No need for either of you to get uppity. You're both kinda right. Jack can't touch anything when I'm down there, but I'm within the parameters to have him observe. And since that makes two of us in the water and you," He pointed at Jill, "manning the surface, we get her done faster than a knife fight in the back of a pickup."

"Do you have a suit I can use?" Jack asked.

"You're probably an extra tall, but I think we got one. I didn't mean any offense, not askin' you, Jill. Did you want to dive?"

"No, thank you. I don't have to go out on the water, do I?"

"Nope. Technology takes care of that. You can sit right in the van and watch on TV."

"That sounds good to me."

"All right," Country clapped Jack on the back. "Let's do this."

Forty-five minutes later, Jack and Country slipped off the side of the boat. While they treaded water, Country ran down a list of instructions and checked their gear. Jack made a mental note to call and thank his father. Ted Stratton had drilled it into his son to take advantage of every training opportunity that came his way, and Jack listened. Now, he was about to embark on an underwater adventure that he would have missed out on if he hadn't taken the scuba diving classes in the Army.

Country cleared out his mask. "You ready?"

Jack wracked his brain for the most southern expression he'd ever heard and replied, "Does a fat baby fart?"

Country laughed so hard he stopped treading water. His head disappeared beneath the surface, and he came up coughing and spitting water. "Gad night a livin'! You done almost killed me, Stratton. My daddy used to say the same thing, and it broke me up every time, too."

Jack winked, pulled his mask over his head, and headed down. Jack followed Country, holding onto the rope attached to the buoy above and the car below with a magnet. The water was cold, but the wet suit and adrenaline kept him from freezing. The great thing about diving in early spring was the clearness of the water. They only went a few yards, and the car's outline appeared.

A fine layer of sediment covered the vehicle. With the lake so clear, the sediment must have been kicked up when the car struck the lakebed. Country flicked his headlamp on, and Jack clicked the handheld one he carried. The outline of a two-door Honda Civic made Jack's heart pound in his chest. The car's wheels sat on the bottom of the lake. Spots of red showed through the sediment, blanketing the vehicle.

Country swam around the vehicle, slowly inspecting it but not touching anything. Once he made a complete pass, he swam back to the trunk and motioned Jack over.

Jack focused his light on the covered license plate.

Country waved his hand back and forth, sending a cloud of fine particles swirling in every direction.

Painfully slow, the cloud cleared, and the white license plate became visible — 568 712. Jack gave Country a thumbs up. They'd found Tyrell's car. But now they needed to get it out of the water.

Twenty minutes later, Jack stood beside the van, toweling dry his hair.

"I called my Chief and Morrison to let them know you found Tyrell's car," Jill said.

"We found it," Jack corrected her.

Jill flashed an appreciative smile. "Duly noted. They agreed to send a wrecker out to retrieve it. I explained that you'd need to stay here, Jack, because Country can't dive alone."

"No need for that, Hollywood." Country jumped down from the back of the van. "My guys are finished at the fire scene. They want to take a dive to get the stink off of them. They can help me get the car on the wrecker if you've got to be somewhere, Jack."

"Part of me wants to stay here, but we need to interview some potential witnesses. Besides, this isn't your first rodeo, Country. You certainly don't need my help."

"But I'll take it anytime. Are you really interested in joinin' the team?" Country quickly held up a warning finger. "My ribs are still killin' me, so don't go bringin' up that fat baby again."

Jill's mouth fell open. She stared at Jack like she hoped he'd provide a translation, but he couldn't explain what Country was talking about without cracking up.

"I'd love to join the team," Jack said. "One thing before we go, I noticed both windows were up on the car, which is good because we're looking for a small jewelry box that may be inside."

"We won't crack open the car until it gets to forensics. Once it's on the wrecker, we wrap it, and they take it, but I'll double-check that there aren't any big openings. Are you certain there ain't a body in there?"

"The body was dumped at another location," Jill said.

Country scratched his chin and looked back at the buoy. "That don't make a lick of sense. Why would someone haul the body someplace else when they coulda just kept it in the car when they drove it into the lake? Where did they dump the body, anyway?"

"Outside my apartment in the trash bin," Jack said.

Country whistled low. "That should make you as nervous as a cow with a buck-toothed calf, Jack. You've been makin' some mighty big collars lately, so I'm sure you're buildin' an enemy list fast as all get out. Someone's gunnin' for you."

"We don't know if the killer dumped the body as some kind

of message to Jack," Jill said. "The proximity to his apartment could be a coincidence."

Country shook his head. "If someone dumps a corpse on your porch, they sure are sendin' you a message. Mark my words, Jack, start watchin' over your shoulder. You're in someone's crosshairs."

Chapter Twenty

Alice spent the next two hours driving down every street and through every parking lot between the K-Mart and Sonic. There was no sign of Scoops' car. Since Scoops had driven away from Sonic, he had to have stopped somewhere before getting chased by the police.

But Scoops' car was nowhere to be found. And if his car wasn't here, there was only one other place she thought it could be. Turning back onto the main road, Alice headed to the edge of town. Her blue Volkswagen zipped along the back roads. She rolled down her window and let the cool wind chill her skin. As more miles separated her from the dark alley and creepy man, Alice started breathing easier, but keeping her doubts at bay was harder. Maybe she should look for a computer job?

Alice cringed at the thought. She loved everything techno, but the idea of being locked away in a basement for eight hours with no human interaction felt like voluntarily committing herself to solitary confinement. On the other hand, this morning, she had almost gotten killed — or worse. She shuddered.

She reached over and pressed her phone, which was sitting on the passenger seat. It flickered to life, and Jack's smiling face brought a grin to her own. She had the best teacher. She could do this.

Alice stopped in front of the auto yard's two enormous gates, secured by a thick chain and padlock. A brand-new sign proudly proclaimed she had arrived at Sullivan's Junkyard. She gave three loud blasts on the car horn, reached into the glove compartment, pulled out a large brown bag, and exited the car.

Bells jiggled from inside the fence. Rounding a totaled pickup truck, a large pack of dogs raced toward her. She couldn't even count the number of animals but knew there were nine junkyard dogs—enormous, muscular beasts as intimidating as they come. They rushed the gate without sound except for the little bells around their collars, panting breath, and pounding gallop.

Alice held up the bag and ordered, "Stop!"

Like furry synchronized dancers, the dogs all skidded to a halt.

"Sit!"

Again, they obeyed.

Alice entered the gate code and walked through.

The largest dog turned to stare at Alice's car and whimpered.

"I'm sorry, Dasher, but Lady's not here today. I still brought all of you a treat." She reached into the bag and took out one of Mrs. Stevens' special treats. Calling each animal by name, she felt like Santa, or at least one of his elves. "Dasher, Dancer, Prancer, Vixen, Comet, Cupid, Donner, Blitzen, and little Rudolph." The runt of the pack came up to her so excitedly his whole body wiggled. The poor guy had an overbite, which made his canines protrude, giving him a particularly frightening appearance, but he was the sweetest of them all.

Alice strode to the trailer, leaving them to munch on their desserts. As she went, she scanned the yard for any sign of Scoops' car but didn't see any. Sullivan's Junkyard was the towing department for both the Sheriff and the city police. If someone had towed Scoops' car, they would have brought it here.

A TV blared inside the trailer, and Alice rang the bell. A second later, the noise shut off, and Sully jerked open the door. "Alice!" The elderly man dressed in dark blue overalls took her hand in both of his and smiled. "Is it Thursday already?"

Every Thursday, she brought Lady by to play with the other dogs. Jack had come up with the idea after the dog owners at all the other parks in town were too scared to let their dogs around Lady. The poor girl was so rejected she stopped eating. Now, she waited by the door every Thursday, eager to roughhouse with some dogs who didn't mind if she was a giant.

"It's Wednesday, Sully. But I'm looking for a car you may have towed. It's a blue Toyota Camry. It would have been parked near the old K-Mart."

"I picked up that one myself. Andy was sick, and it's been a while since I drove the wrecker. Still got my moves." He winked and nodded, sending his wild, white hair bobbing back and forth.

"Is the car still here?"

"Sure is. Let me show you. Why are you interested in it in the first place?" He pulled the door to the trailer shut behind him and descended the three steps to the gravel.

"I've taken over for Jack as a bounty hunter, and the guy who skipped bail owns the car. Where did you find it?"

"It was on the side of the road and beneath the big sign. It looks like he pulled off and parked right there. But it got two tickets, so they called me, and I went and got it. It makes sense it was someone on the run."

"Why do you say that?"

They walked past a few cars parked in a line and stopped in front of Scoops' Toyota. Alice took out her phone and took pictures.

"For starters, they left the driver's side window open. I shut it, but it had rained, and the arm console got filled with water. Don't know if the electronics will work now, but it ain't my fault."

Alice cocked an eyebrow as she typed what he said. "How did you raise the window? They're power windows, right?"

"That's the other funny thing. The keys were in the ignition, and a hamburger and onion rings were on the passenger side floor. I thought there was no way anybody would be foolish enough to leave their keys, but they done it. I figured it was some insurance scam where it was some leased job, and they were hoping someone would steal it."

"Do you mind if I take some photographs?"

"You can take all you want from the outside, but I can't open the car until I get my camera. Part of the procedure I follow is to take a video of the inside, then bag and inventory the contents before anyone does anything to the car. I don't want someone claiming they left a couple of bars of gold in there if you know what I mean."

Alice held up her phone. "I can do that for you now if it's okay."

"That'll save me some work, and since I'm right here, no harm, no foul."

"You're the best, Sully. Oh, I almost forgot." Alice reached into her coat pocket and took out two packages of chocolate Mallo Cups.

Sully's eyes lit up. "You are an angel. My Dad used to bring these home for me when he got done with work."

"A friend named Kiku taught me that a little kindness can go a long way."

"It certainly can!" Sully stuck one pack in his pocket and grinned as he opened the other.

While he ate his snack, Alice photographed the inside of the car. She removed the half-eaten hamburger and found the car's registration lying underneath. After photographing those items, she took everything out of the glove compartment, laid it on the hood, and snapped pictures of both sides of each object.

"Do you mind me asking why you're doing that?" Sully said. "Not meaning to pry, just curious."

"You never know where a lead is going to turn up. Once, Jack tracked down a skip because he left a receipt for a hotel restaurant in his car."

"That's smart thinking. Jackie is a sharp fella."

Alice nodded, hoping some of Jack's wisdom had rubbed off on her.

Sully scratched his chin. "Any idea where this guy you're chasing ran off to?"

Alice shook her head. "That's the million-dollar question."

Chapter Twenty-One

As he drove away from the lake, Jack glanced at Jill sitting in the passenger seat, staring out the window. She hadn't said a word since they left, and she balled her hands into fists on her lap.

"Everything all right?" Jack asked.

"Sorry." Jill sat up in her seat. "What?"

"You seemed preoccupied. Is everything okay?"

Jill leaned away from him and crossed her arms. "Didn't you hear what Country said? You thought about it earlier, but it makes way more sense now. What if Tyrell's killer is sending you a message?"

Jack gave a one-shouldered shrug. "I already have a habit of looking over my shoulder. If someone wants to kill me, they have to take a number and wait in line."

"That's not funny."

Jack held up his hand, his index finger and thumb close together. "It's a little bit funny."

"Don't you realize they may be saying you're next?"

Jack nodded. "I can't let that freak me out, though. People have wanted to kill you, right?"

"No. Why would someone want to kill me?"

"When you arrest people, they don't threaten to kill you?" Jack asked, genuinely puzzled.

"That's a felony. And no, no one has ever said that to me."

"I had an instructor in the army who said I had the uncanny ability to make people angrier than he'd ever seen. I thought he was kidding, but people say they want me dead a lot. Dozens."

"And you don't know why?"

"Mostly, I thought it was because I was locking them up. But since no one has threatened you for doing the same thing, I might have to look at my methods."

"Maybe you should."

"I will. That way, I can share them with you."

Jill cringed like she had taken a bite of lemon. "This may come as a shock, but it's not a good thing that you get people so mad they want to kill you."

"I think you're looking at it all wrong. For one, I make *criminals* so mad they want to kill me. That's a good thing. Frustrated, angry people rush and make mistakes. They don't think clearly. It's the same thing in sports. If you irk your opponent, they're much more likely to screw up. And I'm very irksome."

Jill chuckled. "I can agree on the irksome."

"It's a good thing that my superpower only affects criminals. To everyone else, I'm quite charming."

"I suppose your wife tells you that?" Jill said.

"And my mother, my birth mother, and my foster mother."

"You have three mothers?"

"Like I said, I'm special." Jack winked and pulled into the parking lot of the Waffle Shack. "It's a long story."

"I'm intrigued. Once we finish the case, you'll have to bring me up to speed."

Jack glanced through the restaurant windows and noticed the tables were all empty. "Are you hungry? I'd like to approach this one low-key."

"Sounds good to me. I'm starving."

"I don't know if it's lunch or dinner for you, but I'm buying," Jack said.

Jill held the door open. "I have eaten nothing all day, so I'd keep your hands away from my plate if you like your fingers."

Jack laughed and stopped at the podium set up next to the door.

A tired-looking waitress with blonde hair and extra-long, false eyelashes got up from a chair near the kitchen. She rapped loudly on the stainless-steel counter and strolled over, carrying two menus. "Two? Booth or table?"

"The counter is fine." Jack nodded toward the ten stools in front of the old-fashioned bar. "That way, you don't have to walk far."

"You are an angel." The waitress set the menus on the counter. "What can I get you to drink?"

Jack took a black coffee, and Jill ordered water, orange juice, and the lumberjack special, pointing at the menu's cover.

"You want any food, darling?" The waitress asked Jack.

"Coffee is fine."

Jill unbuttoned her jacket and reached for a sugar packet. "I'm so hungry I might start with this."

"You should have said something."

"I didn't think of it until I realized where we were going." Jill rubbed the back of her neck with both hands.

The waitress returned with their drinks. She glanced down at Jill, and her eyes narrowed when she noticed her shoulder holster. "You're cops?" She put her hand on her hip. "And here I was, starting to like you."

Jack couldn't tell if she was kidding or not. "We're not cops. We're Detectives."

"Those are cops who have ripened a bit."

Jack laughed. "That's a good one. I'm Jack. This is Jill. What's your name?"

"Waitress."

"Works for me." Jack continued. "I get it that public opinion of the police is at a low point, but we're trying to do someone right. There were two guys in here Sunday night. A big black guy and a South American. Do you remember seeing them?"

The waitress's eyes narrowed. She stared at Jack for almost a minute before giving a curt nod. "They were here. Oh, no." She closed her eyes and set both of her hands down flat on the counter. "Was it the young kid? The one getting married? Please tell me it wasn't him."

"Why would you think something happened to him?" Jill asked.

"They don't send the suits out unless somebody got killed. And he flashed that ring. I knew I shouldn't have said anything. But he was so happy, and it was a little rock."

"You saw it?" Jack said.

She nodded. "Everyone did. Even Pete. He's the cook."

"Thanks for getting me involved, Marcia Gentry!" Pete yelled from the kitchen.

Marcia placed her elbows on the counter and stared at Jack. "He's dead, isn't he?"

Jack nodded. "Besides you and Pete, who else was here?"

"The kid met with a wide fella. Hispanic. Older. Gray haired. Hey," Marcia called back to the kitchen. "You know those two guys who work at Alpha Machine Works that were here Sunday? What are their names?"

Pete muttered something under his breath, and a moment later, a very grumpy-looking, bald man appeared in the kitchen window. "And thank you for making me even more involved. No offense, officers."

"Detectives," Jack said. "And none taken. We would have called you out here anyway, so don't get mad at Marcia."

"Doesn't do any good anyway," Pete grumbled. "Yeah, they were here Sunday. The black guy is Gerald Adams. I went to school with him. The other guy is Puerto Rican, I think."

"No, he's not." Marcia shook her head. "He's Filipino or Hawaiian."

"That's what I meant," Pete said. "They call him Dan, but I don't know if that's his real name."

"Speak of the devils." Marcia pointed toward the front of the restaurant.

Jack and Jill swiveled around on their stools.

Two men in gray coveralls strolled across the parking lot toward the front door. When they noticed Marcia pointing at them, they both stopped. Dan's eyes widened, and he took a step back.

"He's gonna rabbit!" Jack raced toward the door. "Jill, take Gerald. I got Dan."

Dan turned and bolted.

Jack ripped open the door and leaped off the steps. "Halt! Police!" he bellowed.

Gerald raised his hands and stayed still as Jack dashed past him.

Dan darted between two buildings and disappeared from sight.

Jack felt the fiery glow of adrenaline course through his veins. His lungs filled with air, and blood rushed to his muscles as he sped up. Dan ran full out, but Jack was faster and quickly gained on him as they raced across the parking lot and behind a phone store. The hard ground was easy for Jack to run on, but Dan's work boots slowed him down.

"Freeze!" Jack shouted. "Give it up before you make it worse."

Dan stuffed his right hand into the pocket of his coverall.

Jack drew his gun. "Show me your hands! Show me your hands!"

Dan stumbled. He pitched slightly forward, his right hand jerked out of the pocket and rose in front of him. He held something in his grasp.

Jack's trigger finger remained on the side of the gun. He couldn't see what was in Dan's hand. It could be a weapon. Maybe it wasn't.

Dan flung something away from himself. It flew into the air, toward the side of the building. Dan's legs tangled over themselves, and he pitched forward. He crashed belly-first into the ground and slid in the dirt.

Jack raced up and stood over him with his gun aimed at Dan's back. "Do not move!"

"I'm not armed. I'm not moving."

Jack fought to get his breathing under control as he patted Dan down. "Hands behind your back."

"Please don't arrest me. Please don't."

"You're not under arrest, but until I sort out why you ran, I'm putting you in cuffs." Jack handcuffed Dan, jerked him to his feet, and searched him again. He had nothing on him.

"I'm so sorry."

"Shut up. Sorry doesn't cut it when I almost shot you." Jack jerked Dan over to the spot where he tossed the object. Jack stared down at the wallet lying open on the ground. He picked it up. "Why would you throw your wallet?"

Dan hung his head.

Jack opened it up. It contained seventeen dollars, a library card, and an ID. "This ID is fake."

Dan nodded.

"You admit it?"

Dan nodded again.

"What's your real name?"

"Kainalu Fepuleai."

"I'm going to run you through the system. Do you have any warrants?"

"No."

"Then why the fake ID?"

"I don't have any papers. I needed the ID to get my job. I'm sorry. Please let me go."

"I can't do that until I figure out who you are."

The young man's eyes widened. "I can't go to jail. I have to go to work. I'll get fired! I have a meeting with immigration next week. Please! I've never even had a ticket."

"Why did you run?"

"I thought you'd arrest me for drug dealing. They'd deport me then, for sure."

Jack picked the joint off the ground as he debated his next question. "Did you say you have to go to work tonight?"

Dan's lip continued to quiver. "Yes. I'm so sorry. Please let me go. I can't get fired."

"Do you always work the late shift?"

Dan nodded.

"Did you work the late shift Sunday night? Both you and Gerald?"

"Yes. We get something to eat before we start. They discount items at night."

Jack ran his hand through his hair as his once-hot lead fizzled out. "Can anyone account for you being there?"

Dan vigorously nodded. "Ten people. They have cameras too."

"When does your shift start?"

"Eight o'clock."

Sirens in the parking lot in the direction of the Waffle Shack made Jack turn. A city police cruiser skidded to a stop. Calvin Green jumped out carrying his shotgun.

"I've got the situation under control," Jack called over.

Calvin jogged up to Jack. "Reyes has the other perp back at the Waffle Shack. You need backup?"

"I'm good," Jack said as he turned Dan around and uncuffed him. "I need to verify Dan's identity, but his running was a misunderstanding."

Calvin grabbed Jack's wrist. "Resisting arrest is more than a misunderstanding. It's a felony."

"There's a lot of range in that charge. Anything from a class A misdemeanor to a class D felony. Speaking of which, I suggest you let go."

Calvin released his grip. "You're going to let him walk? Really?"

Jack removed the other cuff from Dan. "You're not free to leave yet. I still have more questions. Stand over there and face the wall."

Dan opened his mouth, thought better about whatever he was going to say, and did what Jack asked.

Calvin stepped forward and got right in Jack's face.

Jack was three inches taller than him, but Calvin had forty pounds on Jack.

"I heard you were supposed to be some kind of badass, Stratton. And seeing what happened to Michelle, I never would have thought you were a bleeding-heart liberal."

Jack's eyes blazed. He knew Calvin had lost his daughter, but that didn't give him a free pass to stab Jack in the face.

Footsteps rang off the pavement as Emmett Wilson jogged over. "Hold on a second there, Calvin. You're stepping over the line."

"I'm not the one who doesn't see the line." Calvin glared at Jack. "Why are you going to let some scumbag walk, Stratton? Do you care more about that guy than Michelle? Or is it because she wasn't your real sister?"

Jack's hand balled into a fist, but before he knocked Calvin's teeth in, Emmett slapped Calvin across the face.

Calvin's head jerked to the side, and his hand moved slightly toward his gun.

All three men froze. The argument had gone nuclear, and they knew it.

Calvin stared at Emmett like he was ready to kill him.

Disappointment and shock flashed across Emmett's face.

Calvin turned and stormed across the parking lot and back to the police cruiser.

"He didn't mean it, Jack," Emmett said, staring at his hand. "Emma's death is slowly killing him."

"You're his supervisor. I'm suggesting that you place Calvin on leave."

"That *would* kill him."

"You've got a responsibility to him and the public. He needs more time off to deal with what he's going through. If you don't do it as his supervisor, do it as his friend."

Emmett sighed. "He's off for four days. I'll talk to him."

As Emmett walked away, Jack couldn't help but wonder if there had been other times.

Chapter Twenty-Two

Jack walked into the kitchen, toweling off his hair, and the wonderful aroma of roast beef filled his nose. Andrew stood behind the stove, stirring a large pot. Lady sat on her haunches on the kitchen floor, staring at him with large brown eyes.

"Andrew, that smells unbelievable, but you don't have to cook for us. I appreciate it, but you don't have to." Jack said.

"Nonsense, Jackie. I'm so grateful to both of you. And please, call me Gee-Gee. You take care of my Kaya Kukla and are part of my family."

"I'm glad you're here. You've made Alice so happy."

Andrew set the wooden spoon he held down and stared at Jack thoughtfully. "I'm worried about something, Jackie. You're taking so many showers, and that made the light go on." He snapped his fingers over his head. "How are things in the bedroom between you two? You are newlyweds, so you should be exhausted and smiling, but you both seem frustrated. Normally, in my country, this talk would fall to my wife, but God rest her soul since she's looking down on us; it is my responsibility. When it comes to matters in the bedroom, do you need some... what is the word? Coaching?"

Jack shook his head so vigorously it sent water flying. "We're good. I'm good. Really. In America, what goes on in the bedroom is kind of a private topic that people don't discuss."

"I know! But that is one of the things I don't like about America. If someone has a problem, it's a family problem. We're family, so we're free to discuss everything."

Lady trotted over to the front door. The lock rattled, and Alice opened it. She took one look at Jack holding the towel and pouted. "I hope you left me some hot water. I so wanted to jump right into the shower."

"I knew I was right!" Andrew held up the wooden spoon like it was a scepter.

"Right about what?" Alice asked.

"I was just asking Jackie about how often you two are love-making. I'm worried it's not enough. You're newlyweds. You should be dragging each other into the bedroom."

"Grandpa!" Alice's cheeks flushed bright red.

Jack cleared his throat. "Your grandfather explained that where he's from, families discuss everything, including that."

"Of course we do. Families help each other, and I love you both. I made pot roast." He looked at Jack. "Meat, spinach, tomatoes, all things to help with your impotence."

Jack's mouth fell open, and he pointed at his chest. "I don't have that problem."

"Sure, you don't." Andrew gave an over-the-top wink.

Alice chuckled.

Jack scowled and followed her to the bedroom and shut the door. "It's bad enough that your grandfather wants to discuss our sex life or lack thereof, so don't encourage him. You know I don't have that problem. If anything, I have the opposite, but do you really want me to tell him that the issue with us not making love is his being here?"

"You can't say that, Jack! He might move out."

"So, I've got to listen to him thinking I'm impotent?"

Alice grabbed his waist and pulled him close. "Does it matter what anyone else thinks when I know what a stud you are?"

"I'm feeling the need to prove it." He reached for her belt, but she shied away and headed for the bathroom. "After the day I had, I have to shower first. After dinner?"

"I'm going to hold you to that."

Alice bit her bottom lip, nodded, and closed the bathroom door.

Jack walked back to the kitchen.

Andrew dropped the spoon into the pot. "What are you doing out here? I got you two talking about lovemaking. You should be in there with your wife right now."

"She had a rough day. She wants to take a shower."

"Then take one with her. Soap her back. Towel her off. Carry her to bed after." He wiggled his eyebrows.

Lady barked and raced to the front door. Someone knocked twice.

"Hold on a second," Jack said. Jack could guess who it might be from how Lady wagged her tail.

Mrs. Stevens, their landlady, had fallen in love with the giant dog, and she spoiled Lady rotten. She brought her treats, took her on walks, and volunteered to dog-sit. Jack couldn't believe there was ever a time when Mrs. Stevens and he didn't get along, although Jack still recalled the weekly threats of getting evicted. Mrs. Stevens had an excessive fondness for rules, while Jack had a violent allergic reaction to orders. Thankfully, after Alice and Lady became tenants too, and they moved into a bigger apartment in the building, Jack broke fewer rules, the need for his apology gifts became rare, and they had all grown genuinely fond of one another.

Lady whined until Jack opened the door. Mrs. Stevens stood in the doorway with two large brown bags. Her bob of red hair bounced back and forth in synch with Lady's tail. "There's my baby. I've got treats for you." She looked up at Jack. "What is that heavenly aroma?" She hurried over to the kitchen as fast as her large frame allowed.

Andrew took the roast out of the oven. His eyes widened as he noticed Mrs. Stevens.

Jack shut the door. "Mrs. Stevens, this is Aino Oja. He's —"

"Enchanted." Andrew wiped his hands on his apron as he crossed over. He took the bags from Mrs. Stevens, set them on the table, and encircled her hand with both of his. "Please, call me Andrew."

Mrs. Stevens blushed. "I'm Jan. *Miss* Jan Stevens. Are you the chef who created that amazing scent?"

Andrew magnanimously led her over to the roast. "You flatter me. It's a simple dish I whipped up for Alice."

"Are you visiting long?"

"Possibly. I'm a family friend. I was thinking of relocating to the area, and that idea has suddenly grown very attractive to me."

Mrs. Stevens giggled.

Jack felt his eyebrows traveling in opposite directions. Was it even possible for Mrs. Stevens and Alice's grandfather to have the remotest interest in one another? "Could you excuse me for a moment?" Jack said. He didn't wait for an answer and hurried into the bedroom, closing the door behind him.

Alice opened the bathroom door and peeked out. "Is everything okay?"

Jack shrugged. "I don't know. Mrs. Stevens stopped by with some more dog treats."

"Oh, good. I'm out. I stopped by Sully's."

"Why? It's not Thursday." Jack sat on the bed.

Alice came out of the bathroom, pulling on a shirt. "I was looking for Scoops' car."

"Did you find it?"

"Sully towed it from in front of the old K-Mart." Alice crossed her arms and leaned against the bureau. "Can I ask you to do a favor for me? I spoke with Tibet Olsen, and she saw Scoops running away from a cop behind the K-Mart. Her story checked out, but there's no police report on it in either the Sheriff's system or the city's."

Jack cocked an eyebrow. "Tibet may be mistaken. If a patrolman gets in a foot chase, it's procedure to call it in. That would generate a report from dispatch in the least."

"This creepy homeless guy saw the cop, too."

"Was it the city or Sheriff?"

"They were too far away for Tibet, but she swears it was a cop, and the homeless guy didn't technically see him."

"How'd he know it was a cop if he didn't see him?"

Alice made a face. "He said you guys sound like the bad ice cream truck coming into the neighborhood. Your gear jingles and the sound of your shoes are distinct."

"Guy's got a point. I'll have to change my footwear, so I'm more incognito. What did he say happened?"

"He said the cop chased Scoops to this fence at the end of the property. Scoops jumped over it, and the cop stopped and left without saying anything. I've got pictures and video if you want to see them."

"You are exceptional."

Alice sat on the bed next to him and held up her phone. "I had an outstanding teacher."

For the next ten minutes, Alice walked him through her conversations with Tibet, the homeless man, and what she found in the car with Sully, showing him all the photographs and videos she had taken.

Jack stared at the glove compartment's contents spread on the hood of Scoops' car — a box of hand wipes, the owner's manual, a flashlight, napkins, a tire gauge, and a pair of sunglasses. Then he returned to the photograph of the car's registration lying on the floor. "Was this how you found it?"

"Yes. You can see when I found it in the video. It was underneath the hamburger on the passenger side floor."

"Where did Sully say he found the car?"

"On the side of the road and beneath the tall K-Mart sign. Do you know the spot, or do you want me to pull it up on a mapping program?"

"I know exactly where it is. There was a busy crosswalk there because of the K-Mart. People used to run the red light. I issued dozens of tickets there. Sully said the driver's side window was down?"

"Yes. It rained, and water got into the car. You're thinking of something. What is it?"

Jack scrolled back and pointed at a picture. "Why is the car registration on the floor?"

Alice's face scrunched up, and she shrugged. "People usually keep them in the glove box or behind the visor."

Jack swallowed down his growing unease. "What happens when a policeman pulls you over?"

"They get out of the cruiser, and you power down your window." Alice gasped. "Then they ask for your license and registration! Scoops' window was down, and the registration was on the floor. But why didn't the policeman file a report?"

"Maybe it wasn't a cop."

Alice closed one eye and leaned away like Jack had poked her in the face with his finger. "You just said a policeman pulled him over. How can it be a cop and not a cop?"

Jack stood up and pulled out his phone. "I think we're looking for a fake cop. That's why they didn't call it in or file a report."

"I just watched videos of guys doing that on the internet. They dress up and everything. But what happened to Scoops?"

Jack dialed Jill's number. "I'm worried about that, Alice. Because that may be what happened to Tyrell Miller."

Chapter Twenty-Three

Jack paced in front of the Kent building, staring at the entrance to the parking lot and debating about going inside without Jill. He was about to head in when Jill's car appeared through the early morning fog clinging to the ground. She drove straight to the front spaces and parked as Jack jogged over.

"I hope this is an emergency. I haven't even had a cup of coffee yet." Jill opened her door and stared at the darkened building. "Is anyone even here?"

"The building doesn't open until nine, but I called in a favor with Monica Sweet. She's the latent print examiner. Mei is going to meet us afterward."

Jill locked her car and followed Jack down the walkway. "You must owe a lot of people favors," she said, brushing errant hairs out of her face as they climbed the steps. "Did I mention I'm not a morning person?"

"You're the one who wanted me to call if I was going to speak to someone about the case. I'm fine with letting you sleep in."

"Not on your life. Where you go, I go, partner." Jill held the front door open for him.

The evening lights in the foyer were still on, casting a subdued glow across the tiles. A tired-looking security guard stared out the glass doors. Jack and Jill flashed their badges, and he unlocked the doors.

"Thanks." Jack smiled.

The older man nodded and locked the door behind them.

Did I tell you my wife is a fugitive recovery agent?" Jack said as they headed for the elevators."

"No. That I would have remembered. Really?"

"She's going to be better than me at it. Right now, she's trying to find a skip named Oren Dorcey. He goes by Scoops. Alice found two witnesses who claimed a police officer was chasing him on foot behind the K-Mart Friday night sometime around nine."

"That explains why you had me run that search last night. There were no reports filed, and no calls came into dispatch."

"Nothing was reported to the Sheriff's department either. And there's more. Scoops' car was towed to Sullivan's Junkyard. He runs the impound company for both departments. Alice found the car there and photographed everything."

The elevator doors opened, and Jill marched inside. She jammed the button for the bottom floor with her finger and raised an eyebrow, fixing Jack with an icy stare. "So, you're admitting that your wife contaminated a crime scene?"

The doors closed, and Jack smacked the stop lever with his hand.

"Hold on, Eliot Ness. Before you go accusing anyone of something, check the facts. Right now, that car isn't a crime scene. They towed it for illegal parking. Sully owns the junkyard, videotapes, bags, and inventories everything inside the car. He was there with Alice and asked for her help."

Jill crossed her arms. "That makes sense. You should have explained that."

"You should have given me the chance." Jack shot back. "I have a habit of jumping to conclusions. I apologize." She reached out and pulled out the stop button. The elevator began moving again. "I'm surprised the alarm didn't go off," Jill said. "I take it you've done that before."

"Not in this elevator. I thought the alarm would go off, too. I didn't care."

Jill's brows arched in disbelief.

The elevator dinged and the doors opened. Jack headed to the left.

"What would you have done if security came?" Jill asked, following.

"Told them you bumped into it. Monica's in here. But wait a second." Jack stopped. "They video and photograph every vehicle taken to impound. They did the same to Oren's car and discovered the registration on the floor. And when they found the car, his driver's side window was lowered."

"So, you're thinking it was a cop?"

"A police impersonator. They didn't radio in the stop or call in the foot chase. That's why I'm eager to see what Tyrell's car holds." Jack opened the door.

The basement garage was an area reserved for vehicles, small boats, and any other large pieces of evidence that technicians needed to process. The large, bright room was filled with worktables, cabinets, and various high-tech machinery. Monica Sweet, 30s, thin, tall with black-framed glasses and her long hair pulled up in a bun, stood beside a table and turned when the door opened.

"Detective Stratton." Monica strode quickly across the painted cement floor, her unbuttoned lab coat revealing jeans and sneakers beneath. "And you must be Detective Reyes. Monica Sweet."

"Jill's fine. Nice to meet you."

Monica smiled. "Jack and Jill, how funny. Coffee just finished if you need a cup." She pointed to the far counter.

"You are sweet." Jill made a beeline to the corner of the room. "Pun intended." She called over her shoulder. "Jack, do you want a cup?"

"All set," Jack replied. After a minute of small talk, Jack looked expectantly at Monica. "What did you find?"

She crossed over to the table she had been standing at earlier. Less than a dozen items lay on it — a cell phone charger, the car's owner manual, a small black box, a flashlight, napkins, six ketchup packets, a tire gauge, a large rock, and a small pile of change. "The rock was wedged between the gas pedal and the transmission bump out of the firewall, pinning the gas pedal to the floor."

"What are the odds of that happening accidentally?"

"Mathematically zero." Monica raised her hand and showed a bandage covering two of her knuckles. "Someone stomped it in place. I had to use a crowbar to get it out."

Jack's focus shifted to the small black box. "What about the jewelry box? Did you open it?"

Jill hurried over, careful not to spill her coffee.

Monica sighed. "You never know what will hit you in this job." She touched her chest with her finger. "There's an engagement ring inside. Opening the box and seeing that, I felt like someone stabbed me in the heart. I didn't sleep last night. It's so sad."

"Looks like we can rule robbery out as a motive," Jill said.

Jack pointed at the items on the table. "Is that everything? There was no registration in the car?"

"None. Tyrell's wallet was also inside. I've got it drying out upstairs. There were eighty-seven dollars in assorted bills. There are four receipts, but we can't read them yet, and assorted credit cards. His license is missing."

Jack and Jill exchanged knowing glances.

"Do you think you can get prints off anything?" Jill asked.

"There's always a chance, but nothing yet," Monica said. "Once we can see where those receipts are from, I'll send you the data."

"I owe you, Monica. Thanks again." Jack said.

"You don't owe me, Jack. Do me a favor and get this guy. This one really hurt."

Jack and Jill headed out of the garage and to the elevator. Jack pressed the button for the third floor. "I asked Mei to double-check the injuries on Tyrell. She should have the results ready."

"Did Alice find anything more regarding Oren?"

"No. He's still in the wind."

"Or worse, if the two cases are related."

"I'm hoping he got away. I grew up with him, and he's not a bad guy. Neither of the witnesses heard shots fired, but now I really want to talk to Scoops."

"Why do they call him Scoops?"

"Whenever we went to the ice cream store as kids, he'd beg for two scoops. He only had the money for one, but he would get down on his knees and cry if he needed to. Most of the time, it worked."

"I have to ask you something, Jack. If we find Oren alive, will you let him go, or are we taking him in?"

Jack stopped in the middle of the hallway. "Why are you asking that?"

"You let Dan go at the Waffle Shack. He was in the country illegally and ran. We could have charged him and sweated him out in a cell."

"There was nothing to sweat. His manager said he and Gerald showed up for work at their regular time. I checked his story. He's got an appointment with immigration, and he's working now."

Jill crossed her arms. "What about Oren? You said you hoped he got away."

Jack laughed in disbelief. "I want him to get away from the killer, not us. Don't get me wrong, if Oren committed a crime, I want him to pay. I don't want to see him get shot over parking tickets."

"I don't want to see anybody get hurt, either. It's just back in California, everyone is looking the other way now. Even good police officers. Did you see the video making the rounds of the shoplifter running past the group of four cops? The guy is carrying an armload of Gucci bags, but not one of the cops did anything to stop him. It's going viral."

"Was it that bad out there?"

"Worse, and it's going downhill. Every time someone steals and doesn't get punished, it's like they get a reward for doing wrong. It emboldens them. And now stores are closing, and drugs are all over the place. It's like a dystopian future. That's why it bothers me when you say it's only unpaid tickets. How many crimes does someone commit that we don't see?"

"I agree with you there, but you also need to consider other things. Oren would have paid off the tickets. He's trying to turn his life around."

"Do you believe him? Come on. How many prisoners say that? All of them."

"Our job isn't to judge. We catch them. But I do like to think that people can change. It means there's hope for me and my black heart." Jack stopped and knocked on Mei's door.

Mei quickly opened it. "Good morning. Please follow me." Excitement filled her voice as she rushed across the room to an enormous desk with a computer and a large monitor. "After receiving your email last night, I ran the photographs of the bruising on Tyrell's wrists through several enhancement programs. On most points of contact on his skin, the cause of the bruising was inconclusive. But on his right arm, at the terminus of the radius bone, the bruising made a clearer impression." Mei wiggled the mouse, and the screen brightened. "This is the original autopsy photograph."

A close-up image of Tyrell's wrist appeared. The bruise was distinct, but Jack still couldn't tell what caused it.

Mei clicked the button and an inverse of the photograph appeared with the contrast enhanced. "You'll notice the distinct hard lines here and here. And, at this point, there is a circular indentation. I compared the imprint with several objects, and it's an exact match with a standard-size pair of metal handcuffs."

Jack crossed his arms. "We're looking for a fake cop."

Chapter Twenty-Four

Alice sat in the driver's seat of her Bug parked on the side street behind a three-story duplex, staring up at the third-floor apartment. The back shades and the curtain on the large slider leading to the rear entrance were drawn. The apartment belonged to Scoops' friend Francis Kelly. Francis, who went by the nickname Frosty, and Scoops were tight enough that Frosty would hide him.

The apartment, having two exits, created a problem for Alice. Cursing herself for agreeing to Titus's terms of flying solo, she drummed her fingers on the steering wheel as she contemplated what to do. If Bobbie was here, she could take the front door while Bobbie watched the back. Without a backup, she could only cover one door. If she went to the front and Scoops was inside, he'd rabbit out the back. But if she went to the back door, Frosty may think she was a neighbor, and they'd let their guard down.

She angled her dashboard camera to view the back parking lot and pressed record. After double-checking her gear, she got out and locked the car. She doubted Frosty and Scoops would ever do anything to hurt her, but you never knew how a desperate person would behave when cornered.

The wooden staircase swayed as she climbed the three flights. By the time she reached the top, she was out of breath. She wanted to kick herself. She hadn't paid attention to her breathing and should have stopped on the second floor until she was ready.

Pushing her self-critique aside, she moved to the edge of the slider and knocked.

Silence.

She peered through the gap in the curtain. Frosty's unkept room looked like a dorm after spring break. The living room was a chaotic mess, with clothes and trash strewn across the floor and furniture. Empty beer bottles and pizza boxes covered every surface. The furniture was mismatched and worn, with a large screen TV hanging on the wall and a game console on a coffee table in front of it.

Alice stood peering in the window when a woman calling out beneath her made her jump.

"Can I help you?" The woman yelled up from the parking lot below.

Alice rushed to the railing and said as softly as she could while still trying to be heard, "I'm visiting Frosty."

"That's the fire escape. That's my apartment beneath you, and you probably scared the life out of my Pookie."

"Sorry. I didn't hear him bark."

The woman jerked her head back. "It's not a dog. It's my husband! Next time, use the front door." She pressed her key fob, and a car horn sounded.

Alice slipped back to the slider and peered through.

Frosty, tall as an NBA player and thin as spaghetti, strolled through his living room. He glanced out the open curtain and froze.

Alice flashed a huge smile and waved.

Like a deer in the headlights, Frosty stood pinned to the spot. He appeared to be debating if he should run or not.

Alice reached out for the slider but didn't open it, as that could unleash a host of legal issues. She called out, "What's up, Frosty? Got a sec?"

Frosty hurried over, jerked open the slider, and shouted, "How are you, Alice Stratton? I'm glad it's only you."

Alice's smile spread. Even as a kid, Frosty couldn't lie to save his grandma. Scoops had to be in here.

"How's Kim?"

Beads of sweat dotted Frosty's brow. "Who?"

"Your date you brought to my wedding? It was only a few months ago."

"Oh, yeah." He swallowed and put his hand on the back of his neck. "That didn't work out. But your wedding was really nice. How's Jack?"

Alice glanced over his shoulder. The door in the hallway hung open a crack and moved slightly. "Jack's doing great. He's a detective now."

"I heard." Frosty wiped his forehead with his shirt sleeve. "And word is you're taking over for him with Titus. But Scoops isn't here, and I've got no idea where he could be."

Alice nodded understandingly. "Sure. Then you won't mind me checking around."

The door in the hallway slammed shut.

Alice raced forward. "Give it up, Scoops!"

Frosty grabbed for her.

Alice ducked underneath his arms. Sprinting forward, she shoved open the hallway door, revealing a cluttered bedroom. The front window was up, and Scoops was climbing out.

"Freeze!" Alice shouted.

To her surprise, he did. Straddling the window frame with

one leg inside and the other outside, his upper body remained in the room.

Alice gasped as Frosty tackled her from behind. They crashed onto the bed.

Scoops fled out the window.

"Let him go, Z!" Frosty yelled, using her old nickname.

"Let *me* go, you idiot!" Alice attempted to break free.

They rolled off the bed and tumbled onto the floor. Frosty landed on top of her. He pinned her left shoulder to the floor with one hand, and the other slammed palm first onto her face.

The back of her head smashed off the hardwood. Her lip split, and she tasted blood.

Childhood friendship or not, Frosty crossed a line. Alice's training with Jack flashed through her mind. Her pistol Taser was useless at close range. The barbs needed time and space to deploy correctly. And unless she dropped the cartridge, the pistol Taser wouldn't operate manually. Alice ripped her stun gun from its holster, jammed it against Frosty's side, and pulled the trigger.

Frosty stiffened and screamed.

Alice bashed him across the face with the butt of the stun gun.

Frosty pitched sideways off her.

Alice scrambled to the window and climbed out onto the deck. She scanned up and down the street, but there was no sign of Scoops. Besides a few cars driving by, there wasn't any foot traffic.

Muttering beneath her breath, she climbed back in the window.

"I'm sorry! I'm sorry!" The shirt Frosty held against his bloody nose muffled his voice. "I didn't mean to hit you."

Alice drew the pistol Taser and aimed it at him.

"You've got two different ones? Don't tase me again! That hurt so bad. I didn't mean it. You and me are friends."

"I thought we were until you smashed my face and bashed my head off the floor."

"I fell. I was trying to catch myself but grabbed your face by mistake."

Alice scowled. "Am I supposed to believe that you didn't tackle me? What did you do then, trip?"

"That I meant to do. I didn't want to lie to you, but Scoops is my friend. He's nuts. He's scared out of his mind. I kept trying to get him to turn himself in, but he kept saying he'd kill himself. He's lost it, Z."

"Where'd he go?"

Frosty shrugged. "I swear I don't know. I've got no clue what's going on in his head."

Alice glanced around the cluttered room. "He's been hiding here for days and hasn't told you why he's hiding out?"

"Will you put that thing down and let me explain?"

Alice lowered the Taser. "You should put some ice on that nose."

"Is it broken?" Frosty leaned down so she could get a closer look.

"It's a little swollen, but it's not busted. I didn't hit you that hard."

"You pistol-whipped me!"

"It's a plastic polymer handle, and you had just smashed my head off the floor." Alice pressed her hand to her lip, and it came away bloody. "You don't hear me crying."

"That was an accident." Frosty's eyes widened. "Don't tell Jack. Please! He'll kill me."

"I won't. You're sorry, and I'm sorry. Let's get some ice, and you can tell me what's going on."

Frosty nodded and headed for the kitchen. After filling two

baggies with ice, he handed one to Alice, held the other against the side of his head, and leaned against the counter. "I was out of town driving a rig, and Scoops called me a few days ago. He said he was in trouble and asked if he could crash at my place. He told me not to tell anyone where he was. I thought he got in a fight with Imani until I got home last night."

"You didn't talk to him until then?"

"He wouldn't talk, and I'm driving long haul, so I was all over upstate. I couldn't come right back, but I figured it was nothing. Scoops would chill and play some games. But I got back at like two in the morning and saw he had trashed my place. Scoops is passed out in my bed, and when I wake him up, he's a freakin' mess. He fell off the wagon, and he's drunk as a skunk. He was crying and saying his life was over, and he was going to kill himself."

"And he didn't say why?"

"He wasn't making any sense. You know my drunk Uncle Matt, who lived with us? It was like that. Drunk speak with lots of tears and mumbling. So, I figured I'd talk to him this morning. Bobbie G. wakes me up by pounding on the door, and after he leaves, you show up."

"Why was Bobbie here?"

"He said he was looking for Scoops. I lied, but you get why. Bobbie said he had to find Scoops fast. He warned me..." Frosty cringed. "Oh, snap. He told me not to say anything to you. Please don't tell him I told you. He will kill me."

Alice's eyes narrowed. Scoops was her bounty, and Bobbie knew she wouldn't get the job if she didn't catch him. "You don't have to worry about that."

"Why do you think I don't have to worry about Bobbie?"

"Because I'm going to kill him."

Chapter Twenty-Five

Jill stared up at the statue of General Patton outside the supply store and gave a salute.

"Were you in the service?" Jack asked.

"Navy. Four years. What about you?"

Jack held the door open. "I'm allergic to bellbottoms, so I went for the Army."

"Ha-ha. Do you know that there are good reasons for bellbottoms? For one, you can roll them up when you swab the deck. Two, it speeds up removing them if you go overboard. And three, you can use them as a flotation device. The navy is practical."

"And well dressed." Jack grinned.

"I have an allergy to mud and bullets." Jill shot back.

Jack laughed. "Touché."

Jill crossed her arms. "I'm giving a lot of thought to your theory about it being a fake cop. Why couldn't it be a real cop?"

The question hit Jack like a slap in the face. He wanted to point out that he knew all the Sheriffs and most of the cops personally. He'd worked, hung out with them, and placed his life on the line for them. And they did the same for him. He wanted to deny it was possible, but he couldn't. "It could be a real cop, but we still have to check all the angles. Agreed?" He held the door open.

"Agreed." Jill strolled through. "You know I can get the door for you, but I figured it's force of habit for the Army to make way for the Navy."

Jack laughed.

"Detective Stratton?" A young man appeared from around a rack containing assorted flashlights. "I thought that was you."

Jack recognized his face but didn't recall his name, so he was grateful it was written on his name tag. "Hey, Brad. This is Detective Jill Reyes."

"I know." Brad shook both their hands. "Detective Reyes spoke at the Citizen's Academy, too."

"That's right." Jill smiled. "I forgot you were kind enough to give me that discount card."

"How's business going?" Jack asked.

"We're getting ready for another sale," Brad's father, Bud, interjected as he set down a case of ammo at a display close to them. "Ten percent off ammo. But seeing how you're in law enforcement, there's another ten percent off for the men and women in blue! Brad, get two more boxes of nine-millimeter hollow points from the back."

"Yes, sir. Nice seeing you two," Brad said.

"After you grab those boxes, I have some questions for you, Brad," Jack called after him.

"Is there anything I can help you two with?" Bud asked.

"You must be Bud Templeton. I'm Detective Jack Stratton, and this is Detective Jill Reyes."

"Jack and Jill?" Bud laughed. "That's funny. But you're not here about jokes." He glanced over his shoulder. "But I'm glad you came in. Could you do me a favor? You know my boy Brad wants to join the force. He was going to apply, but someone in the Citizen's Academy he went to advised him not to. It broke the kid's heart. He'll make a great cop."

"I'm sure he will," Jill said. "If I remember correctly, you're talking about Emmett Wilson. Brad asked a question in class about the physical exam. Emmett only said that he should make sure he could pass it before applying. He wasn't saying not to apply."

Bud chuckled. "That makes a lot more sense. I'll have to thank Emmett when he comes in. I've been trying everything to get Brad to put down the game controller, and now he has. He's even joined a gym."

"That's great," Jack said. "I'm sure he'll be ready in no time. And it is better to pass on the first try than retake the exam. But there is something you can help us with, Bud. We're investigating a situation where someone could be impersonating a police officer. We're hoping you could tell us if you have any customers who would fit that description."

"Seriously?" Bud chuckled. "Look around. Most of my customers aren't cops, but this gear is primarily tactical, military, or law enforcement. I could give you my entire client list because there's no way of narrowing it down."

Jill folded her hands in front of herself, "Brad mentioned you were in law enforcement. The person we're looking for would be the type who —"

"I know exactly the type of guys you're looking for. We get them in all the time, and I try to weed them out." Bud looked at Jack. "Ask your wife. She was buying gear the other day, and when I saw the car spotlight she picked out, I asked if she was a whacker. What did they do? Do you have a description?"

"We're not at liberty to say," Jill said.

"Like you said," Jack smiled. "You know the type we're

looking for. Has anyone recently purchased materials that could be used to impersonate a police officer?"

"Without knowing something about what they look like or what they're doing, it's going to be tough to narrow it down." Bud snapped his fingers. "If you give me a few hours, I can review past sales and generate a list. Would that help?"

"Immensely." Jack handed him a business card. "You can email it to me here."

Brad came back and called to his father as he approached. "You got a call in the office, Dad. It's Joe Dugan."

"Oh, I have to take this." Bud grinned. "We're putting in an outdoor shooting range. It will be huge—tactical, skeet, and cowboy areas. People need a place for their long guns, and that's the one area we're limited in. I'll get you that list by the end of the day!"

"Much appreciated." Jack nodded.

"Is there something I can help you with, detectives?" Brad asked.

"Your father is making a list, but we wanted to know if you are aware of any customer who would impersonate a patrolman?" Jill asked.

Brad's forehead puckered as he fiddled with the button of the box cutter in his hand.

Jack looked Brad in the eye. "Is there someone you've met who you think may pretend they're a cop?"

Brad stepped closer. "Don't say I said anything. This guy comes to the range every week and was also in the class with me. He's into all that sovereign citizen, conspiracy, and militia stuff. He's not a bad guy. I mean, he's got a little girl who goes to school down the street that he's always talking about, but he's on the fringe. You know?"

"Do you remember his name?"

"Nate, something. He always comes in the store, and my dad likes him, so please don't say I said anything."

"Hey, Brad!" Bud called from the back. "I just had a million-dollar idea! What about adding a zombie targeting section to the new range? You watch all that stuff. Come here and talk to Joe."

Brad rolled his eyes and chuckled. "Who knows? Zombies do sound kinda cool." He turned and hurried down the aisle.

As they left the store, Jack handed the keys to Jill.

"Where are we headed?" Jill asked.

"When I gave my talk at the Citizen's Academy, there was this guy named Nathan Rowe. He said it was his fourth time taking the class at the Sheriff's department."

"He was there when I gave my talk. White, big guy with a crew cut. About five foot ten?"

"That's him. I want to run a background check on Nate. Then I'll pull Bud Templeton's service record."

"Bud, did he raise red flags with you, too?"

"More like flashing red and blues."

Chapter Twenty-Six

Alice drove with the window down and the cool spring wind stung her cheek. She rubbed her eyes and made another mental note to pick up some drops. She'd spent the whole day driving all over the city searching for Scoops, and her eyes were dry and burned from staring. From his friends' and family's homes, to the bus stop and train station, she'd taken the side and back roads, constantly scanning people's faces.

Her cut lip throbbed, and her head pounded, but she didn't want to stop. But it was getting close to dinner, and if she was late, she'd disappoint her grandfather. Food seemed to be his way of expressing his gratitude and love. In some ways, having him in her life added to her stress. He did nothing wrong, but she'd never had an older male figure in her life. Aunt Haddie raised her. She had done her best, but Alice had always been keenly aware of her lack of a father figure. Between that and her abuse, she had many father issues. Thinking they'd go away when her grandfather showed up was naive. They didn't disappear. If anything, his presence shined a light on all of her trouble spots and what she'd missed out on.

Alice was ready to turn around and head home when her eyes widened.

Bobbie G.'s enormous, green Humvee sat parked in front of Hannigan's Pool Hall and Bar.

Alice cut the wheel and skidded into the parking lot. She'd been so discouraged about not finding Scoops she'd forgotten Frosty letting it slip that Bobbie was hunting for Scoops too. Bobbie knew Titus was testing Alice. Why would he go behind her back and try to catch Scoops? If he did that, she wouldn't get the job. Did Bobbie not want her to succeed?

Alice marched through the door of Hannigan's Pool Hall and Bar and stopped. The smell of stale beer and cigarettes deepened the scowl on her face. Underneath the odor was a hint of musty old wood, a reminder of the age of the building. The pool hall and bar were dimly lit, the low lighting casting deep shadows in the corners. Neon beer signs and vintage posters adorned the wooden walls, giving the place a nostalgic feel. The countless drinks served over the years had worn the bar counter down and covered it in scratches and stains. The bartender glanced at Alice's grimace and quickly looked away.

Somewhere in the back, Boomer's voice rose above the sound of the constant clacking of pool balls and the clinking of glasses.

Alice followed the sound until she spotted Boomer leaning against a pool table, cue in hand, studying the layout.

"Boomer is on fire!" he shouted. Boomer was only five foot two, but you wouldn't know it from how he strutted around. He'd gotten his nickname when they were kids because he loved explosions and enormous crashes. He'd blow up or destroy almost anything—bottles, cans, old TVs, fireworks—he loved making things go boom.

Sitting on a stool in the corner was Bobbie G. At six-four and over three hundred pounds, Bobbie Gibson didn't have to show off his massive biceps, but he always rolled up the sleeves on his army-green T-shirt for maximum effect. He noticed Alice and broke into a broad grin. "Alice!"

"Hey, girl!" Boomer launched into a complicated set of fist-bumping and handclapping that ended when he grabbed Alice's wrist and dragged her forward for a hug. "How you doin', married woman?"

"It's nice to see you, Boomer. Can you give Bobbie and me a minute?"

Boomer took one look at the hardened expression on Alice's face and said, "I suddenly feel like playing a little pinball. I'll be over there when you're done."

"Thanks."

Bobbie stayed sitting and re-crossed his arms.

Alice picked up the cue ball, and Bobbie shifted uncomfortably. "I thought we had a deal. Titus said I had a week. Why are you going after Scoops?"

Bobbie's brow knit together. "Do you think I would try to screw you over?"

"I didn't. You're one of the last people I thought ever would. Are you saying Frosty was lying?"

Bobbie hung his head and muttered something.

"So, it's true?" The betrayal cut Alice to the core. Her eyes watered, and her grip tightened on the cue ball. "Why? I thought you wanted to team up?"

"I do!" Bobbie stood.

Alice stepped forward and glared up at him. "Then why did you go looking for Scoops? If *you* bring him in, Titus won't hire me."

"What Titus is doing to you isn't fair. Or safe. Jack and I teamed up in plenty of bounties. Making you fly solo isn't cool on so many levels."

Realization dawned in her mind. "You were trying to help me?"

Bobbie nodded.

Alice turned and set the ball down on the table. "Why didn't you say something?"

"You would have said no."

"Thanks." Alice moved the cue ball back to where it had been. "I'm sorry I questioned you. The truth is, I've been doubting myself. I don't know if I'm cut out for this."

Bobbie sat back on his stool, holding his cue in both hands, and resting the bottom on the floor. "That's not Alice talking. You're letting people get in your head."

"Maybe they're right. Look at you! I must have been crazy thinking I could do what you could. I'm not big enough or strong enough."

"Taking down a skip is only part of the job. Most of the time, it doesn't get physical."

"But sometimes it does, and I'm not looking to set the women's movement back, but I'm not able to overpower most men unless I tase them or use pepper spray."

"That's why the conditions Titus set for you to get onboard are so unfair. The original deal we worked out would have been great."

"Would it have?" Alice walked over and leaned against the wall next to Bobbie. "Or would you have been doing most of the work?"

Bobbie blew a raspberry. "That's you listening to Titus. His name may be on the sign, but Titus doesn't know diddly about catching skips. You said it yourself: you need my muscle once in a while. But what about finding them? Do you know that Jack started catching twice as many skips when you started helping him?"

"Really?"

"Yeah. Finding them is the hard part. And you, with all your computer knowledge and street smarts, know how to run them down. I need you as much as you need me. My eyes light up when I think of the scratch we'll pull in. We'll be making bank together."

Alice crossed her arms. She still had her doubts, but what he said made sense. "Thanks, Bobbie."

"That was sweeter than a Hallmark!" Boomer yelled from the end of the pool table, carrying three beers. "You all gotta hug. Go on. Hug it out."

Bobbie glared at Boomer. "This was a private conversation."

"Who am I gonna tell?" Boomer brought the beers over.

"Thanks, but no thanks," Alice said. "My family friend is still in town, and he made us dinner. I have to jet."

"We cool?" Bobbie asked.

Alice gave him a hug, followed by a fist bump. "Totally. But don't go looking for Scoops anymore. Of course, if you hear something, let me know. Now that I've chased him out of Frosty's, he has to be heading somewhere else."

Bobbie jumped to his feet.

"Whoa!" Boomer cried, stepping back as the beer in his hands sloshed.

"Scoops was at Frosty's? Frosty lied to me?" Bobbie stood with his feet shoulder-width apart, and his large hands balled into fists.

"Don't be mad with Frosty," Alice said. "He's worried about Scoops. He fell off the wagon and is saying he might harm himself. Frosty was trying to convince him to turn himself in."

Boomer laughed. "Ain't that something. Bobbie didn't find him, and you did!"

Bobbie whacked Boomer on the back of the head, spilling more beer.

While the two friends talked smack back and forth, Alice said her goodbyes and headed out the door. But the confidence she gained from her talk with Bobbie faded as she reached her car. She always believed that she could do the job if she had backup, but the problem was that to get the job, she needed to do it on her own.

Alice slumped in the front seat. She may be able to find Scoops by herself, but would she be able to bring him in?

Chapter Twenty-Seven

"I wouldn't expect a warm welcome," Jack said, pointing at the rusted metal gate and the surrounding trees with several signs hanging on them.

Jill tipped her head to the side like she was studying a painting. "I think my favorite is that one. No trespassing. Violators will be shot. Survivors will be shot again."

Jack pointed to one hanging from the gatepost. "How about that one? Due to price increases in ammo, don't expect a warning shot."

"Nope. New favorite. Now I lay me down to sleep. Beside my bed, a gun I keep. If I wake and you're inside, the coroner's van will be your last ride."

"Looks like Nate's a poet and paranoid. I'm getting my vest."

"Good idea." Jill followed Jack to the trunk.

They both moved to opposite sides of the car to remove their shirts. Jack laid his shirt on the car's roof while he adjusted the vest's straps.

"I see why they call you a bullet stopper now," Jill called over. "I take it you were point man of your fire team?"

"You peeked." Jack gazed down at his scarred chest. "They're mostly from shrapnel."

Jill swore. "I was talking about the exit wound in your back. You got lit up."

"The wounds in the front are mostly from a suicide bomber. It killed my brother." Jack cinched his vest tight. "The one on the back is an entry wound. An old partner shot me."

"By accident?"

"Nope." Jack put on his shirt and tucked it into his suit pants. "She wanted to kill me."

"I can see why you're a little wary of me." Jill walked around the car with an expression that Jack hated — pity.

"You squared away, squid?" Jack said, eager to change the subject.

"Let's pull chocks."

"Isn't that Air Force lingo?" Jack circled the gate.

"I think it's both. I was stationed on an aircraft carrier for a bit."

They discussed how to approach the interview as they walked, but his senses were on hyper-alert with each step Jack took. He scanned the woods on either side of the road, listening for foreign sounds. They rounded a bend in the driveway, and an old ranch house appeared. It had seen better days but must have been charming once. The faded yellow paint gave it a jaundiced look now. The lawn was mowed, but clumps of grass grew high around the old birdbath and bench beneath a tall oak tree.

In the window to the left of the door, a curtain moved.

"Left side. Second window in." Jack said.

"Got it."

As they stepped onto the walkway, the front door opened.

Nate Rowe was in his early thirties. He wore a plain olive t-shirt, jeans, and sneakers. Resting on his hip was a holstered big-bore Desert Eagle Mark XIX pistol. People used the gun to hunt bears.

"Good afternoon, Nate," Jack said. "We're in the middle of an active investigation, and I was hoping you could help us with something."

Nate lifted a skeptical eyebrow and waited.

"I recall that you attended the Citizen's Academy. Was there anyone in the class who wanted to become a police officer?" Jack asked.

Nate's head rocked to the right. "This time around, it was mostly blue-haired types. There were two little old ladies who probably watched too much *Murder She Wrote*. Two county commissioners took it. Some thriller writer wannabe was there. Oh, do you know a guy named Brad Templeton? Young guy. Big, but kinda flabby?"

"I do. From the questions you asked in class, I know you're a guy who knows how law enforcement operates. So, I'm not going to try to puff you up or beat around the bush. What's your opinion of Brad? Did you talk with him at all during the academy?"

Nate gave a one-shouldered shrug. "I talk to everybody. His old man bought Patton's. I go to the gun range a lot, so I talk to them both there, too. Brad is all gung-ho about becoming a cop."

"Just how gung-ho is he?" Jill asked. "Did he talk about any police gear he'd bought? Maybe a uniform?"

Nate smiled like he just solved a riddle. "Are you wondering if I think Brad may be a little too impatient to wear the blue, so he got a jump on the academy and deputized himself?"

"Which he can't do," Jill said.

Internally, Jack cringed. Jill was overplaying their hand and giving out too much information. And the last thing you want to do with a guy like Nate is have them think you're correcting them.

Nate inhaled through his nose and then looked down it to glare at Jill. "Is that so? Are you aware that we used to have a citizen's militia? We have every right to defend ourselves, our families, and our land."

"You do." Jack nodded. "But *you* have training and experience on your side. Brad is wet behind the ears. If he or someone in your class is acting as a citizen patrol, I don't want to see them get hurt, and I'm sure you don't either."

"The tree of liberty must be refreshed from time to time with the blood of patriots and tyrants." Nate set both hands on his hips, his right hand close to the huge silver pistol. "And I say if that's what he's doing, good for him. The world is crazy, and the police are going right along with it. You guys quit doing your job long ago. Fishermen are supposed to be catch and release, not the cops."

Jill lifted her chin and leaned forward. "Easy for you to say when you're sitting on the sideline. We do our job."

Nate gave a sarcastic laugh. "Society's blue knights have all given up. Now, they're in the job for the benefits and retirement plan. You guys are letting criminals go left and right."

"If the DA won't prosecute, we can't bring them in." Jill's voice rose in volume and lowered in tone.

"We're not here to argue about the justice system, Nate." Jack motioned for Jill to step back, but she ignored him. "We're trying to stop a crime, and you can help us with that."

"Help you stop a fellow freedom fighter? Are you kidding?" Nate stared at Jack. "I would think you would understand what he's doing more than anyone. Think about it, Stratton. If Emmett had done his job, your sister would still be alive."

The words blasted into Jack's mind so hard his eyes slammed shut, and he grabbed the railing to keep from tumbling off the stairs. "Emmett Wilson? What are you talking about?"

"Emmett didn't tell you?" Nate scoffed. "What a guy."

Jack wanted to grab Nate by the throat, and it was all he could do to control himself. His hands balled into fists. "What are you talking about?" Jack demanded again.

Jill moved slightly between Jack and Nate.

"I'm a frequent flyer on ride-alongs. I like to keep tabs on where my tax money is going. A couple of years ago, I was on one with Emmett. We were in the Mission Hill section when he lit up a silver BMW. A young college guy was driving it. He gave Emmett a sob story of how the stress of finals was getting to him, and he came there to buy a joint and I smelled weed. He even let Emmett pat him down. But Emmett never searched the car. And, in the spirit of community policing, he let the poor, misunderstood kid go. It turns out that kid was the guy who killed Michelle. He was a serial killer trolling for victims. He probably had one in the trunk when we stopped him. If Emmett had done his job, your sister Michelle would still be alive."

Jack stepped back onto the walkway. It felt like iron bands encircled his chest. He tried to take a deep breath but couldn't. Sweat ran down his back. His fingers shook. He couldn't think straight.

Jill's hand touched his shoulder. She talked to him as she led him along the driveway, but Jack couldn't hear what she said.

Was it true? Had Emmett pulled over Michelle's killer? No. Nate was wrong. But why would Nate lie about something Jack could check out?

Chapter Twenty-Eight

Jack leaned against the railing in front of the Kent Building, watching the sun rise over the tops of the trees. He sipped the black coffee in his right hand, and another one for Jill sat at his feet. After she dropped him off yesterday, he'd spent a sleepless night going over every record in both the city and Sheriff's department computer systems. There had been no reports filed of the stop Nate said Emmett made. But Nate had accompanied Emmett on an overnight ride-along before Michelle was murdered.

What if Nate was telling the truth? Did Emmett have a chance to catch Michelle's killer before he murdered her? Had Emmett just let him drive away?

Jill pulled into the lot and parked in the front row.

Jack waited for her to climb the steps and handed her the coffee. "Sorry about having you come out here so early, but Mei said it was an emergency. I also wanted to apologize for my behavior the other day."

"There is absolutely zero need." Jill placed a gentle hand on his arm and met his stare. "I hope you don't mind, but I checked at the police station for hard copy reports. Nate did go out on patrol with Emmett, but Emmett didn't record a stop in Mission Hill."

"If he let the guy walk, I'm not surprised there's no report filed."

Jill's lips pressed together, and she placed both hands around her coffee cup. "I read about what happened with your sister. I have no idea how hard that must have been for you, but if you ever need an ear, I'm available."

"Thanks."

"Are you going to talk to Emmett?"

Jack nodded. "My sister's story was all over the front page, including photographs of the killer. If Nate recognized him, Emmett must have, too. I don't understand why he didn't say anything to me."

"Would you?" Jill shook her head. "From that look on your face, I'm sure you would, but what about someone else? Put yourself in Emmett's shoes. He thought he stopped some college kid looking to get high. The DA wouldn't do anything even if they found a joint, and there was no reason to search the car."

Jack's eyes hardened. "Emmett had probable cause for a search when he smelled drugs in the car."

"A good lawyer could fight that."

"Still, what might have been?" Jack took a deep breath. "Dwelling on the past won't change anything. Let's see what Mei has for us."

As they made their way into the building and downstairs, Jill said, "Thanks for forwarding that client list that Bud sent you. How are we going to narrow it down?"

"That's not the client list. It's a list of all the customers who purchased items used in, or similar to, law enforcement."

Jill's mouth hung open as they waited for the elevator. "Are you kidding me?"

"Nope. But don't get the wrong idea. Manufacturers make products to sell, and when the product looks like military or law enforcement, it sells. I know over fifty names on that list and I'm sure they didn't buy that stuff to pretend to be a cop."

"Maybe we can sort it by items or cost. Either way, we'll need some help to cull it down."

"I'll talk to Bob about it later. There are some deputies I trust to help."

"And you don't trust the city police to handle the job?"

The doors opened, and they got into the elevator.

"The goodwill I bought the coffee for didn't last long." Jack pressed the button for the basement. "And it's not that I don't trust the city police. It's just that I know a few deputies in the sheriff's department that I know could work on this competently."

Jill held up her coffee. "Sorry. Did I mention I'm not a morning person?"

"No worries. Just do me a favor. Stop assuming the worst about me."

"I will. I'm not making excuses, but trying to explain. Before I left California, morale had gotten so low in the department that everyone started to turn on each other. You'd think being attacked by the media and the people you're trying to help would bring us together, but it had the opposite effect. Going to work felt like going to Thanksgiving dinner at a dysfunctional family. Everyone gossiped, and no one trusted each other."

"I bought you coffee." Jack grinned.

"And that's supposed to earn my unwavering trust? Had there been a chocolate scone included, that would be another story, but coffee only gets you so far."

"I pulled Bud Templeton's service record."

"You don't trust anyone."

"Trust and verify. Bud retired after nineteen years on the force. There was no disciplinary record, and he left clean."

"So we take him off the suspect list?"

Jack smirked. "We move him down. I don't take anyone off the list until the case is solved."

Jill laughed.

The doors dinged and opened. Jack and Jill crossed the room to Mei, who was standing beside a body laid out on a stretcher covered with a sheet.

"This one is pretty rough. Would you rather review the report?" Mei asked.

Jack looked at Jill, his gaze searching her brown eyes. "Are you sure you want to do this?"

"Yeah," Jill said, shaking her hands at her sides like a gymnast about to charge the parallel bars. "I'm ready."

Jack squared his shoulders. He was a soldier and had seen things no one should witness. He nodded.

Mei pulled back the sheet. The stench of sulfur was both acrid and sweet. Jack's stomach clenched. The corpse was burned beyond recognition, and parts of bone gleamed white.

"The deceased is Matthew Yates, male, Caucasian, thirty-six-years-old. The official cause of death is a bullet wound to the face that penetrated the brain. There were three more gunshot wounds to the abdomen. The caliber of the bullets are nine-millimeter. They found the victim in the front doorway of his home." Mei explained.

"Was Yates shot before or after the fire?" Jill asked, then started coughing and took a step back. "Sorry," she muttered, moving further away.

"The fire was burning while he was alive. He had a significant amount of smoke damage to his lungs. The angle of the bullet wound to his head was downward."

"Yates could have been on his knees?" Jack said.

"My initial calculations and the position of the body suggest that."

Jill marched back over and stood beside Jack.

Mei glanced at Jack silently, asking if she should continue. He nodded, not wanting to say anything to help his partner save face.

"If you look at the stomach wounds..." Mei shined a penlight on the corpse's abdomen.

Jill leaned forward, her holster bumping the gurney. It was only a slight impact, but it jolted the table, and the corpse's left ear fell off and onto the sheet. Jill covered her mouth and rushed out of the room.

Mei followed her, but Jack placed a restraining hand on her elbow.

"She'll be okay. She needs a little time." Jack said, then turned back to the table.

Mei shined the red dot on three holes, grouped less than two inches apart. "I've extracted all four bullets and sent them to ballistics. The bullet that struck his cheekbone splintered and went into the brain. Of the ones recovered from the abdomen, two are intact."

"How did you identify the body?"

"Mr. Yates has an extensive criminal record. I had to reload the paper when I printed it out. His fingerprints are on file. His body covered his right hand so I could lift a usable set for identification. I've requisitioned his dental records from the prison database to cross-check."

"Was there anything out of the ordinary in your findings?"

"I'm still waiting on toxicology and several other lab reports, but no. I can conclusively say that he was murdered."

Jack crossed his arms as Mei pulled the sheet back over what was left of Matthew Yates. "Does ballistics have the bullets now?"

Mei adjusted her glasses. "Not yet. I wanted to let you know my findings first."

"I appreciate that, Mei. I better go check on my partner."

"You can tell her she doesn't have to come in here. I'm more than happy to present my findings in a different way that's not so disturbing."

"I'll remind her of that. Thanks again."

As Jack made his way to the exit, the acrid stench of burnt flesh clung to him. But that wasn't the reason for the tightening knot in his gut. He now had two victims killed with the same caliber gun, both with extensive rap sheets, and both shot at close range with three rounds in the stomach. He had two murders, but he was looking for one killer.

Chapter Twenty-Nine

"I apologize," Jill said as she rode in the passenger seat with her window down. Her black hair streamed back as she continued to take deep breaths. "I have a squeamish stomach, but I've never had to run out of the room before."

"That was a nine out of ten on the horrifying scale." Jack turned onto the one-lane road leading to Matthew Yates's house. "Mei doesn't mind putting together photos and a package. That way, you can take your time and not get the aroma."

"If it's another fire victim, I think I'm going to take her up on that." Jill brushed the hair out of her face, revealing her coloring was still light green. "I'll never forget that smell. How do you deal with it?"

Jack scratched his eyebrow as images of the horrors of war flipped through his memory. "I can't even tell you how many dead bodies I've seen. Each one burned itself into my head until they cauterized something in here." He tapped his chest. "I still care. It still tears my heart out to see a person lifeless, but I focus on the job. I have to look if I'm going to figure out what happened to them."

"And you think these killings are related?"

"They had the same caliber murder weapon, the same criminal history for both victims, and they were both shot at close range on their knees, then three times in the stomach. The killer might as well have left a calling card."

"They also have a lot not in common." Jill pointed out. "Different races. One was dumped, and the other wasn't. They killed Tyrell out at the pond while they shot Yates in his trailer."

"Speaking of which," Jack pointed when the burned-out shell of Yates' trailer came into view. "Who did the preliminary fire investigation for the city?"

"Detective Adam Carr. He forwarded me his notes. He didn't get far into the investigation since he was waiting for the M.E.'s and fire department's reports. Crime scene took photos, but at the time, they were thinking it was a simple house fire, not murder."

Jack parked the car and got out. The fire had gutted the trailer, leaving only the floors, studs, metal grated door, and barred windows behind. The police had taped the perimeter off, and the smell of old fire hung in the air.

Jill swallowed.

"You okay?"

"Memories." She lifted her chin. "I'll be fine. "Who puts a barred door on the front of their house?"

"Maybe he was homesick for prison?"

Jill laughed. "It does make it look like a cell. But seriously. I wouldn't think Yates would be the kind to worry about home security."

"That's exactly what it's for, but I suspect it's because there's no honor among thieves. Yates was probably worried about someone on his crew double-crossing him." Jack started down the walkway. "Yates was a merchandise man. He upgraded from B and E's to Smash and Grabs. Then he jumped on the shoplifting bandwagon currently sweeping the nation. We're not talking about one-off items. He got arrested at Outdoor Sports World for loading a canoe with over five grand in gear and strolling out the front door. He would have gotten away if his truck had started."

"And he's walking the streets?" Jill curled her lip in disgust. "I hate saying it, but a lot of what Nate said is true. I knew California was bad, but I hoped Darrington was different. What do we have to do to keep them locked up?"

"Our job is catching them and giving the DA the best case possible. And the DA here isn't soft on crime. She's actually a real hardnose."

"Then why did Yates walk?"

Jack stopped at the bottom of the stairs. "I only know about the story because it's the kind of thing that goes around the whole department. Yates went into Outdoor Sports world by himself and found an open display with a bunch of tech gear. He saw the opportunity but got greedy. He hid the high-priced stuff at the bottom of a canoe and covered it with even more gear. The only problem was that he didn't think about how he would get the canoe out of the store by himself. The store manager sees Yates trying to figure out what to do. Yates says he paid for everything but needs help to get it out of the store. The manager and Yates carried the canoe to Yates's truck, but the truck wouldn't start. One of the cashiers knew Yates didn't pay and called the police. Yates claimed he would pay, and since the manager had helped him, Yates' lawyer threatened to sue and take it to trial. The store dropped pressing charges."

Jill chuckled. "I shouldn't laugh. Think about how many crimes Yates has committed that he hasn't been arrested for. The few times he gets caught is the tip of a huge freaking iceberg only the victims know about."

"I agree with you. But even if he was a scumbag, we've got to get the guy who killed him." Jack walked up the steps and stared at the bent railing.

"I checked with the fire department. The accelerant used came back as gasoline."

Jack touched the metal barred door with his foot. It squeaked but still opened easily.

"With the bars on the doors and windows, Yates was barricaded inside." Jill continued. "Maybe the killer started the fire to drive Yates out?"

"I don't think so." Jack pointed at the railing. "The firefighters said when they arrived, the barred door was open. And that railing is bent *in* toward the house. If you tied something on the railing to the barred door, Yates wouldn't be able to get out."

"He wanted to burn him alive? That's sick."

Jack crouched down to stare at the outline left by Yates's body. The floor at the foot of the door was darkened but not burned. "The fire would have killed Yates. Why shoot him?"

"Maybe the killer wanted Yates to see him. With this kind of hate, it has to be personal, right?"

Jack stood. "A few years ago, I would have agreed with you. But there's so much hate in the world now, I don't know anymore. It seems like people are getting to where they don't need a motive to hate."

"What's that saying? Stop the world from spinning. I want to get off this ride." She glanced inside the house. "The fire gutted the place. I don't know what we'd find left in there."

"We should have the techs comb through it. They've got the gear to deal with that environment. We should canvass."

Jill glanced down the road. "Unfortunately, I don't think it will take us long. This is the end of the road, and we only went by two other trailers to get here."

"Let's hope they've got cameras."

Jack drove back down the road, stopping at a white trailer with a neatly mowed, fenced-in square of lawn in front. They parked in the gravel parking space next to a small red pickup. As they approached the house, the front door opened, and a young man appeared with his back to them, trying to keep two yapping dogs inside. He shut the door, turned around, and gasped.

"Sorry. We didn't mean to startle you." Jack said. "I'm Detective Jack Stratton, and this is Detective Jill Reyes. We want to ask you a few questions."

The man glanced at his truck and then scratched his chin. "Is this about the fire? I'm running late for work. Can I catch up with you later? I won't be much help anyway. I wasn't home when it happened."

"It should only take ten minutes, tops," Jill said, handing him a card. "And if you like, we'll speak to your employer."

"Thanks. But I can spare ten minutes. What do you want to know?"

After getting Kip Dunn's contact information, Jack asked, "Do you have a doorbell camera?"

"I do! I watch videos online about people catching things on their cameras all the time. I don't know why I didn't think of it. But I don't know how much help they'll be. One faces the street, and the other covers the backyard."

"We'd still like to review the footage," Jack said.

"Does it store in the cloud?" Jill asked.

Kip nodded as he took out his phone. "Yeah. I have a website I can upload it to and send you the link. I have a graphic design side business. Oh, here." Kip handed them two cards with only a printed QR code on them. "Scan the code and add a slash and the word FIRE. I'll put the video on that page."

"I appreciate that," Jack said. "What can you tell us about Matthew Yates?"

Kip's expression hardened, but he kept working on his phone to bring up the camera video. "My neighbor is the reason I got the cameras. I couldn't prove it was him, but anything I left in the yard not chained up disappeared."

"Why do you think it was Yates who stole it?" Jill asked.

"When I first moved in, he stole my lawnmower. I caught him mowing his lawn with it the day after it disappeared. He said he found it on the side of the road. I took it back and tried to give him the benefit of the doubt, but then my seed spreader and some tools I had out back vanished. The thefts stopped when I told him I got the cameras. Wait a second!" Kip's eyes widened. His hands shook as he held his phone up for Jack and Jill to see. "Look at this! That's right before the fire."

Jill stepped next to Jack as Kip played the video. A car passed by in front of the house, but the bushes almost totally obscured it. The only part of the vehicle you could see was when the porch light reflected off the roof. The emergency lights mounted on top of the car shone a bright blue.

"That's a cop car." Kip's voice rose high. "And fifteen minutes later, you can see the fire reflecting off the trees. See? And now the cop car comes back. Why didn't it stop at the fire? The cop must have seen it."

"Listen, Kip," Jack said. "Until we get this video to our lab and have them analyze it, we don't know what kind of vehicle that is." Kip opened his mouth, but Jack cut him off. "Yes, it has emergency lights on top, but that doesn't make it a police cruiser. Please do us a favor and keep this to yourself until we figure it out. Would you do that for us?"

"I won't tell anybody. I swear it on my mother's life."

"We appreciate that, Kip." Jill smiled.

"I'm gonna upload that video now," Kip said. "I gotta get going to work."

"We understand. But after seeing that video, we will need all of your recordings. We want to go through everything you have."

"Sure. I can get you them after work." He thought about it momentarily. "I can do it from work with the app, but it depends on how busy we are."

"I'm going to ask you to make that a priority," Jack said. "We can go speak with your employer."

"No. She'll understand. This is big, right?"

Jack nodded. "But I also need you to keep this between us. Okay?"

Kipp swore again on his mother's life that he wouldn't tell a soul.

After thanking him, Jack and Jill returned to the car and watched Kip drive off.

Jill clicked her seatbelt on. "That confirms it. We're looking for a cop."

Jack started the car and slowly shook his head. "Maybe."

"Every fake cop I've ever encountered has made their car look undercover. None of them have ever driven around with emergency lights roof mounted."

"There are exceptions. I've heard about guys who drive around in police cars where you can't tell them apart from the real thing." Jack pointed out.

"But what if it is a rogue cop? What will we do then?"

Jack took a deep breath. "I wouldn't care if the killer is the mayor. When we find him, we're taking him in."

Chapter Thirty

Alice sat across from the frail old black woman with thin salt-and-pepper hair and stroked her hand. Her eyes were bright, but her face was lined with concern.

"I'm so glad you came, Alice." Aunt Haddie squeezed Alice's hand tighter. "What's wrong?"

Alice took a deep breath and forced a smile. "Nothing."

Aunt Haddie's lips pressed together. "Do you think I can't tell when you're lying just because I'm getting older?"

"I haven't said anything!"

"That's not true. You said nothing was wrong, but whatever is bothering you is written all over your face. Do I need to go get a mirror?"

Alice laughed. When she was little, and Aunt Haddie had first said that, Alice had run off to the bathroom to check. "There's no need to burden you with my issues."

Aunt Haddie shook her head. "I used to think that way when I was younger. But do you know why the good Lord is keeping me here? So, I can pray for you and offer what little wisdom God's given me. You know I'm going to get it out of you, eventually. Or do you want me to call Jack?"

"That's playing dirty."

"I never play fair." Aunt Haddie winked. "Dish."

Alice pulled her chair closer and leaned her elbows on her knees. "It's my new job. Titus wants me to prove I can do it without Jack or Bobbie's help. But I'm striking out. I found Scoops hiding at Frosty's, but he got away. I would have caught him if I had a partner to watch the front door, but I don't."

"If it is a partner you're worried about, once you get the job, that problem will be fixed."

"*If* I get the job. I don't think I can catch Scoops by myself."

Aunt Haddie rolled her eyes. "Sometimes you need to learn from your mistakes, and other times you need to look back at your victories. How many people have you caught?"

"That was different. Jack was with me. I haven't caught anyone by myself."

"You said you almost caught Scoops once. I'm sure you'll do it again."

"You may be sure, but I'm not." Alice frowned. "Every lead I've followed has dried up. I've tried every trick Jack taught me, and I still can't find him."

Aunt Haddie leaned forward and took Alice's hand. "You're not Jack."

Alice's lip trembled, and her eyes brimmed with tears.

"You're Alice, a child of the Most High—a princess. Jack may be a prince, too, but Jack does things that work for Jack. You need to do things that will work for Alice. Take Jack and Chandler, for instance. They were two peas in a pod, but up here." She tapped the side of her head. "As different as night and day. Jack acts, then thinks, while Chandler would do the opposite. There's good and bad in both. But I remember a time when they seemed to switch like something out of a movie. You know the Disney one where the folks' minds go into each other's body?"

"Freaky Friday?"

"That's the one. Jack started over-thinking everything, and Chandler would just react to a situation. It was pure chaos. Jack ended up with a zero on a test at school. It was one of those tests where you filled it in with a pencil, and a computer scanned it. He kept changing all his answers so often that it became a big smudge. Chandler flunked because he filled it out as fast as he could. What I'm saying is, don't try to be anyone else. You be Alice, and everything will work out."

Alice sat back and crossed her arms.

"Uncross your arms, honey." Aunt Haddie said.

"I'm being Alice."

"You're being fresh."

Alice uncrossed her arms. "But I don't know what Alice would do. Jack is so much better at this."

"Haven't you been listening? That's not true. God made men and women different for a reason. Maybe you should start thinking about how to catch Scoops the way a woman would go about it."

Alice opened her mouth to protest, but one raised eyebrow from Aunt Haddie was enough to make her close it and think for a minute. "I've checked with Scoops' girlfriend and all the guys he hangs out with. I've checked all of his old addresses. And I even made a list of everyone that likes Scoops, then spoke with each one." Alice's eyes widened. "I haven't checked with people who don't like Scoops!"

Aunt Haddie's brows knit together. "Why would you do that?"

Alice spoke as a plan formed in her mind. "Scoops' friends

won't tell me where he is because they like him. But, if someone who doesn't like Scoops heard where he is or knows somewhere he'd go, they'd tell me." Alice grinned. "I need to speak with Tessa Burton. She's Scoops' ex-girlfriend, and she can't stand him."

Aunt Haddie chuckled and clapped. "Now you're thinking!" She draped her arms around Alice and gave her an enormous hug. "When will I see you again?"

"The end of the week."

Aunt Haddie kissed Alice's cheek. Alice stood up and hurried for the door. Just as the nurse reached out to open it, an old woman in the corner waved Alice over.

"Alice, do you have a moment?" she called out.

Alice looked at the nurse, who shrugged. "Her name is Mrs. Hayes. She's harmless," she whispered.

Alice walked over to Mrs. Hayes, who sat in an overstuffed recliner. The old woman sat up straighter, but her back was still curved. She peered out at Alice with big, blue eyes behind thick lenses.

"Is your husband the tall, handsome detective who comes to see Haddie?"

Alice grinned. "He is."

She looked Alice up and down and then settled back into the chair. "You want some advice?"

Oh no. What a day.

Alice had a feeling that no matter what her answer was, she was going to get some advice. "Sure."

"That boy comes in here, and not that I'm eavesdropping, but all he talks about is you. Now, I've lived a long time, and I learned something about men."

"And what would that be?"

Mrs. Hayes held her hands together beneath her chin and smiled. "You're like his sun. He revolves around you."

"And you think that's a bad thing?"

"A bad thing? Oh, no. That's what you want. Very few women are so blessed. I'm telling you to hang onto that boy and never let him go."

Alice grinned. "I never will."

Chapter Thirty-One

After dropping off Jill at the city police station, Jack drove back to the Kent Building. Jill said she wanted to brief the Chief on the latest developments, but Jack suspected she wasn't eager to come anywhere near the morgue. He couldn't blame her. The smell of death clung to his clothes. Even with the window open, he couldn't escape the odor. But he wasn't going to the morgue.

Once inside, he was so grateful to be heading up instead of into the tomb that he took the stairs. He jogged up the steps and reached the third floor, a little winded. He went down the hallway and made a mental note to get back on his jogging schedule. The corridor was brightly lit with fluorescent lighting, casting a clinical glare on the white walls and gray carpet. Doors lined either side, each identical except for the text on the nameplate. He passed by the offices of toxicology and odontology until he reached ballistics.

He knocked and opened the door. The ballistics lab was sterile and organized, with white counters and cabinets lining the walls. Microscopes and other equipment were neatly arranged on each counter. Fluorescent lighting filled the room, making everything seem a little too bright. On the right stood a wall covered with hanging guns, each labeled with evidence tags. The scent of gunpowder and metal filled the air, a strong and distinct odor that brought to mind firing ranges and police training academies. The smell of chemicals and disinfectant lingered as well, a sign of the lab's cleanliness and attention to detail.

Kevin Reed sat behind a desk in the room's corner with his back to Jack.

"Evening, Kevin," Jack called out as he strode over. "Glad you're still here."

Kevin didn't turn around.

"Hey, Kevin!" Jack called out loudly as he crossed the room.

Kevin's head sagged forward, his chin resting on his chest. His grey and thinning hair hung almost to his eyes, which were open and staring at his desk.

Jack touched his shoulder.

Kevin screamed. His legs shot up, and his feet smashed the desk so hard that everything bounced. Kevin yanked his earplugs out and glared at Jack. "Not funny!"

Jack burst out laughing.

"Giving me a heart attack isn't funny, Jack! And it's your case I'm working on. What is wrong with you?"

"I didn't try to scare you, Kev. I called out a few times. You freaked me out, too. I thought you were dead."

"I was thinking!" Kevin tossed the earplugs onto the desk. He glared at Jack again, then chuckled and punched Jack in the shoulder. "I think I broke my toe."

"Sorry again." Jack tried to cover his smile with a cough. "I'm glad you're still here."

"I tend to work the night shift. Why Ballistics doesn't have its own building is beyond me. Only a bureaucrat could think that discharging guns in an office environment is a good idea. How's married life treating you?"

"Happiest man alive." Jack grinned.

Kev scratched his chin. "I can't figure you out, Jack. If I were thirty years younger and looked like you, I would have ridden the bachelor train for at least another decade."

"I'm glad to disembark. What do you have for me?" Jack asked, eager to change the subject.

"I don't know if it's good or bad news, but let me show you." Kevin walked over to stand beside a massive monitor on the wall. He pressed the computer's keyboard on the table before it, and the screen flicked to life.

The picture showed the images of two bullets side by side. "You hit the jackpot with these bullets. They're perfect for comparisons because they struck muscle, organs, and fatty tissue." He clicked a few more buttons, and the 3D images spun until the grooves on the sides lined up.

"They match," Jack said.

"One hundred percent. No question about it. You find the gun that fired those, and no defense attorney could get anyone that would state otherwise."

"I don't know about that. I know some defense attorneys that could put experts on the stand who'd testify that the bullet fired the gun."

Kevin laughed. "True. Since you're here, you can save me a trip and an email. I was about to reach out to Mei. I found a fiber on one bullet from the Yates homicide. It's not readily identifiable. What was the victim wearing?"

"We don't know. The killer set fire to the victim's home. Mei may be able to tell you something. You guys do things I didn't even know were possible. But seeing the state of the corpse, I doubt any clothes survived."

Kevin gave a one-shouldered shrug. "I'll have to send it out for analysis. It will take some time, but I'll get it to you."

"Thanks, Kev. I'd appreciate it if you'd expedite it. Did you glean anything else from the bullets? Manufacturer?"

"Besides them being nine-millimeter and fired from a barrel with rotary, hammer forged, polygonal rifling, not much."

"I could be looking for a Glock?"

"The newer models have it, and some from Walther, Styer, Desert Eagle, and some European manufacturers use it too. You'd have to find the gun so we could compare rounds."

Jack exhaled. "Well, as Johnny Cash said, time's a wastin'."

Kevin crossed his arms. "You said you didn't know how we did what we do. The same goes for me. When I think about how many people live in a radius of here, I don't have the slightest idea how you're going to catch the killer."

"As Detective Clark used to say," Jack lowered his voice to sound like Clint Eastwood after he smoked a few cigars, "Facts. Put together the facts, and it all falls into place."

Kevin laughed. "You ever see Derrick around? I don't know why he didn't move someplace warm after retiring."

"We grab coffee now and then. I'll let him know you were asking about him."

As Jack left the office, he pulled out his phone and texted Jill. They were looking for a single shooter in both murders. Searching for one man made their job easier but also a lot more dangerous. They were hunting a serial killer, and it may be an actual police officer. Trying to catch a murderer was hard enough. Catching one who knew firsthand how the system works could be deadly.

Chapter Thirty-Two

Jack opened the front door of Tullie's Cafe so a woman could exit. She smiled, and he returned the gesture with a slight incline of his head. As the door closed behind him, the little bell overhead chimed. A few regulars sipped coffee, read, or chatted inside the cafe. An extended counter and stools ran the length of the front window, and six round tables the size of extra-large pizzas dotted the middle of the room. Sitting at the one in the corner was Derrick Clark.

The grizzled, retired detective wore his hair buzzed short. No longer gray, it was thick but pure white. Despite being off the force for years, he wore a white shirt and a crisp, dark gray suit. He stood and gave Jack a firm shake. "Detective Stratton." He grinned. "How are you?" Clark's voice sounded like a cement grinder chewing up rocks.

"I'm good. Before I forget, Kevin Reed says hi."

"I'll have to call him. The gold badge looks good on you."

"I wouldn't be wearing it if it wasn't for you. Thanks for coming to see me."

"Are you kidding? It feels good to be needed. Do you want something to eat? That water is yours." He pointed at a glass.

"I'm good. Besides, I think our house guest is making us dinner again."

"I should get me a house guest. I'm getting tired of frozen pizza." Clark sipped his coffee. "Something big is bothering you. I'm still on the books as a consultant for the Sheriff's Department, so whatever we discuss is permissible. Talk."

Jack set his elbow on the table and ran his hand over his mouth. "Just the facts, right?"

Clark nodded.

"Sunday night, I'm taking out the trash and find the body of Tyrell Miller in the dumpster. He was twenty-eight years old with an extensive rap sheet. The original crime scene was out at the lake. According to his fiancée and her father, Tyrell was trying to get his life together. He was about to propose and had a small diamond ring in his car when he was killed. We recovered the car from the lake with the ring still inside. They shot Tyrell at close range with a nine-millimeter—one in the head, three in the gut. We found two sets of tire tracks and only two sets of shoe prints. Searching the car revealed no registration in the glove box."

Clark stared into his coffee cup while listening to Jack relay the case details. Occasionally, his eyes would narrow, and his lips pressed together, but he said nothing.

"The second victim is Matthew Yates, thirty-six years old, a longtime thief with an extensive criminal history. Firefighters discovered his body after a trailer fire. Bars on all the windows and a gated door trapped Yates in the trailer. It appears the killer fastened something to the outside railing to keep the door from opening. Yates was also shot once in the face at close range and three in the gut. We pulled the video off the neighbor's doorbell camera that shows what appears to be a police cruiser with cherries and berries on top driving by."

Clark took a long sip of his coffee, stared into the cup, and took another sip. He set it down with a slight click on the table and waited for Jack to continue.

"We may have a possible third victim. Oren Dorcey jumped bail, and a warrant is out for his arrest. His car was discovered abandoned outside the closed K-mart with the driver's window down and the keys still in the ignition. We found the registration on the floor. Multiple witnesses reported seeing a uniformed police officer chasing him, but Oren got away. We currently have an APB out for him. We've talked to a potential whacker, but the facts point me in another direction. What are they telling you?"

Jack's heart thumped heavily in his chest. He crossed his arms, sat straight, and waited for his mentor's response.

Clark chewed on his bottom lip, tilted his head, and eyed Jack like he was sighting up a pistol target. "Are you positive it was a light bar mounted on the roof?"

Jack nodded.

"You don't need me to tell you what you already know."

Jack took a deep breath and set his elbows on the table. Thinking about what he was about to say made his stomach sour. "I'm looking for a real cop. Do you have any recommendations on the best way to go about interviews?"

"From a long distance." Clark chuckled sarcastically. "There is no good way, Jack. What you need to do is try to minimize the fallout. You're about to go dancing in a minefield. This is one of those things that can tear a department apart. We're talking Civil War — brother against brother."

"I forgot one thing that complicates it further."

"Complicates it? How is that even possible? It's already as bad as it gets."

"My prime suspect works for the city police department. This is a joint investigation, and I'm paired with a city detective."

"That is worse. There is no best way to go about this, Jack. But you've got a job to do. And if you're asking me how I'd handle it, I'd offer one word — fairness. Treat everyone the same. That means you interview everyone. From the sheriff to the chief to anyone with access to a cruiser in both the Sheriff's Department and the City Police Department, you pull them all in. Do it in a way that you can defend what you're doing by not singling out one person. They'll accuse you of it anyway, but you'll have the defense of saying we're talking to, and looking at, everyone."

Jack nodded in agreement. It was a huge task, but it would be worth it if it minimized the emotions he was about to unleash.

"You also need to prep yourself for what is coming your way. You've had experience with internal affairs. None of those fellas get invited to have a beer, go bowling, or go to holiday parties. They're looked at like piranhas and rats. Until your investigation is finished, and probably for the rest of your career, your fellow officers could view you that way. Are you ready for that? Because you could turn this over to internal affairs."

Jack clenched his jaw. He met Clark's gaze with a cold, hard stare. Jack's father raised him to never push a job off on someone else so he could take the easy route. Besides, he couldn't guarantee that Internal Affairs would do the right thing. "That's not going to happen."

Clark chuckled. "Ever since you were a kid and I took you on that ride along, I knew you'd make a great cop. There is something inside you, Stratton, that doesn't care about what the world thinks. You do what's right and damn the consequences." Clark lifted his cup in a silent toast and drained his coffee.

"Thanks for coming and the advice. I better head home. I think I'm going to have a long day tomorrow."

"Tell your parents I said hello." Clark opened his mouth and closed it. He thought for a moment, then looked Jack in the eyes. "I was about to ask if you could trust this detective you're teamed up with, but even if you did, it doesn't matter. As of right now, don't trust anyone. You can't. If you do, you could be the next victim."

Chapter Thirty-Three

Jack sat with his arms casually resting on the sides of the chair in front of Sheriff Morrison's desk. Jill sat beside him, nervously tracing a circle on her left hand with her fingernail.

Bob hurried over to his office window and pulled the shade down. He stared at Jack, deep crevices forming on his forehead. "You want to interview everyone? In the entire Sheriff's Department?"

"Only the people who have access to police cruisers with a light bar," Jack said.

"You're talking about suspecting the men and women who work for me." Bob crossed back behind his desk but didn't sit. "Do you have any idea how low morale is right now? Every day, there are articles after articles on the Internet criticizing policing. There has to be a way to approach this without placing suspicion on everyone." Bob sat, then set his elbows on his desk and rubbed his temples.

"If we interview everyone, they'll be comfortable enough to provide their locations for where they were during the three separate incidents. After that, we can vet their stories. If we pull in one suspect, he'll immediately lawyer up. And this way, no one can accuse us of targeting anyone specific."

"So, there is someone you suspect?"

Remembering Clark's warning, Jack said nothing.

"We could pull reports on everyone who is recorded to have taken out emergency vehicles with light bars," Jill said. "That would narrow down the list of people we interview."

"But we would miss anyone who didn't officially check the car out when they took it," Jack said. "I think it will help minimize the negative impact on personnel if we stick to the plan and interview everyone with access to the cruisers."

Jill pursed her lips. "If the black-and-whites have computers, we could pull the vehicles' GPS records."

"The issue is that the GPS is engaged only when the computer is on. It won't work for those computers not running."

Bob leaned back in his chair and looked at Jill. "What does Chief Hill think about this?"

Jill scowled at Jack.

"He didn't take it well at all," Jack said. "But right before he slammed the door, he said he'd get back to us."

"So, you went to him first?" Bob looked hurt.

"Because I thought you would be more likely to understand and agree," Jack said. "I don't like this any better than you, but we have to do something."

Bob snatched his pen off the desk and began rapidly clicking the end. "I'm well aware of that, detective, but I also have a sheriff's department to run. And it's not just about morale. Public trust in the police is at an all-time low, too. If you pull in everyone, it will hit the news."

Bob's phone rang with a high-pitched ringtone. "Excuse me. I need to take this."

Jack and Jill stood up.

"Hello, Madam Mayor." Bob said, motioning for them to

get out and close the door. "No, I haven't spoken with Chief Hall yet. I wasn't aware of that either. I apologize, Madam Mayor, but I'm only learning about it now. Why is that? Uh..."

Jack pulled the door closed.

"I thought you said he would take it better than my Chief," Jill said.

"At least he didn't slam the door. Did I ever mention that I hate politics in policing?"

"Want a coffee? It's on me." Jill headed down the hallway toward the break room, with Jack walking beside her. "What's the new plan?"

"I was hoping to keep this from blowing up from the start. That's failed. And neither Morrison, nor Hall, is keen to pull in everyone. It doesn't make sense only to interview the people who checked the cars out. There's plenty of times where I took a car home after patrol or even grabbed one before and didn't record it."

"You said you had a suspect. Care to share who and why?" Jill asked.

"I don't want to bias you by naming them. It's your call, but I think it would be best if I held off telling you until after the interview. I want to see what you think when we're done. But like I said, that's your decision. If you want to know, I'll tell you."

Jill blew out her cheeks as she poured herself a cup of coffee, then handed the pot to Jack. "I appreciate that. Maybe you're right in holding off. When do you think we'll get an answer about how we can proceed?"

The intercom on the ceiling buzzed to life. "Detectives Stratton and Reyes report to the Sheriff's office. Attention, Detectives Stratton and Reyes report to the Sheriff's office immediately."

"That's a bad sign," Jack said, finishing pouring his coffee.

"The shorter the call from the Mayor, the more trouble I'm usually in."

Jill shook her head. "I take it that calls to the Sheriff from the Mayor about you aren't a rare occurrence?"

"They're kinda like rainbows in Florida," Jack grinned despite the pit in his stomach. "They're a fairly regular thing. Any word from your Chief?"

Jill checked her phone and shook her head. "I think I've been abandoned."

"Let's go face the music."

When they rounded the corner, Bob stood in his office doorway waiting for them. He waved them inside, shut the door, and closed the shade. "All hell has broken loose. Chief Hall called the Mayor and threatened to go to the head of the police union. While the Mayor was on the phone with him, the *Darrington Star* ran a front-page Web story about the Blue Light Killer. That's what they're calling him. They have the photographs of the emergency vehicle headed to Yates' trailer, and they're implying in news speak that a police officer is behind the murders. The Mayor is ballistic and wants to release a statement that we think it's a vigilante."

"Say something about it being an ongoing investigation, and we're not ruling out any possibilities, including a vigilante, which is true," Jack said. "But I can't exclude the fact it could be one of our own. We can't let politics influence our decisions."

"Are you listening to me, Jack? Politics is already influencing them. But I will not let it derail any investigation, and I won't shelter any of my men if they have broken the law. Now, on one hand, I agree with you that pulling everyone in might be a more thorough option."

Jack opened his mouth to protest, but Bob cut him off.

"But we no longer have that choice. The union is up in

arms, and so is Chief Hall. What I'm asking for is a compromise. You said you had a suspect. Who?"

Jack thought back to his conversation with Detective Clark. He was grateful he heeded the retired man's words. Jack figured he'd better have multiple backup plans when he kicked the hornet's nest. But Jack needed to give credit to his father, too. Ted Stratton taught him that if you were going to ask for something unpopular, ask big, but put what you really need in second place. That way, you'll walk away with something when they shoot down your first request.

"Calvin Green."

Jill gasped.

Bob's expression turned stone cold.

"I don't know about that, Jack," Jill said. "He's already gone through so much."

Jack took a deep breath. "I can't even fathom what it must be like to lose a daughter. But that's also the reason that made me suspicious of Calvin. You know better than anyone, Jill. A three-strike felon with an extensive rap sheet murdered Emma in a botched carjacking. Our two victims have long criminal records. And Tyrell Miller was the getaway driver in a carjacking."

"That's thin, Jack," Bob said. "Calvin is a decorated officer. I'm going to need more than that to pull him in."

"Right now, I only want to pull Calvin in for *questioning*," Jack emphasized the word. "There was also an incident in the field that concerned me regarding Calvin's fitness for duty. Emmett Wilson will back me up on that fact. All I'm asking for is an interview. And since Calvin had a cruiser all three nights, he's on top of the list for asking for his specific whereabouts."

Jill thrust an accusatory finger in Jack's face. "You asked me to put together the vehicle records, but you already pulled them! And the duty sheets!" She shoved her chair back as she stood. "I read all about Jack Stratton and believed you were a smart cop. But you're a grandstander looking to grab all the credit for yourself." Her anger shifted, and she glared at Bob. "You promised me full cooperation with your department. Does this look like full cooperation to you?"

Bob's wrinkles deepened, and he seemed to age before Jack's eyes. "Do you have an explanation, Detective Stratton?"

"There is no explanation for keeping me in the dark." Jill's tone was a low growl.

Jack sat up straight. He longed for the days under Sheriff Collins when Jack would stand at attention when he delivered his report. That way, if Jill tried to hit him, it would be easier to block the blow. "I purposely kept Detective Reyes in the dark because I would also like to question Detective Jill Reyes."

If it wasn't such a serious matter, the expressions passing across Jill's face would be comical — shock, disbelief, anger, hurt, and fury all played out. Her hands balled into fists.

"Jill was the lead investigator in Emma Green's murder." Jack continued. "Her bond with Calvin alone was reason enough for me to keep my suspicions to myself, but there's also the issue of her car."

"What about her car?" Bob's focus was now on Jill, too.

"I'm currently driving an old cruiser with a light bar on top." Jill sat back down. "In California, detectives are all provided with vehicles. The Chief compromised when I took the job and allowed me full access." She reached into her pocket, pulled out her phone, and laid it on Bob's desk. "The pin is 7304. I have location tracking on. Check my where-abouts." She glared at Jack. "You could have asked me privately."

"This way, I can say that I treated my partner the same as everyone else."

"That's something to brag about." Jill crossed her arms.

Bob reached out and took her phone. "Thank you for this. Before we continue, do you want to speak to your representative?"

"I'm an open book." Jill continued to stare at Jack.

"Then you won't mind giving Bob your smartwatch, too?" Jack said.

"I don't know if I should be impressed or further offended." Jill took off the watch and handed it to Bob. "I use the same pin. Do you want me to take a polygraph?"

"That won't be necessary," Bob said.

"Why not?" Jack shot back. "If she takes one, we can ask Calvin to do the same and save ourselves a lot of trouble."

"He's right," Jill said. "I'll head there right after we're done here. I want to be ruled out as soon as possible. But I have a question for Jack. Why would Calvin dump the body outside your apartment?"

"It's no secret that Calvin doesn't like me, but I don't think that would be why he did it if he is responsible. And listen, I'm looking to rule Calvin out, not pin this on him. But if I were to draw up a profile of the murderer, it would fall into two categories. One being a whacker and the other being a cop who recently suffered a triggering, traumatic event. If you take emotions out of it and put all the facts together, we have to talk to Calvin. Are you both on board with that decision?"

Bob and Jill thought for a moment and nodded.

"I'll call Chief Hall. He won't argue about this," Bob said.

"Thank you, sir." Jack stood up, suddenly aware that sweat plastered his shirt to his back. "I have no issue with Detective Reyes watching the interview on camera, but considering her relationship with Calvin and the fact that they may be working together in the future, it would be best if I conduct this interview alone."

Jill surprised Jack by saying, "I agree."

Bob stood. "You two have permission to call me at any time. I don't need to tell you that internal investigations are an ugly business. Be careful."

"Thank you," Jill said, holding the door for Jack. "I need a moment alone with the Sheriff."

Jack left the office, eager to get outside and into the fresh air. The building's once magical glow had faded as he walked through the department. These people were his family, and this was his home. But now he was investigating one of them for murder. In a way, it felt like he was the one who was the betrayer.

Chapter Thirty-Four

Alice sat on the picnic table behind the strip mall, waiting for Tessa Burton. The table was across the street from the building on a small grass strip bordering the woods. With the sun shining, it was a cute place to take a break or eat lunch.

A pink door labeled Beautiful Queens opened, and Tessa hurried out wearing a pink apron embroidered with a gold crown. She was a tall woman, but the first thing you noticed was her hair. A three-inch strip on both sides of her head was shaved. She dyed the remaining hair white, but the ends were a combination of reds, oranges, yellows, and blues, creating a fire effect. She waved at Alice as she crossed the back lot, pulling out a vape.

"I didn't know you were working," Alice said. "It can wait until later."

"Don't worry about it. You gave me the perfect chance for a break." Tessa put the vape in her mouth, and a moment later, an enormous cloud of smoke swirled into the sky. "And I needed one. What a day. How've you been?"

"Great. I just got married."

"Let me see the rock!" Tessa stared at Alice's upheld hand, a strained smile appearing on her face. "Oh, a band. That's pretty."

"Jewelry isn't my thing," Alice admitted.

Tessa shuddered. "The only way a guy gets me is if he gives me a stone so big, I gotta wear my arm in a sling." She laughed at her own joke. "What brings you by?"

"I'm trying to find Oren. I—"

Tessa's lips curled like she'd tasted something foul. "You're looking for Scoops? Why don't you go asking that scrawny butt backstabber Imani where he is? I don't care if he's on the moon, became president, or hit the lottery. I hope he's dead and buried in the sewage plant. That's where he belongs."

"You think Imani is a backstabber? Did Scoops cheat on you with her?"

"Cheat on me?" Tessa set her four-inch fingernails lightly against her chest. "No man cheats on me. But just because I don't want him doesn't mean I want someone else to have him. How dare she go date him after I dumped his sorry butt?"

Alice was about to say that she thought Scoops had broken up with her but caught her tongue.

"Did Imani send you? Because if she did, I want you to tell her that I think she's—"

"Imani didn't send me." Alice held up her hands.

Tessa's lip curled. "You're looking for Scoops for you? Why? You caught yourself a stud. Scoops is the scum at the bottom of the gene pool."

Alice chuckled. "I'm working for Titus. I'm a bounty hunter, and Scoops jumped bail."

Tessa's eyes opened so wide her false eyelashes touched her bangs. "Oh, that's different. Why didn't you say so?" She chuckled wickedly.

"I'm kind of learning as I go." Alice took out her phone to bring up the list of places she had already checked. "I found him hiding at Frosty's, but he ran, and I couldn't catch him."

"Chicken man. That's what they called him when he'd run. Sticking his butt out and his arms dangling behind him in the wind. Why I ever stooped so low is beyond me."

"Do you mind if I tell you the places I've looked?"

"Mind? Are you kidding? Seeing him back in prison would be nicer than seeing him dead. Go for it."

While Alice ran down her list, Tessa gave feedback regarding each person Alice had visited. When Alice reached the end, Tessa took a deep drag off her vape, blew out an immense vapor cloud, and crossed her arms.

"How long have you been doing this?" Tessa asked.

"This is my first job on my own," Alice admitted.

"If I ever skip, I hope someone besides you gets my case. You've checked everywhere I'd look."

Alice grimaced. Tessa was her last, best hope. She was out of ideas. She'd failed.

"I'm sorry I couldn't be more help. I woulda loved to see him rotting behind bars. But don't feel bad. He's a snake that's only good at hiding and lying. Scoops used to lie so much that I'd never go where he told me he'd be when I needed to find him. He'd be hanging at Frosty's, sitting on his lazy butt, playing video games. He's a rat, and that's a rat's nest. I'm not surprised you found him there. But I can't think of any other place he'd go. Sorry."

Alice's body jolted like it had been shocked. "He's a rat!" she shouted and started walking for her car. "Thanks, Tessa. You just gave me a great idea."

Tessa shrugged, her puzzled eyebrows confirming she didn't know what she had said that Alice found helpful. "See ya. I hope you catch him. If you do, take a few snaps and send them to me!" She laughed, waved, and strutted across the lot.

Alice hurried back to her car. A plan was forming in her mind, but for it to work, she needed backup. Titus said she couldn't have Jack or Bobbie help, but he didn't say anything about her asking a girlfriend for a hand.

Chapter Thirty-Five

Jack checked the interview room camera to ensure the red light was on. His heart felt like it weighed ten times as much as it usually did. Each beat thrummed in his chest like the reverberation of one of those enormous drums they sounded by rocking a massive beam suspended on chains into it. His stomach alternated between flipping and clenching, and his mouth was dry.

The door to the room opened, and Jill walked inside, shutting the door behind her. She stared at Jack for a moment before speaking. "I understand."

"Thanks."

"I passed my polygraph."

"I thought you might."

Jill chuckled. "That's not a ringing endorsement. Do you still not trust me?"

"Don't take it personally. I don't trust anyone. Lying is in people's nature. Even the people you love will sometimes lie if they think it's best for you. Besides, I spent the first seven years of my life being raised by drug addicts, thieves, and prostitutes. Being suspicious is in my DNA."

"That's a story I'd like to hear sometime. Are you still okay with my listening to the interview?"

"Absolutely. I'm trying to minimize the impact on you after the investigation is done." Jack admitted. "If we clear Calvin, you'll be working with him down the road."

"I heard you're a white knight, but I can fight my own fights."

"I'm not doing it because you're a woman or even just for you. I'm thinking about Calvin. He lost his daughter. He doesn't need this on top of that. If he's innocent, he'll need people to talk to — including you."

Jill bit her bottom lip and nodded. "I wish I could give you some angle to go at him with, but I can't think of one. In all of my dealings with him, I spoke with him as a grieving father, not a suspect. I'll be in the other room. They're about to bring him in."

"Thanks again for understanding," Jack said, moving over to take a seat so he would appear less confrontational. Once again, his mouth went dry, and Jack took a sip of water. He had turned the air conditioning up, but sweat ran down his back, and he wiped his damp palms on his pant legs.

The door opened again, and Calvin Green stood glaring at Jack. Donald Pugh stood behind him.

"Morning Calvin. Thanks for coming. Donald." Jack motioned Donald to stand next to the door.

"Did I have a choice?" Calvin stomped into the room, dragged the chair opposite Jack back, and sat down. "I didn't think I did the way the Chief put it."

"If you want, you can have your delegate here and a lawyer," Jack said.

"I have done nothing wrong, so I don't need either."

"You know the drill. Everything is being recorded." Jack reached over and pressed the record button on the digital device on the table. He pointed to the corner of the room. "It's also on camera."

"It's the drill for perps, not cops. What do you want to know, Stratton?" Calvin crossed his arms and stretched out his long legs.

"I only have a few general questions for you. We're investigating the location of emergency vehicles. Seeing how you have access to them, I need to know your whereabouts on three separate dates — Friday, Sunday, and Monday night. Between 6 PM and midnight."

"Home." Calvin snapped as he flexed his arms, causing his massive biceps to bulge.

Jack took a deep breath and laid his hands flat on the table. "I'm asking you these questions not to implicate you but so we can clear you from the list of people we need to talk to. If you tell me something that doesn't check out later, you'll find yourself right back in that chair, facing many more questions. Think about it for a minute and tell me where you were between 6 PM and midnight Friday, Sunday, and Monday night."

Calvin's nostrils flared as he inhaled through his nose and glared at the table. He tapped his shoes together, the click echoing off the cement walls. "Probably out."

"Generalizations won't help. I need specifics. Let's start on Friday night. Did you go out then?"

Calvin nodded.

"I need audible responses," Jack said.

Calvin glared at Jack. "You're just eating this up, aren't you, Stratton? You get off ordering me around."

"Not at all. I'd rather be eating sand than doing this. Did you leave your house on Friday night?"

"Yes. I went for a drive."

"What time?"

"I finished my shift sometime around four. I went home and went out a little after that."

"How long after? Half an hour? An hour? Two?" Jack asked.

"I don't know. Maybe an hour. An hour."

"Where did you go?"

"Out. I told you I drove around."

"How long were you out?"

"A while. I don't know. A few hours, maybe." Calvin's eyes became darker as he spoke.

"Did you stop anywhere?"

"No."

"So, Friday night, you left your house sometime around five or six o'clock and drove around for a few hours, stopping nowhere?"

"I'm a cop. Driving around for hours is what I do." Calvin said.

"And that's normally called patrol, and you get paid while you do it. I don't know what to call driving all over Darrington for a few hours for no reason."

"Sightseeing." Calvin laughed. It was as forced and strained as the smile on his face afterward.

"What were you driving?"

Calvin cocked his head and sat staring at Jack, blinking like he hadn't heard the question.

"Were you driving a police vehicle, Calvin?"

"I took one home, yes."

"That's not the question I asked," Jack said. "When you went out driving on Friday night, were you driving a police vehicle?"

"Yes. So what? My chief allows us to do it."

Jack pretended to think about his next question, but it was

the one he was dreading asking. "What were you wearing when you went out for a drive?"

"What was I wearing?" Calvin repeated. "Clothes. Do you think I went out naked? Is that what this is about, a naked driver?" Calvin laughed again.

"On Friday night, when you went out for a drive, were you wearing your police uniform?"

Calvin shrugged. "Maybe? I live in this thing." He pulled at his shirt.

Jack folded his hands. "I need you to be as specific as possible. I don't want to pull you back in here to ask you questions. When you left your house on Friday night, were you wearing your police uniform?"

"Yes."

The pit in Jack's stomach tightened even further. He resisted the urge to glance at the two-way mirror but imagined Jill's shocked reaction to the news.

"Let's move on to Sunday night," Jack suggested. "Did you go for a drive Sunday night between the hours of 6 PM and midnight?"

Calvin uncrossed his arms and sat up straighter. "Sunday night? You know I was working because I was at that dump scene outside your apartment." His eyes widened. "And Monday was that trailer fire. What are you trying to pin on me, Stratton?"

"I'm not trying to pin anything on you, Calvin. I'm looking for answers. And so far, the answers you're giving me are creating more questions. Like, why would you go out driving for hours right after getting off patrol?"

"There's no crime in it, and it's not your business!"

"It is my business. And unless you want to get dragged back in here, you better level with me and tell me what's going on."

"Does this have something to do with the story in the *Star*?

Do you think I'm the Blue Light Killer? Have you lost your mind? I'm a good cop. Why would I throw twenty years away for a couple of scumbags?"

Jack relaxed his shoulders and tried to sit in a way that would convey calmness and understanding. "This job can get to people. The grind of catching criminals only to see them walk is one of the most frustrating parts of the job for me."

"Are you confessing, Stratton? If anyone is crazy enough to go around killing frequent flyers, it would be you! What reason would I have..." Calvin's eyes rounded like Jack had kicked him below the belt.

"I can't understand what you've gone through, but I want to try. With Emma's death—"

Calvin's right fist smashed down on the table so hard that Jack expected he might have broken a bone. "Keep my daughter's name out of your mouth. Don't even say it." Calvin stood. "I had nothing to do with any of those dirtbags."

Donald stepped forward.

Jack gave a slight shake of his head. "I'm just doing my job, Calvin. I need to interview everyone who may have been at those locations at those times."

"That's a bunch of bull, Stratton. I know I'm the only one you dragged in here."

"That's not true. I've already interviewed and cleared Detective Jill Reyes. I was able to do that because she provided full cooperation. She gave us access to her phone and smartwatch and volunteered to take a polygraph. Why don't you do the same so we can put this behind us?"

Calvin blinked rapidly. "I didn't take my phone with me."

Jack wanted to ask why someone would drive around for hours without a phone but nodded understandingly. "That's fine. We would still like to look at it, and if you'd take a polygraph, that will go a long way."

Calvin placed both hands flat on the table and glared down at Jack. "Those things are inadmissible."

"Still, your cooperation would help me stop looking at you so I can focus on catching whoever is responsible for these murders."

"Not me. And if you want more help than that, talk to my lawyer, my delegate, and the Chief. You even try to get in my face, and you'll regret it. Am I free to go?"

"You are."

Calvin stomped by Donald, slamming the door as he left the interrogation room.

Jack set his elbows on the table and rubbed his temples. Calvin had certainly not done himself any favors in the interview. Even before Jack spoke with him, Calvin had been at the top of the suspect list. Now, he'd have to put one of their own under surveillance.

Chapter Thirty-Six

Alice had parked the Charger on the side street behind Frosty's duplex. She sat in the driver's seat, staring at Frosty's third-floor apartment. The back shades and the curtain on the large slider were drawn.

"Okay, here's the deal," Alice said. "Scoops is a rat, and I chased him out of his nest. But being a rat, he's got nowhere else to go, so what would a rat do? It runs around for a bit, lies low, and then returns to the nest." Alice opened the glove compartment and pulled out a brown bag. "I need you to cover the back and stop him if he comes out. Understand?"

The car rocked on its chassis as Lady leaned over to the front seat and nudged Alice's shoulder.

"Yes, you do." Alice gave her one of Mrs. Stevens's special dog treats. "You wait here until I give you the signal."

Lady gulped the treat down and turned expectantly toward the door.

"Wait here. I'll call you. Wait."

Alice exited the car but didn't put the key fob into her pocket.

She needed it out for her plan to work. Heading around to the front of the building, Alice stopped at the end of the sidewalk. With the range extender she installed, the key fob was supposed to operate at a distance of a hundred feet. Alice pressed the door button.

The back door of the Charger opened, but Lady stayed in the car. She pressed the button again, and it closed. They had trained Lady well.

"Best dog in the world."

Alice walked to the front entrance of the three-story duplex and climbed the steps to the second floor. She stopped to catch her breath and focus. After tasing Frosty last time, she doubted he'd try anything again, but if he did, she'd be ready. She admired the wooden sign next to the closest apartment door. 'Spring Has Sprung!' was painted in bright letters with green leaves and flowers surrounding it. Above the door, another sign proclaimed, 'Welcome to the Murray's.' Alice quietly headed upstairs and made a mental note to add some decor to her apartment entrance.

When she reached the third floor, she listened at the door—the muffled sound of a TV and two people talking filtered through. Alice knocked softly and, raising the pitch of her voice, yelled loudly, "Frosty? It's Sue Murray, your downstairs neighbor. I need a favor!"

Frosty opened the door.

"Back up!" Alice shouted, holding her Taser gun toward his chest.

Frosty stumbled and fell on his back in the middle of the living room rug.

Sitting on the couch with a game controller in his hands, Scoops' eyes flew open, and his jaw dropped. He flung the controller at Alice and raced for the back door.

Alice bolted after him.

Scoops shoved aside the kitchen table, knocking it over and sending bowls and coffee cups shattering on the tile floor.

Alice aimed the Taser at Scoops's back, but she couldn't get a clean shot with everything on the table now flying in the air.

Scoops yanked open the slider and headed for the stairs.

Slipping on the liquid, Alice slid across the wet tiles. She grabbed hold of the countertop before slamming into the wall. She darted onto the balcony, aimed the key fob down at the Charger, and pressed the button.

Scoops reached the second-floor landing.

The back door of the Charger flung open.

"LADY! ROCK AND ROLL!" Alice shouted.

The car rocked and rolled on its chassis as Lady bounded out. She landed on the sidewalk and let out three deafening roars.

Scoops reached the parking lot and bolted toward the back alley.

Lady's ears flattened against her head, and she sprinted forward. Her claws scraped the tar. Like a lioness chasing its prey, she raced low, her fluid motions a beautiful thing to behold.

Alice took the stairs down two at a time.

Lady flanked Scoops, cutting him off.

Scoops screamed and scurried sideways toward a van.

Lady pounced, bounding forward as she barked loudly.

Scoops grabbed the roof rack of the van and pulled himself on top.

Lady leaped up, her jaws chomping the air beneath his sneakers.

"I give up! I give up!" Scoops shrieked.

Alice smiled triumphantly as she jogged across the parking lot and clicked Lady's leash onto her collar. "Don't think about running, or I'll let her go."

"I won't." Scoops peered down at her. "But you can't take me in. You'll be killing me, Alice."

"Get down here." Alice held onto Lady as Scoops slid off the van roof.

He landed hard on the ground and fell forward, catching himself on his hands. He straightened but swayed back, almost falling over again.

Alice took out her handcuffs.

"Please, Z! He'll shoot me. You can't bring me in."

The stink of alcohol coming off Scoops smacked Alice in the face.

"You're drunk, Scoops. Just shut up, okay? No one is going to shoot you." Alice cuffed him and pushed him toward the Charger.

"If you take me in, I'm a dead man. He'll kill me." Scoops stopped.

Alice looked to Lady. "Meany face."

In an instant, Lady went from a lovable dog to a Hell Hound. Her teeth flashed, her ears lay back on her head, and she chomped at the air, sending spit flying.

"I'm going! I'm walking!" Scoops jogged unsteadily for the car.

Alice put Scoops in the backseat, and Lady jumped in next to him.

"You can't leave me back here with this thing. It'll eat me."

"Only if you try to run," Alice said, getting in. "So, don't."

"Seriously, Alice. You know me. I was Chandler's friend. I took Michelle to the junior prom. Would I ever lie to you? If you take me in, he'll kill me. You have to let me go."

Alice rolled her eyes. "I'm not falling for it, Scoops. No one is going to hurt you."

"He wants me dead. He already tried to shoot me. Look at my face." Scoops leaned forward.

Lady growled, and Scoops fell back against the door.

"It's okay, Lady," Alice said, turning on the dome light and twisting around in her seat.

Scoops cautiously leaned forward and turned his head toward the light. The left side of his face was red and dotted with small blisters. "The gun went off, but the bullet didn't come out. It burned." Scoops' eyes were red-rimmed and watered. "I swear, Alice. If you take me in, I'll be dead by morning." Scoops hung his head and sobbed.

Alice tried for several minutes to get Scoops to tell her who he was worried about, but his drunk speak only got worse. She shifted the ignition into drive. Scoops might not tell her what was going on, but there was someone Alice knew he'd confide in.

Chapter Thirty-Seven

Jack paced the bedroom and checked his phone. There was still no word from Alice. He called again, and it went straight to voicemail. "Hey, Babe. I'm hoping you're coming home soon. Your grandfather is up to something. He's making this elaborate dinner, and he's set four places. He keeps singing and smiling, and it's kind of creeping me out. Call me, okay? Love you."

Jack hung up and stretched. After dinner, he should go for a run. He'd been so tense today that his muscles felt cramped like he'd taken a cross-continental flight. Between worrying about Alice and his undeserved guilt at investigating a fellow police officer, he was mentally exhausted, too.

"Dinner is ready!" Andrew called from the living room.

Jack opened the bedroom door and walked out as he spoke. "Do you want to wait for Alice or..." His words trailed off as he stopped in the doorway and stared at the table in the corner of the room near the windows. Andrew had covered it with a white tablecloth, set four places, and lit a candle centerpiece, but that wasn't why Jack's eyes felt like they were about to pop out of his head.

Andrew, dressed in a bright white shirt and dark slacks, sat next to Mrs. Stevens. She had her red hair styled and up in a bun. She wore a green dress that, to quote Garth Brooks, he was sure she hadn't worn in quite a while.

"I prepared a plate for Kaya Kukla. Who knows when you kids will be home?"

"Kaya Kukla?" Mrs. Stevens asked.

"It means little doll. It is my nickname for Alice."

"That's adorable. How long have you known Alice?"

Jack's internal warning radar siren went off. Mrs. Stevens was the prying type, and if Andrew weren't careful, she'd see right through his charade. "This smells and looks amazing." He pointed at his plate as he hurried over and sat. "Is it chicken?"

"It is a simple dish I whipped up. Roasted duck with a blackberry balsamic reduction sauce, stuffing with Anjou pear and mushroom, and sautéed Broccoli Rabe with garlic and red onion."

"Simple? Maybe for Gordan Ramsey." Jack said, then winced as both Andrew and Mrs. Stevens kicked him in the ankles.

"Sorry." They both said as one, then chuckled.

"I meant it as a compliment," Jack said.

"Of course." They both spoke in unison again before laughing loudly.

"Since I need them, I'll ask the blessing." Jack folded his hands, but the sound of tires screeching to a stop outside on the street made him turn.

The front window shattered as a red brick smashed through it and bounced across the floor.

Mrs. Stevens screamed.

"GET DOWN!" Andrew shouted as he shoved the table aside and dove toward the middle of the living room. Plates, cups, and duck were still flying through the air as Andrew landed on the brick like it was a hand grenade. "GET OUT! Jackie, get her and get out!"

Jack rushed to the window and watched as a dark truck sped away down the street. "It's not a grenade, Andrew. It's a brick."

"No." Andrew felt around beneath his stomach. "What?" He rolled over and held up a red brick with something written on it in black marker. "Why would someone throw a brick through your window?"

"Oh, Jack has lots of enemies." Mrs. Stevens found her voice as she brushed some stuffing and broccoli off her face. "There's been shootings, a fire, and dead bodies. A brick isn't so bad."

Andrew handed the brick to Jack and rushed to her side. "Are you alright? I thought it was a bomb."

Mrs. Stevens' mouth fell open. "You threw yourself on a bomb to save me?"

Andrew took both her hands in his. "I wouldn't let anything happen to you."

Mrs. Stevens' knees shook.

"Sit down." Andrew held her hands and helped her back into her seat. "Did you get hit by flying glass?"

She opened her mouth, but no words came out. She shook her head.

"Jackie, go get her water," Andrew said as he picked a napkin up off the floor and began wiping the food from her face.

Carrying the brick, Jack headed to the kitchen. He was pretty sure that Mrs. Stevens was only suffering from attention overload, but he filled a glass of water and brought it back. Turning the brick over, he read the single word written on it.

"What does it say?" Mrs. Stevens said.

"Trator," Jack responded.

"Is that an English word?" Andrew asked.

"I think they meant to write 'traitor,'" Jack said.

"Jackie has a way of getting people so mad they don't think very clearly." Mrs. Stevens added.

She's calling me Jackie now, too?

"I've never met anyone that can make people so mad." Mrs. Stevens continued. "He gets under their skin, and they go unhinged. You should have seen some of the rows with his old girlfriends. I remember this one girl, Gina, she—"

"Andrew doesn't need to hear this, Mrs. Stevens."

"No. It sounds fascinating." Andrew quickly tore himself away from Mrs. Stevens to glance back at Jack. "But I'm still confused about the brick. Why would someone do that?"

"I'm investigating a case where a police officer is a suspect. That's why they called me a traitor."

"That's ridiculous!" Mrs. Stevens said. "No one is above the law. You should be commended for doing your job."

"Thanks for saying that."

Andrew shook his head. "That still doesn't answer why they threw only a brick. If you were investigating corruption in my country, they would throw grenades or fire rockets, not a little brick with a word on it."

Mrs. Stevens gasped. "Do you think they'll come back?"

Andrew puffed out his chest. "Do not worry. I will see to your safety." He walked over to the table lying on its side. Jack expected him to set it upright, but he reached underneath the top and pulled a shotgun out of its breakaway straps.

"You hid a shotgun under my dining table?" Jack asked.

"It's a good thing he did!" Mrs. Stevens stood. "I think it's time that I should get one. I don't even know how to fire a gun."

"Jackie hasn't taught you how to shoot?" Andrew asked in disbelief.

"No. Jackie's never offered."

Andrew shook his head and stared at Jack. "In that, I am disappointed in you. Everyone should be prepared to defend themselves."

"I agree." Mrs. Stevens stepped closer to him. "But I'm helpless."

"You have nothing to worry about. Tonight, I will not leave your side." Andrew wrapped an arm around her shoulder, cast another frown at Jack, and walked her out of the apartment.

Jack stood in the middle of his trashed living room, blinking in disbelief at the closed front door. *I'm the one who gets a brick tossed through my window, and somehow, I end up being the bad guy?*

Jack walked to the closet, grabbed an old cardboard box, and crossed to the window. He stared at his reflection in one of the unbroken panes. Were his eyes really so dark, or were they reflecting what was inside his soul? The sense of betrayal he felt whenever a police officer broke their oath tore at him. As a boy, he believed the police were the last remnants of knights, protecting the innocent from the demons that preyed on them. It was a childish fantasy, but he believed it was true so intently it burned into his core. Jack knew well that in every profession, you had a rotten element. In every field, from doctors, teachers, and clergy to dentists, contractors, and brokers, you'd find people who would ruin someone's life for personal gain.

But this was different. Jack wore the shield of a brotherhood of men and women sworn to uphold the law. If Calvin broke his oath, Jack wouldn't let anyone, or anything, stop him from taking him down.

Chapter Thirty-Eight

Alice rang the doorbell of the little cottage home and stepped back. A moment later, Mary Boyd opened the door. Scoops' sister was tall and thin like her brother.

"Why Alice Campbell! I haven't seen you in ages. What are you doing here?"

"I'm sorry to stop by like this, but I have Oren in my car. He's passed out."

"What? Oh, no. He quit drinking. He was doing so well. Is that why he took off?"

"It's a long story. I should take him to jail, but—"

"Jail?" Mary shook her head and stepped out onto the front steps. "Imani's father was straightening everything out. He doesn't have to go to jail, does he?"

"That's where I'm supposed to take him. Oren jumped bail, and I work for the bail bondsman. But I don't want to take him there until I get his side of the story. And he's not making any sense right now."

"Let's get him inside, and you can tell me what's happening. I'm so sorry about all of this."

"Me, too."

Mary followed Alice to the Charger parked alongside the curb.

Alice opened the door and had to catch Scoops from tumbling out.

As Mary stepped closer to help, she looked inside the car and shrieked.

Lady started barking, and Mary screamed louder.

"It's okay, it's my dog."

"That's not a dog!"

Alice grabbed Scoops around his right arm and dragged him from the car.

Mary took hold of Scoops' left arm. "Why is Oren in handcuffs?"

"Because he's wanted, and he keeps trying to run," Alice said.

"Mary?" Scoops slurred and then broke into a smile. "Happy birthday!" He gagged and threw up at his feet.

"Eww!!!" Mary stepped as far away from her brother as she could while holding him up.

"Let's get him inside." Alice started for the house.

Between the two of them, they steered Scoops down the sidewalk and up the steps.

"Oren, you're an idiot," Mary muttered.

"Did I miss the party?" Scoops asked.

"What party? My birthday isn't until August."

"Oh..." Scoops leaned against the door. "Great. I'm early!"

"I see what you mean about him not making sense," Mary said. "The living room is to the right. Ready?"

"I've got this side," Alice said. "Okay, Scoops. Let's get walking."

"Okie-dokie." Scoops stumbled through the door.

Pushing and pulling, Alice and Mary led him to the couch.

"Wait," Alice said as she grabbed his handcuffs. "I'm going to take these off and put them on in front of you."

"Please keep them off," Mary begged. "He can't sleep in handcuffs."

"He sleeps in handcuffs, or he's going to jail. I'm not risking him getting away again."

"That's fine." Scoops grinned. "No jail. No more shooting."

Alice removed one handcuff and quickly reattached it in front of him.

"What happened to your face?" Mary asked.

Scoops flopped onto the couch. "Boom! Fire!" He mumbled before falling sideways.

Mary removed his shoes, placed a throw over him, and said, "I'll be right back. I have to run to the bathroom."

"Don't tell anyone he's here," Alice called after her.

While Mary left the room, Alice texted Jack. She let him know she was fine but wouldn't be coming home. A pang of guilt washed over her for not getting into details, but right now, she knew nothing.

Mary hurried back into the room. "Can I get you anything?"

"I need to bring Lady inside."

"That moose? In here?"

"I don't want to take Oren to jail before I hear what he has to say. He wasn't making any sense drunk, so I'm willing to let him sober up. That means I've got to sleep here, and if I'm going to do that, I'm not leaving Lady out in the car. It's your choice."

Mary bit her thumb as she watched her brother sleeping on the couch. After a minute, she nodded.

Alice took her keys out as she walked to the front door. Standing in the doorway, she pressed the key fob, and Lady bounded out of the Charger. "Lady is a very sweet dog. She'll stay by my side. Come here, girl!"

Lady bounded down the walk and leaped up the steps. She marched into the house and pressed against Alice, knocking her back slightly.

"That is the biggest dog I've ever seen," Mary said.

"She's my backup." Alice patted her neck. "She weighs almost 150 pounds and is 32 inches at the shoulders. That's typical for males of the breed. So, she's like the Alpha Queen. Do you have a minute to talk?"

"Is the kitchen okay?"

"Sure." Alice pointed to the living room. "Lady, watch him."

Lady trotted over in front of the couch. She circled twice and lay on the carpet with her face on her paws, staring at Scoops.

"She certainly is well trained."

Alice followed Mary down the hallway lined with photographs of Mary and her husband.

"Doug is in New York doing a trade show. He won't be home until Sunday." Mary said.

The kitchen was filled with rich, dark wood cabinets and countertops, polished to a high shine. Gleaming brass pots, pans, and utensils hung from a rack over the island. A large window above the sink framed a view of the backyard garden, where herbs and vegetables grew in neat rows.

Mary sat at the round table, and Alice took a chair opposite her. Mary's hands clasped together, and her chin puckered. "Oren was doing so well. I don't know what happened. I spoke to him a few days ago. He loved his job. He's dating Imani Wilson. They're getting along great. I couldn't believe a policeman would let Oren date his daughter, but Emmett saw how much Oren had changed."

"Did you know Oren had been arrested?"

"He turned himself in. It was all a mix-up. Oren wasn't worried about that at all. Emmett said he'd take care of it. Something else must have triggered Oren. Did he say anything?"

"He said someone was trying to kill him."

Mary rolled her eyes and laid her hands flat on the table. "Oren doesn't have a single enemy. He's a loveable goof. It must be the booze talking. When Oren drinks, he gets crazy."

"Crazy violent?"

"Oh, no. Incoherent ramblings. When he's drunk, he transforms into a conspiracy theorist and usually ends up crying in the corner. It's horrible but not violent. Embarrassing, really."

"Witnesses saw Oren running from a police officer. Do you know if he fell back into illegal activity?"

"If he's drinking again, anything is possible. When he's drunk, he's not Oren."

"I guess the only thing to do is wait for him to sober up," Alice said.

"You can't sleep in the living room. I can make up the guest bedroom for you."

"No, thank you. Oren has already run twice and escaped from me once. I won't take that risk. Do you mind if I sleep in the recliner?"

"I'll bring some blankets. It goes almost all the way back." Mary stood up. "Are you sure I can't get you anything to drink? Are you hungry?"

"That's very nice of you. I'll eat anything you have." Alice bit her bottom lip. "Lady will need something, too. You wouldn't have any dog food, would you? I have a bag of treats in the car, but it would be like giving a kid a bag of Halloween candy."

"I have some ground beef I need to cook. How about hamburgers for the three of us?"

"That sounds wonderful."

"Shoot!" Mary took her phone out of her pocket. "I promised to call Imani if I heard anything."

"Don't do that." Alice's voice took a hard edge. "Oren wasn't making any sense, but I believe the powder burns on his face. Someone did try to shoot him. Until we figure out who, don't let anyone know where he is."

Chapter Thirty-Nine

Jack parked Alice's Bug behind his Charger in front of the address Alice had texted him. He rubbed his eyes, took another sip of coffee, and got out. He thought he'd get some sleep with the bed to himself, but he spent all night staring at the ceiling and thinking about the case. Something was bothering him, and he couldn't put his finger on what.

The front door opened, and Alice waited for him on the landing. "You look tired." She kissed him. "Did my grandfather keep you up?"

"He wasn't home. You look beat, too."

"What do you mean he wasn't home? He didn't go after whoever threw the brick through the window, did he?"

"No." Jack resisted the urge to tell her to lower her voice, seeing how that would only escalate the situation. "He slept at Mrs. Stevens'."

"Why?"

Jack shrugged. "After the brick came through the window, she freaked out, and he turned into Prince Galahad. He promised to protect her and vanquish all foes. He was acting weird ever since he invited her to dinner."

Alice's mouth formed an O. "You don't think..."

"I try not to, but they're both acting like middle-schoolers with the Enchantment Under the Sea dance coming up. Andrew got onto me about not teaching her how to shoot a gun."

"With all that happens at our house, you should have."

"You too?" Jack rubbed the back of his neck. "Why don't you tell me what's going on here before you give me a hard time about something else?"

"I'm not giving you a hard time. I'm only saying that it's a good idea to teach her how to defend herself later."

"I think the golden bachelor will take care of it for me. Anyway, what's up?"

"I caught Scoops at Frosty's yesterday." Alice grinned.

"That's outstanding. I have to go to the jail to talk to him." Jack turned around, and Alice grabbed his arm.

"He's not at the jail."

"Did he get away after you caught him? I'm so sorry. What happened?"

"He didn't get away. He's inside on the couch."

"You left him unsupervised?" Jack asked.

"Lady's watching, and I kept him cuffed."

Jack inhaled and tried to keep his voice normal. "Please don't tell me that instead of bringing a fugitive to jail, you brought him here and left him in handcuffs all night."

"It was that or jail."

"No, it wasn't. It was jail or jail. You don't have a license to kidnap someone."

"I didn't kidnap him."

"Handcuffing a person and taking them somewhere they

don't want to go is the definition of kidnapping. Whose house is
this?"

"Scoops' sister, Mary. He begged me to take him here."

Jack pinched the bridge of his nose.

"Look," Alice grabbed him by the hand. "We're both tired.
Talk to him, and you'll see why I did it. Someone tried to kill
him."

"Is that what he told you?" Jack didn't budge, even though
Alice tugged on his arm.

"It's what he *showed* me. He has powder burns on his face."

Jack followed Alice inside and into the living room. Lady
trotted over to him, and he patted her head as he looked at
Scoops sitting beside Mary on the couch. "Scoops. Mary. Sorry,
this isn't under better circumstances."

"Thank you for coming over, Jack." Mary gave a weak
smile.

"Hey, Jack." Scoops swallowed. "Can you please tell Z to
let me go?"

"No can do, Buddy." Jack sat in the chair opposite them.

"If you take me to the police station, he'll kill me."

Mary took her brother's hand in hers and gripped it. The
handcuff chains rattled. "You can trust Jack. Tell him the
truth."

"Why don't you back up and tell me what happened after
you left Sonic?" Jack said.

Scoops blinked rapidly. "Oh, yeah. I forgot I went there. I
didn't even finish my burger."

"What happened after you left?" Mary asked.

Scoops got a faraway look in his eyes. "The special was a
triple cheeseburger with extra sauce and onions, but I couldn't
eat it without getting it all over the steering wheel. I pulled into
the old K-Mart to park. I was only there for a minute or two
before I saw the blues in my rearview. You know the drill they

always ask for — license and registration. So, I grabbed my registration, but because of the burger, I dripped some sauce on it. I was trying to clean it up when I got the cop knock on my window."

"Cop knock?" Mary asked.

"He smacked the glass real hard with his knuckles. He was wearing a ring, which made me jump because it was so loud. I thought the window was gonna bust. It freaked me out so bad that I dropped my burger."

"Stop talking about the food!" Mary snapped.

"Mary, please don't interrupt your brother," Jack said. "Look at me and nod."

"Sorry." Mary nodded.

"What happened after they knocked on your window?" Jack asked.

"It freaked me out. I wasn't doing anything wrong. I'm parked, so I couldn't have been speeding. Then it hits me: it's probably Imani's father busting on me."

"Emmett pulled you over?"

"I didn't know then, but that's what I thought. You know? Like, Emmett was driving around on patrol and saw me eating, so he's playing with me. I power down the window, turn my head, and then BLAM!"

Mary flinched, and Lady sat up.

"There was this bright flash, and the side of my face felt like it was on fire. Remember that time that Boomer lit the deodorant can on fire, and it exploded? It felt like that. I was standing next to Boomer and—"

"Stay on target here, Buddy," Jack said. "Are you sure it was a gun?"

"A hundred percent. Afterward, he was pulling at that top thing because it jammed. I couldn't see that good because the flash kinda blinded me."

"Was he pulling on the gun's slide? The piece on top of the gun that goes back and forth?"

"Yeah. The thing that makes the noise. Click-clack. He was pulling on that, so I beat feet. I dove out the passenger side, and I was gone! You know how fast I can run."

Scoops always believed he was the Flash, but the truth was that Scoops came in dead last in every running game. The image of Scoops as a child racing across the playground like a chicken with his butt out and his arms dangling behind him made Jack want to laugh, but he kept his composure and nodded.

"I was moving like a bolt of lightning, but somehow, he kept up with me. When I got out back of the K-mart, I freaked. There's this barbed wire fence. But I see a gap in the wire near these pallets. I leap over the fence like Superman, but my jacket gets snagged on the barbed wire. That's when I thought I was dead for sure, but I fell out of my jacket. I ran all the way to Frosty's. Then Alice found me."

"Did you see who tried to shoot you?" Jack asked.

Scoops hung his head.

"If I'm going to protect you, I need you to tell me who it is."

"It doesn't matter." Scoops whispered. "My life is over. Even if he doesn't kill me, Imani will never forgive me."

"Of course, she will. But we need to figure this out first."

"She won't." Scoops sniffed. "I don't understand what I did wrong. I thought he liked me."

"Who tried to shoot you?" Jack asked again.

"It was Emmett. Imani's father."

Chapter Forty

Jack, Jill, Bob, and Donald Pugh stood watching Emmett Wilson through the two-way mirror. Emmett sat at the interrogation table with his hands folded in front of him, but his leg was nervously bouncing up and down.

"He certainly is sweating," Bob said.

"We've taken his service pistol and backup from him," Jack said. "He doesn't know what is coming, but he's been around the block enough to know it's serious."

"Is Ballistics checking his guns?" Jill asked.

Bob nodded. "I had them stop everything to get it done. Why would Emmett try to kill Oren? Why would he murder two men?"

"Emmett was Emma Green's Godfather. Calvin named Emma after Emmett." Jack explained. "Seeing how Emma was killed by a criminal with a long history, released without bail, he may have decided to take the law into his own hands. We won't know until I speak with him."

Jill crossed her arms. "Emmet was so supportive of Calvin,

I never even thought about how her death affected him. He may have just snapped."

"He's not guilty yet," Bob said, the muscles in his jaw flexing. "But Oren's eyewitness testimony is something we can't ignore. Oren has no reason to lie."

"I'm not a hundred percent sold on Oren's identification," Jack said. "The flash from the gun would have screwed up his vision. There's a possibility that Scoops expected it to be Emmett, and his brain filled in the details."

"Or it is what it is, and Emmett was the person Scoops saw," Jill said. "Emmett has the motive, means, and opportunity."

Bob turned to Jill. "You agree you should sit this interview out?"

Jill nodded. "My being in there isn't an option. I'll wait here."

"Do you need anything, Jack?" Bob asked.

Jack stared through the window at a man who had worn the badge for over half his life. It was Jack's job to walk in there and figure out if Emmett had broken his oath, killed two men, and tried to murder another. If there were any other way out of this situation, Jack would take it, but if he didn't question Emmett, the job would fall to someone else. Besides, Tyrell Miller deserved justice.

"I'm good. Donald will come with me." Jack exited the observation room and stopped in the hallway. Pausing, he bowed his head. *Lord, please give me wisdom so I don't jack up an innocent man.* He turned the handle and entered the interrogation room, with Donald following.

Emmett's brown eyes were large and questioning. He nodded at Jack and Donald but said nothing.

"I need to go through some procedural things before we

start," Jack explained while Donald sat beside him. "You understand, right?"

Emmett nodded.

After reading him his rights and detailing the additional provisions available to him as a police officer, Jack met Emmett's gaze. "We're investigating the location of emergency vehicles. I need to know your whereabouts on three separate dates — Friday, Sunday and Monday night, between 6 PM and midnight."

"You asked Calvin the same questions." Emmett blinked rapidly.

"I did. But now I need to ask you those questions. Let's start with last Friday night."

"I was home, probably watching TV. I don't know."

"I need you to be specific, Emmett. Were you home or not?"

Emmett took a deep breath and shook his head. "No. I went out."

"Where?"

"I went over to Calvin's."

Jack's pen hesitated over the notepad. Calvin said he wasn't home Friday night. "So you hung out with Calvin? What time was this?"

"I went over there around five or six. Calvin wasn't home, so I tried a few places he might be but didn't find him. Then I went home."

"When did you get home?"

"Ten, maybe?"

"You spent four hours looking for Calvin?"

"No. I picked up some groceries and stopped by the bookstore. I swung by Calvin's house again, too."

"Was he home?"

"No. But I went home after that."

"What car were you driving?"

"A patrol car. I got off work but wanted to see if Calvin wanted to grab dinner."

"So you were still in uniform?"

"Yes. I live in this thing."

"Calvin said the same thing." Jack wrote that down. "Did you know Tyrell Miller?"

Emmett nodded. "I arrested him before. He did time for it."

"Do you remember the charge?"

"Carjacking. He was the getaway driver."

"When was the last time you saw Tyrell?"

"Probably in court during the trial. It was a long time ago."

"How about Sunday night? Where were you then?"

"Working. I was on patrol. I responded to the call outside your apartment."

"We reviewed your log, Emmett. You went off-line between six and eight o'clock. Where were you?"

Emmett clicked his fingernails. "Dinner. I took a long dinner break."

"Where?"

"I parked over near the interstate and ate while I read. I had packed my own meal. Afterward, I wanted to talk to Imani."

"So, you went home? Imani can confirm that?"

"No. I changed my mind."

"Did you go someplace else? Speak with anyone else?"

"I went back on patrol. I drove through the Cedar Grove Cemetery. They had an issue with kids up there."

"There's no report of you doing that."

"I forgot to call back in."

Jack made a note to check if security cameras were at either cemetery entrance. "What were you going to speak with Imani about?"

"She was worried about Oren. She hadn't heard from him since Friday. But I changed my mind, and I went back to work."

"What made you change your mind?" Jack asked.

"What was I going to tell her? I didn't know where he was. I thought if I talked to her, it would just get her more upset."

"How would you describe your relationship with Oren? Did it bother you a felon was dating your daughter?"

"I certainly wasn't happy about it initially, but I gave him a chance. Lot of good that did. Have they caught him yet?"

"We'll get to him. What about Monday night? Where were you then?"

"That was the night of the mobile house fire. Matthew Yates was murdered. You asked Calvin about that, too."

"Let's concentrate on you, Emmett. Did you know Yates?"

"I arrested him a few times."

"Nine times, to be exact. He walked on all but one of those arrests."

"I don't need you telling me my history. This isn't about emergency vehicles. Miller was murdered, and so was Yates. The *Star* ran a story saying it was a cop. The Blue Light Killer. Do you think a cop did it?" Emmett exhaled loudly and ran his hands through his hair.

"You can see the situation you're in, Emmett. We're looking at two homicides and a missing person. Help me understand what is going on here. I want to help you. I know you've been hurting about Emma."

Emmett stared down at his hands like he held the answer to all of Jack's questions there. He closed his eyes and balled his hand into a fist. Setting his elbow on the table, he rested his forehead against his knuckles. "Emma." He whispered.

Jack glanced at the mirror. Emmett was on the edge, but this was the most critical time of any interview. Jack preferred to let the person talking keep talking and take that step over the side of the cliff. He watched a thousand interviews on video, and whenever the interview was pushed too hard at this point, the accused would shut down.

Emmett sat up straight and placed both hands on the table. "I confess. I want a lawyer."

Chapter Forty-One

Jack clicked the handcuff around Emmett's wrist. Jill, Bob, and Donald Pugh stood silently in the interrogation room. After Emmett requested a lawyer, he didn't say another word.

"I want to do this as discreetly as possible," Bob said.

Jack frowned. "We'll have to go through the main office to get to the stairs and take him to processing. There's no other way."

"Do you want Jack and I to clear out the office?" Jill asked.

Bob removed his handcuff key and turned to Emmett.

Donald cleared his throat. "I don't want to overstep, sir. But the procedure states that they must be secured when transferring suspects to processing."

Bob undid one cuff. "You don't need to tell me, Donald. I'm the man who wrote the procedures." He reattached the handcuffs so they were now in front of Emmett. "But this isn't a perp walk." He picked up the yellow legal pad on the interview table and draped it over Emmett's hands, covering the cuffs.

Emmett flashed Bob a sad but appreciative nod.

"Donald, you're on point to get the doors and then Jack. Emmett will move next, then Jill and me. If anyone does approach, Jack and Jill will deal with them. Donald, you stay with me."

The group of five marched down the hallway. Jack tried to focus, but his growing unease with the situation bothered him. Why would Emmett confess and immediately lawyer up? All the unasked questions buzzed in his mind like hornets eager to escape a shaken nest.

Donald opened the door to the main office. Rows of cubicles stretched out. A few people stopped what they were doing and glanced their way. Donald headed to the right, toward the stairs in the corner.

Jack passed through the doorway, his eyes sweeping the room. Standing outside Bob's office were a dozen uniformed city Police Officers, including Calvin Green. "We've got a problem, sir. Nine O'clock."

Bob swore under his breath.

Calvin noticed them and hurried to cut them off. The other cops followed him like a pack.

"Keep walking," Jack said. "The door will lock behind you."

"Hey!" Calvin broke into a run. "I want to talk to Emmett."

Emmett planted his feet and shouted, "Don't say anything to anyone, Calvin! Talk to my lawyer."

"Keep moving!" Bob dragged Emmett forward.

The legal pad covering Emmett's handcuffs fell off.

Calvin's face contorted in anger. "Oh, hell no."

Jack stepped in front of him. "Don't escalate an already bad situation."

Calvin grabbed Jack's shirt with his left hand and drew back his right fist.

Jack sidestepped and grabbed Calvin by his collar and belt.

He pulled Calvin against his leg, twisted his body, and pivoted his hip, leveraging the much heavier cop off the floor.

Calvin gasped as his feet went over his head. He soared through the air like a basketball player whose slam dunk had gone terribly wrong before crashing into a cubical wall and knocking it down.

Pandemonium erupted.

Two cops rushed Jack. One grabbed his left arm, and the other held his shirt.

Jack didn't want to start throwing punches, but Emmett's coworkers didn't have that reservation. A fist slammed into Jack's jaw.

Jill leaped into the fray. She fired off three rapid jabs into the face of the guy holding Jack's arm. The cop's nose gushed blood, and he stumbled back.

Bob dragged Emmett toward the door but was quickly surrounded by cops.

"Get to the Sheriff!" Kendra Murphy charged down the corridor with a grin like she'd hit the lottery. The Muy Thai kickboxing junky went full-on Crouching Tiger, Hidden Dragon. Unleashing a flurry of strikes, she dropped two men before another caught her by her ponytail.

Jack grabbed a cop, trying to get Jill in a headlock. As he wrestled the man off her, Calvin made it to his feet.

Calvin's massive bicep bulged as he cocked his arm.

Jack tried to block, but someone bashed against his side, trapping Jack's arm.

Calvin's fist slammed into Jack's jaw.

Stars and fireworks erupted behind Jack's eyes as he stumbled sideways.

"ENOUGH!" Bob shouted. "Is this any way for law enforcement to behave? It's bad enough how we get treated by other people. Are we going to start cannibalizing ourselves?"

Everyone stopped fighting.

Calvin, his hands still balled into fists, glared at Bob. "You're one to talk. Why are you arresting Emmett? On what charge?"

"He confessed to two murders."

Silence slammed down on the room. Everyone froze. All eyes shifted to stare at the one police officer none of them would ever believe would commit such heinous crimes. Emmett was a role model to them, not only as a cop but as a father and a friend.

Emmett slowly turned to meet Calvin's stare. The partners seemed to have a long conversation without saying a word. Calvin looked away. Emmett hung his head.

Bob motioned for the police to step aside, and they did. He pulled Emmett toward the stairs.

"He didn't do it!" Calvin shouted.

Bob kept walking.

"He didn't do it!" Calvin turned to Jack. His eyes were rounded and filled with fear. "I did. I confess." He held out both hands. "Arrest me."

"He's lying!" Emmett screamed, pulling against Bob as Bob tried to hold Emmett back. "I did it. Don't listen to him."

"I did it, Stratton. Arrest me. Arrest me!" Calvin yelled louder.

"Shut up, you idiot! He wants a lawyer." Emmett shouted. "I heard him. He said it." He looked at the police. "Tim! Amy! You heard him, too, right? Calvin requested a lawyer! Tell him to shut up."

The police officers Emmett had called looked helplessly at Jack.

Bob and Donald dragged Emmett, still shouting, over and out the door to the stairs.

Silence once again descended on the department.

Jack removed Calvin's gun from the holster. "Are you requesting a lawyer, or will you help me figure out what is going on?"

Calvin's eyes met Jack's. Hurt, fear, and desperation all showed in the older man's face. He hung his head and whispered, "I want to talk to a lawyer."

Chapter Forty-Two

"That couldn't have gone worse," Jack said, sitting beside Jill in front of Bob's office desk.

"The fallout has only begun," Bob said. "Once this hits the news, the media will turn this into a circus. Emmett's face is already all over town in community outreach material for the police department. And now he's charged with murder?"

"Calvin confessed, too," Jill said.

"He's obviously covering for Emmett," Bob said.

"Is he?" Jack asked. "Or is it the other way around?"

Bob opened his desk drawer and pulled out a tub of antacids. "Oren identified Emmett as the man who tried to shoot him in the face, and Oren likes Emmett. Why would he lie?"

"Oren isn't lying," Jack said. "He thinks Emmett is the one who shot him in the face, but a 9-millimeter firing next to your head is enough to make anyone see triplicate. And with the powder burns he got, I don't know if Oren could tell the difference between Jill and Emmett."

Jill laughed.

"That's not funny." Bob glared at Jack.

"I'm not trying to be funny. But after almost getting his head blown off, Oren could easily be mistaken about what he saw. When he noticed the police cruiser pull in behind him, he thought it was Emmett playing a prank on him. Maybe his brain filled in the details."

Bob dropped the antacids into the drawer and took out a bottle of aspirin. "If Emmett is not the shooter, why would he confess to two homicides?"

Jack turned to Jill. "You said it yourself. You felt guilty for not seeing the warning signs with Emmett. What if that's what Emmett thought about Calvin? Emmett didn't see how far down Calvin had spiraled over the death of his daughter. Now he's doing what he can to protect his partner."

Bob sat back and crossed his arms. "Do you think Emmett would take a murder conviction for Calvin?"

"I do," Jill said. "They're like brothers."

"Or," Jack continued. "You heard Emmett begging Calvin to shut up and talk to a lawyer. Emmett may be trying to stall for Calvin so Calvin can work out a deal."

"It's a reach, but they're not both guilty," Jill said. "What if Calvin is covering for Emmett? Calvin could be having that same sense of guilt for not seeing the red flags with Emmett."

Bob rubbed his temples. "Do you know I was going to take a vacation this week, but I wanted to wait for warmer weather? Worst decision I've ever made."

"No, it wasn't," Jack said. "If you were on vacation and we had to arrest a cop, you would have come back."

Bob begrudgingly nodded. "Is anyone who was involved in the office fight pressing charges or seeking medical attention?"

"No one from the Sheriff's department," Jack said.

"Or the police," Jill added.

"What about you two?"

They both shook their heads.

"That's one problem out of the way. How would you recommend that we proceed?"

"Our best hope is ballistics," Jack explained. "Kendra brought Calvin's gun over so they could compare his bullets to the ones retrieved from the bodies. They're still working on Emmett's ballistics test. I'm also going to check with Cedar Grove Cemetery. Emmett stated that at the time of Tyrell's death, he was patrolling there. A month back, there were some reports of damage to grave markers at the Cemetery, and I asked them to install security cameras at both entrances."

"You did?" Jill's eyebrows rose. "That's a bit of a coincidence."

Jack's throat tightened. "My brother and sister are buried there."

"I apologize," Jill said.

"No need. Hopefully, they followed my advice. If we can poke holes in Emmett's story, maybe he'll tell us the truth."

"Both of them lawyered up." Bob stared at the phone on his desk. Every line on it flashed an angry red. "There will be no more talking with either of them."

A knock on the door made them all turn.

"Come in." Bob waved Kevin Reed into the room and pointed to the chair in the corner.

Kevin's face was flushed a splotchy red. "Tried to call." He panted as he sank into the seat. "Left messages."

"We've had a rather eventful morning," Bob explained. "Catch your breath and tell me what's going on. Did you get Calvin's gun?"

Kevin nodded as he gulped for air. "Sorry. I took the stairs. We have a match. Barring a couple of anomalies, which is typical, it's almost perfect. I can say definitively that the gun we tested matched the bullets retrieved from both the Miller and

Yates cases." Kevin swallowed. "Because of the volume of bullets recovered and their pristine conditions, it's a slam dunk."

"Which gun?" Bob stood up.

"I'm a hundred percent positive. The bullets were fired from Emmett Wilson's service pistol."

Chapter Forty-Three

Jack sat on the couch in his darkened living room, looking out the window. Normally, after arresting a murderer, everyone headed out to celebrate, but no one was rejoicing this time. This was the last thing the already low morale of law enforcement needed. Two distinguished cops were under arrest, and the media was in a feeding frenzy. The grief both men shared over losing Emma to violence would now be turned into fodder for headlines and clicks.

Closing his eyes, Jack let his head tilt back and rest against the wall. There was never a debate for Jack whether he should go into law enforcement. The gold shield, emergency lights, and the crackle of a radio dispatching him to save the helpless were as impossible for him to resist as a siren's song. He could never understand why other people didn't see things the same way he did.

The door to the bedroom creaked open, and Alice whispered, "Jack?"

"I'm on the couch."

"Were you sleeping? Why are the lights off? Where's my Grandfather?"

"No. Thinking. Mrs. Stevens'."

Alice slipped out of the bedroom and stood before him in a bathrobe with a towel covering her wet hair. "You've gone full-on caveman speak. Talk to me." She didn't need to ask him what was wrong. She knew what was bothering him without him saying a word. It was another reason he loved her so much. She sat next to him and placed a gentle hand on his arm. "Emmett made his choices, and so did Calvin. You did your job, and I'm proud of you. What do you think will happen to them?"

"Bob and the Police Chief are working on one of them to recant, but they're both refusing. If it goes much further, they're both going to flush twenty years down the drain." Jack stared into her green eyes. "Emmett is the one who's going to get charged. The bullets match his gun, and Scoops ID'd him. The DA will take that to trial."

"Then Calvin is trying to help his friend. Can you talk to him?"

"Calvin hates me."

"A lot of people don't like you at first, but you win them over."

Jack raised an eyebrow. "That sounds like a backhanded compliment."

"It is not. Look at Mrs. Stevens. She couldn't stand you and was ready to throw you out, but you turned her around." Alice sat up. "Mrs. Stevens has a single bedroom. Where's my grandfather sleeping?"

Jack wiggled his eyebrows.

Alice punched his arm. "Don't be ridiculous. He's being sweet and protective, that's all."

"That's all? You should have seen how they were fawning all over each other." Jack raised his voice and spoke in a high falsetto. "Oh, Andrew. You cook like Julia Child but look like Gordan Ramsey." He lowered his voice to a deep rumble. "That is nothing, Jan; in my country, I used to bake a roast with my left hand and fight off Cossacks with a wooden spoon with my right."

"Stop it!" Alice laughed and hit him again.

"I'm teasing. It's nice. His wife passed away twenty years ago, and Mrs. Stevens is all alone."

Alice crossed her arms. "Are you being serious? Do you think they're attracted to each other?"

"That goes without saying. You don't have a problem with it, do you?"

"No." Alice leaned against him. "It just caught me off guard. I'd be happy for them both. I don't like thinking about anyone going through this world alone."

"You've got a good heart." Jack wrapped his arm around her shoulder.

Alice placed a hand on his chest. "I'm sorry you're hurting." She opened a button on his shirt. "Is there anything I can do to make you feel better?" She undid another button and slipped her hand inside.

The touch of her skin on his sent a warmth coursing through his body. But when he closed his eyes, the image of the bars of a cell swinging closed and the echo of the lock slamming into place ruined the mood. He exhaled in frustration and stared up at the ceiling.

Alice continued to caress his chest. Her lips tenderly kissed his neck. Soft, warm, wet, her mouth traveled up to his ear. She pulled herself closer to him. "We have the house to ourselves."

Desire pushed aside his dark thoughts. He grabbed her by the hips and swung her around, so she was straddling him.

Her hands grabbed his belt and quickly unbuckled it.

The front door opened, and Andrew turned on the light, temporarily blinding them. "I need to pick up a few things. Oh!"

Alice jumped off Jack, pulling her bathrobe tightly around herself. She turned several shades of red, mumbled something neither man understood, and darted to the bedroom.

Jack deftly yanked the throw off the back of the couch and covered himself with it. "How are you, Andrew? How's Mrs. Stevens?"

Andrew grinned as he backed out of the apartment. Holding the doorknob with his right hand, he pointed to the bedroom with his left. "Go after her! I am like a gust of wind that will put her fire out. Go, kindle the embers, and the flames will come again." He winked and shut the door.

Jack rushed to the bedroom, hoping his grandfather-in-law was right. But when he opened the door, Alice sat in bed with the sheets pulled up to her chin.

"That was probably the most embarrassing thing that has ever happened to me." She said.

"Are you kidding? Aunt Haddie and her Bible study group once caught me buck naked with Whitney Hogan in the back of her station wagon."

Alice's mouth fell open, but her green eyes blazed. "Do you have any idea how mean Whitney was to me?"

"Whitney? She was sweet."

"To boys, she was sweet. To girls she didn't like, she was a snake. She and her flying monkeys beat me up behind Henesy's News."

"Whitney did that? You wouldn't tell Michelle, Chandler, or me what happened?"

"I'm not a fink, and I handled it myself." Alice crossed her arms and glared. "But you had sex with her?"

"No. Aunt Haddie dragged us out of the car. Then, after her pastor had a long talk with us, Aunt Haddie drove Whitney home." Jack shook his head. "Whitney was so mortified that she never spoke to me again."

"Is that supposed to make me feel better?"

"I thought it would."

"You thought wrong."

Jack pulled back the sheet, but stopped when Alice's scowl deepened. "I'm going to go write some stuff down that's rattling around in my head." He kissed her head. "Sorry."

Alice sighed. "All's forgiven." She scooted over. "Come to bed."

Jack shook his head. "I killed the mood, and if I don't start making a list, I'll never sleep. I love you."

"I love you, too."

Jack slipped out of the bedroom and crossed to the kitchen. He opened the cabinet, but his eyes traveled to the large bottle of vodka on the shelf when he reached for the glass. Jack didn't keep alcohol in the apartment because the temptation to finish the entire bottle was too strong. It must be Andrew's. Alice would never put it there.

Jack's hand hung suspended in the air, and he licked his lips. Maybe he could have one drink. One really enormous drink. He could use his forty-ounce thermos, which could hold the bottle. It would be so easy for him to forget all about this case. His fingers closed over the long neck, and he pulled the bottle from the shelf. Crossing to Andrew's room, he opened the door, set the bottle on top of the bureau, and shut the door.

No. The last thing he needed was to get drunk. He had work to do.

Filling up a glass with water, he headed over to the computer desk. He opened the drawer and pulled out a pad of paper. There was something about the tactile feedback loop between his hand and brain when he used pen and paper that helped him think. At the top of the page, he wrote the advice Detective Clark gave him years ago — FACTS, NOT FEELINGS.

Something was wrong with his case, and he needed to figure out what.

Chapter Forty-Four

Jack sat in the corner of Tullie's Cafe across from Detective Clark. Jack's notebook lay open on the table.

"Thanks for coming, Detective Clark. I really appreciate it."

"The tables have turned, Jack. I remember when you were a little kid, and you'd beg me to take you on ride-alongs. Now that I've retired, I'm the one who's grateful to get out of the house. I heard you made an arrest."

Jack didn't expect any congratulations, and Clark didn't give any. Jack wasn't surprised. Arresting a fellow law enforcement officer wasn't a thing to celebrate. It felt more like something to mourn. "There were two confessions." Jack filled Clark in on all of yesterday's events.

Clark sipped his black coffee and listened intently. Once Jack was finished, he waited momentarily before saying, "Thanks for bringing me up to speed, but I don't see where you need my advice."

"I don't think they're guilty."

"They? Most detectives dance a little jig and pat themselves on the back when they get a confession. Am I understanding that you want to throw both confessions out?"

"Calvin's confession is bogus. We were taking Emmett to booking and Calvin came over to us. Once Calvin saw Emmett in handcuffs, he got this pained expression. You could see it in his eyes. He confessed only to save Emmett."

"You're going on a feeling?"

"No." Jack turned around his notebook so Clark could see the first thing written there. "Facts, not feelings. A very wise man taught me that."

Clark nodded appreciatively. "What facts do you have to rule Calvin out? He's got the motive, opportunity, means, and he confessed."

"Emmett has all of that, plus we have witness identification and ballistics against him. All the evidence points to Emmett being guilty."

"You're saying the process of elimination rules Calvin out?" Clark said.

"Partially. In order for Emmett not to be the killer, that would mean someone else fired Emmett's gun. If Calvin committed the murders, why would he have used Emmett's gun to do it? The only reason I can think of would be to frame Emmett. But if that was Calvin's intention, why would Calvin confess once Emmett was caught? That makes no sense."

Clark nodded. "Good point. So, you've ruled Calvin out. But all the facts point to Emmett as the murderer. How do you get past a witness claiming Emmett tried to shoot him in the face?"

"When I interviewed Scoops, he said when he saw the police lights, he thought it must be Emmett busting on him because Scoops is dating Emmett's daughter. When Scoops powers down his window, he expects the cop to be Emmett but gets a face full of powder burn instead. The flash would have screwed up his vision. I think Scoops expected it to be Emmett, so his brain convinced him that's who it was."

While Clark thought about what Jack had just said, the waitress stopped by the table and filled their coffee cups back up.

"Thank you." Clark nodded and smiled at her, then fixed Jack with a piercing stare. "But that's a heck of a coincidence."

"It isn't a coincidence if someone planned it. The bullets removed from the victims match the ones fired from Emmett's gun. If Emmett didn't kill anyone, then someone is trying to frame him."

"Or Emmett is guilty."

"There's a lot of facts that point to Emmett's innocence."

"Such as?"

Jack pointed at his notebook. "I made a list."

Clark chuckled. "Of course you did. But I've got to give credit where credit is due. Yes, I said facts, not feelings. But your dad started you on the habit of making lists."

"They help!"

"I know. That's why I do it, too. Don't tell Ted that. I don't want him to go getting an ego."

Jack smiled. "Okay. Let's look at what happened with Scoops because I know the most details about that. We know the killer aimed the gun at Scoops' face, but the gun misfires. Fact, the killer's gun jammed. That, in itself, is odd. Emmett takes meticulous care of his gun and uses premium ammo. But say it did happen. How long would it take you to clear a jam on your service pistol?"

"A second. Two tops."

"Worst-case scenario? A minute?"

"I'd have retired if it took me that long. And if it did, I'd holster the gun and use my backup."

"Exactly. And that's what Emmett would do. He's a good

cop, and he knows his firearms. He's got a backup .38 he carries inside the trauma plate pouch on his vest. Why didn't he go for it and shoot Scoops while Scoops was getting out of the car and running across the parking lot?"

"I don't have an answer for that. It's a red flag."

"And there's the fact that the killer almost caught Scoops on foot. Scoops may run like a chicken and was always slow, but there is no way Emmett, who's got thirty extra pounds on him and is nearing fifty, almost caught Scoops. It would never happen."

"But again, you have a witness."

"I have a witness that saw someone dressed as a police officer chasing Scoops. It was too far for them to make an identification. But again, why didn't Emmett draw his backup .38 while he was running?"

Clark leaned forward, setting his elbows on the table. "Go on."

"The two murdered victims were both shot at close range in the face. But then the killer fired three shots in the abdomen. Why?"

"Rage. Classic overkill."

"I could see that if it was the other way around. If the killer put three in the stomach to make them suffer, I'd say it was rage. But he kills them and then shoots them in the stomach? Does that make sense?"

Clark's eyes widened.

Jack watched understanding dawn on the old detective's face. "The killer wanted us to recover those bullets."

"That's why he shot into soft tissue."

"Exactly. And that's my next point. Tyrell and Yates were both skinny guys, yet out of six nine-millimeter bullets, not one goes all the way through?"

Clark's fingers drummed the table. He stared down, his brows pulling together. "How many hit bone?"

"None. And none went through. All rounds fired into the torso were recovered and identifiable. The bullets that struck the skull shattered."

"So, someone packed underpowered rounds?"

"I think that's why the gun aimed at Scoops misfired. The bullet held a partial charge."

"You're saying it's a setup? You think someone framed Emmett?"

Jack nodded.

"But how did the killer get a hold of Emmett's service pistol?"

"That's what I need to find out."

Chapter Forty-Five

Jack stood in the hallway of the jail, leaning against the wall. His eyes were wide open, but even if he'd been brought in here blindfolded, he'd know where he was. The mix of cleaning chemicals, the stink of unwashed humans, and the constant noise would confirm the fact that he was in a giant cage. Although the concrete and tiles looked like they belonged in a university, it was like walking into a morgue.

Every part of the prison set Jack on edge, from the cold, indifferent tone of the guards to the prisoners, who glared at him with nothing but hate. When the first heavy metal gate clanged shut behind him and the unseen lock sealed it with a loud click, Jack recalled what he detested the most about this place: he was trapped and locked behind steel doors and concrete. The feeling of panic rippled through his entire being as flashbacks from his childhood rolled through his mind.

Jack flexed his hands, and his breathing sped up. It felt as if the floor was rolling out from under him. His eyes clamped shut as tightly as the door. Everything inside screamed at him to turn around and run—to tear the door open and barrel outside.

Sweat ran down his back, and his arms shook. He stretched his hand out and felt the cold concrete.

Get out! Yelled a voice in his head.

His eyes snapped open, but his feet didn't move. He had a job to do. If Emmett and Calvin were innocent, he couldn't leave them caged in here and a killer out on the streets. He smacked the wall with his fist and started walking again.

There was no doubt in Jack's mind that he would go mad if he were ever put in here for any length of time. His chest tightened. Cops were typically kept isolated—for their safety. General population wasn't exactly kind to former law enforcement.

Jack froze when he reached Calvin's holding cell. The huge man lay on his cot, curled into a fetal position. His shoulders shook as he softly sobbed into the balled-up blanket. He turned his head and noticed Jack standing there.

Like a rhino charging a car, Calvin moved quickly, catching Jack off guard. His arm darted between the bars and Calvin seized Jack by his shirt.

Jack stepped back, ready to break Calvin's elbow using the leverage of the bars.

"Please, help him!" Calvin begged. "Stratton, please." Calvin sobbed, his fingers going limp as he released Jack from his grip. "It's all my fault. Please." No tears ran from his red-rimmed eyes. Maybe there were none left?

"You invoked your right to an attorney. I can't speak with you unless—"

"I waive it."

Jack didn't ask a second time. Instead, he re-Mirandized Calvin, ensuring he understood he was waiving his rights to a lawyer. After Calvin agreed, Jack said, "I'll be back in one second," and then raced to the end of the hallway.

The guard on the other side approached the door.

"Call in and request a uniform for assistance with an interview and transport," He shouted to the guard, who nodded and repeated the request into his radio.

Jack hurried back to Calvin's cell.

"I know what happened to you," Calvin said.

"You're going to have to clarify what you mean. A lot of stuff has happened to me."

"Michelle. When she died, did you feel responsible?"

The muscles in Jack's back tightened, pulling his shoulders back and lifting his chin. He met Calvin's questioning gaze with a cold, hard stare. "What's your point?"

"You weren't." Calvin's eyes rounded in pain. "But you felt like you were, somehow, right? That's how I feel with Emma. I was her father. I swore to protect her. But I failed."

Jack wanted to turn away from the man's prying gaze but couldn't. Calvin was right. The burning ache in his chest caused by his failure still smoldered inside him. "Michelle wouldn't want me to, but I blame myself."

"My Emma would say the same thing. That's why I'm trusting you, Stratton. Please help him."

"To help him, I must rule you out because you confessed. But before we talk about anything, you need to go on the record. We're going back to the interrogation room. Okay?"

Calvin nodded.

Twenty minutes later, Jack sat across from Calvin in the same interrogation room they had spoken in earlier. Jack had left two voice messages for Jill and texted her multiple times, but she hadn't responded. He wanted to talk to his partner before proceeding, but he wasn't about to wait and risk Calvin changing his mind about talking.

Jack asked Kendra to stand at the door and witness the interrogation. She was eager to do it, hoping to run one herself in the future. She stood at attention, watching, and listening to everything.

After starting the recording and Mirandizing Calvin again, Jack asked, "Do you want to recant your confession?"

"Yes. I didn't kill anyone. Neither did Emmett. I don't know why I said I did. When I saw him in cuffs, I panicked. I knew he only confessed to the murders because of me."

"Back up, Calvin. Let's start with your alibi, or lack thereof, on the nights of the murders."

"I don't have one. I told you the truth when I said I was driving around. That's what I do." Calvin's chin dipped down to rest on his chest. "I can't stand being in that house. I think Emma will come around the corner any minute, and it will all have been just a nightmare. But she doesn't. Then I go looking for her. When I can't find her, I leave."

Jack swallowed. He felt the same way when he'd gone to Aunt Haddie's, and neither Michelle nor Chandler were there. "Where did you drive?"

"Up to the mountain. I took the back roads, too, so no one could see me."

"Why did you do that?"

"Because I didn't want anyone asking why I was doing what I was doing. It sounds crazy, right? Because it is. But what would happen to a cop if someone reported that I spent hours aimlessly driving around? Psych evals. Desk duty. Those would drive me up a wall, so I didn't want anyone to know. I tried to keep it hidden and deal with it myself."

Jack grimaced. So many people needed professional mental health help but tried to overcome it on their own. They were like a swimmer caught in a riptide. The water kept dragging them further out from shore, and when they finally wanted to call for a lifeguard, it was too late to save them, and they drowned.

"So, you have no alibi for either murder or the attempted shooting?" Jack said.

"Yes."

"And you were in uniform and driving a cruiser all three nights?"

"Yes."

"You arrested Tyrell Miller previously?" Jack asked, already knowing the answer.

"It was over seven years ago, but yes. Twice."

"And Matthew Yates?"

Calvin held up four fingers.

"I need an audible response."

"Yes, I arrested Matthew Yates four times."

"How about Oren Dorcey?"

"No, but I hated him." Calvin shifted in his seat. "It wasn't because of anything he did—Oren's a goof but not a bad guy. Emmett liked him. He was good to Imani. But I couldn't stand him."

Jack's throat tightened. Calvin's talking wasn't doing himself any favors. If anything, the more he talked, the guiltier he made himself look. Calvin started the interview by recanting his confession, and now his answers were painting him into a corner. "Why did you hate Oren?"

Calvin's hard stare focused on a spot on the metal table. He inhaled and gave a slight shrug. "Imani is the same age as Emma. They were best friends since they were kids. They used to play together. Now, everything Imani does punches another hole in my chest. They deserved the best."

"So, you didn't want Imani to date Oren?"

"It goes without saying that a guy with the street name of

Scoops isn't the best in anything. He's not even on the top one-hundred list. So, no, I didn't want her to date Oren."

"Did you do something about that?"

"I told you I didn't try to kill him. But Emmett thinks I did."

"Why would Emmett think you wanted to kill Oren?"

"Emmett confronted me about the fight behind the phone store. He thought I should take time off. He asked me what I was feeling, and I told him."

Jack nodded and waited. Silence descended upon the room. A minute ticked by.

"Rage. All I feel is rage." Calvin continued. "I hate everything now, including myself." Calvin stared at Jack. His eyes were empty. Not in a cold way, but like a gas can that had run out of fuel. "Emmett asked me if I had anything to do with the murders and with Oren. I lost it."

Jack's mouth was so dry it was hard to breathe, but like a hunter in the brush, he remained motionless—worried that the simple movement of taking a sip of water would spook Calvin and he'd stop talking.

"I called Emmett every name in the book for letting Oren date his daughter. I told him he was a fool. If Imani were mine, Oren would be dead. That's why Emmett confessed. He thinks I snapped."

"What about the other two men?"

"I said something about them, too."

"Such as?"

Calvin closed his eyes, but when he opened them again, they burned with pain and rage. "You know what it's like. How many times does someone have to commit a crime before they get caught? Five? Ten? It's probably way more. And then how often does the case get tossed by some moron of a bleeding-heart DA who cares more about the criminal than the victim?

So yeah, I said I was happy they were dead. I was glad they couldn't hurt anybody else."

"You said that to Emmett?"

Calvin nodded. "It sounds like I did it, but I didn't, Jack. I swear. I swear, for Emma's sake. She loved Emmett as much as she loved me. And he loved her right back. He didn't want me to name a girl after him. He thought she'd hate it, but she didn't. But I know he didn't kill those men."

"Do you have some proof of that? Because I need to level with you, Calvin, you look guilty. What facts do you have that Emmett is innocent?"

Calvin touched his chest. "I know Emmett."

Jack leaned forward. "That's not going to go anywhere in court, Calvin."

"Then you need to find something. Emmett is innocent. I know the man."

Jack crossed his arms. Ballistics matched the bullets to Emmett's gun. If Emmett didn't fire the shots, the killer must have used Emmett's gun.

"What kind of service pistol do you use?"

"A Glock 17. They're department-mandated. Chief Hall insists everyone who carries use that model so we can swap ammo and mags if things go south."

"What about attachments?"

"I have an Acro P-2 red dot reflex sight and a compact nightstick light. Emmett uses a DeltaPoint pro red dot and an O-light mini."

Jack ran his hand through his hair and thought for a moment. "Can you think of any times when you saw Emmett's gun out of his possession?"

"Emmett has a quick-release safe at home. I have one, too. If he's not wearing it, he stores it in there."

"Has Emmett had it serviced recently?"

"No. We run drills at the range every Monday and clean them after. They've always been reliable."

"The gun range at Patton's Supply?"

"Yeah. We go at 10. Emmett takes stall 16. I use 15. We shoot drills for half an hour, then get an early lunch while we clean our guns before our shift. It's our jam."

"Is anyone else there?"

"A few people drop in, but nobody is regular except Nate."

Jack sat up. "Nate?"

"Nate Rowe. He's a military-wannabe, sovereign citizen whack job. Don't get me wrong, he's kinda pro-police, but only as long as we're on his side."

"Can you expound on that? Did he say something?"

"Say something? We always have to tell him to shut up. You'd figure he'd get the hint, but he's got the memory of a goldfish, and every thirty seconds, he's back railing against this or that. Do you know I even had to point out that Emmett and I were black?"

Jack raised an eyebrow.

"I don't play the race card, and I'm not doing it now. I think the guy hates everybody. Black, white, purple, it doesn't matter. When I pointed out something he said was racist, he turned around and said racist stuff about everyone on the planet. He even bashed Eskimos. Who says bad stuff about Eskimos?"

"Besides, at the range, have you had any dealings with Nate?"

"At the Police Citizen's Academy. I gave the community policing talk, and he wouldn't shut up. He interrupted me so much that Emmett had to take him out to the hallway to talk to him. He's done a dozen ride-alongs with us, too. He said he wanted to see how his tax dollars were being spent. The Chief hoped it would quiet him down, but it had the opposite effect. I responded to a call out at his place once, too."

"When and for what?"

"It was a month ago. Nate called 911, saying he heard someone in his backyard. Nate has an arsenal of weapons, but instead of checking the noise out himself, he calls us and hides in his kitchen."

"What happened on the call?"

"Nothing. I responded and swept the perimeter. The yard was clear. But Nate was an idiot. I was standing near the back porch, and he came creeping up behind me with a pistol. I think he was trying to use me for cover! He's lucky I didn't shoot him."

Jack crossed his arms as he weighed the facts. Serial killers all begin somewhere. Some start with animals. Others build up to that with other acts of destruction. Had Nate's 911 call been genuine? Or had Nate lured Calvin out there? Jack wondered if Calvin had it wrong, and it wasn't lucky that he didn't shoot Nate. Maybe it was the other way around?

Chapter Forty-Six

Jack parked at the side of Patton's Supply and checked the time on the dash — 9:43. The store was open, but it would still be fifteen minutes before the gun range did. Seeing that it was Monday, he hoped Nate was as much a creature of habit as Calvin and Emmett.

The bell above the door chimed, and Brad glanced up from behind the counter. The usually excited man waved unenthusiastically and stayed sitting on his stool.

"Did I tell you, or did I tell you it wasn't a whacker?" Bud called out from the ammo row.

Jack wanted to point out that Bud hadn't made any prediction but instead said, "Thank you for emailing that list."

"Lot of good it did. I can't believe you arrested two cops. Having been on the job, the last thing I can stand is a dirty cop." Bud waved Jack closer.

Jack walked down the aisle to where Bud rearranged ammo boxes on the shelf.

"Can you do me a favor?" Bud whispered. "Talk to Brad. He went on a couple of ride-alongs with that lunatic, and now he's second-guessing going into law enforcement. I kept telling him not to put anyone on a pedestal, but the kid wouldn't listen. Hero worship is what it was. When I was on the force, I could pick a dirty cop out by looking at them. And I knew when I met Emmett he was so crooked he could hide behind a corkscrew. No one's that nice."

Jack rubbed the back of his neck. He wanted to ask why Bud let his son go on ride-alongs with someone he felt that way about, but he thought about what he'd be going through if he'd been in Brad's position. "I'll talk with Brad. I'm also going to use the range after."

"Sure. It's free for you today. Use it as long as you want. I appreciate it." Bud held out his hand, which Jack shook. "Do you have any kids?"

"No. Not yet."

"When you do, you'll realize what you're doing means to me. Thanks."

Jack nodded and headed for the back of the store.

Brad typed with two fingers on the keyboard and didn't look up. "Hey, Detective Stratton."

"I'd ask how it was going, but I don't have to be a detective to see something is wrong. What's the matter?"

Brad shrugged. "Nothing."

Jack cocked an eyebrow and stood there, waiting.

Brad sat on the stool and crossed his arms. His broad shoulders sagged. "I heard you arrested Emmett," Brad said. "I don't want this to sound bad, but I wish you were wrong. Emmett seemed like the perfect cop. I wanted to be like him."

"Right now, we don't know the whole story. But I understand a little of what you're going through. When I was at the police academy, there was an instructor named Joe Callahan, who I thought was a supercop. Until he was arrested, he had planted evidence on a suspect. Of course, Joe tried to justify it, saying he'd arrested the guy before and knew he was now dirty. They sentenced him to five years and kicked him off the force."

"No offense, but that didn't make me feel better."

Jack chuckled and put his hands on the counter. "I'm going to sound like my foster mother, but you're looking at it the wrong way. She said that the Devil waters sin, hoping it will blossom and its seeds would be carried into other people's hearts as an example or to discourage them."

"Emmett being a killer has certainly discouraged me."

"But that's what I mean when I say you're looking at it all wrong. Instead of depressing you, Emmett's arrest should act as a reminder to you not to be that guy. He should be like the ghost of Christmas future to you."

"The what?"

Jack shook his head. "Old reference. Did you see the second *Star Wars*? *Return of the Jedi*, not the other one."

Brad nodded.

"Yoda told Luke, once you start down the dark path, forever will it dominate your destiny. Consume you, it will."

Brad sat up straighter. "So you're saying, don't give in to the dark side?"

"Exactly!" Jack held out his fist, and Brad bumped it.

"It just came as such a shock. Emmett was a cop's cop."

"You still don't get it!" Bud stepped out from behind a display of holsters. "You pick the wrong role models. You thought Emmett was a good cop because he's on the posters plastered all over town. That's like thinking Bill Cosby is a good dad because he played one on TV."

"I'm not having this conversation again, Dad." Brad puffed out his cheeks. "I'm gonna take a break and get something to eat."

Bud watched his son stomp off and shook his head. "There I go, sticking my whole leg in my mouth."

Jack wanted to agree with him but wasn't going to kick him when he already realized he'd made a mistake. "Give him time." Jack glanced at his watch — 10:05. "I've got to get to the range. Can I please have a box of nine and a couple of targets?"

Bud rang Jack up, didn't charge him for the range or targets, and gave him a twenty-five percent discount on the ammo. "Thanks for trying."

"He's a good kid. He just needs to process it. Give him time."

Taking his targets, Jack headed through the back door and across a covered patio to the large concrete building out back. The generic-looking single-story building resembled a cattle barn from the outside. Inside, it was almost empty. Sixteen separate partitions created lanes for firing pistols. The stalls had two walls on the left and right, with a waist-high table where you could place your ammo and firearm. A hundred yards of open space lay between the stalls and the far end of the building to provide shooters plenty of distance for their targets. Peering down the lanes, Jack couldn't see the bullet traps at the end because of the lack of lights, but he knew they were there— a collection of steel plates that prevented bullets from exiting the range.

Jack was the only person there. He grabbed a hearing and ear protection set off the wall and strolled down to the last stall — number 16, which Emmett used every Monday. After clipping his target on the wire, he held down the red button on the stall's wall. Machinery whirled, gears clanked, and his target, attached to a pulley, traveled out to twenty yards.

A familiar excitement built inside him as he donned his PPE and drew his pistol. With each trigger pull, brass flew upward, fire and smoke roared from the muzzle, and gunpowder filled the air.

Jack pictured the bullets hurtling toward the target. They'd shred the paper, continuing until it shattered inside the bullet catcher in the back. It was one of the reasons Jack liked shooting inside. It was nice not having to worry about what stood behind your target.

He dropped one magazine and slapped the other into place with lightning speed. He'd practiced the movement so frequently that it was now reflexive motion. After unloading those bullets, he dropped that magazine, clicked another in place, and holstered his gun.

10:15.

He looked down the row of empty stalls. It seemed that Nate had broken his habit. Drawing his gun, Jack stared at the weapon. He pictured Emmett standing in this exact spot practicing. He quickly did the math in his head. If Emmett came every week, he was looking at a hundred dollars in ammo and other expenses. What would that cost over twenty years? Of course, people don't think of that when they vote to slash police budgets. And what about the time he'd spent on training? And for what? Now he's accused of murder.

Jack exhaled. A police uniform could be faked. So could a whole cruiser, for that matter, but the gun? No way. The bullets recovered came from Emmett's pistol. If someone were trying to frame him, it would be impossible to steal his gun, use it, and put it back without Emmett knowing it was gone.

With blinding speed, Jack drew and fired at the target down range. He aimed for the silhouette of the head. Flames shot from the barrel, the gun kicked back into his hands, gleaming brass arced through the air, and the faint ping of the rounds striking the bullet catcher in the back echoed in the empty room.

The slide of Jack's pistol stood open, signaling he'd emptied the magazine. But Jack stood as motionless as a statue. The smoke drifted and curled up to the ceiling. Like the last gong of a Church bell, the ringing of the bullet striking steel faded into silence.

Jack leaned to the right and peered past the target and down the lane. There were no lights past the targets at the end of the building, so it was cloaked in shadows. Jack ducked under the counter and started walking. He flicked on the attached light on his pistol.

Benny Duggan, the previous owner of Patton's Supply, was a safety nut. He had insisted the range be made with high-end steel bullet traps. Located at the end of the range, all projectiles that enter the opening of the narrowing trap are directed into a vertical cylinder that decelerates the bullet until it loses its inertia and falls harmlessly into a bucket.

Jack's shoulders slumped. A crazy idea had popped into his head. What if the killer hadn't stolen the gun but had collected the bullets after they were fired? Emmett used the same stall at the same time every week, so it would be easy for someone to isolate his rounds. Staring at the pitted steel plate and the shattered remains of bullets at the base, he realized that was impossible. When the lead hit the steel, it would become so malformed that it could not be fired again without being melted down and recast. And if you did that, you'd be creating a new bullet, and there would be no ballistic match.

Jack turned, but something inside the bullet catcher reflected the light and caught his attention. Focusing the beam, his eyes widened. Something yellow was caught on one of the bolts. He reached in and removed three pieces of plastic thread caught between the steel plate and the bolt. Pulling an evidence bag from his pocket, he placed the fibers inside.

Maybe his idea wasn't crazy after all?

Jack snapped off his light, holstered his gun, and hurried back to stall 16. Gathering up magazines, he grabbed his ammo and rushed outside. The door clicked closed as he crossed the patio.

"Congratulations, detective." A voice behind Jack made him stop. Nate Rowe sat in a chair in the corner of the patio, smoking. A metal toolbox lay at his feet. "I heard you arrested that whack job, Emmett. Good work."

"Morning, Nate. How've you been?"

Nate took a long, slow drag off his cigarette. The tip glowed bright red. He closed his mouth, and two streams of smoke blasted out of each nostril. "What were you doing inside the range?"

Jack hesitated. He'd been so focused on the fibers he may not have heard the door to the gun range open. Had Nate come inside and seen what he'd been doing? Or was it simply a generic question? "Practicing."

"Why were you looking in the bullet traps?" Nate set his cigarette down on the wooden arm of the chair. The ashes dangled off as the smoke curled upward.

Jack eyed the big-bore Magnum Desert Eagle pistol on Nate's hip. "Why are you so interested?"

"Going past the stalls is very dangerous. If I hadn't seen you down there, I could have accidentally killed you."

The corner of Jack's mouth ticked up in a challenging grin. No matter how often he tried to change, sticking his thumb in a bully's eye was ingrained in him. Poking the bear was foolish, but whatever part of his brain was necessary to stop it had been broken during a beating when he was six.

Jack's mother's pimp had kicked and punched Jack to the point where Jack not only thought he was going to die but wanted to. Jack's nose was broken, his eyes were blackened, and the man lifted him off the kitchen floor by his throat to scream in Jack's face.

That's when Jack first flashed a bloody, crooked smile. Then Jack started laughing.

The pimp, high on drugs, freaked out. He set Jack down on the floor and backed away like Jack was possessed. Then he turned and fled out of the apartment.

Jack met Nate's gaze with an unflinching stare of his own. "What are you doing here, Nate?"

"I come here every Monday to shoot. You can't be too prepared."

"I agree. But why don't you go to the range closer to your house? What's it called?"

"Bullseye Gun Club."

"I was thinking about trying it out. I heard they had a good cowboy shooting setup."

"They do, but I have my daughter on the weekends, so I drop her off at school on Mondays, and then I come here."

Jack furrowed his brow and pretended to think. "Every Monday at this time?" He checked his watch.

"I get something to eat first. So what?"

"Seeing how you're here every Monday at 10, you'd be here when Emmett and Calvin were practicing, right?"

Nate stood up, knocking the cigarette off the chair and to the ground. "What's with the third degree?"

"I'm just asking questions, Nate. Did you ever talk to them while they were here?"

Nate reached down and picked up the cigarette, which had burned down to the filter. He flicked it toward the corner, pulled out his pack, and lit another one. "Not really. I focused on what I was doing. They were busy milking the clock."

The jab got under Jack's skin. "They weren't on duty when they were practicing."

"They were in uniform."

Jack let the comment go. "You must have spoken with them

a little, right? Good morning. How are you doing? That kind of thing?"

"Of course. But we weren't fishing buddies. Besides, I always knew Emmett was whacked. That's why I kept an eye on him. It was only a matter of time before he snapped."

"Why do you say that?"

"I told you that he was responsible for letting your sister's killer go. And you should have seen him on patrol. He knew all the scumbags that he should have been arresting by name. He knew their families and what was going on in their lives. It was disgusting."

Jack would have pointed out that what Emmett was doing was called community policing and was the sign of a good police officer, but instead asked, "Did you know that Emmett has one of the highest arrest records in the department?"

"He probably forged the records. Nobody on the street was afraid of him. You won't make busts if the crooks laugh at you behind your back."

You don't want people to fear the police! Jack knew the truth would be wasted on Nate, so he swallowed his disdain and asked, "I'm sure you three talked about guns while you were here. That's what shooters do, right? Especially with your Desert Eagle. You must get a lot of questions about it."

Nate took a deep drag and nodded. "No one believes I bought it in L.A. I had to buy the .44-mag version because the .50 caliber is on the banned gun list, which is stupid seeing how you can purchase the upgrade kit — which I did."

With how much Nate smoked, Jack was surprised he had the lung capacity to talk so much. "Did either Emmett or Calvin shoot it?"

"I let both of them fire off a magazine apiece," Nate smirked. "They couldn't handle the recoil of the 50. To put it bluntly, they sucked."

Jack forced a chuckle but doubted either experienced officer, both past winners of cowboy shoots, would have that much difficulty with the gun. "That was nice of you. What about reciprocity? Did you talk about their guns?"

"Vanilla Glocks? What's there to talk about?"

"Ammo, sights, grips — the usual fare. You never fired either of their guns?"

Nate's eyes narrowed. "Why are you asking?" His hand moved to his belt and closer to the Desert Eagle on his hip.

"Relax. Like you said, I arrested Emmett. I'm just putting a bow on the case."

Nate spit. "Bull. I know how cops work. The thin blue line, right? You protect your own. Is that what you're doing now? You're looking for some angle to cut Emmett loose and sweep the mess under the rug?"

"What are you talking about, Nate? Like I said, I arrested Emmett."

Nate gasped and started coughing. He pointed an accusatory finger at Jack. "You're trying to pin this on me."

Jack shifted his right foot back slightly to give himself a clear draw if he needed it. "Calm down, Nate. No one is accusing you of anything."

The door to the main building opened, and Brad ran out. He wore a pistol on his hip. "Hi." His Adam's apple bobbed up and down as he swallowed and nervously looked at Jack. "Is everything okay?"

"Everything's fine. Right, Nate? You were standing up to go in and use the gun range."

Nate's eyes traveled from Jack to Brad and then returned to glare at Jack. "I don't feel like shooting at targets anymore. I'm leaving." He grabbed the box at the foot of the chair and stomped to the door leading back to the store. He opened it and turned around.

"It's men like you and Emmett that are turning this world to crap. How much are they paying you to let a guy go who killed two men but also could have saved your sister?" Nate spat on the ground and stomped inside.

Brad exhaled loudly and grabbed onto the fence. His hands shook, and he appeared ready to fall over. "I saw it all on the security feed." Brad pointed to the camera mounted on the corner of the building. "I thought Nate was going to draw. What was that all about? There isn't any audio."

"I asked him a few questions that bothered him, but I don't think anyone has ever accused Nate of being mentally stable. I appreciate the backup, Brad. Good job."

Brad smiled.

Jack opened his mouth and closed it. He eyed the security camera. "Do you have cameras in the range?"

Brad nodded.

Jack wanted to ask Brad to pull all the security footage, but he needed to follow proper channels and get a warrant. "Thanks again, Buddy. I owe you one."

"Anytime Detective Stratton." Brad's smile wavered and disappeared. "I'm not telling you anything you don't know, but if I were you, I'd be careful. I've never seen Nate so mad, and like you said, he's not right up here." Brad tapped the side of his head. "He's also the type of guy who holds a grudge."

Chapter Forty-Seven

Jack drove across town to Jill's apartment complex. She hadn't returned his messages or texts, and he was now officially concerned. He parked in the visitor's lot and headed for Building 2. The apartment complex consisted of four brick buildings with a row house design. The units were two stories tall, and each building held six units. It was finished a few years ago and, with its clubhouse, gym, pool, and walking trail, was marketed to the higher end of renters.

Jack rang the bell on unit 3 and waited. A few moments passed, and he was about to ring again when a lock clicked, and the door opened.

Dressed in sweats and fluffy socks, Jill's hair was pulled back. Her eyes and nose were rimmed red.

Jack stepped back. "Are you sick?"

"Of this world." Jill cocked an eyebrow. "What are you doing here?"

"I got worried about my partner."

She rolled her eyes. "The case is closed. We're done working together."

"I'm opening it back up. Do you have a second?"

Jill glanced over her shoulder. "My place is a pigsty."

"I got my shots." Jack walked past her and headed to the couch heaped with blankets. A trash can was on the floor with a pile of tissues in and around it. He headed for a wide leather chair and sat down.

"Make yourself at home," Jill muttered as she shut the door.

"Before I tell you what's going on, talk to me. What's wrong?"

Jill stopped and stared at him like he had three heads. Her upper lip rose, revealing her teeth as her brow pulled forward. "This case is a hand grenade going off in an ammo factory. Tyrell Miller was engaged to be married. His fiancée is heartbroken, and his once future father-in-law just checked himself into a mental health facility."

Jack's shoulders slumped. "I didn't know."

"I couldn't bring myself to tell you. I called to check on Rosa, and she told me her father is blaming himself. He felt something bad would happen, and he didn't warn Tyrell. Rosa said he hadn't slept for days, and he started talking about self-harm."

"It's good she got him help."

"Can you imagine what she's going through? She lost her fiancé and now is trying to take care of her father, but who is taking care of her? And what about Imani and Oren? How is that relationship supposed to work after Oren identified Emmett? And Matthew Yates' grandmother called me. It was horrible. She's such a nice woman and thought the world of her grandson despite what he'd done. She's having nightmares about him trapped in the fire. Last night, I did, too."

"It sucks."

"It's not over. What about Calvin and Emmett? They lost Emma, and now they're lost. Emmett is going to jail, and

Calvin is out of a job." She pressed her hands against her head and gritted her teeth. "I want to smash something. And if one more person tries to offer me advice, I'm going to strangle them."

Jack smiled.

Jill held her arms out and pantomimed strangling him. Her fingers tightened so much that the muscles in her forearms flexed.

"You're pretty jacked. And if you had Darth Vader's powers, I'm sure I'd be choking right now. But, can I offer a word of advice to a squid?"

Jill's arms dropped to her sides, and she stared at him in disbelief. "I think I actually will kill you." She glanced around the apartment.

Jack didn't know if she was looking for her service pistol, so he talked fast. "You need to do two things." He held his right palm upward, then made a fist. "Embrace the suck. Everyone is going to tell you to forget about the pain or ignore it or some other crap, but do you know what? What happened to everyone involved in this case was wrong. Horribly wrong. It sucked. Hold your hand out like me."

"This is stupid."

"No, it isn't. Trust me. Hold out your hand."

Jill did.

"Now, put all of that wrong in your hand and embrace the suck." He closed his fist and squeezed. "Acknowledge that wrong. Hate it. Say it. Tyrell Miller being murdered was wrong. It sucks. He was a young guy trying to make a life for himself and to be cut down like that makes no sense, and I hate it."

Jill's body trembled as she crushed her fingers tightly together.

"But the second part is as important." Jack turned his fist

over so the fingers were facing the floor. "Let it go." He opened his hand. "If you don't let the hate go, it will consume you. That's what fire does, so you have to let it go."

Jill opened her hand. "That's the hard part."

Jack noticed the wedding ring now on her finger and sat up straighter. "Is that a good sign?"

"What? Oh," Jill removed the band and flicked it across the room. It pinged off the wall and fell someplace out of sight. "No."

Jack felt like a mackerel on the docks, with his mouth opening and closing and no sound coming out. "Sorry." He finally managed to say.

"Don't be." Jill crossed to the couch and flopped down. "To quote Randy Travis", she sang the lines with a very nice voice and in tune, 'I was digging up bones. Exhuming things better left alone. Resurrecting memories of a love that's dead and gone.'"

"Good song. Good advice unless you haven't dealt with them."

"I've dealt with it." Jill placed one foot on the couch. "My husband was a history professor at a prestigious little university in California. The marriage got rocky, and he blamed my career. He was partially right — long hours, low pay, high stress. He gave me an ultimatum: quit my job, or he quits the marriage."

"And you chose the job?"

"No." Jill chuckled sarcastically. "I wrote up my resignation. Before I handed it in, a young blonde college student showed up at my front door, wanting to talk. It turns out my dear husband was having not one, not two — four affairs that semester alone. How blind could I be?"

"You did find out."

Jill shook her head. "I was told. There's a big difference. I confronted him, and he admitted it and promptly handed me divorce papers. In a way, I'm kind of glad he did. It saved me from being the sap who sticks with someone like that."

All Jack could think of saying was, "At least it was amicable."

Jill laughed. Real, hard, and for a full minute. "You stink at this, Stratton. It was amicable until I turned the nanny cam confession I recorded over to the college. After that, it was definitely un-amicable."

Jack laughed, but it clipped off. "Nanny cam? Did you have kids?"

"No, but it being California, you put a nanny cam in your living room to watch thieves steal your belongings while you're at work."

Jack laughed again.

"I'm serious!" Jill said.

"I know. That's what makes it funny."

"Why are you here?"

Jack told Jill his theory and reiterated all of his points. She listened intently and asked a few questions, but she stood up when he pulled the bag with the three yellow fibers out of his pocket.

"You didn't have a warrant. Those aren't admissible."

"That's why I'm going straight to Morrison when I leave here. Are you with me?"

"Ready to lead, ready to follow, never quit."

Jack smirked. "I think that middle part is why I didn't join the Navy. I'm not too good with the whole following thing."

Jill stopped halfway up the stairs. Jack expected her to come back with a sarcastic comment, but instead, she gave a slight nod and said, "Thanks, Jack."

While she got ready, Jack crossed to the corner of the room and found her discarded wedding band. He carried it to the end table next to the couch and set it on the coaster. As he stared at the simple golden ring, he agreed with Jill. "Letting go was the hardest part."

Chapter Forty-Eight

"Before we talk to Bob, I want to run these fibers by Kevin Reed in ballistics. I hope he'll be able to compare them to the foreign material found on the bullet from the Yates's crime scene."

"Have you spoken with Bob at all?" Jill held the door open.

"Not yet." Jack headed for the stairs. "I'm sure he'll agree, but this case is so convoluted already it will be a mess. Two false confessions? Have you ever heard of that?

"No. But as Dwight Yokum says," Jill sang in perfect pitch as they jogged up the stairs. "There's a first time for everything."

"I take it you're a fan of country music." "I'm a fan of both kinds of music — country and western."

Jack laughed as he held the door open at the top of the stairs. "The Blues Brothers. Funny movie. Wait a second, how come you didn't tell Country that?"

"He tried to give me the nickname Hollywood. Who knows what he would try to call me if he knew I loved Johnny Cash."

"Good point."

They stopped outside the lab and knocked. The door was locked.

Jack knocked louder.

A moment later, the door whipped open, and Kevin Reed stepped out. He was in such a hurry that he didn't even look at them as he locked the door. "I apologize, but I'm working on a priority case. If you call the lab and—" He glanced up at Jack, screamed, and stumbled back into the door. "What is wrong with you, Jack!"

"Wrong with me?" Jack held up his hands. "I'm just standing here."

"I was heading to the Sheriff's department to talk to you." Kevin looked at Jill and smiled. "Hello."

"Kevin Reed, this is Detective Jill Reyes."

Jill shook his hand. "Nice to meet you."

"Great!" Jack pulled the evidence bag out of his pocket. "Now that we have the niceties out of the way, I need you to tell me what these are."

Kevin grabbed the bag from Jack's hand and scowled. "Is this another joke? How did you get these so fast?"

"It's not a joke. I recovered those from a potential crime scene. Do you recognize the fibers?"

Kevin turned to Jill and asked, "Is he being serious? Because if he's pulling my leg after all the work I've done, I won't find it funny."

"He's not being funny."

"I'm telling the truth." Jack held up his right hand in the Boy Scout sign — covering the nail of his little finger with his right thumb while holding the three middle fingers upright.

"You were a scout?" Kevin asked.

"No. But I'm serious about the fibers."

"Then you have got to see this." Kevin unlocked the door and led them into the lab and over to the computer connected to the enormous monitor on the wall. "I couldn't figure out what the fiber was that we recovered from bullet 3 of the Yates crime scene. I sent a portion of it to the state lab, but I contacted my colleagues while waiting for the results. We have an internet forum to ask and answer each other's questions that I frequent."

Jack set the evidence bag on the table.

Kevin wiggled the mouse, bringing the massive monitor to life. "Brad Pitt held the answer."

"The movie star?" Jill asked.

Kevin laughed. "No. He's a ballistics expert for Los Angeles. Can you imagine working right next to Hollywood with that name, but you're five foot three, balding, and have a pot belly? Poor guy. He knew exactly what the fiber was because he's been working with them."

The screen changed, and a photograph of a dozen bullets appeared. The bullets were of various calibers, but they had one thing in common — a melted yellow fiber clinging to them.

"You'll never guess what the fiber is." Kevin crossed his arms and smiled confidently.

Jack squared his shoulders. "A new kind of ballistics medium."

Kevin shook his head like he had water in his ears. "How could you *possibly* know that? I only just found out myself."

Jack pointed at the evidence bag on the table. "I knew the answer because of where I found the fibers."

"They're fascinating stuff. It's bleeding edge. These fibers will replace ballistic gel. You can fire bullets into them, and the bullet retains its shape miraculously. As far as forensic comparisons go, these fibers are a game changer. I can't wait for approval to order some for this lab."

"Let me ask you a hypothetical," Jack said. "With the bullet

294 Jack & Jill and the Blue Light Killer

in such good shape, could you re-pack it in a cartridge and fire it out of a smooth bore barrel?"

Kevin nodded rapidly. "That shouldn't be a problem at all. Of course, if you did that, you'd lose accuracy."

"All the bullets were fired from close range." Jill held her palm up, and Jack gave her a high-five. "Jack Stratton, you're a genius!"

Kevin's mouth hung open. "Are you saying that someone used ballistic fibers to catch the bullets from Emmett's pistol, re-packed in fresh casings, and then re-fired them from another gun?"

"You confirmed it was possible," Jack said.

"That would explain the abnormalities," Kevin said. "The lands and grooves from Emmett's gun remained, but — that's diabolical!"

"I have to see the Sheriff for a warrant. Can you write up an explanation of why ballistics use these fibers and make it fast?"

"Sure. I'll also reexamine all of the bullets from the two cases."

Jack patted the excited man on the back. "I appreciate all your work, Kevin. You just solved this case."

As Jack and Jill headed to the stairs, he called Bob Morrison. "Hey, Sheriff. Are you in your office?"

"I am. What's up?"

"I need to speak with you ASAP. Jill and I are leaving the Kent Building now and can be there in ten minutes. I need approval for a warrant to search Patton Supply and their gun range."

The line went silent for a moment. "I take it you've had your radio off. There's a fire at that location right now, and it's a big one."

Jack swore, and they sprinted for the Charger.

Chapter Forty-Nine

Jack skidded to a stop outside Patton Supply. Three fire trucks and a police cruiser had responded. More sirens sounded in the distance. Black smoke billowed out of the gun range roof, forming an ominous cloud overhead.

Jack and Jill both exited their cars.

"Hey, Mitch!" Jack called over to a firefighter standing next to one of the trucks as he jogged over, and Jill hurried to catch up.

Mitch Holt was Jack's age, tall and thin, built like a runner. Jack didn't know how he carried all his firefighting gear, but from the smile on his face, Mitch liked his job. "What's up, Jack? Beautiful wedding, by the way."

"Thanks for the fire extinguishers."

Mitch laughed. "I thought they were a very unique but practical wedding gift."

"This is Detective Jill Reyes with the city police." Jack's smile faded as he turned to the smoldering building. "How bad is the back of the range?"

"Nice meeting you." Mitch cracked open a bottle of water. "How did you know that the fire was in the back of the range?"

"Because I requested a warrant to search that area for evidence."

Mitch made a face. "That's too bad. The only thing left is the bullet traps. They're steel, so they didn't burn, but all the machinery there did. It's definitely arson. We found a couple of empty cans of gas inside."

"It's now part of a homicide investigation. Can I get you to spread the word for your guys not to touch anything?"

"Sure thing."

Officer Kendra Darcey walked out of the store building. "Hey, Jack. Jill. You guys are going to want to check inside."

As the glass doors swung into place, Jack's stomach tightened. The door on the right had been kicked in. "Don't tell me it's the security tapes."

Kendra's head pulled back, and she made a face like she had swallowed a bug. "How did you know that?"

Mitch leaned close to Jill. "Did anyone tell you that Jack is a psychic?"

Jack rolled his eyes. "If I were, I would have got my warrant before the fire and break-in." He motioned to Jill. "Let's go check it out."

Kendra led the way to the broken front door. "I was the first police unit here. I noticed the kicked-in door but also the sign.

A piece of paper was taped to the front door — CLOSED TODAY FOR PERSONAL HOLIDAY. SEE YOU TOMORROW!

"I made sure the building was clear, but you should see inside."

The three of them made their way through the store and to the office in the back. Jack crossed around the counter and stopped in the office's doorway.

The cluttered office had been ransacked. Wires hung from empty shelves where electronic equipment had once been.

Jill pointed. "Judging by the monitors on the top shelves, someone stole the video security system."

"Oh, no!" Bud swore as his boots crunched the broken glass on the floor. He came into the store with Brad following behind him. "Don't tell me! Don't tell me!" Bud hurried over and looked inside the office. A long stream of profanities poured from his mouth.

"Dad! Dial it back." Brad said. "You're going to give yourself a heart attack."

"Look at my office! Do you have any idea how much those security recorders cost me? And what about the range? Not only does it look like the building has to be torn down, but think of how much revenue I'm going to lose!" Bud flopped on the stool beside the cash register and glared at Jack. "This is all your fault. What are you going to do about it?"

"This isn't his fault!" Jill stepped forward.

"Of course it is. Brad told me."

Jack shook his head. "Everyone, hold on a second. What are you talking about, Bud?"

"Brad told me that you got into it with Nate Rowe. He said you got Nate so mad that he thought you were going to start exchanging bullets, and he had to break you up."

Jill glanced at Jack. "You seem to have forgotten to mention that part."

"Nate was mad, but that was at me," Jack said.

"It started with you, but then Brad came out. When Nate was leaving, he came to the office and said I should teach my kid to mind his own business, and if I didn't, the next time Brad got in his face, he'd teach him. Well, that sure got my dander up, so I said some words, and he said some words back and left."

"Why don't you tell us what was said?" Jill asked.

"I told him to go to hell, and he threatened to teach me a lesson, too. Of course, more colorful language was used, but that's the gist of it."

"It looks like Nate made good on his threat." Brad's hands balled into fists.

Bud stood up. "I'll teach Nate that —"

"You'll do nothing of the kind," Jill said. "This is a police matter, and we'll handle it."

"If you think I'm going to sit on my hands and do nothing, you're crazier than he is," Bud said.

Jack stepped forward so he and Bud were inches away from each other. "If you so much as text Nate, I'll arrest you. This is an active police investigation, and I will handle it."

Brad placed a restraining hand on his father's arm. "If Detective Stratton said he'll handle it, he will, Dad. Just give him some time."

Bud's shoulders slumped, and he sat down on the stool. "I'm sorry. But just look at this mess." He turned to Brad. "Can you go move the car? I parked behind the fire truck, and the last thing I need is for them to back into it."

Brad nodded and hurried out.

"Thank you for understanding," Jack said. "I do have a question for my report. Why was the store closed?"

"I did it to spend some time with Brad. He was so depressed about Emmett, and all we've been doing is working around the clock. I was going to take him fishing but got the call from the alarm company before we left." Bud exhaled, stood up, and started for the office. "I've got to call the insurance company."

Kendra blocked his way.

"I'm afraid you can't go in there until we process the crime scene," Jack said.

Bud shrugged and took out his phone. "I got you. And if it helps you nail that jerk to the wall, take as long as you need." Bud muttered something else as he shuffled off to the front of the store.

"Kendra, secure this scene. Don't let anyone near it until crime scene gets here. This is part of a homicide investigation." Jack said.

"You got it." Kendra nodded.

"What are we doing?" Jill asked.

"I need you to come with me, but you need to grab your vest and shotgun from your car before we go."

Jill's mouth fell open. "Where exactly are we going, Jack?"

"Nate Rowe's."

Jill jogged beside Jack over to their cars. "If I heard Bud correctly, Nate looked like he wanted to shoot you this morning. And now you want us to put on vests. Why aren't we calling in SWAT?"

"Because if we do, Nate is going to lawyer up. Besides, I think he'll talk to me."

"Think? I'd like it if you were a little more certain."

"There's a good chance he'll talk to me. But don't worry. If I'm wrong, I'm the one knocking on the door."

Chapter Fifty

Jack slowed down, shut his emergency lights off, and turned onto the gravel lane. "You know, I've been thinking," Jack said. "How about I take you and Bob out to dinner when this is done? Invite Chief Hall if you want, too."

"That sounds nice, but back up a second, Jack. Seeing how we're about to confront someone I consider to be the primary suspect in two homicides, can you please tell me why you don't seem overly concerned?" Jill asked as she checked her pistol.

"I am worried, but if I get freaked out, I will tense up. If I tense up, I slow down. And if I slow down and something breaks bad, that's not good."

"Why don't we call in SWAT?"

"Because it hasn't risen to that level yet. Yes, Nate got aggressive this morning, but I think Brad got a little dramatic when he told his father what happened. This whole case has been filled with misdirection, and I'm not positive that Nate is responsible for what happened to the gun store."

"If Nate didn't do it, who did? You don't still think it was Calvin?"

"Calvin has an iron-tight alibi — he's still in lock-up."

Jill shook her head. "Bob didn't tell you? The DA charged Emmett this morning. They let Calvin go."

Jack slowed to a stop at the end of the lane and put the car into park. "Why didn't you tell me?"

"I'm so sorry, but Bob told me he wanted to speak to you about it first. Here, I thought you were handling that well."

"We agreed to hold both of them until we figured this out. They both confessed." Jack opened his door.

"But you said you didn't think either of them did it."

"I still don't, but with their confessions, we could have sat on both of them." Jack slammed his door.

Jill held up her hands. "I had nothing to do with the decision. Bob called me and told me he wanted to talk to you."

Jack exhaled. "Maybe he was waiting until I came in to tell me. Do you know if he put a tail on Calvin?"

"He didn't."

"This case keeps getting messier." Jack started walking. "Stay frosty and keep your eyes open. I'll take point. I want you to stop beside the truck in the driveway. I'm going up to the door by myself." Jack pointed to a sign hanging on a tree. "I've got a new favorite." Jack pointed. "No trespassing. Violators will be shot. Survivors will be shot again."

"In light of current circumstances, I don't find that funny."

Jack motioned for Jill to fall back and kept walking. The gravel crunched beneath his shoes and sweat rolled down his back. He searched the windows for any motion, but there was none. A gun nut like Nate would undoubtedly have a long gun and could easily pick Jack off at this distance.

Jack kept his hands out at his sides as he turned onto the walkway and approached the house. "Nate! We need to talk. I'm taking my gun out and putting it down."

"Jack!" Jill's voice rose high. "That's totally against protocol."

Jack slowly unholstered his pistol and set it down in the middle of the walkway. "I'm unarmed, Nate. I'm here to talk, but not about you." With his heart pounding, Jack kept scanning the windows of the ranch house. The window shade to the right of the door was raised all the way.

"I'm unarmed," Jack yelled. His heels clicked off the front steps. He peered through the window.

The interior of the house was surprisingly clean. Jack scanned the room for movement and saw Nate lying on the floor next to the dining room table.

Jack pounded on the door and pushed it open. "Darrington Sheriff's Department! I'm coming in!" He drew his backup .38 and motioned Jill forward. Once Jill reached the top of the steps, they swept the house. Jack headed to the right, with Jill following after him. Room by room, Jack navigated each doorway until they reached the dining area and the body lying on the floor.

Nate lay on his back, his eyes open and staring at the ceiling. On the table sat a picture of him holding a young girl, a broken rubber band, and a piece of plastic wrap with some pills in it.

"Put your gloves on," Jack said, removing some from his pocket. "It looks like fentanyl, so don't touch anything."

Jill holstered her gun. "Did he O.D. by accident, or did he kill himself?"

Jack stared at the empty holster on Nate's hip and then scanned the room. His silver Desert Eagle was sitting on a corner table beside a lamp.

Jill pointed to the table. "He left a note."

Jack moved beside her.

I am the person responsible for killing both Tyrell Miller and Matthew Yates. I shot Tyrell at the lake and set fire to Matt's trailer. They were scum who deserved what they got. I don't apologize to anyone.

Nate Rowe.

"The handwriting is pretty shaky," Jill said. "But look at this." Sitting on the table was a plastic laminated gym membership card that belonged to Tyrell Miller. "Looks like Nate took a trophy."

Jack stared at the photograph on the table of Nate holding his daughter. She was a young girl, maybe seven or eight. Her arms were wrapped around Nate's neck, and they were both grinning from ear to ear.

Jack took out his phone. "Do me a favor and call it in?"

"Sure," Jill said. "What are you going to do?"

"I'm calling a friend of mine. I need a favor."

Chapter Fifty-One

Three hours later, after turning over the crime scene to Mei and her team, Jack and Jill sat in his Charger in the empty school parking lot.

Jack checked his phone and smiled when the reports he requested came through.

Jill took a protein bar out of her pocketbook. "Do you want one?"

"I'm good," Jack said as he watched the entrance to the parking lot.

"Why are we meeting the IT director of an elementary school?"

"Because Nate Rowe was murdered by killing himself."

Jill started coughing so hard that she leaned forward in her seat.

Jack smacked the middle of her back hard.

"OW!" Jill grimaced and pulled her elbows back so far, they almost touched. She continued to cough but waved him off with one hand while taking a sip of water with the other. "I'm not choking."

"Sorry. I thought you were."

"No." Jill wiped her mouth with her hand. "How could Nate be murdered by killing himself?"

"I think someone forced Nate to write that note and take those drugs. Look at the facts."

"I am looking at the facts, and I think we caught our killer. Nate hated law enforcement. He knew where and when Emmett practiced. He had access to the gun range. And he wasn't a big fan of you, which is why he dumped Tyrell's body outside your apartment." Jill held up her hand as she took another sip of water. "Plus, he confessed. He wrote a suicide note."

"I agree with those facts, but there are others that completely change the scenario. Nate would have to sneak bags filled with fibers into the gun range to stuff the traps with enough material to catch Emmett's bullets. I checked with Kevin in ballistics. The trap would need to be packed full of fiber to catch the round undamaged."

Jill nodded. "Isn't that motive for why Nate would set fire to the gun range and steal the video equipment?"

"That's another fact why it wasn't Nate. Why would Nate destroy the evidence and then kill himself?"

Jill thought for a moment. "Guilt. Maybe he realized he'd be caught?"

"It doesn't make sense to get rid of the evidence and then confess. And why did he steal the video equipment? Why not burn the store, too?"

Jill bit her lip. "That's a good point."

"If I were Nate and wanted to get rid of all the evidence, I would have burned everything down."

"Then why did whoever did it set fire to the gun range and not the store?" Jill's eyes widened. "You think the killer is Bud?"

Jack nodded. "Or Brad. Or both of them. Bud is getting bids for a new outdoor gun range. Maybe he wanted to collect the insurance on this one, or he needed a quick way to ensure he got rid of any fibers still stuck in the trap."

"And Bud didn't want to burn his whole store down, so he stole the video surveillance?" Jill exhaled. "But why would Bud or Brad or both of them have killed Tyrell and Yates? Why try to kill Oren?"

"Motive is the hardest thing to nail down, but Bud has a few."

"Such as? His police service record came back clean."

"I hate to say it, but you can't always trust someone's service record. It happens in any profession. Doctors cover for doctors, teachers for teachers, and cops for cops. It's sad because they're passing the bad apple down the line. But why would Bud retire after nineteen years unless they made him? Twenty is the magic number. He lost out on a boatload of cash and benefits by not sticking around for a few months, and you have to ask why his superiors didn't let him."

"That would cause a lot of animosity. So you think he's got something against cops? Why target Emmett?"

"Emmett is the poster boy for the police — literally. And Bud's son was a fan."

"Oh," Jill's lips pursed together, and she nodded sagely as she leaned against the door. "A jealous father will go to great lengths to win his son's love. If Bud did it, is that why you think he dumped Tyrell's body at your apartment?"

Jack nodded.

Jill's eyebrows knit together. "I've got a big problem with your theory. Don't get me wrong, it works on a lot of levels, but what about Nate's confession and suicide? I can't see how Bud could force Nate to confess and kill himself."

Jack pointed to the car, pulling into the parking lot. "That's why we're meeting Tim Grant."

After introducing themselves to the young teacher, Tim showed them inside the school. They strolled through the entrance and into a room just past the main office.

"We keep all the security monitors in here," Tim explained as he unlocked the door. "Since I'm IT, the responsibility fell to me."

"We appreciate you coming on such short notice," Jack said.

"It's fine. I was only grumbling about my responsibilities. Everything seems to have a chip in it or connects to the internet. And if it falls under that umbrella, I own it."

"Sounds like you need a raise," Jill said.

"Tell that to my boss."

Tim turned on the light and pulled two other chairs beside the one already positioned in front of a computer and huge monitor.

"We haven't had any incidents at the school for a while. There are dozens of cameras. Can you narrow down what you are looking for at all?"

"I need the video footage from this morning. Ten o'clock on. Do you have any cameras on the playground?"

"Six. Unfortunately, that area is our biggest security risk."

"What a world we live in," Jill muttered.

A few minutes later, Tim had sectioned the monitor to six videos covering the playground.

"We're looking for a red Jeep or a tan, four-door, king cab truck," Jack explained.

Tim began scrubbing the timeline, and all the videos moved simultaneously.

"There!" Jill pointed at the upper-right corner of the screen.

A red jeep had pulled into a parking space across the street.

"What is that store?" Jack asked.

"It's a home decor type of store. They sell stuff for decorating the house."

"Can you zoom in?" Jack asked.

The jeep had parked parallel to the playground so they couldn't see the license plate. Even if they could have seen it, Jack doubted they could read it from this distance.

"The window is tinted," Jill said. "We can't see the driver."

"What time is this?" Jack asked.

"11:13."

"Can you fast forward?" Jack said.

Tim scrubbed the timeline. Different classes of kids burst out the door for recess and then were ushered back inside by the teachers the way farmers round up chickens.

Jack kept his focus on the jeep.

The window powered down.

Tim zoomed in.

Jill gasped.

Brad Templeton sat in the driver's seat, holding a cell phone, which he aimed at the playground.

"What time is this?" Jack asked.

"1:02."

"Brad waited there for over two hours. Why?" Jill said.

Jack stood up. "Let's go ask him."

Chapter Fifty-Two

Jack sat as Sheriff Bob Morrison paced his office floor. Every few steps, Bob would stop, stare at Jack, and shake his head, but he didn't say anything.

Finally, Jack said, "Have you ever heard the expression, don't shoot the messenger?"

Bob marched over to stand beside Jack's chair and glowered at him. "Do you have any idea what kind of situation this puts me in? The mayor thinks the case is closed!"

"Maybe you should have talked to me about that first," Jack fought to keep his voice from rising to match Bob's volume.

"That wasn't my fault. Chief Hall wanted to speak with Jill, so he drove to the Nate Rowe crime scene. He saw the note and the drugs and..."

"Jumped to the wrong conclusion. But how does that put you under the bus? With my keeping the investigation open, doesn't that stop the bus from backing over you?"

Bob hurried back behind his desk. "You have a good point. I never told the mayor that the case was closed. But I think she's going to hold a press conference."

"If I were you, I'd shoot Madam Mayor a text that says stop the presses."

Bob picked up his phone and started typing. "I'm going to have SWAT bring in Bud and Brad."

"Respectfully, if you do that, you're going to start a gunfight. Bud owns a gun store. He's got enough weapons to start a war."

"I'm not signing off on you doing anything reckless."

"Me be reckless?" Jack smiled.

Bob scowled. "Then how do you propose to get them to come in here?"

"I'm going to ask them." Jack held up his phone. "They've had an arson fire and a break-in. I want to ensure they don't have a problem with insurance, so I want to make sure all the information I have is correct."

"That's good."

"Thank you."

"But if they don't come in, I'm sending SWAT."

Jack thought about it and nodded. "I want Jill with me on the interviews. She headed to the police station to update the Chief but didn't know he thought the case was closed."

"She may be a little busy with Chief Hall. I imagine the crap he is going to get is going to travel downhill."

"You have to run interference for Jill, then. The credit for this case is fifty-fifty. She should be rewarded, not reprimanded."

"I'm not her boss. What am I supposed to do?"

"You can put in a word with the mayor. The mayor can shut down the chief."

Bob's phone rang. "Speaking of which, this is her. And I will. Good work, Jack." Bob picked up his phone. "Madam Mayor."

Jack left the office and texted Jill to come in ASAP. He hit send, and a phone chimed inside his cubicle. Puzzled, he rounded the corner to find Jill in his chair.

She read the text. "Thanks for the warning, but too late." She brushed back her hair and sighed.

"Was your Chief mad?"

"Not as mad as I was." Jill stood up and chuckled. "You should have seen his face when I dumped my coffee on his desk."

Jack's eyes went wide, and his mouth fell open.

Jill laughed. "I'm kidding. I wanted to, but I need the job. The thing that gets me most is it was his mistake. I never even talked to him."

"The genius of management." Jack smiled. "Can I get you a coffee while we discuss how to go at this interview?"

"Bob agreed to you calling them in?"

"He did. Let's hope they show up."

Chapter Fifty-Three

Jack, Bob, and Jill stood at the front desk of the Sheriff's Department, scanning the parking lot. A red jeep turned in and parked in the visitor spot.

Jack grit his teeth when only Brad got out.

"I'm sending SWAT to pick up Bud Templeton," Bob said.

"Understood," Jack said.

Brad hurried up the steps and stopped inside the foyer. "Detectives. Sheriff." He shook everyone's hand. "My dad couldn't make it. He's not feeling well."

"I'm sorry to hear that, Brad, but we appreciate you coming in to help with these forms. Is your dad at home if we have any questions you don't know the answer to?"

Brad nodded.

"I'll let you two take it from here," Bob said before shaking Brad's hand again and walking down the hallway. "I hope your father is feeling better."

"In addition to the paperwork, we need to ask you some questions, Brad." Jill smiled. "Why don't you follow us? We'll do that someplace quiet."

"Sure. Have you spoken with Nate yet? Did he confess?" Brad asked.

Jack held the door open. "We should get these forms out of the way before tackling the Nate situation. Your father was distraught at the store. Are you sure he's okay? Should he be checked out at the hospital?"

Brad waved his hand dismissively. "He has an ulcer. I'm sure the break-in and fire aggravated it."

They made small talk until they reached the interrogation room and led Brad inside.

"Seeing how we're going to be asking you questions about this case, I'm going to Mirandize you and record the conversation," Jack said, sitting on one side of the table with Jill.

Jill picked a pen up off the table. "Brad's familiar with the procedure. He took the Citizen's Academy, right?"

Brad sat up proudly and nodded.

After reading Brad his rights and having everyone say their names and titles, Jack moved the stack of papers he'd previously set on the table in front of himself. "I left the store around 10:30. When did you and your father close up shop?"

"Not that long afterward. My dad said he wanted to take me fishing. A bonding thing."

"That was nice of him. Where did you go?"

"Home to get the gear ready."

"Straight home?" Jack asked.

Beads of sweat broke out on Brad's forehead. He nodded.

Jill said, "Brad, because of the recording, we need all your answers to be said aloud."

"Sorry." Brad cleared his throat. "Yes. I went straight home."

"So you stayed at your house until the alarm company called about the break-in and fire?" Jack said.

Brad sat there blinking rapidly. "Yes. We never made it fishing."

"I'm glad we cleared that up," Jack said, pretending to check off a few boxes on the form and turning the page. "What time do you close the store?"

"Every day at five. Except Saturday, we close at three."

"And you're closed on Sunday?"

Brad nodded. "Sorry. Yes. We're closed on Sunday."

"What do you do when you are done with work, Brad?" Jill asked. "I'm just curious."

"Not much. I was kind of seeing this girl, but she decided to go to school out in Oregon. But I work a lot."

"So, do you go out on the town after work?" Jill continued.

"Not so much. I usually just watch some movies or something."

"You and your father?"

"Sometimes. What does this have to do with the break-in?"

"We're getting to that." Jack touched his pen to the form. "I forgot to ask, was your father home with you all afternoon?"

"Yes."

"What time did he get home?" Jill asked.

"What time did he get home?" Brad looked between Jack and Jill. "Eleven fifteen."

"Eleven-fifteen?" Jack asked as he took out his phone. "I called your dad right before you got here, Brad. So now I'm a little confused."

Brad's eyes widened, and he licked his lips. He looked up and to the right, then shook his head. "No. He said he got home at eleven-fifteen."

"He said he got home?" Jill said. "What does that mean?"

Brad's foot tapped off the floor. "He got home then. I'm positive."

"Did you look at the clock?" Jack asked.

"Yes."

"What room were you in?" Jill asked. "What were you doing before he came into the house?"

"I was in the kitchen. I wanted to get something to eat."

"Really? At eleven-fifteen?" Jack asked.

Brad nodded.

Jack shook his head. "Why are you lying to us, Brad?"

"I'm not lying. What is this about? I thought you had some questions about the reports."

"You are lying." Jack removed the last piece of paper from the stack and set it before Brad. "You don't know when your father got home because you weren't there. You were at the elementary school at eleven-fifteen."

Brad gasped. "I want — "

"Nate Rowe is dead!" Jack's hand slammed down on the table.

Brad stared at Jack in disbelief. He turned to Jill, and she nodded.

"Do you know why your father told you to go to the elementary school?" Jack asked.

Brad pressed his lips together.

"Nate's daughter goes to that school," Jack said. "Your father wanted to try to pin his crimes on Nate, and he used you as an accomplice."

"That's a lie!"

"No, it isn't." Jack continued. "Your father killed Tyrell Miller and Matthew Yates to frame Emmett Wilson. He set fire to the range and stole the security tapes."

"You think my father did that?"

"After I argued with Nate, what happened after I left? Did your father send you home and then call and tell you to go to the elementary school?"

Brad shook his head.

"We're going to pull your phone records," Jill said. "The GPS won't lie."

Brad hung his head, and tears rolled down his cheeks.

"I want to help you, Brad, but you need to get out in front of this train wreck. You have one chance to do that, and it's now. Did you know your father killed those men?"

Brad stared at Jack with haunted eyes.

"Did you know?"

"No." Brad's voice broke.

"Did you know why he told you to go to the elementary school?"

Tears streamed down Brad's cheeks. "He said he wanted to scare Nate into confessing that he broke into the office. I asked him to let you handle it, and he lost it. He..."

Jill reached out and gently touched his arm. "What did he do, Brad?"

Brad shook his head. "He doesn't do it to hurt me."

Jill exchanged a nervous glance with Jack.

Jack lifted his chin, hoping Jill picked up on his signal for her to keep talking. She'd formed a bond with Brad, and he was opening up.

"What did your father do to you?" Jill whispered.

Brad lifted his shirt. His side was peppered with dotted scars two inches apart. Some had thin burn scars between the points.

Jack placed his hands in his lap as they balled into fists. Bud had stun-gunned Brad, and from the scars, the abuse had been chronic and long-term.

"Brad," Jack picked up his phone and texted Bob to send a medic to the interrogation room. "We're going to have someone look at that injury. We're going to need you to provide a statement. But I swear that I won't let your father hurt you again."

"He didn't mean it. He's just trying to toughen me up. Training me so I'll be a good cop."

Jack's phone beeped, and he ground his teeth as he read Bob's reply. SWAT raided Bud's house, but Bud wasn't there. They had issued an APB, but Bud was in the wind.

"He's going to be so mad," Brad said. "He told me to stick to what he told me to say, and if you guys asked me anything else, I should leave. If you didn't let me do that, I should request a lawyer and shut up."

"But you're not requesting a lawyer now, are you, Brad? You want to help us, and you want to help your father."

"He's going to be angry that I spoke with you. He's going to be so angry."

"Don't worry about him," Jack said. "I'll deal with him."

"You don't understand, Detective Stratton. He said he would do something if I didn't come out in half an hour. And my dad is a very dangerous man."

Chapter Fifty-Four

Alice walked through the front door of Titus Bail Bonds, and the little bell over the door chimed. The waiting room was empty.

Shawna walked up to the counter. When she saw Alice, her eyes went wide. She raised her arms toward the ceiling and started cheering. "Here comes the newest bounty-hunting queen!"

Alice felt heat rush to her cheeks but grinned broadly. "I couldn't do it without your help."

"What a load of garbage." Shawna hugged Alice and danced her around in a circle. "This was all you, girl. Take it in. Relish the victory. Savor the flavor."

Alice grinned and raised her fists over her head.

"I think Titus is ready to see you. Are you going to celebrate?"

"I might have to hold off until Jack finishes his case."

"You are the most thoughtful wife. I wouldn't do it. I'd be all over a lobster dinner tonight if it were me, but waiting is sweet of you. Do you know how it's going with Jack?"

"I haven't talked to him all day. But I'm sure he'll figure it out."

"Well, don't let me hold you up any longer." Shawna stepped out of the way and cupped her hand to her mouth. "Make way for the queen of the bounty hunters! Make way!"

Alice marched over to Titus' door and knocked.

"Come in!" Titus called out.

Alice stepped into Titus's office and was surprised to see a banner that read WELCOME ON BOARD, balloons, and Bobbie G. with a sparkly cone hat and a party blowout whistle.

"Surprise!" Bobbie G and Shawna shouted as they tossed confetti into the air.

"Oh, come on!" Titus said. "Do you know how hard that stuff is to get out of a carpet?"

"Don't be a party pooper!" Shawna hurried over to his desk and picked up a folder. "Here is all of your paperwork. You are now an official employee of Titus Bail Bonds."

"Congratulations. Get out." Titus glowered.

Alice chuckled. "I take it you're not happy I won?"

Bobbie laughed. "He's not happy he lost a thousand dollars to me." He grinned and held up a check.

Titus stood up and came around the desk. "Congratulations, Alice. Seriously. I'm glad you're on the team." He held out his hand.

Alice shook it.

Bobbie and Shawna blew their party whistles.

"Okay. Okay. Now you can all get out." Titus grumbled.

The three of them left the office, and Bobbie fist-bumped Alice. "Way to go. Are we going to start making bank tomorrow?"

"You know it!" Alice said. "Thank you for believing in me, guys."

"I never doubted you for a minute. Before you go, I need

your John Hancock on one form." Shawna reached for the pen in Alice's blouse pocket, but Alice blocked her hand.

"That's not a pen. It's a stun gun." Alice proudly pulled it out and handed it to Shawna.

"You got a new toy!" Shawna turned it over in her hands.

Bobbie grinned like a little boy. "I want one!"

"I want to try it out." Shawna eyed Bobbie.

"Don't even think about it!" Bobbie stepped back.

Alice laughed. "I gotta jet. Give me the papers."

After signing the form, Alice finished making plans to meet with Bobbie and then headed back to her Bug. On the ride home, she powered down her window, turned on the radio, and let the spring air widen the smile on her face. She couldn't wait to tell Aunt Haddie. She'd have to visit her tomorrow. And then take Lady to Sully's. The poor girl was overdue for a playdate.

She pulled into the parking lot of her apartment building and parked next to a tan truck with a king cab. As she shut the door, running footsteps made her spin toward the sound.

Bud Templeton ran around the truck, holding a black pistol aimed at her chest. "Turn around and put your hands on the car now."

Alice's mind raced. The only weapon she had was the stun gun in her pocket, but he was too far to use that or kick him.

"I can just as easily shoot you and grab someone else. You'd be easy to stuff in the trash can."

Alice scowled but turned and put her hands on the car.

Bud hurried over and quickly patted her down. He either didn't feel the stun gun in her shirt pocket or ignored it because he thought it was a pen. But having a weapon on her gave her some hope as the handcuffs clicked around her wrists. She still had a chance.

Bud jerked her back toward the truck and opened the door. "Get in."

Alice glanced up at her apartment window. "LADY!" Lady roared. Alice smiled, and then everything went black.

Chapter Fifty-Five

Jack poured himself a cup of coffee in the break room while Jill scanned the snack machine.

"There are a lot of good delivery places," Jack said, pointing to a cabinet. "That drawer is filled with menus."

"I need a sugar fix," Jill said, but the smile on her face vanished. "I can't believe I missed the signs. That bastard must have been abusing that kid for years."

Jack nodded. "I didn't see it either. But with Bud out there, the safest place for Brad is keeping him here."

"When will the DA be here?"

"A couple of hours. He's going to ask our opinions, and I don't think Brad knew what his father was doing."

"Neither do I. You could see it in his eyes when he heard about Nate."

"Still, I want to get proof. I've requested Brad's cell records, and I'm hoping that they come back verifying that Brad was at home at the time of the murders."

"We can also check with his internet provider. If he were home playing video games, they'd be able to tell us that, too."

Jack leaned against the counter. "When you add in the abuse, I can't see the DA charging him. Especially seeing how he is ready to testify." Jack's phone rang with the Darth Vader theme ringtone.

"Who is that?"

"My wife." Jack smiled.

Jill laughed. "Does she know you gave her that ringtone?"

"She's the one that set it up, actually," Jack answered. "Hey, darling."

"Don't say a word, Detective," Bud said. "Your wife is safe, but how long she stays like that is now up to you."

Jack crossed over to the refrigerator and the dry-erase board.

Jill moved to his side.

Jack wrote — BUD HAS ALICE.

Jill clamped her hand over her mouth.

"You are to get my son and bring him to the west fire exit of the Sheriff's Department right now. If you tell anyone what you are doing, she dies. If you come out of the building with anyone except Brad, she dies. You have five minutes." Bud hung up.

Jack stared at his phone.

"I'll get Morrison." Jill started for the door, and Jack grabbed her arm.

"Stop. Bud's outside with Alice at the west side fire exit of the building. He's given me five minutes to come out with Brad."

"You can't do that."

"I know. But I don't want this to turn into a hundred cops against a guy holding my wife as a human shield. I'm going out. Don't tell anyone. Get to a window on the second floor. He wants me to set off the fire alarm so he'll be nearby to make a quick exit. You won't need a long gun. Move."

Jill took off running.

Jack exhaled and started walking to the rear of the building. Every emotion inside him screamed for him to run to the door, but he had five minutes and needed a plan. As the different scenarios played through his mind, he fought down his fears. Alice's life depended on him, and to save her, he needed to focus. He wouldn't fall apart, and he wouldn't panic.

Unbuckling his holster strap, Jack's shoes rang off the tile floor. The west side of the Sheriff's Department road was only used for deliveries. The road ran parallel to the building, twenty yards away from the side. Bud would park there.

Would he stay inside his truck? Would he keep Alice inside or force her out?

But Jack was coming without Brad. That would set Bud off.

Jack flexed his fingers and forced himself to breathe calmly. He made the final turn in the corridor. There were no windows, and he had zero information, so he'd be shooting blind.

Stopping in front of the door, he bowed his head. "Please keep her safe."

He stared at the red paddle of the door. After he pushed it, there was no going back. Whatever happened would change his life forever.

Chapter Fifty-Six

Alice's eyes fluttered open, and she immediately shut them. Her head throbbed, and her body gently rocked back and forth. She was lying across the backseat of Bud's king cab. Her hands were cuffed behind her, and Bud was driving.

Alice took a deep breath and pushed with her left hand while pulling with her right. The metal of the handcuff dug into her skin, but her hand moved upward.

"Hey!" Bud called back.

Alice froze.

"Hey! Are you awake?"

Alice opened her eyes and tried to sound like she wasn't struggling to free herself as she continued to twist and turn her hand. "I'd ask you what you're doing, but I figured it out. You're the Blue Light Killer."

"I'm not going to kill you. If you do what I say." Bud said as he stopped at a light. "Keep your voice down, and don't make any noise."

"Where are you taking me?"

"To talk to your husband. He arrested my son."

Alice's throbbing head spasmed, and she grimaced. "Give Jack a little more time. I'm sure he'll arrest you, too. Maybe you and Brad can share a cell."

"Brad had nothing to do with this."

"So you killed those men on your own?"

"Men? They weren't men—more like feral dogs. The world is better off without them. I did society a favor."

"How come everyone who wants to be a vigilante doesn't understand that Batman doesn't kill people? He ties them up until the police come. Did you ever think about doing that?"

"There's no point. There is no justice unless you take it into your own hands. Look at the police. Calvin's daughter was killed, and what did he do? Nothing. Emmett was worse. Emma was his goddaughter, yet he lets his daughter date a three-strike loser."

"Tyrell turned his life around."

"They never do. People can't change. But if it wasn't bad enough for them to look the other way, they stop my son from becoming a cop? My son! I gave nineteen years to the job, and that's the respect I get?"

"Look. I agree." Alice's winced as the cuffs cut into her skin. "You should be able to kill whoever you want. Why don't you and I find some real bad guys and kill them?"

"Do you think you're funny?" Bud stepped on the gas, and the truck flew forward. "Listen to me. We're almost there. You do exactly what I say, and I'll let you and your husband go. You do anything else, and I'll kill you both. Do you understand?"

"I get it," Alice said, but she knew he was lying. Bud was going to kill them both. She had to get out of the cuffs.

Bud turned again. The truck slowed down. Alice bounced as they drove over one and then another speed bump. He parked the truck and got out, leaving the driver's door open.

Holding onto the handcuff chain with her left hand, she

pulled like her life depended on it because it did. Blood ran down her fingers. She twisted and yanked. The cuff slid, so it was just covering her knuckles. One more pull, and she'd be free.

Bud opened the back door. He grabbed her ankles and dragged her out. His beefy hand seized the back of her neck, and he lifted her and set her down on the tall curb beside the road.

She immediately recognized the Sheriff's Department. She was at the side of the building facing a closed fire door.

Her heart thumped in her chest. Jack was close. It wasn't just a fact. Somehow, she could feel his presence.

"Just do everything I say. Your husband is coming for you."

Alice smiled.

Yes, he is. But he's coming for you, too.

Chapter Fifty-Seven

Jack stood in front of the fire exit. He took a deep breath and slowly exhaled. There was only one choice of action now. He shoved open the door.

The fire alarm blared to life.

Bud's truck was parked twenty yards away, directly across from him. Bud stood on the road behind Alice, who he positioned on the curb. With the added height, Alice made the perfect human shield.

"They already transferred Brad to the police station," Jack said. "Let me call my partner, and you can take me hostage instead. We'll go over there and get your son out."

Bud's face pinched, and his gritted teeth flashed white. He stared between Alice and Jack and shook his head. "I don't need both of you." He aimed the gun at Jack.

Time slowed so much that it seemed like it had stopped.

Maybe it had.

Jack took it all in. He was fast, but his draw was at least a second. It would take Bud half that time since he only needed to aim.

Alice turned toward Bud. Her right hand grabbed his right wrist. Somehow, she'd freed herself from her cuffs.

Jack's gun cleared the holster but he didn't have a clean shot.

Bud yanked his gun arm free.

Alice's left hand pulled back. She was holding something.

Jack aimed, but Alice was still blocking his shot.

Blue light flashed.

Bud screamed. He bashed Alice to the side.

Jack pulled the trigger. Once. Twice. Three times.

More gunfire sounded above him, along with the sound of breaking glass.

Bud staggered backward and fell. He rolled toward the back of the truck.

Alarms went off in Jack's head. All of his shots hit center mass. Bud must be wearing a bulletproof vest.

Alice dashed toward the building.

Bud scrambled behind the front of the truck, firing three quick rounds.

The bricks behind Jack shattered, but he didn't dive for cover. He moved sideways, trying to draw Bud's fire away from Alice.

A blue Volkswagen Bug raced across the parking lot and down the delivery road. Mrs. Stevens' red hair streamed backward as she gripped the steering wheel with both hands. Alice's grandfather sat in the passenger seat, shouting something. He thrust his arm forward like some Cossack General ordering a charge.

Bud turned toward the sound, but it was too late.

The bug smashed into Bud, sending him tumbling through the air. Bud landed in a heap and slid across the grass.

Both the car's airbags deployed, and the Bug skidded to a stop.

330 Jack & Jill and the Blue Light Killer

Jack sprinted over to Bud. Bud's gun lay fifteen feet away in the grass. He was sprawled on the ground with his left leg bent at an odd angle. His eyes were closed, but he was still breathing.

"SHOW ME YOUR HANDS!" Jack shouted, and Bud stretched his arms out.

Alice sprinted up next to Jack, gripping a thick black pen. "Don't move!" She ordered, raising the pen like it was some kind of weapon.

Andrew raced around the car with a shotgun in his hands. He dashed over and leveled it at Bud's head.

"Don't shoot him!" Jack yanked the gun from his hands. "We got him."

"He hurt my Kaya Kukla!"

"But we got him. Go check on Mrs. Stevens."

Andrew dashed back to the bug and opened the driver's side door. He helped Mrs. Stevens out. "Oh my, Mila, are you okay?"

Mrs. Stevens nodded, sending a cloud of white powder everywhere. "How's Alice?"

"I'm fine, Mrs. Stevens," Alice called over.

"What about you?" Andrew tenderly tried to brush the powder off her face. "Are you okay, Mila?"

Mrs. Stevens shook her head, sending more powder showering to the ground. "Mila? What does that mean?"

"My beloved."

Mrs. Stevens's eyes widened, then rolled back in her head, and she fainted.

Chapter Fifty-Eight

Jack held Alice close as the rising sun's rays filtered through the bedroom window. "Are you sure you want to go to work today?" He asked. "The doctor wanted you to take it easy for a while."

Alice's green eyes sparkled. "I'm fine. Besides, it's my first day working with Bobbie. I can't call in sick."

"How's the bump?" Jack peered at the side of her head.

"It's not that bad. I thought getting pistol-whipped would hurt worse."

Jack chuckled. "You're made of tough stuff," he caressed her arm. "But you're so soft."

Alice shook her head. "Not again. We both have to work, and I want to check on Mrs. Stevens before I go."

"Your grandfather is taking care of her. And she's doing great. She only fainted because of what he said." Jack ran his hand back up her arm and along her neck. "My beloved."

Alice softly moaned but slid sideways out of the bed. "You are so bad. I want to go thank them and Lady again before I leave."

Jack rolled over and placed his hands behind his head. "Speaking of which, I owe Lady a steak. If she didn't alert your grandfather, he wouldn't have come to get me."

"How bad is my car?"

"It's in a lot better shape than Bud. I'm sure Sully can get the dent out of the hood. I had it towed over there."

Alice stopped in the middle of the floor. "Oh, no. Can you give me a ride to work?"

"You're taking the Charger."

Alice shook her head. "I'm not going to leave you without a car."

"I took a cruiser home. Besides, I thought you wanted to bring Lady as backup now that Bobbie said he's okay with her."

"I do. Are you sure about me using the Charger?"

"What's mine is yours." Jack grinned. "Did you hear from Imani?"

"She and Scoops are back together. But I'm worried about what will happen with Emmett and Calvin."

"I'm hoping they'll retire. I thought of a plan for them last night."

"And what would that be?"

"I think they should use all of their law enforcement knowledge and do something they love. Since Patton Supply and Gun Range needs a new owner, I was going to check with Brad to see if he'd be willing to bring on Calvin and Emmett as partners."

Alice crossed her arms, and her green eyes got misty.

"What's wrong, baby?"

"Jack Stratton, you are the sweetest man in the world." She rushed over to the bed and climbed on top of him.

"Think you can spare twenty minutes?"

"We may be a little longer."

Chapter Fifty-Nine

Jack sat in a chair in front of Sheriff Morrison's desk, waiting for Bob to finish his phone call with the mayor.

Bob nodded and grinned broadly. "Yes, Madam Mayor. I appreciate that. Of course. I'll let him know. Thank you." He hung up and held his hands toward the ceiling. "You've just witnessed a bit of a miracle. The Mayor said she is indebted to the Sheriff's department. Boy, do I wish I had wiretapped that call. Today, a peacock, tomorrow, a feather duster. But let's savor the victory. Great work, Jack."

"I can't take the credit." Jack handed Bob a piece of paper. "It'll all be in the final report, but this case would never have been closed without Detective Jill Reyes, Dr. Lai, Monica Sweet, and Kevin Reed. And that's only the top tier of people who deserve to be thanked. I've included everyone's names on that list."

"Has my wife been giving you advice on how to deal with me?" Bob smirked.

"Meg called me last week and gave me that tip. She said you like lists. They keep you organized."

Bob's mouth fell open.

Jack burst out laughing.

"You're going to kill me, Stratton. I believed you. Meg's been on this list thing lately. Between shopping lists, to-do lists, and honey-do lists, I have more lists than Santa. I don't want to see another list."

"All kidding aside, the people on that list deserve the credit. Especially Jill. Did you speak to the Mayor about her and try to get the Chief off her back?"

"The Mayor and I discussed it, and I was surprised by the Mayor's candor. She grew up with Chief Hall and is concerned that he'll hold a grudge."

"But it was Hall's mistake. He's the one who jumped to the wrong conclusion about Nate's death. Jill had nothing to do with it."

"Everyone knows that except the Chief. He wanted to assign Detective Reyes to burglary cases on the night shift."

Jack's grip tightened on the arms of his chair. "With all due respect — "

"Hold up, Jack. I'm not Jill's boss, so there was nothing I could do about her assignments. So —"

"It's not right that she is getting jammed up after all of her work on this case."

Bob glanced at the door, raised his hand, and motioned for whoever stood outside to enter.

Jill walked into the office and smiled at Jack. "I came by to deliver my paperwork. I emailed them, too." Jill shook Bob's hand. "Thank you for everything, Sheriff."

"Speaking of email, please sit down."

All three took their seats.

Jack wondered how Jill could have completed her reports so quickly. It was going to take him days. "Can you send me a copy of those reports, too?"

"I already did." Jill smiled. "I thought you'd like to copy them."

"Use them for reference." Jack winked.

"Jill's mention of the email reminded me of something." Bob set his elbows down on the desk. "Detective Ed Castillo emailed me last night. Ed is Jack's partner who was injured in the line of duty during Jack's last case."

Jack leaned over and whispered, "Ed ran in front of a car to stop it, and it hit him. Somehow, he blames me."

Bob frowned. "Ed heard about the shooting incident at the station and Jack's central involvement in it. Ed requested to be assigned a new partner upon returning to his position."

"What? Really?" Jack's eyes widened, and he settled back in his chair. "I mean, that's too bad. But if that's what Ed wants, I'll find some way to manage independently."

Bob shook his head. "I'm not fond of that idea, Jack. Everyone needs a backup, but I made several calls and encountered a problem. It seems none of the other detectives are eager to partner with you. They all cited health concerns."

Jack shrugged. "As I said, I'll manage solo. It'll be hard, but I'm willing to make the sacrifice."

"I haven't finished." Bob picked up his pen and turned it over in his hands. "I even called Chief Hall, and he assured me that none of his men would be willing to partner with you either."

Jack grinned like he'd hit the lottery.

Bob pointed at Jill. "But a female detective was willing to take the risk. Detective Stratton, I believe you already know your new partner."

Jack's mouth fell open. "But that's impossible. She works for the city."

"Not anymore. The Sheriff approved my transfer this morning." Jill sat up straighter and stared at Bob. "But before officially accepting the position, I need to speak to the Sheriff regarding my seniority and taking the lead in all investigations."

"Over my dead body." Jack stood up.

Bob and Jill burst out laughing.

Jack glanced back and forth between them. "Is this all a gag? Are you two pulling my leg?"

"Only about my taking the lead." Jill wiped her eyes. "The part about me transferring is true."

"And she is your new partner," Bob said. "You're not the only one who can joke, Jack. Jack and Jill. That's going to take some getting used to." Bob said.

Jack thrust out his hand and shook Jill's hand. "All kidding aside, I'm looking forward to working with you again." He took his seat.

Jill glanced at Jack sideways. "I didn't think you'd be so happy about having a partner. Why are you smiling so much?"

Jack leaned back in his chair. "I thought it over, and Bob's right. Everyone needs a backup. If I'm solo and something goes wrong, which it will, I get all the blame. Now, I have shared responsibility. And judging by my track record, it won't take long for people to start shooting at me again. And when that happens, having a partner who's friends with the Mayor is a good thing."

"Don't think you're going to use Jill as leverage against me, Jack," Bob said.

"I'd never dream of it."

Bob's phone buzzed on his desk. He glanced down at the screen. "This conversation has to wait. It looks like you two have your first official case."

The End

ALSO BY
CHRISTOPHER GREYSON

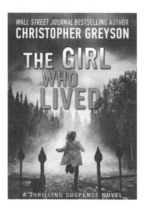

<u>THE GIRL WHO LIVED</u>

Ten years ago, four people were brutally murdered. One girl lived. As the anniversary of the murders approaches, Faith Winters is released from the psychiatric hospital and yanked back to the last spot on earth she wants to be—her hometown where the slayings took place. Wracked by the lingering echoes of survivor's guilt, Faith spirals into a black hole of alcoholism and wanton self-destruction. Finding no solace at the bottom of a bottle, Faith decides to track down her sister's killer—and then discovers that she's the one being hunted.

THE WOMAN BENEATH THE STAIRS

Uncovering her husband's family secrets could cost her everything...

Ally's perfect marriage to Tim Hawthorne is crumbling under the weight of one trial after another. Forced to visit Tim's mother on her secluded island off the coast of Maine, Ally uncovers a sinister secret: years ago, a member of the family was the prime suspect in a young woman's disappearance from the same island. Now, history is repeating itself. Another woman has vanished without a trace. Ally digs into all the dark secrets of the Hawthorne family's past, but what she discovers may cost her more than her marriage — it may cost her life.

ONE LITTLE LIE

A LIE IS A WELCOME MAT FOR THE DEVIL...

Kate had high hopes when she moved to her husband's hometown, but her domestic bliss was short-lived. Blindsided by her spouse's public affair with his high school sweetheart, everything she worked for begins to unravel, along with her sanity. Confused, alone, and afraid, can Kate untangle the web of lies and unmask her stalker, or will she lose everything—including her life?

One Little Lie is a riveting suspense novel set in an idyllic town where money talks, gossip flows, and the court of public opinion rules. Jump on for a fun, fast-paced ride with a book you can't put down!

The Detective Jack Stratton Mystery-Thriller Series

The Detective Jack Stratton Mystery-Thriller Series, authored by *Wall Street Journal* bestselling writer Christopher Greyson, has 5,000+ five-star reviews and over a million readers and counting. If you'd love to read another page-turning thriller with mystery, humor, and a dash of romance, pick up the next book in the highly acclaimed series today:

<u>And Then She Was GONE</u>

A hometown hero with a heart of gold, Jack Stratton was raised in a whorehouse by his prostitute mother. When his foster mother asks him to look into a missing girl's disappearance, Jack quickly gets drawn into a baffling mystery. As Jack digs deeper, everyone becomes a suspect—including himself.

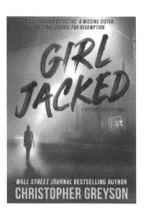

GIRL JACKED

They say a dangerous man is the one who had it all and lost it. But they're wrong, it's the one who lost everything but has a chance to get it back...

Guilt has driven a wedge between Jack and the family he loves. When Jack, now a police officer, hears the news that his foster sister Michelle is missing, it cuts straight to his core. The police think she just took off, but Jack knows Michelle would never leave her loved ones behind—like he did. Forced to confront the demons from his past, Jack must take action, find Michelle, and bring her home... or die trying.

<u>JACK KNIFED</u>

How far would you go to uncover the truth of your past?

Constant nightmares have forced Jack to seek answers about his rough childhood and the dark secrets hidden there. The mystery surrounding Jack's birth father leads Jack to investigate the twenty-seven-year-old murder case in Hope Falls.

A heart-rending mystery-thriller about lost love, betrayal, and murder that will keep you on the edge of your seat.

JACKS ARE WILD

As the body count rises, the stakes are life and death—with no rules except one—Jacks are Wild.

When Jack's sexy old flame disappears, no one thinks it's suspicious except Jack and one unbalanced witness. Jack feels in his gut that something is wrong. He knows that Marisa has a past, and if it ever caught up with her—it would be deadly. The trail leads him into all sorts of trouble—landing him smack in the middle of an all-out mob war between the Italian Mafia and the Japanese Yakuza.

A strong hero, smart women sleuths, and more twists and turns than a piece of licorice.

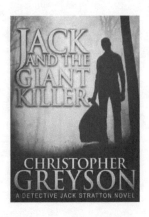

JACK AND THE GIANT KILLER

A serial killer is stalking Jack's town--and no one's safe. But they don't know Jack.

Rogue hero Jack Stratton is back in another action-packed, thrilling adventure. While recovering from a gunshot wound, Jack gets a seemingly harmless private investigation job—locate the owner of a lost dog—Jack begrudgingly assists. Little does he know it will place him directly in the crosshairs of a merciless serial killer.

An action-packed thrill ride until the very end!

DATA JACK

Can Jack and Alice stop a pack of ruthless criminals before they can Data Jack?

Jack Stratton's back is up against the wall. He's broke, kicked off the force, and his new bounty hunting business has slowed to a trickle. He thinks things are turning around when Alice gets a lucrative job setting up a home data network.When the computer program the CEO invented becomes the key tool in an international data heist, things turn deadly. In this digital age of hackers, spyware, and cyber terrorism--data is more valuable than gold. The thieves plan to steal the keys to the digital kingdom and with this much money at stake, they'll kill for it. Can Jack and Alice stop the pack of ruthless criminals before they can *Data Jack?*

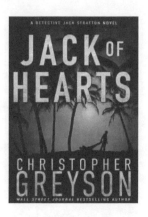

<u>JACK OF HEARTS</u>

Jack Stratton is heading south for some fun in the sun. Already nervous about introducing his girlfriend, Alice, to his parents, the last thing Jack needed was for the dog-sitter to cancel, forcing him to bring Lady, their 120-pound King Shepherd, on the plane with them. The dog holds Jack responsible and wants payback. On top of everything, Jack is still waiting for Alice's answer to his marriage proposal.

When his mother and the members of her neighborhood book club ask him to catch the "Orange Blossom Cove Bandit," a small-time thief who's stealing garden gnomes and peace of mind from their quiet retirement community, how can Jack refuse?

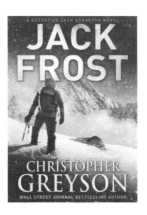

<u>JACK FROST</u>

What do you get when you mix the blockbuster television show Survivor with Agatha Christie's masterpiece And Then There Were None...

Jack has a new assignment: to investigate the suspicious death of a soundman on the hit TV show *Planet Survival*. Jack goes undercover as a security agent where the show is filming on nearby Mount Minuit. Soon trapped on the treacherous peak by a blizzard, a mysterious killer continues to stalk the cast and crew of *Planet Survival*. What started out as a game is now a deadly competition for survival. As the temperature drops and the body count rises, what will get them first? The mountain or the killer?

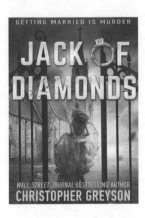

<u>JACK OF DIAMONDS</u>

All Jack Stratton wants to do is get married to the woman he loves—and make it through the wedding. It seems like he is finally getting his wish until he responds to a police distress call and discovers his old partner unconscious in an abandoned house. Investigators insist it was just an accident, but Jack fears there may be more to it. Sketches of women cover the walls, and among them is one sketch that makes Jack's blood run cold —a sketch of Alice, pinned up beside an invitation to a very special wedding—his own.

This time, "till death do us part"
might just be a bit too accurate!

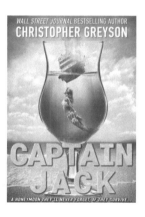

CAPTAIN JACK

Looking forward to some fun in the surf and sand, newlyweds
Jack and Alice Stratton are determined not to let something like
a hurricane upset their honeymoon plans. But the storm's
winds and churning tides unearthed a secret long hidden
beneath the turquoise waters of the island paradise.

A local tour boat captain discovers a lost submarine and offers
to sell the location to a man known only as the Dyab—the
Devil. When the captain is murdered, the police suspect Jack
and Alice and confiscate their passports. Trapped between the
Devil and the deep blue sea, the handsome young detective and
his blushing bride have nowhere to turn and everything to lose
as they set out to prove their innocence and find the real killer.

JACK OF SPADES

The most dangerous killer is the one you don't see...

When a distraught man calls 9 1 1 to report a murder that hasn't even happened, police think it's a hoax or a crackpot until the caller turns out to be a highly respected Doctor. After his warning comes violently true, the killing thrusts Jack Stratton into his first official case as a new detective. Money, sex, and drugs are all motives. Still, these aren't your usual suspects: a tenured professor, a tech CEO, a mathematical genius, and a convicted felon have a million reasons to kill, but who did it? Can Jack follow the trail of victims and catch the mastermind, or will his first case be his last?

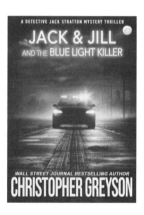

Jack & Jill and the Blue Light Killer

This time, there's murder on Jack's doorstep…

Jack takes out the trash and comes face to face with a lifeless body in the dumpster. With no attempt to hide his crime, the killer left his gruesome handiwork on full display, wanting it to be discovered. Is this chilling message directed specifically to Jack?

When the body count rises, and more suspects emerge, Jack is ordered to join forces with recently transferred Detective Jill Reyes. As they plunge headfirst into the investigation, each new piece of uncovered evidence suggests one of their own may be the killer, leaving Jack to wonder who he can trust. Will Jack be able to outsmart this cunning murderer and catch the killer? Or will he become another victim in their sick game of life and death?

Hear your favorite characters
come to life in audio versions of
the Detective Jack Stratton
Mystery-Thriller Series!
Audio Books now available on Audible!
Listen Now

Fantasy Adventure
PURE OF HEART

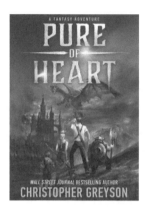

Orphaned and alone, rogue-teen Dean Walker has learned how to take care of himself on the rough city streets. Unjustly wanted by the police, he takes refuge within the shadows of the city. When Dean stumbles upon an old man being mugged, he tries to help—only to discover that the victim is anything but helpless and far more than he appears. Together with three friends, he sets out on an epic quest where only the pure of heart will prevail.

Post-Apocalyptic Thriller Serial
<u>THE DARK - Book 1</u>

If the Dark doesn't kill you, what's in it will.

One year ago, anything with a computer chip; the electric grid; communication; every modern convenience stopped working. Ridgecrest, perched on top of the Highland Plateau, went dark — cut off from the rest of the world. Anyone who leaves never returns, and no one comes into town — until today.

Grab your copy and start reading this electrifying new serial now!

A Post-Apocalyptic Thriller
<u>The Dark 2</u>

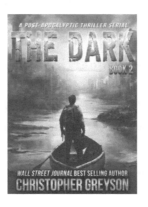

***There are places in this world where even angels
fear to tread.***

In book 2 of the gripping thriller, Cain Haight — a drunk ex-soldier, his opportunist ex-wife, her redneck mother, and a sweet Amish woman are on a mission to rescue two kids from the rebel soldiers who kidnapped them. But they have to survive journeying across the Tennessee landscape filled with nightmarish creatures. The words of Cain's grandmother echo in his ears. "There are places in this world where even angels fear to tread." But that's where we're headed, straight into Hell.

You could win a brand new
HD KINDLE FIRE TABLET
when you go to
ChristopherGreyson.com
Enter as many times as you'd like.
No purchase necessary.
It's just my way of thanking my loyal readers.

Kiku - Rogue Assassin

Award-winning, *Wall Street Journal* bestselling author Christopher Greyson breaks the mold for action-thrillers. Join Kiku as she crisscrosses the globe from Chicago to Hong Kong, the streets of Japan, and the frozen tundra of Russia and takes on the mob, Yakuza, black market, and anyone else who stands in her way!

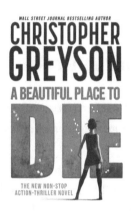

A BEAUTIFUL PLACE TO DIE

When you wound an angel, you unleash a demon.

It was supposed to be a simple assignment, get a DNA sample from a young boy, but it turns into a deadly trap. With a price on the boy's head and a target on her back, Kiku must not only shield him from the ruthless Russian mafia but also from a traitor within the Yakuza itself. Torn between love and honor, duty and scorn, Kiku must decide where her loyalties lie before it's too late.

KINDLE THE FIRES OF WAR

She's outnumbered 100 to 1.
They're going to need more men.

Kiku has gone rogue. Now hunted by the Russian mob and the Yakuza, Kiku heads to Hong Kong's underbelly to rescue her lover. Faced with impossible odds, Kiku must outwit, outfight, and outrun everyone trying to capture her and collect the two-million-dollar bounty. Rats fueled by greed or vengeance, driven by ruthless leaders, run rampant, all hoping to score. The mob, Yakuza, and Hong Kong's black market—they all wanted to fight. Kiku started a war.

DANCE OF DEATH

To save the one she loves,
she'll kill them all.

Kiku's quest to rescue her lover has gone disastrously wrong.
With the odds stacked against her, her enemies think she'll run
and hide to save herself. They're wrong—dead wrong. Kiku
decides to take the fight to them instead. Now the hunter, Kiku,
will stop at nothing to protect those she loves.

The Adventures of Finn & Annie – MiniMystery Series

In these heartwarming short stories, join Finn and Annie as they investigate their way through murder, arson, theft, embezzlement, and maybe even love, seeking to distinguish between truth and lies, scammers and victims. A MiniMystery series that will touch your heart and leave you craving more!

Acknowledgments

I would like to thank all the wonderful readers out there. It is you who make the literary world what it is today—a place of dreams filled with tales of adventure! Word of mouth is crucial for any author to succeed. If you enjoyed the novel, please consider leaving a review at Amazon, even if it is only a line or two; it would make all the difference and I would appreciate it very much.

I would also like to thank my amazing wife for standing beside me every step of the way on this journey. My thanks also go out to Laura and Christopher, my two awesome kids, and my dear mother and the rest of my family.

ABOUT THE AUTHOR

My name is Christopher Greyson, and I am a storyteller. Since I was a little boy, I have dreamt of what mystery was around the next corner, or what quest lay over the hill. If I couldn't find an adventure, one usually found me, and now I weave those tales into my stories.

My love for tales of mystery and adventure began with my grandfather, a decorated World War I hero. I will never forget being introduced to his friend, a WWI pilot who flew across the skies at the same time as the feared, legendary Red Baron. I love to hear from my readers. Please go to Christopher-Greyson.com and sign up for my mailing list to receive periodic updates on new book releases. Thank you for reading my novels. I hope my stories have brightened your day.

Sincerely,

Made in United States
Troutdale, OR
10/29/2024

24230534R00224